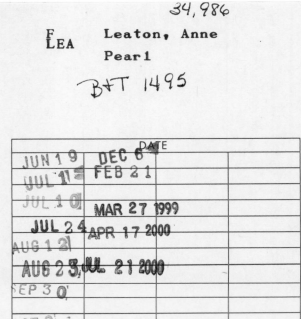

PEARL

PEARL

Anne Leaton

Alfred A. Knopf, New York

1985

THIS IS A BORZOI BOOK
PUBLISHED BY ALFRED A. KNOPF, INC.

Copyright © 1985 by Anne Leaton
All rights reserved under International and Pan-American
Copyright Conventions. Published in the United States by
Alfred A. Knopf, Inc., New York, and simultaneously in
Canada by Random House of Canada Limited, Toronto.
Distributed by Random House, Inc., New York.

Library of Congress Cataloging in Publication Data

Leaton, Anne.   Pearl.

1. Reed, Rosie Lee, 1867–1925—Fiction. 2. Starr, Belle,
1848–1889—Fiction. 3. Younger, Cole, 1844–1916—Fiction.
I. Title.
PS3562.E2614P4   1985   813'.54   84-48538
ISBN 0-394-53923-0

Manufactured in the United States of America

FIRST EDITION

To Frida, again

PEARL

Old Savoy Hotel,
Douglas, Arizona: 1925

The heat was something Ruth Reed could hold in her mouth and roll around on her tongue like a hard candy. It looked from the hotel window on the second floor like a gauzy curtain rising from the street, shimmering with its own life because there was no air stirring. But it wasn't gauzy, it was solid. Solid as a wall, she thought. Ruth Reed had run into this wall every day since April: four months ago.

"Gimme some water."

Ruth turned to the bed behind her, to the woman in the bed, thin red hair against the pillow, fat wrinkled arms lying like beached fish against the dingy sheet. "I'll go get some fresh," she said. She sniffed the water in the pewter pitcher on the table next to the bed: it smelled like trough water into which someone had plunged a rusty horseshoe. "I'll be a minute, not more than a minute," she said to the woman in the bed. "Can you wait? Will you be all right?"

"Ma?" the woman in the bed said. "I waited for years, rotted away waiting," she wailed. "What's a few more minutes?" She sighed. "I thought you'd never come. You took your sweet time."

Ruth Reed clasped the pewter pitcher to her bosom and went downstairs to the lobby of the Savoy Hotel. She stood for a moment directly under the slow-spinning ceiling fan, wiping around the back of her neck with her damp handkerchief. "She wants some fresh cool water," she said to the desk clerk who was watching her expressionlessly from under his green eyeshade. She handed him the pitcher.

He shrugged. "There's a limit to cool," he said. "Fresh we can give you, but it ain't likely to be any cooler. We don't make any guarantees about cool to our guests. We can't hardly do that."

Ruth Reed nodded. With her left index finger she scooped the sweat delicately off her upper lip. "Why don't you people have ice cubes?" she said. "Ice cubes are all over now, they're modern. Everybody's got ice cubes."

The desk clerk shrugged again. "This is Arizona," he said. "You couldn't keep no ice cube frozen in Arizona. It'd melt while you thought about taking it out of its little metal box."

"Then let the water run a long time," Ruth Reed said. "Till it's cool. Do that, anyway. She's a dying woman, after all. It wouldn't hurt you to take a few pains."

On her way back up the stairs to the second floor, bearing the pewter pitcher with the slightly cool water in it, Ruth Reed said, out loud, which was often the way she addressed herself: Things have been running downhill since I was fourteen. Why should I think everything will suddenly be different? Maybe when Jennette gets here she'll make things better. She was always magic that way. She always made things better.

The woman in the bed stirred slightly when Ruth Reed entered. "My God, Ma," she said, "you used to be so fast, Jesus you was like the wind when you rode Venus, even on your two feet dragging all that velvet skirt behind you, you was like lava from one of those erupting mountains—hot and quick, hot and quick. How come it took you so long to get here? How come your baby Pearl's got to wait so long for you to come?"

Ruth Reed put the pitcher down. She blotted her forehead with the ball of her handkerchief and then the forehead of the red-haired woman in the untidy bed. "I don't know," she said quietly. "I don't know why it took so long. Dead women travel slow, I guess that's it. The dead don't pick up their feet very fast, I learned that in St. Louis at Convent Marietta. It was one of the first things they taught me. Look here, Ruth, they said to me: this creature moves like treacle in January, that's because she's dead as anybody can get, dead as a doornail. That's how we know who's living, they step right quick."

The woman in the bed turned her head and the blue eyes

opened wide and stared at Ruth Reed. She looked frightened for a moment. Ruth Reed patted the flabby arm that lay crooked in an awkward right angle. "Don't be afraid," she said. "Fear wears you out."

That's the second thing she had learned in Convent Marietta in St. Louis, she thought. The nuns always counted on it, especially with the young boarders. First fright, then exhaustion, then conversion.

"What's just across the border there?" she had asked when she first arrived.

"Agua Prieta," the news vendor at the hotel had said. "Nothing there. A wide spot in the road, a couple of mangy dogs, a couple of lazy Mexicans. Even the tortillas are no good. Now, when you can't make a decent tortilla . . ."

"What about Douglas?" she had said. "How is Douglas any different? Just a wide spot in the road, a couple of lazy Anglos . . ."

The news vendor had laughed. "Our dogs are livelier," he said. "Our tortillas are tastier. We wash the streets down every week to lay the dust. Now, who could ask for more than that? You must be from a big city. Nobody else would expect more than that."

The train arrived at three o'clock. Ruth Reed had waited at the depot since two. She didn't know why she had gone so early to sit on the one bench under the metal roof next to the one-room station. Was she that eager to escape from the Savoy Hotel and that woman under the crumpled sheets who picked at the bed linens as though she were telling a rosary? Questions questions, never any answers in Ruth Reed's head. She smiled and felt her dry lips stretch painfully over her dry teeth. Ruth Reed, she said aloud, has only questions. She is thirty-one years old, but she has only questions. When will she have an answer or two? Ah, she said, no answer to that.

The half dozen cars of the 3 p.m. train stopped only briefly at Douglas. The engine steamed and groaned for a few minutes as it took on water, and then the train shifted forward in one metallic spasm followed by a ripple of slighter spasms as it moved again toward the desert. When it pulled out of the depot, Jennette Andrews stood tall and, yes yes, Ruth Reed thought, even cool, cool would not be too much to say—on the station platform, waiting for her sister to come forward.

"Jennette . . . ," Ruth Reed said, kissing her sister on the cheek. "It's been such a long time. I can't even remember how long it's been."

Jennette gazed at Ruth steadily, as though from the moon or one of the more distant stars. "Five years," she said. "Exactly, almost to the day."

"You were always good at that sort of recollection," Ruth Reed said. "I never had a head for that."

"How is she?" Jennette said. "Is she dead yet?"

"No, no," Ruth Reed said. "Not yet. She clings. She's been clinging for days. It's too hot to die," she said.

"What a queer thing to say," Jennette said. "But then you always were given to saying queer things, weren't you, Ruth?"

"I'm glad you're here," Ruth Reed said. "I needed somebody to help, somebody to say, all right, Ruth, you can rest now, you can close your eyes this evening. Just sit in the lobby next to the palm trees and close your eyes and rest this evening. Isn't that silly? I could do that on my own, sure I could. But I can't, somehow. I need permission."

"Comes from Convent Marietta," Jennette said, and laughed. "After you've been to Convent Marietta, you've got to have permission to pee." She took Ruth's arm and steered her toward the street. "Where's the hotel?" she said. "Let's get it over with."

"She won't know you," Ruth Reed said, feeling comforted by Jennette's grip on her elbow. "She'll think you're somebody else, God alone knows who. She thinks I'm her ma. For the last two days she's thought I'm her ma."

"Oh, for God's sake," Jennette said. She dropped Ruth's arm.

She stopped dead in her tracks and looked at the solid wall of heat rising from the paved road next to the depot. "What is she doing here, anyway?" she said. She turned to Ruth Reed, her blue eyes sapped to empty in the fierce sunlight. "What's she doing here, anyway?" she repeated.

"Waiting for Belle, I think," Ruth Reed said. "Waiting for Cole. She's gone a long way back from my daddy or your daddy. Maybe that's what women do when they're dying, that occurred to me. I haven't known any other dying women. Maybe that's what they do, maybe they go way back to mamas and papas and even farther back than that, I don't know, maybe so. She was talking about Paso Robles the other day, maybe two days back. You know she couldn't remember Paso Robles and Jim Reed. That was all too long ago. But she said to me—she rose halfway up out of the bed like a mermaid and she said—Ma! The ocean's like glass, it's like blue glass, and when Jim papa kisses me his mouth is like cool well water and smooth as a snake."

Jennette Andrews looked at her half sister with slotted eyes and lips lifted almost imperceptibly at the corners. "We'll see," she said. "We'll see what that's all about."

"It's her heart, you see." He caressed his black leather bag and pursed his lips contemplatively. "It's no good, that's the simplest I can put it," he said. "It's been carrying around this huge body all these years. She's too heavy, you see, no doubt about that. Too fond of her food and drink. Too much good living, that's not very medical, but it's the fact. It's worn her heart out. She's got no strength left."

Jennette studied Dr. Weatherby with the same appraising look she had turned on her sister at the railroad depot. "How long has she got, in your opinion?"

Weatherby gazed at the brass clasp on his black leather bag as though the answer lay cryptically there. "Nobody ever knows such things," he said finally. "The end could come tonight or to-morrow or not for a week. Not for a month, maybe."

"That's not much help," Jennette said. "I have appointments in Chicago."

Ruth Reed laughed and then put her fingers over her mouth. Jennette frowned at her. "A life to live," she said, to no one in particular. "People waiting on me, things that can't be put off."

"I'm sorry I can't be more certain of the hour of your mother's demise," the doctor said, daring to be just slightly offended although times in Douglas were hard.

"It's all right," Ruth Reed said, despite herself. "If you have to go, Jennette, then you have to go. I've seen to everything for the past two years. I can go on seeing to everything. When it's time to make arrangements, I can manage. There'll be people here to help me." She looked at Dr. Weatherby, wondering if he was one of these helpful people.

Jennette waved a dismissive arm. "Don't be silly, Ruth. I came to help you out and I aim to help you out. It wouldn't be fair to leave you alone with all this trouble. I intend to shoulder my part of the burden." She focused on the doctor again. "What can we do for her now?" she asked. "Is there any medicine you can give us that could make her easier?"

"She doesn't seem to be suffering much," Weatherby said. "There's a little paralysis on the left side, I noticed that. But I doubt it hurts her. I'll leave you a little vial of opium for emergencies. You can call me up anytime you need me." He put his hat on and nodded and backed toward the stairway. "Evening, ladies . . . good evening, ladies . . . don't wear yourselves out, now . . . try to rest." Closing remarks, Ruth thought. Always the same closing remarks, like a benediction.

Jennette looked at the vial of opium. "If I can't sleep tonight in this heat, some of this will help."

"Do you want to go in now?" Ruth Reed said. "Do you want to talk to her now?"

Jennette shook her head. "I've seen her, that's enough. Let her sleep. Besides, we've got nothing to talk about, have we? . . . I haven't been living with her these last two years the way you have. She doesn't know anything about me. What could I say?"

"About your life in Chicago?" Ruth suggested. "She might like to hear about that, she might be interested."

Jennette laughed. "Interested in my life in Chicago? She's dying. She only cares about old things now, things that happened before the two of us were even born. You said that yourself. Sometimes I think you're living on the moon, Ruth. She wouldn't know what I was talking about. She never did know what I was talking about, even when I was just a little thing and she'd come to visit us at Convent Marietta." Jennette considered the palms of her hands as though a map lay there. She rubbed the palms together to eradicate the map. "Where can we eat?" she asked Ruth. "Is there any decent food in this whistle-stop?"

"Can we leave her?" Ruth asked. "For that long? Can we, do you think?"

Jennette looked over the stair railing, appearing to listen to sounds from the lobby of the Savoy Hotel. Ruth knew there were no sounds rising from that dead place except the occasional whisper of a palm tree stirred by the passage of an occasional guest. Not to be heard on the second floor. "She's dying," Jennette said, turning to her sister again. "She's not going to get up and run around. We don't have to worry about that. Like Weatherby said, who can ever tell the moment? Meanwhile, we've got to eat. We've got to nourish ourselves against this ordeal." Ruth thought she saw her sister smile slightly when she said this, but she wasn't sure. The light was bad: she couldn't be sure.

"There's a little cafe just across the street," Ruth said. "I was in there one morning, just for a moment, just for some toast, I think it was. I needed to get out of the hotel . . . I really . . ."

"Why are you always justifying everything, Ruth? God doesn't damn you for getting hungry and bored. He understands that better than most, wouldn't you think so?"

Ruth stared at her half sister. "I knew you'd make things better when you came."

"Have I done that?" Jennette laughed her cool laugh.

"Yes," Ruth said. She nodded hesitantly, then more emphatically with each movement of her head. "Yes!" she repeated. "Already I feel lighter, as though air has started circulating around in my chest, blowing out the cobwebs and the dust."

"And the spiders," Jennette said. "Don't forget the spiders."

"The spiders?"

"You said cobwebs, didn't you? Spiders live in cobwebs. Maybe all that fresh air will blow them away too, before they can weave another castle. That's what I used to call them when I was a child—spider castles. It doesn't pay to have spiders in your chest. Look at her, let her be an object lesson. Her old spiders are eating her up."

Ruth Reed and Jennette Andrews ate hard steak and fried potatoes at the Crystal Cactus Cafe across from the Savoy Hotel. Jennette put her face down near her plate and concentrated on the movements of her knife and fork, chewing quickly, her eyes switching rapidly around the room as though she were spotting enemies and exits.

"I remember how you used to do that as a child," Ruth said.

"Do what?" Jennette looked up at her sister. Her jaws stopped moving.

"Eat like a ravenous animal. As if you'd never eaten before and you'd never eat again. I used to think you were hoarding nourishment against a bad time. That was before I knew you couldn't do that, that bodies didn't store up nourishment like that."

Jennette put her fork down and mopped her plate with a square of bread. "Eating is a pleasure," she said. "I take all my pleasures fast and hard." She said it in the same tone she would use to explain to her sister how a machine works, how, for instance, someone might run up a hem on a Singer sewing machine. "Do you want coffee? You've hardly eaten a thing."

"I find eating difficult now," Ruth Reed said apologetically. "It's the heat. I don't think it's . . . Mama, you know . . . just the heat. I never could tolerate much heat, you remember? Even in

St. Louis you used to chide me because I sweated like a long-shoreman."

Jennette nodded. "You think a lot about St. Louis, don't you?"

"Don't you?" Ruth said. "It was our childhood, wasn't it?"

"You were fourteen when Mama took us off there," Jennette said. "Half grown, you might say. I was the child: six years old, just a baby. My whole life was St. Louis in those days and for years after. But your childhood was in Fort Smith." She grimaced. "Dreadful old Fort Smith. Wonder is, you turned out so sane, everything considered." She turned her blue-eyed steady look on Ruth. "You did turn out sane, didn't you?"

Ruth laughed uncertainly. "You always did take me by surprise that way, startle me something terrible with a question. You're the only one who could ever do that to me. I was always prepared for everybody else's questions."

"Listen, Ruth," Jennette said. She leaned intently toward her sister across the small table. "Don't be poetic or philosophical or anything like that. I know that's hard for you to manage, you've never been very practical, but try anyway. Just tell me straight out what Mama is doing in this godforsaken town, dying in this godforsaken town. I understand the dying. You wrote me about the stroke. But why here? You must know. You've been with her for the last two years. You came to this place with her a year ago. You saw things. I know Mama can be kind of secretive some-times, and I know she makes up stories—she's always made up stories, that's the way she lives—but you don't have to be like that. You can tell me the truth."

Ruth studied a cold fried potato on her plate. She shook her head slowly, wonderingly. "I never know how to talk to you, Jennette. I wonder sometimes how two sisters could be so different."

Jennette leaned back in her chair. "Different fathers," she said. "Mine was a lovely fat man as irresponsible as a baby. Yours was somebody rich and mysterious, that's what Mama always said. If they just knew who Ruth's father was, she'd say, wouldn't they all just jump out of their pants. And then she'd laugh that big laugh of hers. You heard her say that a hundred times." She laughed, turning her face up momentarily to the ceiling of the Crystal Cactus Cafe. "My own feeling always was that your daddy was not just rich and mysterious but probably a loony as well, a real honest-to-God loony."

"Why would you say a thing like that to me?" Ruth said, offended. "I would never say such a hurtful thing to you."

Jennette wiped her mouth with her napkin and threw the napkin across her plate, on which steak grease had congealed into a translucent low relief. "We're different," she said. "As you just pointed out a minute ago." She stood up impatiently. "Let's go back to the hotel. This place is beginning to depress me. We can sit in the hotel lobby. It's fairly cool there, shady anyway." She studied the bill and opened her handbag. "This one's on me," she said. "A little celebratory dinner. Two sisters together again after all these years." She smiled at Ruth, who wondered what subtle thing about the smile made it look so unpleasant.

Ruth got up and the two sisters walked with straight-backed dignity to the door, aware that they were being watched by the handful of diners remaining in the Crystal Cactus Cafe.

"Hicks!" Jennette whispered into Ruth's ear as they pushed open the door. "They've never seen a city woman in this burg."

They sat for an hour in the lobby of the old Savoy Hotel. Jennette put her head back against the wicker chair and stared dully at the ceiling fan. She seemed hypnotized by its slow rotation and its occasional shudder. "It trembles violently," she said, "on every third rotation. Have you noticed that? Do you think there's something wrong with its machinery?" She smiled her unpleasant smile at Ruth. "Perhaps it will fall on us," she said. "Kill both of us while we're waiting down here for Mama to die. Wouldn't that be rich?"

Ruth fanned herself with a thin Christian Science magazine she had picked up from a small table near the hotel entrance. "You have a very odd imagination," she said.

"Coming from you that's a real laugh," Jennette said indifferently. She opened her handbag and took out a silver-colored flask shaped like a quarter moon. She glanced at the desk clerk, who had his back to the two women, sorting and distributing a handful of letters, and then she took a long draught from the flask and offered it to Ruth. "It's the best Chicago has to offer," Jennette said. "You ought to try it. See what big city booze is like. Or are you still Little Miss Goody about drinking?"

"I drink a little now," Ruth said. She looked at the flask but didn't take it.

"How could you live with her anytime at all and not drink a little?" Jennette said. "Prohibition could never stop that great thirst of hers, could it?" She took another swallow from the flask and looked at Ruth curiously. "What do you drink?" she asked. "Where do you get it?"

"Rye," Ruth said. "A little rye whiskey. I don't mind a little rye. If you've got any money, if you can pay something for it, a bellboy here can get it for you. I don't know where he gets it, I don't ask. It tastes disgusting."

Jennette laughed. "He probably whips it up in the laundry room. What about her? Does she still drink, even the way she is now?"

Ruth nodded. "It's just as you said. She's got a great thirst. Nothing ever slakes it, as far as I can see. Anyway, why deprive her of her pleasures at this bitter end? Whenever she asks for a drink, I give her a little. She doesn't ask often. She's too busy thinking about other things, remembering." She leaned over and took the flask from Jennette and held it to her lips for a long draught.

Jennette looked surprised. "You *have* changed," she said.

"Things happen," Ruth said, handing the flask back to her sister. "Things happen," she repeated, as though it were somehow an explanation.

Jennette dropped the flask back into her handbag. "I have a bottle of this in my suitcase for later."

"Good," Ruth said. I need something to warm me, she thought. In this terrible heat, this misery of heat, I feel cold somewhere in the bottom of my stomach. She put her hand protectively against her belly and leaned back against the cushions of the huge armchair. She felt the pressure of tears behind her closed eyes. She did not want to weep in Jennette's presence. Jennette had always mocked her when she wept: in the dark crannies of Convent Marietta, Jennette had squatted at her sister's knees, sucking bits of chocolate noisily through her back teeth, saying, Why are you doing that? Only silly women in magazines cry all the time . . . I bet you'll have a wet lap for days . . . maybe it'll sprout mushrooms . . . like in the garden by the fence . . . you'd be good for something anyway . . . Ruth kept her eyes closed until the impulse to weep had passed. When she opened her eyes again, Jennette was standing in front of the enormous window that spanned half the hotel's lobby. "How far is the border?" she asked Ruth without turning.

"Not far," Ruth said.

"Is there anything to see over there?"

"A village," Ruth said. "Name of Agua Prieta. The news vendor who wanders around the streets here told me there was nothing to be said for the village at all. That it was dull and hot, like here."

Jennette turned and looked at Ruth almost angrily. "Are you ever going to tell me why she's here in this godforsaken place?" Jennette said. "She didn't just pick this place off a map the way you play pin the tail on the donkey. It's not one of the country's well-known garden spots. It's a dry stick the desert beats you with, the end of the road."

"I guess that's what she really wanted all along," Ruth said. "A visible sign."

"Don't guess anymore," Jennette whispered fiercely. "Just tell me what you know for a fact."

Ruth leaned forward in the big armchair, stretching her hand out for a moment toward her sister as though she might be appealing to her, then withdrawing it. How simple Jennette made it sound, she thought. As if the fact of a life was like an accounting kept in a ledger.

"We were in San Francisco," she said. "She wrote me in St. Louis to please come out and stay with her for a while, that she needed me badly." Ruth rubbed her forehead, soothing herself. "When I got there I found her living in a shabby little hotel in the Mission District. She weighed about two hundred pounds. Every time she moved she wheezed like a steam engine and pressed her bosom as though it was going to collapse and she had to hold it together. That was in 1923, sometime in the year, I can't remember exactly when."

Jennette sat down again in her wicker chair and leaned forward, listening intently to her sister.

"And she was drinking even more than usual," Ruth continued. "I don't know where she got all that liquor from. Men would come, she never told me who they were. She'd say to them, This is my daughter Ruth. They must have brought the whiskey. She drank every night until she passed out. I couldn't get her to bed, you know. She was a dead weight. I'd have to leave her on the sofa with all her clothes on. I'd just take the shoes off. Some nights she'd wake up and go to her bed, but most mornings she'd wake up on the sofa, hair looking like fat red fingers and blue shadows under her eyes."

"Why didn't you leave?" Jennette said. "Why would you put up with that?"

"She was Mama," Ruth said. "I kept remembering how she used to be, in Fort Smith and when she came to visit in St. Louis. I remembered all that life in her, the laughter, the fun she could make. I couldn't leave her like that. She didn't have anyone else until John Henry came along."

"John Henry?"

"He was a gangster, a booze runner."

"My God," Jennette said. "Just like Belle. She never could resist an outlaw. Things like that must run in families."

"Maybe they do," Ruth said. "After John Henry came along there was never any shortage of alcohol."

"And he liked her?" Jennette said. "Were they lovers?"

"I don't know. I used to wonder how they could be lovers, with her wheezing with every breath and so heavy the floorboards groaned when she crossed the room. John Henry was a tall, slender man. He didn't weigh as much as Mama. He just seemed awfully fond of her. They laughed together a lot, they were always laughing. I'd hear them chatting away and laughing in the parlor half the night sometimes. Then John Henry left."

"Why?"

"I never knew why," Ruth said. "Mama didn't say and she looked too sad for me to ask. She cried a lot after that. That's when she started talking all the time about her ma and Jim Reed and Cole and Younger's Bend—and, oh, everything. All the past, her childhood, Eddie . . ."

"Poor Ruth," Jennette said, pulling her mouth down the way she thought sympathetic people looked.

"It was terrible," Ruth agreed. "I lived with her about a year in San Francisco, every day a little worse than the one before. Downhill . . . everything downhill. I thought every month would be her last. Then she got a letter from John Henry."

"And he said . . . ?"

"He said Mama should meet him in Douglas, Arizona, in six weeks. And from here he'd take her across the border and show her the fanciest hacienda in Mexico. And they'd live in this hacienda together and have a fine time, even better than San Francisco. He said he was on the run, so he wouldn't be able to write her again. But she was to come here to the old Savoy Hotel and wait for him, and in July he'd be with her. That was last July."

"I don't believe it," Jennette said, shaking her head slowly back and forth. "You mean she came all the way to this hellhole from San Francisco to meet this gangster, this hooch runner, on the strength of this one letter of his?"

Ruth nodded. "Mama believes in instinct, you know that. She always goes by her instinct. She said to me, Pack up, Ruth, and help me get out to Arizona. So that's what I did."

"Only John Henry never showed up." Jennette leaned back in her chair and stared at the ceiling fan again. "And she's still waiting for him, is that it? That's why she never could leave?"

"That's why," Ruth said. "Whenever I suggested that she might find somewhere a little nicer to live, a little cooler maybe, a few more of the conveniences of modern life, she'd always look at me and say, You go on if you want to. But I'm staying around here until John Henry shows up."

Jennette pressed her cheeks with both hands as though she were trying to contain something under the skin that was threatening to escape. "What do you think happened to John Henry?"

"Two possibilities come to mind right away," Ruth said. "First is, he's dead. He was on the run, so he could have gotten himself killed along the way somewhere. The second possibility is that for some reason he wanted to hurt Mama and getting her out here under false pretenses was just the way to do it."

"Why would he want to hurt Mama?" Jennette looked up from the molasses-colored floor upon which she was visualizing the ignominies of life.

"Some people," Ruth said, "like to hurt other people just because that's what they like to do. I didn't think John Henry was that kind of person, but I didn't know him that well in San Francisco. There was always something a little standoffish about him, as though he held something back, some private thing. I never could put my finger on it exactly. I just thought that was how men acted who traded in illegal alcohol."

Jennette stood up and sighed deeply. She looked toward the big plate-glass window behind her. "Sun's going down," she said. "Finally."

"It'll start getting cooler now," Ruth said. "It's like the desert here. Nights are cold sometimes."

"Let's go on up to your room," Jennette said, "and start in on that bottle I've got in my suitcase. I really do need a drink, and I can't just sit around here in the lobby swilling it down. I guess they do enforce the law here . . . I guess they've heard what the law is?" She laughed and pressed against the small of her back as though she had been sitting too long and had stiffened.

Ruth arose and led the way to the wide stairs. Jennette sighed again. "In Chicago they've got elevators in some of the better hotels," she said. "A lady doesn't wear herself out climbing stairs all day. Chicago is a civilized place." She raised her voice on the last sentence and turned her face toward the desk clerk, who was writing something in the hotel ledger. He didn't look up.

"Here's mud in your eye," Jennette said, taking a long swallow of the very pale chrome-yellow liquid in the hotel glass. Ruth sipped from her glass and made a face. Jennette laughed. "You don't like it?"

"It's a lot like what we get around here," she said.

"It all tastes like pee with a touch of battery acid."

Ruth had forgotten how uninhibited her sister could be, how she often seemed to say the first awful thing that popped into her head, no matter how unsuitable. Maybe that was part of the magic she remembered, part of whatever it was about Jennette that always seemed to make things better. But perhaps it was all an illusion: planned down to the last flicker of an eyelid, but seeming as natural as a cat taking a stretch. Pearl seemed uninhibited too, Ruth knew. When she was just a child, she hadn't known that in Fort Smith Pearl was considered a force something like a great wind sweeping down from the northern plains: sudden, untrammeled, sometimes leaving nothing standing in her wake. Whenever her mother came to visit Ruth in the apartment where she lived with her keeper (she always thought of the large red-faced woman whose name she could never remember as her keeper), Pearl was always on her best behavior. Never any swearing or foul language, never any allusions to body functions. Pearl hardly touched her, Ruth remembered—it was as though she was afraid she would contaminate the child. For a long time Ruth had believed her mother didn't love her: there was to be no touching of this undesirable creature. And then one day Pearl had come in her elegant carriage pulled by the four fine horses gleaming like black sateen, and she had seemed subtly different to her daughter. Softer, an easier smile, a wisp or two of red hair not properly pinned, an unusual smell on her breath, which Ruth, at eight, had not identified as rye whiskey. Pearl had taken the child onto her broad lap and put her plump arms around her and murmured sounds into Ruth's ear that were the sweetest sounds Ruth had ever heard. It was months before Pearl did such a thing again. On her next visit she was quiet and chastened and fidgeted with the lace on her cuffs and left early after pecking Ruth goodbye on the cheek.

"Go on with your story," Jennette said. "You haven't finished yet."

"I thought I had," Ruth said, drinking the pale yellow liquid with more relish.

"Mama must have known after a few months that John Henry wasn't going to come. She must have known that by August, as a matter of fact. She was never such a fool she couldn't finally see things clear. Sometimes it took her a while, but she always managed to see by whatever light there was."

"She's changed," Ruth said. "She's not the mother you remember from St. Louis. When she came here, she was desperate. I don't think that's too strong to say: she was desperate. There was no place else for her to go. She didn't want to return to San Francisco. There was nothing for her there."

"She could have gone back to Denver," Jennette said, refilling her glass. "She always liked the climate in Denver."

"I mentioned Hot Springs to her once," Ruth said. She swirled the rye whiskey around in the potbellied glass and recalled that awful day. "She hit me such a blow I saw stars, I swear I did."

"Why did she do that?" Jennette said, astonished.

"That's what I asked her at the time," Ruth said. "And she said to me, I wasn't happy in Hot Springs. I was so miserable in Hot Springs, God preserve any woman from such misery in her lifetime."

Jennette considered this, drinking again. "She was in Hot Springs right after she left Fort Smith, wasn't she?"

Ruth nodded.

"That was 1916," Jennette said. She considered, biting her

lower lip. Ruth remembered that her sister always mulled things over in this painful way. "What could have happened in Hot Springs to make her so unhappy? I never knew why she left Fort Smith. I know it was sudden. I always thought she was probably asked to leave. Did she ever tell you?"

"It was one of her secrets," Ruth said. "She had a good many secrets, even though she always left the impression that she told everybody everything. She was always telling stories about her life. People just never realized how many years she left out. It was like studying the Civil War and you'd hear all about the battle of Gettysburg over and over, but there'd never be a single mention of Antietam. But Gettysburg would be so interesting, so colorful, you'd forget all about Antietam. Later on you'd realize there were all these strange gaps in your knowledge." She held her glass out to Jennette for replenishment. "It's tasting better all the time," Ruth said.

"Maybe we're both our mama's girls," Jennette said, smiling, this time pleasantly.

"Maybe we're both just in need of comfort," Ruth said. "I know I need some comfort. Until you came, I thought I wouldn't be able to make it on my own. I thought to myself, When Mama dies, I'm going to sit down next to the bed where she's lying and stare at the bedcovers and not be able to think of a single thing to do. And then when she begins to stink, I'll just get up and go away." She pressed the potbellied glass against her forehead as though she would in this way obscure all the horror that seemed to her to be there. "The last few months have taken a lot out of me," she said to her sister. "I don't know how to describe them to you. I don't even know if you'd believe the description. I feel like an open sore." She sat down suddenly on the bed, feeling her head spin. "I think I must be drunk. I'm not used to drinking quite so much whiskey. Not quite as much as this." And she fell back across the bed, unconscious.

Jennette studied her sister's face for a few minutes, then removed Ruth's shoes and drew her legs onto the bed. She refilled her own glass and pulled the single armchair over to the window. She sat down and peered out into the street where the rising, shimmering wall of heat was beginning its nightly fall to earth.

Downstairs, the lobby was empty (the night clerk was dozing in the small office behind the front desk) except for a man playing "Poor Butterfly" on the upright piano that stood against the east wall next to a music stand and a straight chair on which a violin case rested—there were occasional tea dances on Sunday mid-afternoons. The man was picking casually through the notes, playing certain phrases over and over, beginning again. He stopped in the middle of a passage, swung around on the piano bench and sat slumped with his arms hanging loosely between his legs. He looked at Jennette, who had been listening to the man play and who sat now in one of the large wicker-armchairs with her eyes closed and an expression of sorrow around her mouth. She suddenly became aware that the music had stopped and opened her eyes. In the half-light of the lobby it was hard for her to see what the man looked like.

"Does the nice lady have any special requests?" the man asked. "I play by ear. I can pick out most anything."

"You're very talented," Jennette said flatly. "That's obvious."

The man lit a cigarette and leaned back against the piano keys on his elbows. "I guess you think I don't know a slam when I hear one."

Jennette shrugged. "Call them as you see them," she said.

"Staying long?" the man asked after a pause.

"Not very long," Jennette said. "I'm visiting my mother."

"You don't say. I haven't seen anybody around here lately that looked like anybody's mother."

"You haven't looked in the right bed," Jennette said.

The man looked slightly uneasy. "She . . . sick, you mean? Crippled or something?"

"Dying," Jennette said.

"I am sorry to hear that," the man said.

"I'm sure you are," Jennette said. "Why don't you play another tune? Something melancholy. I like sad songs."

He swung around on the bench again and began to play random phrases, running up and down the keyboard, then dropping into a dark minor key to play a slow, regretful song Jennette didn't recognize. When he finished, she said, "That was very nice. I liked that."

"Out of New Orleans," the man said. "A little tune I picked up down there last year. A blues tune. They're all over the place in New Orleans."

"I think I could sit here and listen to a blues tune all night," Jennette said. "Suits my mood to a T."

"Want me to play another one?"

"Yes," Jennette said. "Play another one. I'm just going to put my head back and close my eyes and drift around in the dark. I won't be sleeping, I promise. I'll just be drifting around in my dark head."

The man studied her for a minute uncertainly. Then he played another blues tune and after that repeated the first one he had played. He turned around on the piano bench again and lit another cigarette. Jennette sat with her eyes closed, breathing gently. He could see that she was smiling slightly, or thought he could see that, but the light in the lobby was too dim to be sure. "Are you asleep?" he asked softly. There was no reply. He got up and stood with his hands in his pockets and the cigarette dangling from his lips for a minute and then he walked over to Jennette and leaned down very close to her face. She put her arms around his neck without opening her eyes and pulled his mouth against hers. The man noticed that her lips were soft and smooth and cool in the middle like the inside of a melon from a shady grove. He imagined those cool lips against his forehead and whispering around his eyes and that seemed to him a sensation desirable above all others. He lifted her from the armchair. She opened her eyes and smiled at him. "I suppose you're taking me upstairs to your room," she said.

"That's right," he said.

She leaned briefly against his shoulder and then straightened up and held out her hand for him to take. "In Chicago," she said, "I always ride up in an elevator."

The next morning when Ruth awoke she saw Jennette standing in front of the bureau mirror and twisting expertly to stare over her shoulder at the seams in her silk stockings.

"Do you feel awful?" Jennette asked, leaning down to make one final adjustment to her left seam.

"Awful is not a suitable word," Ruth said. "I can't think of a suitable word."

Jennette laughed. "Dress and we'll go to the Crystal Cactus Cafe and drink some coffee. You'll feel better after that."

As Ruth stirred in the bed she perceived a new kind of aroma rise around her: warm and musty like a dog's basket in which the creature had slept for days without moving. "I've never spent the night with all my clothes on." She looked around the room and at the other half of the undisturbed double bed on which she lay. "Couldn't you get in the bed? Did I just not leave you enough room, sprawled like the drunken woman I was?"

"I was okay," Jennette said. She was making up her face at the bureau mirror. "I wasn't tired. I got some sleep down in the lobby, catnapping."

"After your train ride and all that?" Ruth said. "And the . . . emotion. Not to say all the rye whiskey. You weren't tired?"

"I caught my second wind," Jennette said. She went into the bathroom and ran the water furiously for a minute. When she returned to the bedroom her blond hair looked brighter and her eyes a deeper blue. "I rejuvenate well," she said, smiling at Ruth. "Friends in Chicago tell me I rejuvenate quicker than anybody they know."

"It helps to be twenty-three," Ruth said. She groaned as she left the bed. "Instead of thirty-one." She studied her face in the mirror. "Except today I look forty-one." She straightened with an effort and took a deep breath. "Last night was the first time I haven't slept on that cot in her room since she got sick. It feels strange to wake up in here with someone walking around, speaking to me. I'm so used to this big mound of stillness in the bed. And when she does talk, it isn't conversation—just ramblings and recollections. I'm never present to her anymore. It's hard to lose yourself that way." She went into the bathroom to splash water in her face. "You go on down," she hollered out to Jennette. "I'm going to wash a little and look in on Mama, and then I'll come right along."

In the hallway Jennette hesitated and then walked quickly to a door just on the other side of the stairway. She opened it and peered in. The shades had not been drawn, so the room was light enough for her to see the shape under the rumpled bedcovers and the thin red spokes of hair appearing above the sheet. She walked over to the bed and leaned down.

"Mama?" she said. "Are you awake? It's me, Jennette."

There was a slight stir within the cavern of the bedcovers. A hand emerged and pulled the sheet away from the white face and puffy blue eyes underneath. The eyes focused on Jennette. "God-damn Dell Andrews," Pearl's hoarse voice said. "You could of hung around after the baby was born, you could of done that for Pearl, but, no, nothing would do but that you make yourself a little trip." Pearl coughed. The cough was followed by a series of loose rales. "All alone for a year, dear old Dell God knows where. Now you want to come back, I guess. Want to come back to old Pearl and get yourself a little comfort, a little loving . . . same old Dell." Pearl coughed again, then pulled the sheet back over her face, so that only a few red strands of hair could be seen on the pillow. Over the hole of her mother's mouth the sheet hollowed and ballooned, hollowed and ballooned, with each breath. Jennette watched this process for a moment, fascinated, and then turned and left the room and walked quickly downstairs to the lobby to wait for Ruth Reed.

"Morning," the clerk said, dusting the front desk with the flat palm of one hand. "Have a nice night?"

His face was inscrutable. Perhaps he had heard nothing from the night clerk. Perhaps it was a simple greeting.

"It was all right," she said.

"Gonna be a scorcher today," he volunteered. He looked around the lobby appraisingly as though signs of the day's impending horror were hanging everywhere in the air. "A real scorcher."

"Just like yesterday," Jennette said. "The days here are all the same in the summertime."

"Some are worse than others," the desk clerk said. "All bad, some worse," he summed up aphoristically.

"A person might wonder how this area ever got settled," Jennette said.

"Ain't it the truth." He laughed soundlessly, everything suffocated in the chest, which heaved slightly to indicate mirth. "Ain't it God's truth. Musta been some dumb pioneers from some such place as Chicago."

Ruth appeared at the bottom of the stairs. "Get Weatherby," she said.

"What's wrong?" Jennette said. "Just a minute ago . . ." She could still see in her mind's eye the hollowing and ballooning of breathing.

Ruth looked blue with illness. Wisps of dark brown hair hung in disarray about her face. She grasped the newel post of the stairs to steady herself. "She's dying, I think. She's turned a strange color and she's gurgling in her throat and this morning she's not even recollecting, she's just babbling, I can't understand anything she says. I think she's truly dying. Go get Weatherby."

Weatherby came with his worn black bag and tired eyes and worked over Pearl for half an hour before he said, "It's no use. I can't do anything for her. You ladies will have to prepare yourselves for the worst."

Ruth, who had been standing next to the bed watching

Weatherby with his stethoscope, with his vials of concoctions, with his hands feeling for the heart, feeling for the pulse, reaching, pulling, heard herself draw a sharp breath without realizing she had done so. "How do you do that? How do you prepare for the worst?"

Weatherby folded his stethoscope and dropped it into his bag. He shook his head, gazing sorrowfully at the woman in the bed, who had acquired a blue glaze to her skin which every minute seemed to deepen. "I don't know how you prepare," he said. "It's just something doctors say. It doesn't mean anything."

Jennette grasped the foot of the bedstead so hard her knuckles turned white. "What are we supposed to do?" she asked, not addressing Weatherby, looking around the room as though she were inquiring of unseen forces there. "Just stand here and wait until she draws one last breath? Just stand here and chat among ourselves? Talk about the weather, maybe? How hot it is . . . how tomorrow they say it might get cooler . . . ." Something in her voice made Weatherby look quickly away from Pearl into Jennette's face. Was she going to be one of those cool-looking women who get hysterical when finally the crisis comes? You could never tell about some women. They were deceptive. This one, maybe. He had thought when he first saw this one that she might be a good help to the other daughter, who seemed less sure of herself, less in control. Now he didn't know. Maybe it was the older girl who would hold the center together when the outside of the circle threatened to give way.

Weatherby opened his bag again, rummaged about and produced a vial. He shook a lozenge into Jennette's hand. "Take one of these," he said. "It'll help you relax."

Jennette stared at the lozenge and then at Weatherby. "This will make everything all right?" she said. "Make everything seem like a bad dream, will it?"

"I don't know about that," Weatherby said, snapping his bag shut. "It'll help you relax."

Ruth stood gazing raptly down at her mother. Both hands were fisted at the base of her throat.

"What about her?" Jennette said. "Don't you think she needs

relaxing? She's been waiting four months for Mama to die. It gets to be a habit, waiting like that. How's she going to feel when the waiting's all over? How would you feel?"

Weatherby remembered his brother Albert, who had been killed in the Great War. There was no waiting for Albert to die. It was all over in an instant. That's what Albert's friend had said later on in a letter he had sent Weatherby: "He was shot straight through his heart and died in the middle of a breath. There was no suffering." Weatherby always wondered how Albert's friend could be so sure. Maybe when someone is shot directly into the heart there is a moment that seems an eternity and in this eternity you suffer as you have never before suffered and you weep for your life and your wasted youth and your young wife. But to a soldier watching this death, it would all seem to happen in a single moment—in the time it would take to say no. "Bereft," Weatherby said to Jennette. "I'd feel bereft. Even a nail through the hand you get used to, you come to count on it being there."

Ruth turned dreamlike from the bed. "I don't need anything to relax me," she said. "What I need is . . . what I need is . . ." and though she struggled to find the words for her need, she couldn't. She wrung her hands in frustration, moving toward Jennette and the doctor, who stood together near the door. She grasped Jennette's two hands and searched her sister's face as though she expected to find a sign there, some message printed in the blue eyes or across the smooth forehead or along the silken curve of the cheek. Her intense scrutiny made Jennette uncomfortable and she moved to arm's length and averted her face slightly to protect it from Ruth's gaze.

"Why are you looking at me like that?" Jennette said.

"I want to see something," Ruth said quietly, still staring intently into her sister's face. "I want to see something."

"What?" Jennette said, looking directly into her sister's face, flushed. "In God's name, what?"

Weatherby watched the two women, mesmerized. His hand was on the doorknob, but he felt unable to leave. "Ladies . . . ladies . . ." he said, not knowing why he said it or what he hoped to accomplish by it. "Ladies," he repeated.

"What is it?" Ruth said, turning to him impatiently. "Do you have something to say?"

"I must go," Weatherby said, so softly he wondered how the woman could hear him. "I have other patients to attend to."

"Go on, then," Ruth said, turning back to her sister. "We'll call you when it's over. We'll call you for the formalities."

What a strange way to put it! Weatherby thought. The formalities . . . He opened the door and went out into the hotel corridor.

Ruth continued to stare spellbound at her sister until Jennette withdrew her hands from Ruth's grip and said, "Shall we both wait or only one of us at a time?"

"We'll both wait," Ruth said. "Neither of us will be spared anything."

"You're so intent on both of us suffering this," Jennette said. "If I hadn't come when you wrote, you'd be all alone. But since I'm here, neither of us is going to be allowed one minute away from the gruesome business."

"Gruesome business?" Ruth said. "That's Pearl in that bed there. That's Mama. How does Mama's death get to be a gruesome business?"

"I don't feel about her the way you do," Jennette said. "I was the last of the line. She sent me away from her when I was only six. I don't remember her the way you do. A few visits to St. Louis . . . a few letters later on when I'd left the convent. She's like a stranger to me."

"That's not true," Ruth said. "That's not the way you spoke of her five years ago. You're making that up because you don't want to feel anything now that she's dying. I understand that, Jennette. Really. But don't lie to me about the way you feel about Mama. I wouldn't be able to tolerate that. I'd hate you for doing that. You just sit and wait with me. It'll all be over soon. She's so blue and sick-looking and still. It can't last long. And then you can go back to Chicago to keep your appointments."

Jennette listened to the sound of her sister's voice and she couldn't find in it any animosity or sarcasm, any sly ugliness under the surface of the words. She walked over to the foot of the bed and stared down at the mass under the bedcovers. The white heavy arms lay motionless across the sheet. The red hair was like spider's web on the pillow. Face thrown back, chin up, mouth ajar: a watery breathing forced its way through Pearl's throat. "Did she ever tell you who your father was?"

Ruth moved to her sister's side. "Of course," she said very softly. "A gentleman from one of the first families of Fort Smith."

Jennette laughed flatly. "And you were happy with that information, I suppose."

"What does it matter who he was?" Ruth said. "I never knew him. He was never anything to me. Pearl was what mattered. If she didn't want to say who he was, I didn't mind. I was alive. She was my mother. That's what counted."

"Which mountains are those over there?" Jennette asked.

"The Pedregosas," Ruth said. "They look blue this evening. Some nights they look pink."

"One of these days we ought to go and take a closer look."

"That would be nice to do," Ruth said. "Mountains up close are very different from what you expect."

The two women sat in Ruth's room side by side on the edge of the bed drinking rye whiskey, watching the one window as though it were the screen in a movie house. On this screen they studied the Pedregosa Mountains in the distance, although their minds were fixed elsewhere.

"All those years when she was surrounded by people, oh hundreds and hundreds it seemed like, all the time. Never a moment alone. To end up like today, planted in that hot terrible little graveyard, earth like brick, not a tree in sight anywhere, just the two of us to say goodbye . . ."

Jennette poured more whiskey into their glasses. "Don't think about it," she said. "Don't dwell on it."

"I can't help dwelling on it," Ruth said. "It's a model, you know. It's what we all come to in the end. Oh, there are all those wonderful days of roses and kisses and laughter, but in the end there's just you and maybe, if you're very lucky, a couple of your babies who've managed to outlive you."

"Ruth," Jennette said, "if you're going to go on in this vein, I swear I'm going downstairs to the lobby and just sit around by the palm plants until I fall asleep."

There was a long silence, then Ruth said, "Tomorrow we'll see about the marker."

"What are we going to put on it?" Jennette said. "Are we really going to put Rosa Reed on it?"

"That's how they knew her here," Ruth said. "And in San Francisco too. Ever since she left Fort Smith she went around under that name. Nine years . . ."

"It's different going around places under a name and being buried with that name on your tombstone forever and ever," Jennette said. "From the beginning she was Pearl. That's her true name. It doesn't seem right that she should be buried as Rosa. You shouldn't have to hide out anymore when you're dead."

Ruth sipped her whiskey. "And for a last name I guess we can take a pick. Reed, for Daddy Jim . . . Starr . . . Erbach for a while . . . Andrews . . . And what was legal and what wasn't, nobody ever knew, maybe even Mama didn't really know. She was never too clear about legalities where men were concerned."

"Let's put Andrews," Jennette said decisively. "She was married to my daddy, and he was the last of the bunch."

"Common law," Ruth said. "Just a common-law husband, your daddy."

"Common law's as good as any," Jennette said. "At least we know who my daddy was."

"Don't start in," Ruth said.

They stared in silence at the Pedregosas.

"Why don't we strip away all the husbands?" Ruth said. "Or near-husbands or maybe-husbands or however you might like to call them. Why don't we go right back to the beginning, to the name she was before anybody else came along to give her another one or before she got reason to change it to something else?"

Jennette put her glass down on the nightstand next to the bed and looked thoughtfully at her sister for a few moments and then said, "That's a wonderful notion. Pearl Younger. That's the way the marker will read. 1867–1925. Rest in Peace."

"She'll never do that," Ruth said. "She never rested in peace while she was alive and all that hard dirt they threw on her today won't make her lie still. There's not enough brick dirt on this globe to make Pearl Younger lie still!" Ruth's voice rose at the end to a triumphant note which made her sister jump to her feet and grab Ruth by the elbows and pull her up and start spinning her around the room.

"That's true!" Jennette sang, her head back, whirling her sister. "That's all true!"

And the two sisters danced around the old Savoy Hotel in Douglas, Arizona, on the day their mother died.

Paso Robles: 1868

The man and woman—the woman holding the child in her arms—came down the road from Harmony in a small open cart pulled by a bay mare. You could see that the man was tall from observing how high his knees rode up in front of his chest as he sat on the wooden cart seat leading the bay mare. He was thin without being fragile, with a sharp Adam's apple and heavy brows that drew almost together above his nose. He wore a shirt the color of blackstrap, open at the collar with the sleeves rolled up to his elbows, and trousers with a small brown check made of material too substantial for the California spring. There was something watchful and uncertain in his manner: he was not accustomed to the role of outlander. He continually turned toward the woman at his side with a half smile, a gesture of question in his shoulders, a movement of one long hand toward the horizon or to something that lay in the stubbled dune grass on either side of the road—driftwood, for instance, or an outcropping of stone. He clicked his tongue at the bay mare and shook the reins now and then to encourage her to move along the hard sand road toward the water which shone like blinding glass just beyond the next rise.

The woman held the child loosely, almost carelessly, in the circle of her right arm. Over and over she swept the wispy red hair back from the girl's eyes and in the same movement leaned forward to kiss her forehead. She lifted her arm and directed the child's attention to the brilliant ocean light just ahead of them. The girl laughed, squinting her blue eyes against the sun. She was happy: she rested comfortably against her mother's knees the way some men lean back in imperturbable ease against bar rails in rich saloons.

When they reached the soft sand, the man reined in the bay

mare and sat for a moment leaning forward with his elbows on his knees looking out over the Pacific. He turned finally to the woman. "I never seen water like that," he said. He scanned the horizon. "Lord God, there's no end to it! No end to it!"

"Oh, there's an end to it," the woman said, and laughed. "Somewhere over there in the East, Japan or some such place. That's where it ends." She narrowed her eyes and gazed across the water as if she could plainly see Japan. Then she turned her glance downward, fondly, to the child. "You want to go into the ocean, baby? Want to wet your sweet little toes in the big Pacific?" The child shrank back, clutching her mother's knees. "Don't be afraid, Pearl baby," the woman said, embracing the child tightly. "Your mama will be right with you every minute. And Jim papa will hold you way up above the waves."

The man stroked the child's head with his long brown fingers. He looked anxious. "Don't want her to get too fond of the ocean, now do we . . . so's she'll miss it when we cut loose from here."

The woman sat very still in the cart, smiling out at the ocean, holding the child pressed to her side. "Oh, we won't cut loose from here for a good long while, Jim," she said quietly. "Not till the Pinkerton men and all those Texas deputies lose interest in your murdering ways or decide you're too much like a cat in the hills to track or just think of some other fool they'd rather find and string up."

The man flushed and looked down at his boots. "I ain't a fool," he said.

"You're all a bunch of fools," she said calmly, smiling at him. "You and that whole Fischer gang—just a collection of almighty fools. Not enough brains among the lot to fill a small derby halfway up." She threw her head back and laughed, grabbing the man's arm and kissing him passionately on the neck just under the line of the jaw where she could see a large pulse beating. "But jolly lads, all of you," she said. "My good boys . . ."

He kissed her on the lips, encircled her waist, pulled her tight against him. "Belle, I swear, someday you're gonna make me so damn mad . . ."

"What will you do, Jim?" She pulled away from him, still smiling. "Shoot me out of my saddle the way you did that boy in Texas you think killed your brother?"

He looked offended. "There wasn't no mistake about that—he killed Tom, all right."

"And the other man you shot? They both killed Tom, did they? Bushwhacked poor Tom, did they?" She continued to smile, clasping the child to herself again. "Had to go rushing off from Rich Hill to avenge poor old Tom." She stroked the child's forehead, pressed her lips to it. "One excuse for killing's as good as another, that's what I always say. And a man don't want to sit around with woman and child too long a while, does he . . . makes him seize up and go all rheumaticky in his gun hand."

He stared at her uncertainly: when she spoke to him in that tone, smiling, always smiling at the same time, he never knew what he should do or what he should say. He knew he should say something because he felt she mocked him, but he could never devise the proper words. Now he slapped his knees in frustration and leapt down from the cart. He grappled his boots off and stood wriggling his toes in the sand and looking out at the ocean as though the woman and child had disappeared and he was all alone at the edge of the Pacific.

"Give us a hand down, Jim," the woman said. And when he turned to her she was gazing at him with an expression of such tenderness and desire that it was all he could do to keep from seizing her in his arms and falling upon her in the soft sand, even though the child stood watching and there might have been strangers just beyond the next dune. "Help us down, then . . ." she repeated softly.

He reached up and grasped her around the waist and lifted her from the cart, holding her close for a moment and studying her face, wondering again what it was in that face that he so fervently and constantly desired. She touched his shoulder. "The child," she said. "Help down baby Pearl."

She drew her own boots off and the girl's tiny slippers and

then pushed the child onto the soft cushion of sand where, laughing with delight, she danced in circles before her mother.

Dr. Woodson James sat at the head of the long table, leaning back comfortably in his high-backed chair, pulling intermittently on his bright red suspenders, and expanding upon his role as director of the Paso Robles Sanitarium. Jim Reed sat midway down the left side of the table and Belle Reed midway down the right. They continued, delicately, to eat: tamales and refried beans. On Jim Reed's left a pale, thickset man with a sweeping downward-turning mustache and a melancholy expression stared reflectively at an orange-colored tamale shuck that lay empty on his plate. At the other end of the table sat a tall, fair-skinned young man with cold blue eyes and a dark, neatly trimmed beard. His clean white hands lay at rest on either side of his clay plate. The lids of his eyes were pink-rimmed and crusty with granulation, and he blinked unceasingly as he stared down the table at Woodson James, listening.

"Lunacy," Dr. Woodson James was saying, "ain't an easy thing to comprehend, no indeed. Many people think a lunatic comes forward in the street and identifies hisself or else looks so strange in his face that no soul could mistake that he means to do somebody harm—hisself or some innocent passerby. Nothing could be farther from the truth, I hasten to advise you of that. Most times it is uncanny hard to tell a lunatic from any other soul until he has perpetrated some scurrilous misery upon another's person."

"Do you have many lunatics in this sanitarium?" Belle asked, wiping her mouth with her fingers in a genteel manner.

"A few," Dr. Woodson James replied. "But mostly we have got here folks with rather pitiful lungs, lungs in some stage or another of rot, and precious little we can do about it. I said to one such unfortunate soul just the other day, I said, Willie, you enjoy each day as much as you can, you go off and look at God's great Pacific, you rest yourself and try and be happy, because someday your soul is going to be nesting in some gob of blood you spit up and that will be the end of it for you."

At the far end of the table the young man closed his cold blue eyes and it was not even possible to see his chest moving with a breath. The expression of the thickset man with the handlebar mustaches did not alter its melancholy attention to the empty tamale shuck.

"My apologies to the lady present," Dr. Woodson James said, "if I have offended her with my picturesque manner of speaking."

Belle Reed acknowledged with a bow of her head this regret of Woodson James.

"However," he continued, "I am a physician and a physician is one that bandies about cruel, or what seem cruel, expressions about another's physiognomy. I have got to be honest with these poor sick souls, you can see the necessity of that."

The young man at the far end of the table opened his eyes again, blinked and resumed his breathing. Jim Reed nodded sagely, picking his teeth, without seeing the necessity of anything except a glassful of decent whiskey. He had finished his plateful of tamales and beans and he was still hungry.

"What if"—Woodson James leaned forward, the huge, grey-haired chest riding out like a cliff over his dinner plate, dwarfing it so that it looked to Belle Reed like a toy plate, like one of baby Pearl's playthings—"I lied to these souls about their miserable bodily conditions? What if I said to Willie, Oh yes, Willie, never you mind about this thing and that left undone in your tiny life. Never you mind, because you are going to get well, you are going to live possibly forever, your rotten lungs will cease to rot and will recover theirself. You have got God's own time to do with whatever you feel like." He looked inquiringly up and down the table. The man with the handlebar mustaches shook his pale, melancholy head. "Indeed, Frank, indeed so," the doctor said. "Then one day this sick creature coughs up one last fistful of odoriferous blood and falls upon the tile floor dead as any man can be, Nurse Milledge to find him stretched out there stinking already in the heat when she makes her customary rounds."

Woodson James exercised his red suspenders and sighed deeply. "My fault, you see," he said. "My fault that this soul dies kinda unshriven. That he ain't been off to look at God's masterpiece the Pacific. That he ain't loved a good woman in so long he has shriveled." He picked up his glass and hollered "Juanito!" at the top of his voice. A small Mexican boy came scurrying in with a large skin of wine and filled Dr. Woodson James's glass and then passed along both sides of the table filling everyone's glass in turn.

Woodson James wiped the moisture of emotion from beneath the sagging skin under his pale blue eyes. "Oh, it's a sad lot to be a physician," he groaned. "To tend these miserable souls, some lunatic and some rotten in other ways God has seen fit to devise. What a thankless task I've been set here!"

The melancholy mustachioed man next to Jim Reed said, "God has seen fit to try us all in one sorrowful way or another, Uncle."

The tall, cold-eyed young man at the far end of the table arose. "God has seen fit to try me with a fool brother who never knows when to keep his face shut, just like a Baptist preacher," he said, and left the room.

Frank James sighed with long-suffering and stood up. "Jesse never has had any manners to speak of," he said to Dr. Woodson James. "That was a real nice supper and we thank you for it."

Woodson James stared at his nephew for a moment as though he were considering some extraordinary notion about him and then he leaned back in his chair again and hooked a thumb in his suspenders. "You boys are entirely welcome," he said. "You and all your friends"—his gesture encompassed the table—"are always welcome at the Paso Robles Sanitarium. Think of this place as your refuge and haven." He bowed his giant unkempt head in a gesture which Frank James interpreted, rightly, as dismissal. After he had gone, Belle Reed said, "Maybe it would be a good thing if we all went on to bed and let you get a little rest, Dr. James."

He raised his head and looked gravely at the woman. "Call me Woodson," he said. "Do you like my red suspenders?"

"Why, yes," Belle said. "Yes, I do."

"You don't think they're unmedical? I don't want the patients

to feel I'm not giving them my very utmost, you can understand
that. But I do like bright colors. Life can be hellish drab, you got
to do what you can for it."

Belle laughed, throwing her head back and roaring up at the
ceiling. Jim Reed looked uncomfortable and pushed his chair back
as though he were preparing to bolt if that should be necessary.
Woodson James smiled tenderly at Belle and took the last of his
wine in one swallow. Then he stood: this gargantuan figure in
bright red suspenders stretched over his behemoth chest, fur
sprouting from his unbuttoned collar like spiky grey cactus, hands
wide as a prairie, fingers like wagon spokes. Belle looked at him
as if he were one of the fine buildings in Philadelphia she had seen
pictured in books. "Nothing about you is usual, Woodson," she
said, rising, smiling at him wonderingly. "Nothing whatsoever."

He took her delicate hand in his. "No, ma'am," he said. "Not
one thing I know of. Ain't I saintly fortunate to be living in a
country that allows the uncle of a cold-blooded little murderer
like Jesse James to minister to the unsound of California?"

"Now, Dr. James," Jim Reed said, also getting up, "you hadn't
ought to speak about Jesse like that. He's a good friend of me and
Belle."

"He has many fine qualities, of that I am assured," Woodson
James said. "He is wonderful with a gun. Why, he can shoot the
eye out of a sparrow at three hundred yards."

Small Juanito entered the dining room as if called by a secret
bell. Woodson James propped one elbow atop the boy's head and
the child steered him toward the door. "I bid you good night," the
doctor said without turning. "I bid you take care when moving
about among the lunatics in these parts. Oh, they can be uncanny deceptive, they can take you in. They go around looking as
sweet and smelling as clean as your baby Pearl." He stopped at
the door and shouted into the wall, "But they stink in God's
lovely nostrils!" He sighed again and patted Juanito on the head.
"I do what I can for them," he said. "A thankless task I've been
set here. Thankless." And he was gone: all the momentum that
carried him down the long tiled hallway seemed to be located in
the boy's thin brown legs.

Jim Reed looked at Belle uncertainly. "Now, then, you talk about the blind leading the blind. My old mama used to use that expression a lot. She was always talking about the blind—"

"Stuff your old mama in your back teeth," Belle said.

In July, Cole and James Younger arrived at Paso Robles, and Jim Reed, full of suspicion, said to Belle, "Did you tell Cole to come on out here?"

"Why would I do that?" she said. "Jesse told him to come."

"Why all of a sudden now?" Jim Reed persisted.

"They're all on the dodge from Russellville, you know that. What's got into you?"

"They robbed that bank in March," Jim said. "Where they been all this time?"

Belle laughed. "In Texas," she said. "Counting their money."

"So goddamn smart," Jim Reed said, not specifying whether he meant Belle or the Jameses or the Youngers.

"Now, listen, honey," Belle soothed him. "That was all a long time ago. I'm pregnant now with your baby, ain't I? Why, I'm going to make you a proud papa in your own right before we leave this pretty place." She stroked his cheek and the side of his throat. "Don't carry on about Cole, now. It just embarrasses everybody."

"I don't like you being with him," Jim said. "I don't like the way he acts with baby Pearl."

Belle crossed the room and poured herself some wine from the carafe that sat on the bureau. She drank it down in two swallows and stood looking at herself in the bureau mirror, which had lost most of its silvering down one side. "Well, honey, she's his baby, after all. Everybody knows that."

Jim Reed's dark brown eyes widened and his light brown skin deepened into Indian red. He made subtle humming noises in his throat, which Belle knew signaled the onset of temper. She watched fascinated as he struggled to be calm, clenching and unclenching his fists, the singing in his throat waxing and waning, the eyes closing, opening again, closing. Finally he said very quietly, "When you have this new baby, Belle . . . is everybody gonna know it's mine?"

She kissed him fiercely on the mouth and pulled him down on the narrow iron bed with the thin husk mattress. "Of course they'll all know," she whispered. "I'll tell everybody that Jim Reed, my own boy, my childhood sweetheart, can do as well as Cole Younger any day in the week. You want me to start at suppertime? You want me to tell Dr. Woodson James that Jim Reed is father to this child in my belly likely to be born right here in the Paso Robles Sanitarium? That not another man in Paso Robles could have done so well as Jim Reed?"

He stared at her face, which was only inches from his own, trying to sort out into words the abundance of sounds in his head, trying to see where the love lay in that face of hers. At last he said, "You hadn't ought to taunt me that way, Belle. You know it makes me mad. You know how I get."

"I know how you get," she said, smiling, lifting her long skirts.

The Paso Robles Sanitarium was composed of two long rectangular adobe buildings—one housed patients and the other harbored Dr. Woodson James and his assorted guests and relations —and two smaller square adobes in which Nurse Milledge and her female assistant lived, suitably segregated from an alcoholic German who tended the grounds and did all the heavy work. Nurse Milledge, her assistant Flora, and Axel the German were all in various ways helped by a collection of Mexicans who lived in the town of Paso Robles and presented themselves at the iron gates of the sanitarium every morning very early. At seven the gates were flung open by red-faced Axel, who wore a leftover uniform from some forgotten Prussian war and who was already drunk. The sanitarium could accommodate fifteen patients. It had never done so. In the spring and summer of 1868 there were nine patients in residence. Dr. Woodson James said that of these nine six were hopeless cases and any day he would announce this to them, at which time there would probably remain only three patients at the sanitarium and suppers would consist primarily of refried beans. "The wine, you see," he explained, "the wine which makes it possible for us to stay sane enough to assist the lunatic, the cost of the wine makes a devotion to foodstuffs regrettable. We must stay as grateful for whatever bones we get as old Rover is."

Paso Robles was on high ground scarcely covered by thin intermittent grass. Standing on the gallery which surrounded from front entrance to back stoop the rectangular adobe in which Woodson James ate, slept and anguished over his charges, it was possible for the doctor and any guests or refugees who joined him there to see a faint luminescence from the Pacific Ocean twenty miles away.

This cool evening in July, Cole Younger wore a sky-blue shirt open wide across his full neck, trousers the color of milk chocolate, and a broad Mexican leather belt spanning the girth of his two hundred pounds. He lounged comfortably against the gallery railing, smoking a thin black cigarillo and squinting his blue eyes into the sunset. Belle thought that his hair was like gold dust in the late sun, but she kept this to herself.

"We got aboard in New Orleans," Cole said. "A big steamer out of New York called the *Manchester*. First-class accommodations all the way to Chagres. Good food. They even had a little band that played at supper, a couple of fiddles, a big bass fiddle and a piano, I think. Nice little band . . . played hell of lively music, but damn! there was nobody like sweet Belle here for a man to dance with." He put his arm lightly around her shoulder for a moment and then withdrew it.

"You trying to tell us you spent those eight days to Chagres without wining and dining some pretty señorita?" Jim Reed said, moving nearer Belle, putting an arm about her waist.

"Well, hell, Jim," he said, smiling. "To get up to any proper devilment you got to have at least the beginnings of a good-looking woman. They was mighty few and far between on this little sea voyage. Mostly men and married ladies with faces like hatchets and bodies like ax handles. It was enough to send me and James to heavy drink." He laughed, clapping Jim Reed on the back. "We passed the time playing monte and hoping the rains hadn't been so heavy on the Isthmus that we couldn't get to Panama City from Gorgona." He frowned, remembering his earlier misgivings. "But they had been," he recalled. "They had been." He sighed. He stared into the setting sun. "How about a little more of that wine, friend Woodson?"

Dr. James picked up the large skin propped against the gallery railing and poured wine into Cole Younger's cup. He refilled his own and Belle's and Jim Reed's. He held his cup up toward Cole. "Your good health, sir," he said, drinking. "Your continued good health."

Cole drank his wine down with a sigh of satisfaction. He brushed his gold-dust hair out of his eyes, caught up in his recollection of the voyage from New Orleans to Morro Bay: the steamer, Mosquito Bay, the Chagres, the Isthmus of Panama . . .

"It took us four days up the Chagres River to Gorgona. Open boats. Rained in our goddamn faces the whole time. I never been so soaked through in my life, me a Missouri boy from Texas. I never seen so much rain. We put up at American houses along the way—we was three nights on the road. We'd draw up, wet as rats, at some mooring and crawl out of the boat thinking, Sweet Jesus, how'd we ever come to be here? What the hell ever are we gonna do? Couldn't see through the rain, it was coming down so steady and heavy . . . then there'd be this fellow come along with a lantern and lead us through a bamboo grove, or something like that, and down a muddy path and onto a wide veranda and there'd be this woman standing there, usually a kinda good-looking woman, and she'd lead us off to a room that was nice and dry with a clean soft bed waiting for us—goddamn, it was like some kinda dream! I said to James once, I said, Listen, James, do you think we're dreaming or is this really happening? This pretty woman and the clean white room with the soft bed and the mosquito netting hanging down over it like a veil . . . I said, James, I know goddamn well I'm dreaming all this. I drowned down there in that god-awful river—water coming up from below and water coming down from above, more water than any damn man oughta ever have to deal with in his life. I drowned down there and I'm dreaming all this."

"And what did James say?" Belle asked.

"He said, Shit, Cole, don't say that, 'cause I'm gonna get that pretty lady into bed before morning and I don't want me no dream between the sheets!"

Everyone laughed but Woodson James. He stood silently in the shadows of the gallery. Cole shook his head indulgently. "Ain't that just like James?" He went on smiling for a moment, recalling his brother's peccadilloes, then he looked somber. "When we got to Gorgona we found out we'd have to go on to Cruces, seven miles upriver. It was so wet James and me, we was wearing boots up to our knees and still the water come in and damped our socks until they squished every step we took. Hell of terrible. Took us four days to cross the Isthmus, instead of the usual two."

Jim Reed made sympathetic murmurs. "That's a real bad trip to make," he said. "Me and Belle sure know that. We traveled that same way, you know. Two months before you. But we beat the rains, we sure as hell was lucky that way."

Cole nodded. "You're a lucky man a lotta ways, Jim. You got away from that Texas deputy and those Pinkerton fellows—hot on your heels, just about grabbing your coattails. You got this sweet lady here. Now I hear you got this kid on the way. Seems to me you got everything going right smartly, Jim. A real good run of luck."

Jim looked solemn. "God's own truth," he said. "God's own truth."

"Now, the next question is, are you gonna begrudge a poor man like me the pleasure of a walk with your sweet lady? Seems to me, with all that luck of yours, with all that plain good fortune, you can afford to be generous. Ain't that so, friend Woodson? Don't it seem so to you?"

Woodson James moved in the shadows like a great whale in the grey water. He shifted into the late rays of the sun and sat down in a blue cane-bottomed Mexican rocker that was painted all over with large red and yellow flowers. "Many's the man can afford to be generous but ain't. Fact of the matter is, a man being able to give makes it about as certain as death he'll see you don't get a second penny to rub against the one you already got. A strange quirk of disposition that I have observed over and over again in my work with the great human herd."

All three looked at Woodson James politely, holding their earthenware cups suspended like begging bowls. "I see you got a real poor idea of folks," Cole Younger said.

"True, true," Woodson James said, sighing. "Guilty as charged. My opinion of mankind ain't very elevated. Comes from seeing too many of the creatures for too many years. God knows, too many years. Oh, the things I've seen transpire in the odd human bosom, the queer fish I've seen floating upside down in the hindmost part of a man's brain . . . I could tell you tales that even God wouldn't credit."

"Well, sir," Jim Reed said, "you're talking lunatics, but now, we ain't all lunatics. Some of us is just good clean white men. Me, now, I never had no lunatic in my family, either side."

"You don't say," Woodson James said. He studied Jim Reed for a moment in the half-light and then turned and stared out across the Santa Lucia mountains toward the ocean. "The tales I could tell," he repeated softly. "Dear God . . ."

After a moment's silence, Cole Younger said, "Well, Jim, how about it? You gonna object if I step Belle out for a little night air?"

"If Belle wants to go walking with you, she's a growed woman, she can do what she likes," Jim Reed said petulantly. "I won't say nothing regarding the matter." He glowered at Belle, turned and went into the adobe.

They all listened to his boots echoing down the tiled corridor. Then Belle said, "I wouldn't mind a bit of a meander in the cool evening air."

Cole took her under the elbow and led her off the gallery and onto the brittle grass. He smiled down at her: fine full cheeks lifting above fine white teeth. "You never did mind a bit of a meander, Myra Belle. As I recall."

"Cruces to Panama City," Cole said, leaning forward and engaging with a keen glance everyone seated at the long dining table, "is twenty-five miles or thereabouts and takes about two days when things is average. But of course with all that rain things wasn't average. Took us four days to get to Panama City. And then there was no boat." He shook his head in remembered disbelief, leaned back in his chair, felt in the breast pocket of his cloud-colored shirt for a cigarillo. "James said to me, Cole, you think God is trying to get across some message to us?"

He winked at Belle and they laughed together. Jesse James rubbed his crusty eyes: it was impossible to tell if he smiled. There was a sad curve of amusement somewhere in Frank James's nether lip. Jim Reed watched Belle and Cole Younger with a stony face. Woodson James, at the head of the table, swallowed the last of his wine and bellowed "Juanito" twice; the small, thin brown boy appeared with the large skin of wine.

Cole Younger lit his black cigarillo and put his wide chin up to blow a cloud of smoke into the still air above the dining table. "I said to him, James, God's been trying to get across a message to us since we was little tykes and we been turning a deaf ear. We're too old to change now. We're gonna sit ourself down here and wait for that boat that's gonna take us to Morro Bay, and if moss grows over us before that boat comes, then damn! we're gonna be two real fine-looking moss men, ain't we?"

"Picturesque," Woodson James said. "Indeed. I can see plainly why it is the ladies take a fancy to the boy. A certain looseness of the tongue. More than a touch of what our French brothers call *joie de vivre*." Woodson James spoke into his clay plate, where lay the remains, mere colors, of his Mexican supper.

"How long did you wait?" Belle said, rolling a cigarette.

"Eight days," Cole said. "Eight whole days. My God, it was

hell of terrible. The heat, mosquitoes the size of quarters . . . the food gave me and James both the dysentery. There was no decent, clean women in Panama City. The whiskey tasted like piss, begging your pardon, Belle, but that's the fact of the matter. Eight days . . ." He sighed and blew another puff of smoke toward the ceiling. "Seemed like eight months. That's why old James been in his room since we got here. He's still sick as a dog, can't seem to get hisself just right again."

"Poor old James," Jim Reed said quietly, making patterns with his knife in his refried beans.

"In my professional opinion," Woodson James began. "In my professional opinion," he repeated.

They all waited. "In your professional opinion," Belle finally said, "it's just a bellyache."

"Exactly," Woodson James said, draining his wine cup.

"And what finally come along," Cole continued, locked suddenly into his terrible memory of the Isthmus of Panama, "what finally come along was just about the worst damn thing I've ever seen floating in water. A Norwegian cattle boat, you could still smell the cow shit on the decks. I said to the captain, You think me and my brother are gonna pay good money to travel on some sonuvabitch ship like this that ain't worth mule pee? And the captain just smiled at me and said, *Ja*, I think so. You pay or you stay here in Panama City. Next time I come through here, he said, you gonna have a hole rotted clean through your neck from the damp. You gonna be mildewed up to your knees, green and rotten to your knees. That's what he said." Cole stared across the table, lost in the horror. "I can hear that goddamn Norwegian saying that like it was yesterday . . . green and rotten to your knees."

Frank James pulled one side of his mustache contemplatively. "Always someone to take advantage of a man in distress, been my experience. I can recall . . ." But Jesse turned his cold blue eyes on his older brother and Frank stopped recalling and stared morosely into space.

"The name of the ship was the *Christina*," Cole Younger said. "Pretty name for such a misery of a tub."

"Get on with it," Belle said. "You always did take God's time to tell a tale."

"James and me, we paid this smiling Norwegian bastard two hundred fifty dollars each for this dirty little cabin size of some old lady's reticule and as full of bugs as a dead man's eyes. Took us fifteen days to reach Morro Bay. I thought to myself more than once I'd be better off with the Pinkerton boys. Ain't no hideout in the world worth sleeping with cow shit in your nose and eating bugs in your stew and watching your feet turn green up to the ankles."

"One of these days soon," Jesse James said from the far end of the dining table, "the transcontinental railroad's gonna be finished, and we can all ride out here to California in style."

"Yessir," Cole Younger said, smiling ruefully at his friend. "Us and the Pinkertons, all nice and cozy."

"Until then," Jesse James said, "we have to put up with this sea trip and the Isthmus crossing. But it's better than hanging, ain't it? Mildew is better than a rope. Turning green is better than jail." He didn't smile. He spoke formally, as if he were delivering a sermon upon a text long considered.

His congregation listened respectfully. Then Cole Younger said, "Well, of course, you're right, Jesse. Just like you always are. The *Christina* sure as hell beats hanging. Thing is . . ." He smiled at Belle across the table. "It don't beat it by much."

He and Belle laughed together until Cole saw Jim Reed's eyes and then he stopped laughing, lit another cigarillo and rose from the table. He bowed toward Woodson James, smoothed down his cloud-colored shirt and tucked it more neatly into his pants. "Friend Woodson," he said, "I do thank you for that nice repast and for seeing that my ailing brother got some nourishment in his bed of pain."

"Entirely my pleasure," Woodson James said.

In February 1868, Belle Reed, full-bodied as never before, gave birth to a son, Eddie Reed, in an empty room of the hospital adobe at Paso Robles Sanitarium. She was delivered of her burden that chill winter day by Nurse Milledge and her assistant Flora, who labored along with Belle Reed for nine hours to produce the small figure wrapped in swaddling with which they finally emerged.

"No woman ought to have to endure such a thing," Nurse Milledge said to Woodson James, who waited at the end of the corridor, leonine and weary. Juanito slept at his heels, cradling the skin of wine. "It is an indignity God has provided woman, and I am at a loss to understand His reason for this punishment."

"They say it's Original Sin that's the cause of it all," Woodson James said, sipping wine from his earthen cup. He watched the sunrise through the east windows.

"Don't talk like a fool," Nurse Milledge said, wiping her hands on her white apron. "If there's any sin at all, none of it's original. Where's the father of this creature here?" She pointed to Eddie Reed, who lay in a basket at her feet with only his red face exposed. He made froglike movements under his blanket.

"Asleep, I believe," Woodson James said, tearing himself away from the sunrise. "Sleeping the blissful sleep of the father whose ordeal is merely to produce semen enough to keep the world moving steadily onward toward the Day of Judgment."

"Quit prattling," Nurse Milledge said, "and go and get him. Smelly bastard . . . least he can do is lose a few minutes of sleep."

"Your language," Woodson James said, "is deteriorating daily. You have lost all graciousness of reference. It ain't enough that you call our patients dolts, dummies and charlatans . . . now you got to allude to the sanitary habits of a guest. Jim Reed smells just like the others—no worse, no better. It's the smell of the male outlaw in his temporary lair."

Nurse Milledge picked up the basket at her feet and set it on a nearby table next to a bedpan of chipped beige enamel. She tucked a few flyaway strands of straw-colored hair back into the knot from which they had escaped. "Jesse don't smell like that," she said through a hairpin in her teeth.

"Jesse must be especially clean in his person because his soul is the most nearly carrion." Woodson James prodded Juanito with the toe of his shoe. The boy pulled himself upright on Dr. James's knee and stood swaying and shivering under his winter serape. "Go and tell Jim Reed to wake up and get hisself over here pronto," the doctor said. "Now, git!" The boy's thin brown legs flashed away down the corridor. "Now," Woodson James said, "if you can find yourself a urine jar somewhere that ain't in use, I'll give you some of this wine to drink and that'll perk you right up, make you forget how you hate everybody but Flora."

Nurse Milledge produced a beaker from the cabinet on top of which baby Eddie lay and held it out for Dr. James to fill. "All the way to the top, now," she said. "None of your mean spirit this morning." She drank down all the wine without lowering the beaker from her lips.

"My God, woman, what a toper you are!" Woodson James said admiringly. "Drink like a man."

"Better than a man," Nurse Milledge said. She set the beaker down next to the baby, adjusted its blankets, peered at it for a moment and then said, "If Jesse's so bad, why do you let him come here—him and all his outlaw friends?"

"He is my brother's boy," the doctor said, leaning back against the whitewashed wall, stretching himself. "It's the revolting power of blood. Maybe someday, Milledge, the day will come when blood kinship don't mean any more than blue eyes or brown eyes. We'll just say, Well, that man's a monster and we don't want him anywhere under our roof, contaminating our dwelling. Blood won't come into it."

Nurse Milledge watched Juanito and Jim Reed through the window as they hurried from the residence adobe. Jim Reed was still buttoning up his shirt. His hair was wild and spiky with sleep. "You think Jesse's a monster, do you?" she said.

"It's a matter of history, Milledge. A matter of history. Consult your newspapers and periodicals, consult your Federal archives. Think about Centralia, Kansas, and the massacre of seventy-five boys in blue. Oh, he wasn't alone, Milledge. He had help. But there was three soldiers afoot and running for their lives and Jesse cut them down like chickens in a yard. No, that ain't true. With a certain pleasure. He took a certain pleasure in it." He sucked in a deep breath and closed his eyes.

Jim Reed loped down the corridor ahead of Juanito. His thin face was anxious. "Where is she? Where's Belle? Where's my boy?"

Nurse Milledge pointed to the basket on the nearby table. Jim Reed approached it hesitantly. "My God," he said breathlessly. "Ain't he red . . . and tiny . . ." He looked at Nurse Milledge apprehensively. "Ain't he too tiny?" he asked.

"Too tiny for what?" Nurse Milledge said. She refilled her beaker without consulting Woodson James.

"It ain't normal . . . is it normal to be that tiny?" Jim Reed asked.

"Did you expect him to spring full-grown from the womb? As it is, he was too big to give his mama much comfort on the way out."

Jim Reed pulled back a corner of the blanket and picked up one of his son's feet. "Ain't they cunning?" he said wonderingly. "God works wonders, don't He?"

Woodson James let a long spiral of breath escape audibly from his wide throat. "Now and again He tries. But it's a losing game. He just plays now out of habit. Even God's got habits, I would suppose."

"Belle's in the last room on the left, if you want to see her, if she's still awake," Nurse Milledge said to Jim Reed.

Jim Reed dropped the tiny foot. "What you gonna do with my boy?" he said. "I mean, right now. What happens to him right now?"

"I give him to Flora and the Mexicans," Nurse Milledge said. "They'll take care of him until his mama's rested up."

He rushed off down the corridor and disappeared into the last room on the left. Nurse Milledge looked after him, caressing her beaker of wine. When she turned around again, Woodson James was staring down the hallway as though he were in a trance. "Are you all right, Woodson?" she asked.

"In a few years we'll be reading about him in the *Police Ga-*

zette," the doctor said. "A dashing young blade who robs trains and shoots bank tellers in small Missouri towns. They'll say about him that his pa was an illustrious outlaw before him and that his ma was once the mistress of the celebrated Cole Younger. Among the other facts of his short history it'll be noted that he was born at the sanitarium of Dr. Woodson James, hisself the uncle of Jesse James—apprentice to the bloody Quantrill and scourge of the Middle Border."

Nurse Milledge ran her short, callused hand over the white mane of Woodson James and said, "Never mind, Woodson. Never mind. Have another cup of wine. Forget tomorrow. That was never anything but grief."

The woman opened Belle's door in the hospital adobe and peered in. She saw that Belle was lying awake in her bed, hair strewn upon the pillow, eyes fixed on some distant point through the north-facing window. "Can I come in?" she asked. "I'm Magdalena."

Belle said, "Sure, you can come in, Magdalena. I'd welcome the company."

Magdalena stood uncertainly by the bed, stroking and smoothing Belle's bedcovers. "They say I've got a mania," she said.

"Who says that?" Belle asked, sitting up in her bed.

"Dr. James says it. And I think Nurse Milledge says it too. I don't know what Flora says. I don't think I've ever heard Flora say anything. She's not talkative. She just works and works, but she doesn't say anything. She's as silent as the grave."

Belle leaned over to her bedside table and picked up her sack of tobacco and began to roll a cigarette. "What kind of mania have you got?" she asked Magdalena while she was rolling. "And what the hell is a mania, anyway?"

"Well," Magdalena said, "it's like a thought you keep having over and over, a thought you can't get out of your head, day and night it keeps sticking in your head like a burr." She looked out the north-facing window and sighed deeply. "It's got something to do with men," she said. "Something terrible to do with men."

"What's it got to do with men?" Belle asked, lighting her cigarette.

"I like them too much, that seems to be the trouble," Magdalena said. "Dr. James says I like them too much for my own good. He says I'd be much better off if I didn't like them at all. If I thought they were all horse dung. Dr. James says it would be a big step forward to health if I thought they were all horse dung." She smiled angelically at Belle. "But of course I don't think that," she said. "I think they're all wonderful. Everybody from Axel to the President. I let Axel make love to me once, and Dr. James was very disappointed in me. He just kept saying, My God, Axel . . . my God, Axel. Over and over." She smoothed down Belle's uncombed russet hair with her two delicate hands. She leaned upon the bed on her elbows. "I don't know why he said that about Axel. Axel was very nice. Oh, he's too old. And he speaks a funny way. He's from another part of the world, that's what Nurse Milledge says. But he's nice. He's very gentle. He's a nice gentle soul, I like that."

"Yes," Belle said, smoking. "Gentle souls are nice sometimes. Although—"

"But Dr. James said Axel wasn't gentle at all. That's what he said to me. He said, Magdalena, Axel is not gentle, Axel is not with us, he is away off somewhere else. He doesn't know the meaning of the word gentle. He said, Axel is so drunk he hasn't got the strength to be vicious. Dr. James got very cross with me and hollered. He said, Can't you take that in? I didn't know what that meant. What does it mean to take something in?"

Belle snuffed out her cigarette in a tin lid on the pea-green table by her bed. "It means . . ." she began. Then she shrugged and gave up. "It don't matter," she said. "Forget it."

"I'm trying," Magdalena said. "I do try to forget things. The sooner I forget things, the sooner I can go home."

"Home?" Belle said. She looked at Magdalena curiously: the

clipped hair, the long blue muslin hospital gown, the bare feet, the brown bird-bright eyes. "Where's your home?" she asked.

"Down there." The woman gestured southward. "Near the border. My family lives near the border. My father's an *alcalde* . . . you know? A governor. Very respected. Everybody respects the *alcalde*. He doesn't like me. That's why he sent me up here to Dr. James. He doesn't like me at all."

"I know about fathers," Belle said. She stared out the window and considered John Shirley. "They're all bastards. They got no understanding of women. Women are like something off the moon, far as they're concerned. They'd sell you to the first man come along with a good Arab pony if it wasn't for your ma hovering there in the shadows with a shotgun of her own. Listen, Magdalena . . ." Belle leaned toward the girl intently. "Let me give you some good advice—you get yourself a shotgun of your own and you keep it by your side. Don't you ever let that shotgun out of your sight . . . you hear?"

Magdalena listened and smiled, plucking lint carefully off Belle's bedcovers. "I will," she said. "I'll get myself a shotgun. I always try to take good advice from women. Nurse Milledge told me that. She said, Magdalena—whatever terrible things you take from men, never take any advice. When you need advice, ask a woman. Nurse Milledge's got no respect at all for my father the *alcalde*. One day she told me he was an imbecile and his mother should have held him under the water tap when he was born. She said that would have been a service to all of California." She laughed. "I never have forgotten that. I think about it a good deal, but nothing comes of it. Nothing ever comes of me thinking about things. It's all very mysterious. What do you think?"

Belle laughed and leaned over and embraced Magdalena. "I think it's all very clear, is what I think," she said. "One of these days Dr. James is going to explain it all to you very clearly and then you're going to be well and happy and go somewhere nice to live. Not with the *alcalde*. Somewhere nice, with a nice man. You'll see."

Magdalena kissed Belle on the cheek and stroked her russet
hair and smiled winsomely. "I'll come and see you again," she
said. "Tomorrow, maybe."

"I won't be here tomorrow," Belle said. She patted the girl on
the shoulder. "I'll be well enough to go back to my own room
tomorrow, and then one of these days I'll be going back to Texas
again. But think of me once in a while, will you do that? Think
of Belle Reed and wish her good fortune. Say: Belle Reed is
twenty years old—give her twenty more good years. Can you
remember that?"

"Oh yes," Magdalena said. "Don't worry. I'll send you good
fortune every day. Where is Texas? Is that near the border?
Would my father the *alcalde* be boss of Texas too? I'd be interested to know that."

It was an uncertain April day in 1868 when the rider appeared
in Cambria, a small fishing village on the California coast. A
squall had blown in from the Pacific and washed the dusty town
into its natural whites and blues, but by midafternoon the sun
was drifting quickly in and out of clouds and dappling everything
in Cambria. For the man on horseback, who was Jim Reed, it
was as though some giant played with the shutters of the sky,
constantly opening and closing them. He didn't like the effect:
it made him feel strange. He had the sense that his eyes were
slightly unfocused and darting about like Mexican jumping beans,
but he rode on, very slowly, down the main street of Cambria
until he reached the First County Bank. This was a red-brick
building about fifteen feet across with a partly glassed front. It
had a tall wooden door and no metal bars anywhere visible, since
the First County Bank had never had any reason to fear for its
deposits. Jim Reed dismounted and flung his horse's reins once,
loosely, around the hitching post in front of the bank. He took
a deep breath and threw open the door of First County. One
hand brought his neck scarf up across the lower part of his face
and the other drew his Colt .44 from its holster. Inside, he

slammed the door behind him, leaned for an instant against it, looking around the interior of the miniature bank with its three grilled teller's windows, and then said, "Reach for the sky, folks —this is a holdup!" It seemed to him unnaturally dark for a bank.

An old woman at the grilled window on the right screamed and dropped her paisley shawl. Jim Reed pointed his pistol at the woman. "Now," he said, "don't do that again or I'll put a bullet through you and I don't like doing that kinda thing to ladies." The old woman moved back and braced herself against the wall. She had forgotten her paisley shawl.

Jim Reed approached the first teller's window and shoved his pistol partly through the grill. "All your cash money in a strong bag," he said. "Real quick, I ain't got all day. No silver, just bank notes."

The teller began stuffing a heavy muslin bag with notes, his eyes huge with astonishment. The other two tellers stood frozen at their windows. One held a pencil upright and in the middle of a page where it had stopped. The old woman still shrank against the wall, hands outstretched to steady herself. A middle-aged man wearing a soft felt slouch hat and carrying a small bag that looked like a medical bag had just completed a transaction at the middle window. He stood with his head down contemplating the small bag. His right hand rested on the ledge outside the grilled window.

"You!" Jim Reed said, and motioned with his pistol. "Over against the wall there with the old lady."

The man in the slouch hat turned and inspected the wall as though he had been asked to paint it and were readying a quotation on the job.

"Now!" Jim Reed hollered. "I don't mean sometime next week, mister."

The man moved over to the wall and leaned against it on his shoulder as if he were enormously tired and could not take another step. The old woman stared at him; he smiled at her apologetically. "I regret, madam," he said, "that the state of my health does not permit me to take any action against this villain."

"Shut your face!" Jim Reed shouted at the man, dragging the

muslin bag to the middle window and shoving it through toward the teller, who stood like a statue on the other side of the grill. "She don't want to know why you're such a coward as you are." He spoke to the teller out of the side of his mouth, without turning toward him. "Fill up this bag just like your friend over there done. And make it snappy!" He ran his left hand over his eyes, but things remained as shadowy as ever. He wondered how a bank could do business in this half-light. "What's the matter with you?" he yelled at the third teller, who stared down at the bulging muslin bag Jim Reed passed through the grill as though it were an exotic artifact from the moon. "Don't you know what to do with that bag? You got no idea what to do with that bag?"

The teller grabbed the bag and inserted a handful of bank notes without glancing down. He looked green. Jim Reed thought it might be the light in the bank. The green teller continued to stuff handfuls of money into the muslin bag as though he were in a trance, his eyes fixed upon Jim Reed and his Colt revolver. He tied together the two strings at the top of the bag and pushed it through the grill toward Jim, who picked it up and turned toward the door. Then he had a second thought: "You, there!" he shouted.

The man in the slouch hat leaned away from the wall but continued looking at the old woman. "Are you addressing me?" he said.

"You bring me over that little black bag you got in your hand," Jim Reed said. "And be quick, I got to get a move on."

The man closed his eyes and pressed his lips together. "I don't think I'll do that," he said, still facing away from Jim Reed.

"You don't think what?" Jim Reed said incredulously, waving his Colt in the air. "What is it you ain't gonna do?"

The man in the soft felt slouch hat turned very quickly from the wall, at the same instant throwing his right arm out briskly as though offering his hand to shake. There was a small slapping sound as a double-barreled Remington derringer slipped into the man's palm from the wide cuff where it was concealed. At the same moment that Jim Reed heard the small slapping sound, he also heard the bullet from the derringer explode against the bone in his upper left arm. He dropped the muslin bag. Hot rivulets of blood streamed down his arm, dripped from the ends of his fingers and made a quick puddle on the bag full of bank notes. Jim Reed stared at the burgeoning puddle in disbelief. He forced his eyes away from the mesmerizing sight of his own blood to the extraordinarily white face of the man in the slouch hat, who still stood fixed in a half crouch, the derringer so concealed within his palm that the smoke from the barrel seemed to emanate from the ends of his fingers. "I have one more bullet in here," he said quietly to Jim Reed, whose pupils had grown as large as his irises, whose face grew paler by the moment. "Get out of this bank and I won't use it," the man said. Jim still couldn't see the derringer. It looked as if the man simply pointed at him accusingly, leaning forward emphatically.

The bank became more and more shadowed. Jim Reed tried to remember what he knew about fainting, which he thought might be near at hand. He recalled it was unmanly, something women did at all critical moments. Nevertheless, the dark was eating away the edges of his eyes and there was a high-pitched humming in his ears. He leaned down to pick up the muslin bag.

"Leave that where it lies!" the man with the derringer said.

Jim Reed dropped his Colt into its holster and clamped his hand around his upper left arm: the blood spurted between his fingers like a fountain. The old woman screamed and left her knotted fist in the open hole of her mouth. "He's going to bleed to death, dear Lord, he's going to bleed to death!" she said.

The man with the derringer straightened up from his half crouch and pulled the little pistol back under his broad shirt cuff. He picked up the soaked muslin bag and threw it onto the ledge of the middle teller's window, where it struck with the soft splash of an overripe melon, freckling the teller's white paper collar with Jim Reed's blood. The man opened the tall wooden door and motioned Jim Reed out of the First County Bank with an almost courtly sweep of his soft slouch hat. He gave him a leg-up to mount his horse and threw a saddle blanket over the bloody arm. Then he slapped the horse on its backside. "Keep riding until you can't see even a trail of smoke from a chimney in this town," he said.

To keep his head upright, Jim Reed propped it against the chin strap of his sombrero. He grasped the horn on his saddle and, rocking back and forth as though he no longer had a spine in his long body, he was carried off in a southward direction. A mile outside Cambria he turned his horse eastward toward Paso Robles. Only a pinprick of light remained in the middle of his eyes, and he could smell his blood like a newly killed animal.

For a week after his horse carried him back to the Paso Robles Sanitarium, Jim Reed occupied that grey zone of the not-quite-dead. Dr. Woodson James called it a miracle that he had not died of blood loss on his way back from fateful Cambria. He wondered why God had singled out Jim Reed to preserve against all odds.

"Maybe He's saving him for something more suitable," Nurse Milledge said. "Like hanging."

Belle came every morning and stood leaning against the glass enclosure of the infirmary, staring fearfully at the pale face and closed eyes of the figure on the iron cot. One morning she brought baby Pearl, who was now two years old.

"Look," Belle pointed, leaning down toward the child. "That's Jim papa there. Go and kiss his cheek."

Pearl gazed with horror at the unmoving body on the cot and then turned and stared at her mother. "No," she said. She grasped the edge of Nurse Milledge's desk. "No," she repeated.

Belle tried to loosen the child's fingers from their grip upon the mahogany, but it was as if Pearl feared for her life and Nurse Milledge's desk was her only hope of salvation. "Pearl!" Belle shook the child by her shoulders. "Go and kiss Jim papa. You may never have another chance to kiss him in this life. Do like I say!"

Pearl burst into tears. She wept until she lost her breath and began to gasp air to restore the rhythm of her small lungs. Her mother stared at her disbelievingly. "What's got into you?" she asked the child.

"She don't want to kiss a corpse," Woodson James said, patting Pearl on the head. "That's natural."

"Jim's not dead yet," Belle said.

"Smells close, though," Woodson James said. "Children got good noses when it comes to dying. They're like little animals in the forest who can catch a scent of fire on the wind while a man's still sitting around his camp drinking coffee and thinking he's got tomorrow ahead of him."

Belle lifted her skirt and wiped her daughter's eyes on the petticoat underneath. She brushed the girl's fine red hair away from her damp forehead and embraced her. "Don't cry anymore, Pearl baby. Don't cry. Your mama's not gonna make you do anything you don't want to do. Come on, now. Straighten yourself up. Be a big girl . . ."

Pearl's eyes clung to her mother's face as though all the world's comfort lay there. She grasped Belle's arm in a tight grip. "Let's go," she whispered. "Let's go, Mama."

"We're going right now, baby," Belle said, smoothing down Pearl's wild hair, tugging her dress into order again. Belle looked at Woodson James and said, "I'll be back in an hour. If Jim should wake up . . ."

"I'll tell him," the doctor said. "I'll give him the message." He watched Belle and the little Pearl hasten away down the corridor.

Nurse Milledge came out of a nearby room, groans at her back. She sat down at her desk and made a note on a long pad lying there. Then she studied Woodson James's face for a moment. "What the hell was he doing robbing a bank in Cambria, anyway?" she said. "Haven't we got troubles enough here without harboring an outlaw some posse may be out looking for? Why don't he save his villainy for Texas and Missouri—he knows something about Texas and Missouri. He don't know a thing about California. He'll be the death of us all."

"There'll be no posse, Milledge," Woodson James said. He sighed and rubbed his forehead and ran his hands thoughtfully through his heavy white hair. "If there was a posse, it'd be already at our door. Nobody's looking for this man lying here."

"Why not, then?" Milledge said. "Why is nobody looking?"

"Why did they let him leave Cambria?" the doctor said, slumping onto a small white metal stool next to Nurse Milledge's desk. "Why did somebody shoot him up like that and then let him go riding off home? What's your opinion on that, Milledge?"

"My opinion," she said, "is that Jim Reed strikes about as much fear into their hearts as a heavy rain."

Woodson James nodded. "My feelings exactly," he said.

"What's Belle think about it?" Nurse Milledge said.

"We ain't spoken of the matter," the doctor said. "I got reason to suspect she don't think overmuch of Jim's capabilities. She talks admiringly about the Younger boys and of course Jesse, but she never says much about Jim Reed. She loves the boy, oh, doubtless that's true, that's true. But love has not blinded her to his shortcomings as an outlaw."

Nurse Milledge tapped her pencil in a regular tattoo on her desk for a minute or two. "The baby's puny too," she finally said. "Scrawny little thing . . ."

Woodson James arose from his low white metal stool. "Well, then, get Flora to tell the cook something special to fix for the child, some fattening delicacy he can't resist. Feed the boy up. I promised Belle it'd be a strong, strapping lad . . . do her proud. You see to it, Milledge."

Nurse Milledge smiled at him with just the outside corners of her mouth. "Well, if you promised Belle, we'll do our best to keep you from looking like some doddering old fool doctor. Flora and I, we'll try our very best."

"One of these days," Woodson James said, "I'm going to send you and Flora away from this place in a very large wooden box addressed to God in care of the Pacific Ocean."

Milledge laughed raucously. "That'll be after Axel has burned the sanitarium right to the ground, will it? Drunk as a lord from potato whiskey and mean and vicious as usual, he'll drop a match in the dry grass and send the whole place up in flames. Then you won't need Flora and me to run this place for you. That'll be about the time you decide to do us both in, will it?"

The doctor sighed deeply. "I've lost all control over you, Milledge," he said. "You was tractable once, that must have been decades ago, so long ago I can't even recollect the time. But I remember a sweet-eyed blond girl I could bend like a willow sapling."

"I remember that girl too, Woodson," Nurse Milledge said. "She died of overwork."

Woodson James shook his great white head. "She died of clear seeing," he said. "She had too damn good an eye, that girl with the honey hair. She saw too many horrors too many times."

"She saw something else too," Nurse Milledge said. "Who did all the work and who did all the talking."

"You got to talk to a lunatic, Milledge," the doctor said sadly. "You never will understand how important it is for me to speak to these lunatic souls. They're perishing for want of the human voice."

"Not for long they're not," Nurse Milledge said, sweeping off down the corridor to the room from which cries had begun to escape a moment before.

After eight days in the grey zone Jim Reed opened his eyes and gazed upward at Nurse Milledge, who was taking his blood pressure. "I'm not dead," he announced.

"That's true," Nurse Milledge said, rolling up her blood-pressure bandage. "It's one of Dr. James's very own miracles."

Jim Reed began to weep softly. He rubbed his eyes in embarrassment. "I thought sure I'd bought it," he explained. "I thought sure I'd never see Belle or the kids again."

"Well, you were wrong," Nurse Milledge said, rising from the side of the iron cot. "I'll tell Belle you're awake. She's been wait-

ing on you to open those eyes for a whole week. Real devoted."
She left the room.

In ten minutes Belle Reed arrived, breathless. "Jim!" she cried
from the door. She threw herself onto the floor next to the cot
and extended her body across her husband's torso, her hands
reaching up to caress his face. "It's so good to see those eyes
open again," she said. She leaned back to study him. "But you're
so thin, Jim! You look like a cadaver in the face, I swear you do.
And you need a good shave, you feel like a cactus patch. I'll get
one of the boys to come shave you."

"Not Cole," Jim Reed said. "I don't want Cole shaving me."

Belle rose from her crouch next to the iron cot. She brushed
her hands over the sides of her hair and back over the knot at
the nape of her neck. "Don't fret yourself," she said. "Woodson
says you got to stay calm and easy."

"Easy for him to say," Jim said. "He's got no shot-up arm.
Cole Younger ain't after his woman."

"Don't start in so soon talking like a fool," Belle said. "You
do what Woodson James tells you to do. He saved your life, Jim.
You know that? Nobody thought you'd live through the night
when you showed up here that day with your arm just hanging on
by a string of muscle and blood everywhere. Your saddle blanket
was soaked clean through. Milledge took one look at you and
you know what she said, Jim? She said, I'll tell Axel to dig his
grave. That's exactly what she said. But Woodson James brought
you in here and poured alcohol all over that arm and bandaged
you up real good and told Flora to get some beet soup down you
any way she could. He stayed with you, or Nurse Milledge or
Flora stayed, every minute you been lying in that bed. He just
plain willed you back to life, is what I think."

Jim Reed thought that over. Then he sighed. "I'm no good anymore, Belle honey. My eyes have gone back on me. I couldn't
see nothing clear that day. It was like I was inside a dark cloud.
I can't even hold up some little tiny bank and get off with a bag
of greenbacks to keep you and the kids fed and covered up
decent."

"Now, don't you start worrying your head about that," Belle

said. She sat down gently on the side of the bed and began to roll a cigarette.

"After all, there's little Eddie now," Jim said, "along with baby Pearl. We got expenses and the money we brought from Missouri is running out. I got family responsibilities, Belle. I got to look after my own." His eyes reddened as though he might begin to weep again.

Belle smoked and studied him appraisingly through her narrowed eyes. "From now on," she said softly, "you let Belle decide where and when, all right? And then you go on in with your big Colt drawn and take what I tell you to take and bring it on back to your little ones."

He stared at her and then turned his head toward the whitewashed wall.

"Now, don't pout," Belle said. "Pouting don't accomplish nothing. I'm not saying you can't outlaw all by yourself as good as you ever could. I'm just saying that maybe the two of us together could do it better. Ain't you always saying how proud you are of me because I got myself an education when I was little? Well, now, you just let me use some of that education to make things better for both of us. All right, Jim? You see how smart that'd be, don't you?"

He looked at her and smiled tentatively. "The two of us together," he said. "That'll be nice."

"Sure, it will," she said. She stepped on her cigarette and then leaned down to kiss him lightly on the forehead. "We'll make them sit up and sing, won't we? All those little bastards in all those little banks . . ."

Jim Reed laughed weakly, taking pleasure in the picture.

"One of these days," Belle continued, stroking Jim's forehead, "maybe we'll get a gang of men to work for us, a real gang, doing just what I say . . ."

Jim Reed lifted himself slightly from the bed, thrusting her hand away. "A gang! Why the hell we need a gang?"

"More banks, honey," she said. "Bigger banks. Bigger bags of money." She smiled at him sweetly, pushed him gently back against his pillow. "But we'll think about that later. Right now you just rest your poor old arm and don't worry your head about a thing. I'll bring you in some supper later on."

Her goodbye kiss was like a feather across his lips.

"The way I understand it," Cole Younger said quietly to Belle as they stood on the gallery of the residence adobe after supper the next night, "is that the man was a gambler, owns the Cambria Elegant, which is a nice saloon over there. I stopped in to check on it myself." He grinned at Belle and touched her face quickly. "This fellow was carrying a whole week's receipts from his saloon in a little bag. He'd just drawed this money out of the bank. Well, naturally, he didn't want to hand it over to Jim, now did he? So here was Jim with this bag full of bank notes, folks in Cambria say he musta had maybe ten, twelve thousand dollars in that bag, and he spies this little bag of the gambler and decides he'll have that too. Only the gambler's got other notions and draws a derringer out of his sleeve and shoots Jim in the arm."

Belle rocked back and forth on her boot heels, looking unhappy. "A hideout gun . . . he was done in by somebody with a tiny little old hideout gun."

"Well, you know, Belle," Cole said, "you just can't see those damned little things until they go off in your face. There oughta be a law against them, is what I say."

"Is that the whole story?" Belle said.

"That's all. Except after this fellow shot Jim, then he takes him out of the bank and puts him on his horse and sends him off home. The citizens over there in Cambria say it was one kindred spirit looking after another—this fellow's spent his whole life holding people up at the faro table or playing poker or monte. He just didn't want to see one of his own kind hanging on a gallows outside his window. At least that's what the townsfolk in Cambria say about it." Cole put his hands into the pockets of his pale brownish-yellow nankeen trousers and sighed deeply. "Makes as good sense as anything," he said.

Belle stared out into the night, preoccupied. "Of course," she said at last, "the real reason might be to show contempt for Jim. Like saying, Well, you can take this man that tried to rob us and patch him up if you can and send him wherever he wants to go, even back here again, because he's so blessed poor a villain nobody's got any reason to be afraid of him."

Cole Younger studied his boots in the moonlight. After a moment's thought he nodded. "I guess that might be so," he said. "It ain't what they say in Cambria."

"You didn't talk to the gambler who shot him, though . . . did you? Now, he's the man who knows."

Cole looked at her thoughtfully, a slight smile on his lips. "Why you want to think so poorly of Jim?" he said. "He made a mistake, all right. But any one of us would have wanted that gambler's little bag and tried to take it, just like Jim did."

"Greed's all right in its place," Belle said. "In its place it's a nice manly trait. But its place wasn't the First County Bank in Cambria with Jim standing there holding a bag already stuffed with enough bank notes to go all the way to Paris, France, and back again half a dozen times. A man ought to learn when it's out of place to be too greedy. He ought to be able to see things like that real quick and clear. You would have seen that, Cole. Nobody'd have to tell you a thing like that twice. Jim just don't have much elementary good sense."

At that moment there was a sound like a crack of doomsday thunder out of the hospital adobe. Belle and Cole turned simultaneously, faces astonished. Across the intervening patch of brown earth illuminated by several coal-oil lanterns they saw a figure emerge from the adobe. The man was erect but wobbled like a puppet on a string. Every few feet his knees bent and then pushed up again—each time a deeper bend, a harder rise. He appeared to be making his way haphazardly toward the residence.

"Ain't that Axel?" Cole Younger said.

Woodson James appeared on the gallery in his union suit, hair standing wildly from the muss of the bed to which he had retreated immediately after supper. He narrowed his eyes and squinted across the space between the two adobes. "What the hell sound was that?" he shouted. He pointed. "And who is that coming there? Is that Axel I see?"

The man had reeled, rising and falling like an ocean wave, to the edge of the gallery upon which Belle and Cole and Woodson James stood transfixed. He grasped the railing with both hands and stared at them, his mouth opening and closing rapidly, emitting only a high-pitched humming sound from the back of the throat.

"Axel!" the doctor shouted, staring at him in horror. "Axel . . . my God, Axel . . . Who put that hole in your chest? Who was it did that, Axel?"

The high-pitched humming sound approached the lips, intensifying. Axel wore a soiled Prussian uniform jacket with intermittent gold braid unbuttoned down the front and no trousers. Just above his navel there was a hole the size of a California mango. From this hole there streamed a red-and-yellow substance, the force of the stream increasing each moment. Axel stared at Dr. James in terrified amazement. The high-pitched hum gathered and emerged from his mouth as a scream which made Belle Reed shrink back against Cole Younger and lift her arms to ward off whatever horror might be presaged by it.

Woodson James moved with the quickness of a giant cat to Axel's side and, grasping him under the arms, began to drag him back toward the hospital adobe.

"Nein! Nein!" Axel shouted, waving his arms like the wings of a windmill. "Nichts da! Nichts da! Geh' nichts!" He slumped to the ground on his knees and fell forward on his face. Woodson James leaned down and turned the German's head slightly to the left, scooping dirt out of his nostrils. "Now, breathe, you German fool!" he hollered. He looked up wildly at Cole and Belle, fixed like two stone figures on the gallery. "Cole!" he shouted. "I need you! Come here!"

Cole Younger stirred as though waking from a dream. He ran to Woodson James's side and the two of them managed to lift Axel upright. He hung like a rag doll between them.

"I did as you said, Belle!" The voice came from the front entrance to the hospital adobe. The doctor and Cole Younger stopped where they were and gazed toward the shadowed area, the motionless Axel still dangling between them. "Belle?" Magdalena stepped into the lantern light. She bore a shotgun as though it were a sheaf of flowers. She smiled, looking past the two men bearing the rag-doll Axel, searching out Belle in the darkness. "Are you over there, Belle?"

Belle stepped off the gallery and out into the light. She moved slowly toward the hospital, holding her skirts up a little as though she feared to dirty them. "I'm here, Magdalena," she said.

"I took your advice," Magdalena said. She lifted the shotgun above her head. "You see, Belle? I got a shotgun of my own and I keep it by my side. Axel got it for me, but then he wanted to make love to me again, even though I told him how disappointed Dr. James was about the last time. I told him I'd have to wait for a younger, prettier man, or the doctor would be very displeased." She looked at her bare feet and then across the space at Cole and Woodson James, who stood watching her curiously, not moving. Below Axel a pool of the red-and-yellow liquid was forming and growing. "He wouldn't believe me when I said no. He was just like my father the *alcalde*. Whenever I said no about anything to the *alcalde*, he would just frown and say, Ignorant girl, ignorant girl."

Belle Reed took the shotgun very carefully from Magdalena. She put one arm about the girl's waist and pulled her gently toward the hospital adobe. "The *alcalde* was wrong," Belle said. "You're not an ignorant girl. You know just what you're up to, ain't that true? You come with me, now, and we'll take you back to bed. You look real pale and tired. You need to sleep." The two women moved slowly inside the hospital, their heads slightly bowed and close together: they could have been two friends returning from an afternoon walk. Woodson James saw a kerosene lamp flare up in the interior and illuminate the two women as they entered: Milledge, he thought. Milledge has come.

"Drag him now, Cole!" the doctor shouted. "Before the carcass is cold as a stone, we got to get him to the infirmary. Pull!"

The two men half dragged, half pushed the bloody Axel to-

ward the hospital, groaning with exertion. Near the entrance
Woodson James dropped Axel's left side and leaned against a
wooden support post, breathing heavily.

"Just a minute, wait a minute . . ." he said to Cole. "Put him
down, just lay him down on the ground. Let me have a look. I
sense we're too late. I got this feeling we're lugging dead guts."
He got down and pressed his ear to Axel's chest. He opened the
German's mouth and listened into the dark cavern. Then he stood
up. He nodded, wiping his bloody hands on his union suit. "Dead
as a doornail," he said. "Not a breath, not a gurgle." He shook
his head. "It's amazing to me how silent a man can get. You'd
think the blood would keep on running for a second or two, but
it stops in its tracks. Not a swish of it, not the least little splash
against the side of a vein."

Cole Younger wiped his mouth with the back of his hand.
"What do you want to do with him?"

"We'll carry him into the infirmary and cover him over and
leave him for the night. Tomorrow morning I'll get some of the
Mexicans to dig a hole for him. They'll be pleased. They never
liked him a damn's worth."

Cole Younger grasped Axel's bare feet and Woodson James
his square military shoulders and they carried him into the hospital. Nurse Milledge met them in the corridor with a lamp. She
stared for a moment at the burden stretched between them. "The
old fool," she said. She led the way to the infirmary, where they
deposited Axel on a metal table from which Nurse Milledge
stripped the sheet just before the body touched it. "No point in
bloodying things up unnecessarily," she said, throwing the sheet
over the dead man.

"Dear God!" they heard Belle scream, and all three ran out
into the corridor. Belle stood in the doorway of Magdalena's
room pointing to the infirmary's glass enclosure, through which
baby Pearl—standing on the white metal stool and wearing a
nightdress the color of ripe peaches, with white ribbons at the
neck—watched the sheet covering Axel slowly turn red and
yellow.

. . .

"I don't hold you responsible," Woodson James said to Belle Reed. "How was you to know the girl would get herself a shotgun and blow it off into Axel's chest? Lunatics seize on odd things we say to them and only the dear God knows what they'll do with them. The Mexicans won't say nothing about these events. They know I require discretion, that's one of the cardinal things I require. And, besides, they don't like the authorities. They stay strictly away from the authorities. Here, let me fill up your cup."

Belle held her cup out and the doctor tipped the skin of wine into it. She sighed. "What will become of Magdalena?" she said.

Woodson James shrugged. "She'll stay here as long as the *alcalde*'s money holds out," he said. "I calculate the *alcalde*'s sons and grandsons will be rich men when I've been moldering in my grave a hundred years."

"I mean about Axel," Belle said.

"Oh, that," the doctor said. "Well, that don't matter. Axel's dead and that's an end to it. We've already put him into a nice hole over by the eucalyptus tree. Ordinarily I'd look for some exceptional blooms in that vicinity, but Axel was so pickled in alcohol he'll probably poison the ground there and kill the roots of all the foliage."

"No marshal or sheriff will be coming around here?" Belle said.

"They've never come up here yet," Woodson James said. "They're all afraid of my loonies. That's the main reason Jesse and Frank started coming here to hide out. It's a long and arduous way, but once here they're about as safe as a soul might be that sat in a church for high mass."

"And nobody will come for Magdalena?" Belle said.

"Nobody wants Magdalena." Woodson James drained his cup and set it on the floor at his feet. "Nobody wanted Axel and nobody wants Magdalena. When I come to write my magnum opus someday on the lunatic and infirm, all I'm going to say is that nobody wants them. They're just the trash of our marvelous world. I thought it was going to be a much longer book when I was a young man."

Within two months Dr. James replaced Axel with another German, a tall, skeletal, hairless man named Denker, who drank only a little Mexican beer in the evenings after supper and who worked noiselessly like an ant. Twice a week Denker went into Paso Robles for hospital supplies, provisions and wine. One Tuesday afternoon he returned to the sanitarium around five in the afternoon, left his laden wagon and horses by the hospital adobe and sought out Jim Reed in the residence building. He found him in the cool, shuttered sitting room, where Jim was stretched out on a settee with his chin buried in his black shirt-front and his boots elevated on the armrest. Belle Reed was pacing the room, smoking, stopping in her course now and then to memorize with one hand the contours of her face.

"Excuse that I interrupt," Denker said.

"Well, what is it?" Belle said.

"I am coming only now from the village and there have I heard news you will interest yourself in."

Belle Reed crushed out her cigarette on the tiled floor. "For God's sake, get on with it then!"

Denker removed his wool hat and cleared his throat. "I have heard at the Golddust Saloon that a posse will soon arrive here in search of the Herr Reed." He gestured toward Jim on the settee, who sat up quickly and swung his boots onto the floor.

Belle narrowed her eyes and focused on the German. "Who told you that?" she asked.

Denker stared at the wool hat in his hands, turning it steadily to the right like a cartwheel. "I do not know the men who have spoken," he said. "There were three of them." He cleared his throat again and read his text off the ceiling. "They said, That place out there is a nest of them. We have got to clean that place out. Jim Reed is out there. He is wanted in Texas and now he has robbed the bank in San Luis Obispo. We will go out and get him." Denker dropped his eyes from the ceiling to Belle Reed. "Finished," he said. "Now I must go." He turned and went toward the door.

"Wait a minute!" Belle Reed said. She approached him, her arms outstretched. "It was real good of you to warn us like this," she said to Denker. "We thank you, Jim and me—we truly thank you. Maybe we can do you a good turn someday."

Denker nodded and smiled his cool, thin smile. "I do not like police," he said. He put on his wool hat and left the sitting room.

Belle stood for a moment facing the door through which Denker had just disappeared. Her whole body was an arc of electricity; it seemed to hum; even her russet hair seemed charged. Jim Reed, standing now, involuntarily moved back a few steps, his face growing more and more anxious. When she whirled to look at him, her brows were a black bridge across her face. Her lips were pulled back against her teeth. Her skin had reddened with anger. "Goddamn fool!" she shouted at Jim. "Goddamn fool!" She darted at him, slapped him across the face with such force that he staggered backward until he struck the wall.

"Now, just a minute here . . ." he said, rubbing his face, regaining his footing. "Now, hold on here just a minute . . ."

"Didn't I tell you this would happen?" she said. She glared at Jim Reed blackly. "Didn't I tell you? You was supposed to let me do the planning, ain't that right? Didn't we agree on that? But big man Reed here has got to go on out and rob his own bank his own way, mighty stupid way, dear God, who'd believe how clumsy, why, a man would give more thought to buying a pair of nankeen trousers."

"Listen, Belle . . ." Jim Reed began, pulling himself up to his full height and glowering down. "Ain't I got away with four thousand dollars from that bank in San Luis Obispo? You seemed pretty happy when I walked in with that four thousand dollars, as I recollect."

Belle Reed threw herself down in an armchair and stared up at Jim, shaking her head slowly back and forth. "Anybody's glad to get four thousand dollars, Jim. We needed the money and four thousand is four thousand. But if you'd waited and let me plan it all out, you could have come back with twice or three times four thousand. You never stop to think. You're just like tumbleweed, you just blow hither and yon, hither and yon."

Jim Reed looked miserable. He fumed. He stuffed his hands in his pockets and walked stiffly around the room, casting an occasional glance at the woman in the armchair, who sat with her head thrown back against the chair and her eyes closed. He stopped walking and considered. "I guess we'll have to run for it," he said.

Belle opened her eyes and stared upward at the ceiling. "You guess we'll have to run for it," she repeated in a resigned, unpleasant tone.

"Well, what do you think?" Jim Reed said petulantly. "It ain't safe here anymore, if that Prussie's telling the truth. We got to make tracks."

Belle rose, looked casually around the room until she had located her cigarette fixings and then began with ease and deliberation to roll herself a cigarette. After a minute she said, "Someday, Jim Reed, something real bad is gonna happen to you because you ain't careful enough, you don't take thought."

The comment seemed to freeze him where he stood. He turned pale and sat down suddenly on the settee. "Ah, Belle," he said. "Don't tell me things like that. You know what store I set by what you tell me."

She nodded. "I tell you what's true, Jim. What's true is, you're a sweet lad who don't take thought and someday you'll pay a bad price for that." She was perfectly calm now. She smoked, blowing a veil upward that drifted over the room, leaving a sweet, dark smell in the air. "Now I'm gonna go see Woodson James."

"Goddamn!" Jim Reed said, rising from the settee, regaining his color. "I'm sick and tired of you always running off all the time to see Woodson James, hanging on every word the old coot says, like it was something out of the Holy Book . . . why"— his voice rose—"you got more use for all that shit he talks than you got for anything I say to you, ain't that so!"

Belle studied the burning tip of her dark cigarette for a moment. Then she looked at Jim unsmilingly. "That's so," she said. "Woodson James is a man that takes thought. He'll be sitting out here tippling wine when your own boy Eddie can't remember your face."

"Damn you, Belle!" He took a menacing step toward her.

She lifted her right arm in warning. "I got one of those little hideout guns you never do see hidden right here in the cuff of this dress. It's got one bullet in it for any man lays a hand on me in anger."

Jim Reed stepped back, startled.

"Now," Belle said, "I'm gonna go say adios to Woodson James." She moved to the door of the sitting room. Then she faced Jim again. "We'll leave tomorrow for Sacramento. From there we'll get ourself a train, now that we live in modern times and have a transcontinental railroad. We'll use some of that four thousand you stole to go first-class to Ogden in one of Central Pacific's Silver Palace sleeping cars. I do like a little taste of luxury on my tongue now and then, Jim. I'd like baby Pearl to get to know a little something about luxury too, to get a little bit familiar with it—she's gonna be a lady when she grows up and ladies ought to know a little something about luxury. Even little Eddie ought to have some idea of what a good life is about, don't you think so, Jim? He might have a fool for a daddy, but he's got a mama knows her way around a bucket."

FIRST INTERLUDE

Tom Hill, Outlaw

We rode up to the North Canadian River to find this old Creek Indian who was supposed to have thirty thousand dollars in gold hid away somewheres. Belle said she was sure as hell coming along and there was no way Jim Reed and Will Dixon and me was going off without her on such an adventure and besides she had to come along to make sure she got her share of the gold, that's what she said and I didn't notice she smiled when she said it.

Belle dressed up in some of Jim's britches and one of his old shirts and she put a poncho over everything and tucked all that hair up under a sombrero and wore a kerchief high up on her neck and damned if she couldn't of passed for a man if you didn't look too hard. She carried a six-shooter on each hip and she rode her fine mare Venus. She never rode any other horse but Venus if she could help it.

We traveled for five days before we reached the old Indian's sod house in the Nations. He was out by his well drawing water when we got there late in the day. He didn't run away or nothing and you couldn't tell from his face that he was scared, but you know how it is with Indians—most of the time you can't tell a thing by looking at their faces. Hell, I've seen an Indian ready to cut you into pieces, didn't look any different than if he'd been boiling jackrabbit for his supper. Of course, we didn't look like we meant the old Creek any harm. We just rode up nice and easy, so maybe he didn't think there was any reason to run in the house and grab hisself a shotgun. Jim asked him if he'd mind sharing his water with strangers and maybe letting us sleep on his land overnight. He just looked at us and nodded his head and then he handed the bucket of water up to Jim and made a kind of a circle movement with his other hand to show that he meant Jim to pass the water to all of us. Jim took a dipper of the water and drank it down and then passed the bucket on over to Belle. She handed it on to me without drinking and just went on looking at the old Indian with this kinda funny smile on her face. She got down off Venus and walked over to the Creek and asked him where he'd like us to camp down for the night. He said something to her I couldn't hear and she laughed and turned around to Jim Reed and said, He wants us to move on. He don't much want us hanging around these parts. Now, I wonder why that's so . . .

The Creek made a run for his cabin and Jim fired off his shotgun just in front of the Indian's moccasins. The old man stopped dead in his tracks. When he turned around again, his face looked grey. There was this face naturally the color of tobacco and it'd gone grey as ash.

We spent two days at the Creek's place. The old man just wouldn't say where the gold was hid. At first he said there wasn't no gold, but when Belle picked a hot brand out of his fireplace and said she was gonna burn out his black eyes with it unless he told us the truth, he wailed, Lord, it was like some awful animal cry, and he threw hisself onto his knees and lifted his arms up like he was praying to his gods for help and I guess that's what he was doing, all right. Belle waved that firebrand across his face until his eyebrows smoked and his eyes got so red I swear I thought that any minute they was gonna leak blood onto his face. Jim Reed finally said, For God's sake, Belle, don't kill the old man! We won't find out nothing from a corpse. She stopped then. But her eyes was just shining, I remember that. Her skin was flushed like some kinda rose and she was sweating like she'd been drinking tequila all night, she'd even sweated through Jim's old heavy shirt, and her eyes was shining like she'd seen some kinda real lovely thing that made her happy. We all looked at her like we was in a trance. Belle could do that to you sometimes, sort of put you under a spell, it was like she gave off something powerful that just kept a man rooted like a stump, with his mouth hanging open like he was a dog on a dry day. But that time she scared hell out of me. If I'd been that old Creek, I'd of told her anything she wanted to know quick as spit.

By noon of the second day we was getting pretty tired of asking the old man and not getting anything out of him but a lot of wailing and strange noises. I was about ready to give it all up and ride back to Texas. Will Dixon was feeling the same. We just thought it was all a waste of time, we thought the old Creek was gonna die before he told us where the gold was. Maybe there wasn't no gold, Will and me thought that might be so, even if Belle didn't believe it. Belle *knew* there was gold hid some-wheres, she was sure as God about that and wouldn't hear no arguments against it. Jim Reed didn't say much one way or another. He just looked uncomfortable, like he had a cactus spine sticking in one of his boots. He watched Belle pacing around that Indian's cabin and you could see from his eyes that he expected her to get up to something soon and he was wondering if he could maybe not deal with it when it happened.

Finally she walked over to the old Creek and took him by his long, scraggly white hair and pulled him off his little three-legged stool and onto the hard mud floor on his knees and hit him a terrible blow across the face with that Mexican quirt of hers she always carried around. Streaks of blood came on his left cheek right away. She didn't say a word to him. She just pulled his head back again and went on hitting him in the face over and over with that quirt and everywhere those tight-braided leather strips hit him the blood started pouring out, until finally his whole face was like new-killed beef and all you could see besides the blood was these two black eyes the size of silver dollars.

Jim Reed stood over by the fireplace with his hands on his guns, watching everything like he was in a dream. Then he seemed to wake up all of a sudden and he ran over to the old man and grabbed his arms from behind and held him up while Belle went on hitting him with that quirt. You old devil! he kept saying over and over. You goddamned old devil! I thought it was kind of a funny thing to say, since it was Belle acting like a devil, not the old Creek.

Will was outside tending to the horses. I went out to see could I help and, besides, I wanted to get out of that cabin. All I could smell in there was blood and that smell always made me feel sick to my stomach. A nice clean bullet through the chest or between the eyes, that's what a man oughta have when it come time to call it quits.

In a little while Jim come out of the cabin with this little smile on his face and walked over to where Will and me was brushing down the horses. He said, Boys, we're all rich men.

The old Indian had his gold hid off in a hole downstream a ways on the Canadian. He drew a map and Jim and Will went right off to dig up the money, while Belle and me kept watch to see the Creek didn't get hisself a shotgun or some such from a hide place and try to blow all our heads off. But I thought to myself it wasn't no need to stand guard over the Indian, since he was more dead than alive. He wasn't going no place at all by the time Belle Reed got done with him. I never seen any woman take such pleasure in doing a man in.

It wasn't no thirty thousand dollars in gold. That was somebody with drink in him talking. There was about ten thousand dollars. Will Dixon and me got a thousand dollars each and went on our way. I was glad to go. Jim and Belle went on back to their little place in Texas. I never set eyes on either one of them again. That was all right by me.

Bertha Jenkins, Resident of Scyene, Texas

Oh, it was a wondrous thing to see Belle Reed ride into Scyene, I can tell you that. Wondrous. I remember the first time I saw her. It was early evening in the springtime. That would have been about, oh, 1871 or thereabouts. I'd been to Bartlet's General Store doing some shopping and I was on my way home when I looked to my left and straight out on the north road and I saw this woman on horseback coming into town. It just took my breath away. She was riding the most beautiful mare I'd ever

seen, black and shiny as ebony with a wonderful proud head, and
when she trotted she picked her hooves up just so and put them
down again like she was walking in very high grass. I found out
later on that the mare's name was Venus. I guess she knew who
she was carrying and that's why she looked so grand.

When Belle got to the edge of Scyene she slowed Venus to a
walk, so we could all get a look at this woman we knew was an
outlaw living among outlaws on this little farm outside town. Jim
Reed's woman, everybody said. Cole Younger's mistress before
that. And oh she was something to see. My husband, Herman
Jenkins, always remonstrated with me about admiring the sight
of Belle Reed, but I didn't see any sense in turning a blind eye to
beauty just because it was on the other side of the law. Herman
never understood my reasoning.

That first day I saw Belle she was dressed in velvets the color
of burnt chocolate and wearing a rose-colored chiffon waist. She
had on a creamy white hat with swept-back sides, pulled down a
little over her right eye to give her a kind of rakish look. It was
the kind of jaunty wearing of a hat that said, Look at me, you
poor old country folks! I'm Belle Starr! Of course, she wasn't
Belle Starr then, she was Belle Reed still. It'd be a while yet before they started writing about her in *Fox's Police Gazette* and
places like that. But she always acted like she knew all that fame
was just around the corner.

On top of the hat I recollect there was a tall snow-white ostrich
plume that leaned down so low in front that it almost touched
Venus' mane. Belle sat sidesaddle with her long velvet skirts
pulled up from the bottom and draped over one arm. When she
rode past me I caught a flash like diamonds from her black
leather boots. She wore a six-shooter at each hip, hanging from a
cartridge belt.

Sometimes she'd bring the little girl Pearl with her. She was a
pretty child: hair color of a sunset, blue eyes, skin fair as milk.
Belle would dress her up in silks and lace and put her astride a
little Appaloosa pony that trotted along next to her. They were a
handsome sight, though I know I was very near alone in thinking

so or at least in saying so out loud. The citizens of Scyene didn't
prize Belle Reed and her kin too high. I used to say to Herman
Jenkins, They're jealous, that's all the matter is. And Herman
would harrumph and splutter and say, Why in God's name would
they be jealous of a woman like that? Style, I would reply. You
ever heard the word, Herman Jenkins? I would say. You any kind
of idea what that word means?

John Whitehouse,
Proprietor of the Long Bar Saloon,
Scyene, Texas

Belle Reed would come into the Long Bar once or twice a week
and sit herself down at one of the faro tables and announce to
everybody that there was no limit to the betting. She'd put that big
hat of hers with the feather on it at the side of the table and she'd
smooth back that reddish sort of hair she had—fingers flashing
when she did that, on account of she wore a lot of rings, gold and
silver with little bright stones—and she'd say, All right, who's
gonna challenge Belle Reed? And some fool always would. I say
fool because she won most of the time. She was lucky. Fortune
always seemed to shine on her, that's how it looked to me. She'd
call for whiskey and drink it down like a man. Spend a good part
of the day in the Long Bar, playing faro for high stakes. A lot of
money would change hands in an afternoon. Some said she had
thousands of dollars hid out to the old farm where she lived with
Jim Reed. But nobody wanted to go out and look, I can tell
you.

As the sun was going down she'd get up and put on her big hat
with the feather and throw down one last shot of whiskey and get
her pistols fixed just so on her hips. She'd look over to me and
smile this kinda tight little smile and then turn around and stride
on out of the Long Bar like she was queen of the whole damn
county. She'd get onto Venus and then she'd give whoever was
watching—and somebody always was watching—a kind of salute

to the hat with that riding quirt of hers and then she'd give Venus a little spur and away she'd go. Sometimes when she got to the edge of Scyene she'd fire off a couple of shots from her pistols and then go galloping off real fast.

It was better than any traveling show ever came through Scyene. Ed Baynes used to say he'd move out of Scyene for good if he knew Belle Reed wasn't gonna come to town anymore.

L. J. Thompson,
a Deputy Sheriff of Travis County

In April of 1874 Jim Reed, along with Jesse James and Cole Younger, robbed the San Antonio-to-Austin stage and got off with a fair number of greenbacks belonging for the most part to the Pederales Mining Company. They didn't shoot nobody, but the sheriff and the U.S. marshal was so mad it was hard to see how it could of been any worse. Dick said to me, L.J., you get on out there and you find that bunch or I'm gonna get me another deputy, there's one waiting around every corner and don't you forget it.

I didn't see how I was gonna do what no other man, including the Pinkertons, had been able to do. I said so to Dick. His look would of withered tall corn in the field. You just go out and do it, he said. At that precise time I thought that I should of gone on working as a hand on the Cross-4-X Ranch.

But I had a piece of luck. I caught old Ed Flay rustling a few cows and he said if I'd think about letting him off, he'd tell me where he seen Jim Reed lately and how Reed was bragging about all the greenbacks he and Jesse'd got off with. So I let Ed Flay go and he said he'd seen Jim Reed down Dallas way at the old Shirley place, where Belle Reed's mama still lived. I rode on over that way, feeling that by next morning I would most likely be dead. I guessed I didn't mind too much getting killed. I was thirty-five years old and I'd done had me a damn fine life. Still, I would of liked a little bit more time for drinking bourbon whiskey and whoring, the two things I most appreciated next to a real fine horse with a double-rigged Texas saddle and fancy stamped taps to put my boots in.

I got to the Shirley place late, about maybe ten o'clock, and I seen a coal-oil lamp burning in the kitchen and so I went around there and looked in. Lo and behold, there sat Jim Reed hisself, talking to Belle across the kitchen table. Old Miz Shirley was standing at the bake oven spooning biscuit out of a pan. I said to myself, L.J., nothing could be this easy. Death's playing some kinda joke on you, watch out, now. But I threw open the door and fired off a warning shot and rushed in shouting, Jim Reed, put your hands over your head or you're a dead man! He just stood there with his mouth hanging open, holding this biscuit with a bite gone out of it. Belle screamed out, Goddamn it, Jim . . . and made a leap for her pistols, which was hanging across the back of a chair. But I fired off a shot in her direction, not much caring if I killed her or not, and she just froze as hard as the Red River in February, not a hair moved. I thought she'd stopped breathing. I thought I'd shot her through the heart, but she hadn't fell down yet.

I thought Dick'd be real pleased when I come in with Jim Reed, but what he said first thing was, Where the hell's the greenbacks? I told him I'd looked real carefully all over the house and hadn't found a bank note anywheres. I said, Maybe Jesse and Cole is holding the money. Dick give me another one of them looks that'd blight the crops and said, Well, in that case, why in hell you bringing me this feller here? You think he's such a handsome feller we need to have him in the jailhouse to pretty up the place? Or what? Dick was a real trial to me, had a real mean tongue in his head.

Anyways, a bunch of us rode out to the Shirley place and we went through it like calomel through a trail hand and there wasn't no greenbacks to be found. No money sacks. No stage boxes. Nothing at all. Old Miz Shirley just stood around with her hands folded under her apron, saying, I don't know what you want here, please don't ruin the sideboard, that sideboard's older than any of you. People always said Miz Shirley was a very refined woman but never knew which side was downwind of a polecat.

When we was getting ready to ride off, I looked over to the side of the house and there was this little girl, maybe seven, eight years old, pretty red hair, face white as a cloud, standing there watching us. She had one arm across the shoulders of a brown-haired boy about her same age. They just watched. They didn't say nothing. No hellos. No goodbyes. No please spare our papa. I guess Jim Reed was their papa, who the hell knows. Old Miz Shirley come out of the house and shooed the two children inside like they was chickens.

We had to let Jim Reed go, on account of there wasn't no evidence against him to be found anywheres we looked. Belle Reed come to the jailhouse to collect Jim. She was leading his horse alongside her own. She looked at me like I was some kinda boy had fits and wasn't too clean. Well, she said to me, did you really think you was gonna lock up Jim Reed for ten years? A little old nothing nobody like you? That'll be the day.

We never could find no trace of Jesse or Cole Younger or the greenbacks. I guess Jesse and Cole went on back to Missouri to rest up—after all, robbing banks and stages is tiring work. We did find ourself a boy who sometimes rode with Jim Reed and knew all about the San Antonio-to-Austin stage robbery, and the U.S. marshal said, Now, don't worry, boy, you help us get the goods on Reed and we won't prosecute you for nothing, you'll be free as a bird from now on.

But this boy was nervous and high-strung and half the time drunk besides and always firing off pistols at anything that moved. One night Jim Reed moved when he shouldn't of, I guess. Because that boy blowed his face right off and Jim Reed fell down dead as a stone. That was in August that same year, 1874. Dick said to the boy, Listen, you shit fool, we told you we wanted some evidence against Reed so we could put him in jail until he was an old man. Did we tell you to blow his head off? What's the matter with you? You wearing your hat too far down over your ears? Or maybe you're too stupid to piss standing up.

And the boy said, Well, he just made me mad, that's all. And I thought to myself, They're gonna hang him anyways, so it don't matter if I shoot him. So I shot him.

And I said to myself, Anyways, it wasn't me got killed, not this
time. I got a little while to go yet.

Miss Greenleaf, Teacher of Piano and Dance, Dallas

Mrs. Reed was a woman who thought well of herself, I could see
that, but she was always pleasant to me whenever we had occasion
to meet, which wasn't too often. She'd generally bring Pearl by
my studio in a buggy and let her out and then come back in the
buggy in two hours and wait by the gate for the child to run out
to her. Once a month she'd come in to pay me for the lessons and
to inquire how Pearl was doing. I was real frank with Belle Reed:
I said right out that although Pearl played the piano passing fair
and probably would get some better on that instrument as the
years passed, she would never make a dancer. I said, Mrs. Reed,
the child just don't have the build for a dancer. She'd always just
smile at me, a kind of unpleasant little smile, and say, We'll just
have to see about that, won't we? I think she thought her little
Pearl could do anything, it was just a matter of taking her to the
right place and finding her the right teacher. She used to mention
St. Louis now and then, like it was a magic place where little
Pearl was going to turn out to be a famous ballerina.

What I didn't tell Belle Reed was that Pearl was about as
interested in being a dancer as she was in learning to speak the
Comanche tongue. She was ten, eleven years old when I taught
her, sort of a plump little red-haired girl, full of vim and vigor. A
good deal of mischief showing in those blue eyes, I used to think,
although she was always well behaved with me. She liked to play
lively things on the piano, gay little dances and suchlike. Whenever she had to practice a serious piece, she'd look peeved and
stare at the keyboard and sigh a lot. But she wouldn't refuse. She
wanted to please her mother. She never refused to do anything
that would please her mother. I said to her once—this was after
she'd spent an hour struggling to do one little pirouette correctly
—I said, Pearl, why don't you tell your mama you don't like to

dance? Maybe she'd let you stop taking lessons, maybe you could take extra piano instead. And she just looked at me, sweat running down her little white face and breathing real hard from all that effort, and she shook her head and said, Ma wants me to be graceful. There ain't no other way but dancing.

Miss Mirabeau,
French Teacher, Dallas

Quite hopeless, quite, quite hopeless. The child could not even speak her native tongue properly, although she was twelve when her mother brought her to me for lessons. After two weeks I say to her mother, Madame, she cannot learn French, she is not suited to the tongue, you must please take her away from me. For a moment I think this woman will strike me to the face. She grew very pale and trembled. Then she say to me, That is too bad that you think this, you are mistaken. And she seized the child to the arm and took her away. I was relieved. The mother, she was very nervous and she had dark circles under the eyes. Sometime later a friend was saying to me that this woman was bad, very bad, a breaker of the laws. That her husband has been shot down like a dog. I think, Poor child, poor, poor child, who has such a *maman* and who has seen the father killed like a dog. It has made me very *triste*.

Miss Sherman,
Founder-Director of the Sherman
Academy of Elocution and Drama, Dallas

It was to have been a gala evening. First, there would be select recitations by a few of the best junior girls. Then the older pupils would present *The Heart of Her Rival*, which was a well-known theatrical piece, but not so often performed as to be uninviting to an audience. A goodly crowd was expected, since enrollment at the Sherman Academy that year—it was, I vividly recall, 1881—

was above average and almost all the girls' parents and relatives, even friends of the families, had promised to attend the theatrical showing. For the senior pupils the evening was to be their Dallas stage debut; I fully expected certain of the more gifted girls to continue their advanced studies at academies in the Midwest or East.

I had been worried about Pearl Reed from the beginning. She had been cast as Leonora—not the lead but a very prominent role that required vitality and the projection of considerable *joie de vivre*. Pearl Reed was, as we express it in theater circles, a natural. In first rehearsals she was excellent and confirmed again and again the wisdom of my choice. Yet the closer we came to actual performance, the more nervous the girl became: she would forget lines in which she had been the week before letter-perfect; she would stand stock-still upon the stage, staring into space as though she saw there something unspeakably awful; she began to move about the stage as though sleepwalking, completely without her earlier vigor and élan.

I questioned her about these changes. I said, How is it, Pearl, that such a saucy girl as you has suddenly become so subdued and so nervous? Are you ill? Is something amiss with your health? She just stared at me with her mouth hanging slightly ajar and shook her head. I noticed that tears sprang into her eyes. Pearl! I cried. You must tell me what's wrong! Confide in me! Perhaps I can help you. But again she shook her head, gazing at the floor. I opened my arms to her, saying, Pearl, my dear child . . . and she came rushing against my bosom in a flood of tears. I consoled her as best I could, not knowing the cause of this misery, and finally she brought herself under control. Now tell me, I admonished her, what the matter is. She pressed both her temples between her two small white hands and said, My head hurts. When? I said, beginning to feel alarmed. All the time, she said. It hurts all the time like a pickax is sticking in it.

I consulted Dr. Mead, a good friend and a supporter of the Academy. In his opinion the girl, fourteen years old, was suffering the not uncommon problems of the menarche. I chafed silently under this diagnosis, although I respected Jonathan Mead. In his opinion Pearl Reed would be all right and honor both herself and the Academy in *The Heart of Her Rival.* I could not bring myself to unqualified agreement. I continued to worry.

I wrote her mother a letter, which I sent by Pearl, since I did not know for certain where she lived. I asked that she please call on me to discuss her daughter's problems. I emphasized the urgency of the matter. In three days' time Belle Reed appeared at the door of my office at the Academy. I had never seen her before, since arrangements for Pearl's enrollment had been made by mail and since the child arrived every afternoon as though by magic carpet and was spirited away in the early evening by equally invisible means: one moment she was present and the next moment she had simply vanished, to reappear the following afternoon.

I am Belle Reed, she said to me that spring afternoon. I was struck by the way she said this—it did not seem to me so much a matter of announcing a fact as proclaiming an event. She was indeed a striking woman: dressed all in maroon crepe de Chine, wearing a plumed black Canton silk hat over heavy auburn hair, there was an arrogance in her every movement. Every lift of her dark eyebrows, every turn of her head bespoke the woman accustomed to the stares of others. But she was very pale and she rouged too heavily to compensate for her pallor. She seemed to me like a charge of gunpowder waiting for the hammer of a pistol to strike. She was unable to sit still for very long in the chair I offered her on the other side of my desk; she paced my office, pausing now and then to stare out the window at the sadly rudimentary garden at the side of the Academy.

I told her as succinctly as possible of her daughter's behavior and asked if she could offer any explanation for it. She turned a profoundly dark expression upon me and said, She lost her daddy seven years ago.

I pointed out to her that many girls at the Academy had lost parents or relatives, that we lived, unfortunately, in reckless, lawless times. But, I said, these children do not complain of a continuous pain in their heads like a pickax.

Pearl is a gifted child, she said to me, as though I had not spoken. She should be in St. Louis or Chicago, not Dallas.

I said that she was free to take Pearl out of the Sherman Academy of Elocution and Drama anytime she chose and that I was sorry she was discontent with the course of instruction.

Pearl will be fine, she said to me. Again, it was as if I had not spoken. As if she were responding to an unseen interlocutor. She repeated the statement: Pearl will be fine. She will grow up to be an accomplished lady. Someday you will be surprised to see what social circles she moves in.

I sighed, because there seemed little else to do, and thanked her for coming to see me. I asked if she herself intended to be present at Pearl's debut upon our stage. She looked at me from the door of my office, for the first time that afternoon with a slight smile, and she said, Wild horses couldn't keep me away. I expect it to be a triumph for my baby Pearl. And then she opened the door and swept out, leaving a heavy scent of oleander in her wake.

My feeling was that Belle Reed was ill. Perhaps that was the reason for Pearl's strange behavior. The girl had lost her father, perhaps she now feared the loss of her mother and the condition of orphanage that would follow. It was at least a reasonable explanation, the only one I had been able to muster.

As the night of the premiere of *The Heart of Her Rival* drew closer, Pearl went through yet another metamorphosis: she seemed to enter a state of perpetual fever. Her white cheeks glowed, her blue eyes looked glazed, her glance seemed unfocused. She smiled constantly, babbled ceaselessly and seemed unable to live a moment without touching someone—another of the girls, me, even the cleaning women; her hands fluttered over everyone like butterflies, alighting a moment here, flying away, finding another flower. I took Elsie Broadhurst aside and quietly told her to take especial care in understudying Pearl's role. I did not want all my girls to be crushed with disappointment should something untoward happen before opening night.

And indeed my premonition was correct. The first act of our play went well enough. Pearl took to the stage with something approaching hysteria, although I felt confident that the audience interpreted it merely as the high spirits associated with the part. Standing in the wings, I noted the presence of Belle Reed (who had thoughtfully removed her plumed hat) not too far beyond the footlights of our small stage. When I saw her I realized that I had for several days been silently praying that she would not attend.

We were in the second scene of the second act when it happened. Pearl, elaborately dressed, was to come downstage and deliver a rather long and impassioned speech beginning, I am, as you see, a lady of the high country . . . She fairly shone as she moved downstage center. She seemed to glisten, as though some kind of internal luminosity pressed against her flesh. She turned her eyes toward the right, where I stood in the wings, but I have no sense that she saw me. She smiled that lately very strange bright smile of hers and opened her mouth and said, I am, as you see . . . Then she grasped her head vigorously either side, screamed with such pitch and volume that everyone in the theater was doubtless transfixed, and fell first to her knees and then prone upon the stage. I rushed out from the wings, as did other members of the staff, and we gathered her up and bundled her backstage to a convenient, however ancient, divan. Her mother appeared almost at once, pushing her way through the crowd of girls, crouching next to the divan and tenderly brushing the child's hair away from her pale, hot forehead.

Jonathan Mead was in the audience and came with lightning speed to see to the girl. He studied her gravely for a few moments and then pronounced that from the look of her she had suffered a brain hemorrhage. Belle Reed arose from her crouched position like a spring unwinding. You fool sawbones! she cried at Dr. Mead. You wouldn't know a brain hemorrhage if it leaked red on you!

That is what she said. That is exactly what she said. It was appalling. The girls all stood in a circle staring at the woman. Then someone tittered nervously and restored me to the reality I had for a moment lost. I asked her please to apologize to Dr. Mead. She ignored this request, staring intently down at Pearl.

She finally rushed away, hurling over her shoulder the admonition that we were not to move the child in her absence, which would be brief.

I began to hear restive sounds from the audience. I sent Mrs. Fitch to announce that the play would continue after a brief interval and to ask for patience.

In a period that could not have exceeded ten minutes Belle Reed reappeared with a man at her heels the like of which I had never before seen: a tall Indian dressed head to toe in cowskins and wearing soft moccasins, so that he moved as silently as a cat. One long black braid hung down his back. He carried a knife on one hip and a pistol on the other. He looked at me briefly, his black eyes narrowed, as though I were merely part of the wall. Belle Reed nodded toward Pearl and the Indian picked her up, flung her over his shoulder as though she were the weight and character of a blanket, and departed—followed by Belle Reed.

Miss Cumbie, whose head was a ragbag of gossip and rumor, whispered into my ear: She's married to that Indian, can you imagine . . .

It was my first and last glimpse of Sam Starr. I was never to see any of them again. I often used to wonder whatever happened to poor Pearl. Whether she ever managed to pluck that terrible pickax out of her brain. Whether in the end it killed the child.

Younger's Bend: 1881

Baby Pearl [she wrote],

My dear little one; it is useless to attempt to conceal my trouble from you, and though you are nothing but a child I have confidence that my darling will bear with fortitude what I write.

I shall be away from you for a few months, baby, and have only this consolation to offer to you, that never again will I be placed in such humiliating circumstances, and in the future your little tender heart shall never more ache, or a blush be called to your cheek, on your mother's account.

The trial of Belle Starr in the courtroom of Isaac Parker—called the Hanging Judge—for horse stealing had been that winter's titillation for the ladies of Fort Smith, Arkansas, where Belle was by then as well known as she had been in Scyene. She wore her finest velvets, her tallest feathers into court. She swept down the aisles of the courtroom like a queen entering her privy chamber, head high, acknowledging with slight turns to the right or left the murmurs of fascination which greeted her appearance. People at the back of the packed courtroom stood on the benches to follow the progress of her plumed hat through the crowd to the defendants' table in front. A battery of lawyers accompanied her like courtiers. In their wake the cat-footed Cherokee Sam Starr—handcuffed; a lawman steered him forward by the elbow.

"How could I possibly be guilty?" Belle had asked Judge Parker with a smile. "Do you imagine I could support Younger's Bend on the niggardly profits of a few stolen horses?" At the mention of the magic name Younger, with all the licentious images that called up, a sound of pleased scandal ran around the room.

"It is a strange defense, madam," Isaac Parker had replied, "to suggest that you are innocent of stealing horses because you are

involved in more profitable lawbreaking." The audience in the
courtroom laughed and clapped. Belle Starr smiled. Even Judge
Parker's face lightened from the ingrained sobriety that accom-
panies the hanging of eighty-six men. Sam Starr's face continued
to look as impassive as sleep, only the eyes awake.

Belle Starr was the first woman to be tried for a major crime in
Judge Parker's court. The trial lasted four days. The jurors re-
tired for an hour and returned to announce that they had found
Belle Starr guilty on two counts of horse thieving and Sam Starr
guilty on one. There were those who said later that not even Isaac
Parker could resist her: he sentenced her to a mere six months.
As if to confirm this opinion, the judge gave Sam Starr a year.
Sam neither smiled nor frowned when he heard this sentence
from the high bench: spectators said there was not the slightest
batting of an eyelid nor twitching of a lip.

Now, Pearl [she continued], *there is a vast difference between
the House of Correction at Detroit and a penitentiary. You must
bear that in mind and do not think of your mama being shut up
in a gloomy prison. It is said to be one of the finest institutions of
its kind in the United States, surrounded by beautiful grounds
and fountains and everything that is nice. There I can have my
education renewed, and I stand sadly in need of it. Sam will have
to attend school and that is the best thing ever happened for him.
And now you must not be unhappy and brood over our absence.
It will not take the time long to glide by, and when we come home
and get you we will have a nice time.*

We will [she concluded] *get your horse and I will break him,
and you can ride Venus while I am gentling Loco. We will have
Eddie with us and will be gay and happy as the birds.*

Belle was released for good behavior after serving only three
months of her sentence. She spent her time in Detroit weaving
cane chair bottoms. Sam Starr, shuddering in the Michigan cold,
worked on the road gang, splitting rocks with a sledgehammer.

Belle returned to Younger's Bend—sixty-two acres with three
one-room cabins, a corral and barn, and several hideout caves on
the Canadian River in Indian Territory—by way of Carthage,
Missouri, where she fetched Pearl from her auntie's house.

"Was it just awful in that place?" Auntie Bethel said to Belle, patting her niece's arm, halfway between commiseration and fascination.

"It was a puking degradation," Belle said. "The law will never touch me again, I can promise you that." She shook off her auntie's hand and rode away to Younger's Bend with baby Pearl, who was sixteen years old and had passed the time in Carthage with a grey-eyed, black-haired apprentice horse thief named Frankie.

When Pearl came into the cook cabin one of the men straddling a chair at the long table down the middle of the room almost from one wall to the other smiled broadly and made a small lip-smacking sound and said, "Well, lookee here at Belle's little girl . . . ain't she something? Where'd you get them blue eyes, Pearl?"

"From her daddy," Belle said insouciantly from the far end of the table, where she sat chewing a leg of boiled chicken. "Where'd you think?"

The big man who had spoken laughed along with the others: three men opposite him, tipped back in their chairs, digesting; a small half-breed next to him, assiduously picking his teeth, eyes fixed unseeing on the empty tin plate in front of him.

"You're a goddamn brazen hussy, Belle," the big man said. He continued to eye Pearl with an appraising smile. "When you gonna marry off this one?" he said.

"She ain't," Pearl said, reaching for a brown biscuit from the plate in the middle of the table. "I'm gonna marry off myself, when I get good and ready."

Belle dropped the bare chicken leg onto her plate and began licking her fingers. "You keep a tongue in your head, missy," she said. She poured whiskey into a tin cup and swallowed it down noisily. Pearl guessed that Belle had had several whiskeys already and calculated the care each of those would exact in her dealings with her mother.

"I didn't mean nothing by it," Pearl said. She carefully nibbled her biscuit. "I just come in to ask if I could ride out for a while on Loco. Not far, maybe just down the river a little ways."

Belle studied through narrowed, lustful eyes the small half-breed on her right as Pearl spoke. She rolled herself a cigarette inside paper the color of bitter chocolate. The little part-Creek struck a long wooden match and lit it for her. "You go on and take a little ride," she said to Pearl without turning her gaze from the half-breed. "A nice little moonlight trot, now won't that be nice . . ." She laughed, and Pearl knew it had nothing to do with her riding her horse Loco down the Canadian River.

All the men in the cabin were looking at Belle Starr now, their eyes bright in that way Pearl had come to know meant they wanted her mama and they were imagining what it would be like to roll with Belle into that hard little bed in the cabin where she stayed with Sam Starr—when he was at Younger's Bend—and her daughter and her son Eddie. Pearl grabbed a handful more of brown biscuits and moved quietly toward the door. Just outside the cabin she heard a roar of laughter behind her and then a murmur of voices and as she made her way to the corral to saddle Loco she heard the men leaving the cook cabin where they had been eating: she thought the sound was like a very big animal of some kind, she couldn't think what to call it—like twenty buffaloes yoked together—turning over in its sleep.

Two of the men made their way to the small barn back of the corral, where they would bed down in the warm straw that smelled of horse sweat and dung. The other two ambled off toward the hideout cave half a mile distant and concealed behind heavy brush. They spoke to each other in low voices and now and then laughed quietly. They were smoking thin cigars, and Pearl, hidden in the shadows of the live oaks, could see against the moonlight a pale cloud drift from their mouths and encircle their heads. She thought they looked devilish. At the Sherman Academy she had once seen pictures in a book of creatures consigned to Hell and they moved around in pale clouds like these two she watched. Neither the small half-breed nor Belle emerged from the cookhouse. Pearl waited, her breath caught in her throat, until all the men had disappeared from sight and there was no murmur

of voices, no laughter, no pale cigar smoke. Finally the door of
the cookhouse opened and the half-breed appeared, Belle at his
side. He had his arm about her waist and she swayed against him,
laughing softly. Midway between the cookhouse and the cabin
where Belle slept they stopped in the clearing and the Indian
kissed Belle's throat greedily, the way Pearl had always seen him
eat, as though he wanted to swallow everything down all at once.
"Bastard," Pearl said aloud, quietly. "Goddamn little 'breed
bastard."

She waited until Belle and the Indian had crossed the clearing
and closed the door of Belle's cabin behind them and then she
made her way across the corral to Loco's stall in the barn. The
two men Belle had dispatched to the barn were already asleep,
snoring heavily. Pearl saddled Loco and led him through the
corral and down to the river's edge. She held his reins and waited
for a moment, listening, before she mounted the horse and rode
west along the pale moonlit water. About a mile down the river
she drew up her horse next to a scrubby mesquite. Loco snorted
contentedly and bent his neck to crop grass. A few minutes later
Willie appeared as though by magic on a small mustang pony. He
smiled at Pearl, his teeth shining like little moons.

"I thought you wasn't coming tonight," he said.

"I had to wait till she went off to bed with her new half-breed,"
Pearl said. "Little brown bastard . . . waited till she'd had too
many whiskeys to tell the difference between him and a stump
. . . or him and Sam."

"You hadn't oughta talk like that to a half-breed about a half-
breed," he said. "Makes me feel real bad to hear you talk about
'breeds like that."

Pearl leaned over and grabbed his arm. "You know how I feel
about you, Willie. You know I love you. You're not like a 'breed
at all." She looked around, anxiously studying the terrain. "Where
can we go? Back there in the brush? You got a place picked out?"

Willie bared his brilliant teeth and leaned across to take Loco's
reins. "I show you where we go," he said. "New place." He
turned both horses toward a nearby clump of trees.

When the two horses were tethered, blowing happily through

their noses as they fed on brown grass, and Pearl and Willie were stretched naked, hardly visible in the pale moonlight that flattened everything to grey, upon Willie's saddle blanket, Willie said, "When we gonna speak to your ma about the marrying?"

"Soon," Pearl said, stroking Willie's brown tight thighs. "Next week, maybe. Sam'll be home. She'll be in a good mood. We'll speak to her then."

"I want to marry soon," Willie said.

Pearl nodded. "It'll be nice," she said. "We'll get our own place, a few cows."

"Who the hell wants cows?" Willie said, leaning back on his folded arms and staring up at the moon. "Nobody at Younger's Bend keeps no cows. Cows is for stupid farmers. I'm gonna run stolen ponies through the Nations, the way your ma and Sam do. Make some silver like that."

"You'll end up in jail like Ma and Sam too," Pearl said. "Or like my daddy, Cole Younger, sitting up there in Minnesota for twenty-five years. Now, ain't that nice . . . You think I'd wait for you twenty-five years, Willie? Ma, now, she loved Cole like nobody else, why, she thought Cole Younger hung the moon, but she ain't sitting around waiting for him to get out of jail, is she? She ain't doing without a man, you can see that. She got a man every night she wants one, if it ain't Sam it's some little red half-breed. You think I'd wait for you twenty-five, thirty years outside the jailhouse door? You think I'm better than Ma?"

Willie turned and stared at her blankly. "Don't race your mouth," he said. "Plenty of time to talk on it later. Right now we gonna make love." He squinted up appraisingly. "Moonset soon."

Pearl put her arms around his thin, square shoulders and kissed him on the mouth. "That's nicer than talking about cows and horses," she said.

Belle sat with three men in front of the cabin where visitors slept. A lush cloud of smoke rose above the group. Belle smoked her thin black cigarettes and laughed brightly at a story John Jason was telling. Sam Starr stood just behind Belle on the porch of the cabin, his eye traveling from one outlaw's face to another, listening, seeing—as everyone always said—everything there was to see. Now and then Belle turned and smiled up at Sam. Once she took his hand and held it briefly against her cheek. Sam stroked her hair with his other hand, but his eyes never stopped moving across the faces of the three men.

Belle rose at the conclusion of John Jason's story. "Now, you boys all go on off and do whatever business you got on hand and when the sun goes down, we'll eat. China Po's made us a nice pot of stew, plenty of beef around for everybody. And don't forget that one of you has got to take the watch in an hour. We can't get too relaxed and easy here at the Bend. We got to keep a lookout on the pass every minute, or some goddamn sheriff will come riding in here with a posse. That sort of thing can ruin a lady's day."

The three men who constituted her audience laughed and shook their heads in wonder. "That Belle . . ." John Jason let the rest of his comment hang in the air as he wandered away toward the corral. The two other men idled toward their tethered horses.

"We don't need them to watch," Sam said. "Starrs will guard the pass. Creeks make the best lookouts."

"That's true, Sam. But these boys have got to have something to do to keep them busy. They can't just hang around here telling stories and drinking whiskey and waiting for China Po to lay the table. They'll get to fighting among themselves in no time." She smoothed her hair down and stared off across the clearing. "Who's that coming along with Pearl?"

Sam studied the pair approaching on horseback. "Looks like Willie Brownleg."

"Who the hell is Willie Brownleg?"

Sam shrugged. "He's a 'breed boy, lives over there near Whitefield with his uncle."

Belle kept her eyes fixed on the riders nearing the cabin. "Brownleg his real name?" she said.

Sam laughed. "Close as we need to get," he said.

Pearl dismounted not far from her mother. She cast a nervous glance at Willie, who still sat astride his mustang, staring fixedly at Belle. "Get down, for God's sake!" she whispered to Willie. "Don't just sit there like you seen a ghost!"

Pearl walked toward Belle and Sam. "I want you to meet somebody, Ma."

Belle half closed her eyes, so that all Pearl could see were two dark liquid slits glittering like lizards in the sunlight. "That so . . ." she said.

Pearl beckoned to Willie, who had dismounted and stood holding the reins of his mustang and staring at Belle with his mouth hanging slightly ajar. "Come here, Willie," Pearl said. "Come over here and meet Ma."

Willie came forward, removing his hat, holding it respectfully over his belly. Pearl grasped his arm and smiled uncertainly at her mother. "This here's Willie Brownlow," she said. "We been keeping company for a good while and now we want to marry."

"Do you, now?" Belle continued studying Willie through the bright slits in her face. Her dark eyes seemed to Pearl awash. The girl wondered how the lids could contain all that glistening water.

"He'd be good help to you and Sam around here," Pearl continued. "He's strong and a hard worker."

"You don't say," Belle said quietly, a small smile turning her lips up just in the corners. She looked up at Sam. "Hear that, Sam?" she said. "A hard worker. Do we need a hard worker, Sam?"

Sam laughed and stuck his hands underneath his belt and waited, the way someone might wait for the next act of the touring company show.

Belle picked up her Mexican quirt and snapped it quickly against Willie's cheek. It made a singing sound like a breeze through a broken slat and left a thin bloody welt behind.

"Ma!" Pearl screamed. "Why'd you do that?"

Belle's bright slits of eyes had opened now to their fullest. They focused first on Willie and then on Pearl. "You been keeping company for a while, have you?" Her voice was like a snake rustling over a rock: it was quiet, it slid over the rock with a soft *shushshush*. Who could imagine the snake had just struck someone, just emptied its venom sac? "Now you want to marry, do you?"

Willie stood transfixed, one hand pressed to his wounded cheek. "Now, Miz Belle . . ." he began.

The quirt sang through the air again and flicked its tongue against Pearl's white cheek. Sam's eyes gleamed. He folded his arms and leaned back against the porch post.

Now Belle's voice rose like the wind before a storm. "You fool girl!" Each word like the blow of the quirt again. "You damn fool girl! You think I brought you up like a lady, sent you to all those wonderful schools in Dallas, gave you every privilege in the world, so you could throw yourself away on some half-breed trash? You're as empty-headed as one of those squaw women sitting around Fort Smith selling geegaws on the street!"

She turned to Willie like a mountain cat, lips drawn back against her teeth. "And you! Think you was going to marry into this family and fall into good times all at once? Get to be Belle Starr's new son and come into your fame and fortune early . . . that what you thought, was it? Well, laddie, you think on things again. Because you ain't never going to wed my baby Pearl. She's going to marry a rich gentleman from the city, which you ain't and never will be in a thousand Indian years. Now . . ." She lifted the quirt above her head. Willie flinched and backed toward his mustang. "You get off my property, 'breed. If I ever see signs of you at Younger's Bend again, I'll have Sam cut you so no woman'll ever look at you twice. Your keeping-company days are over."

Willie threw his leg over his horse, pulled the stallion's head sharply to the right and dug his heels heavily into the horse's soft flanks. "Haw! Haw!" he cried and, stretching out almost flat over the horse's mane, rode away at full gallop. The dust rose and settled in Pearl's eyes like a stinging mist. She could feel grit like broken glass between her teeth. She put her hand up and ran her fingers down the thin ridge the quirt had left on her face: they came away bloody. Pearl stared at the blood in disbelief. "You marked me," she said to Belle. "I'll have a scar on me forever."

"Maybe that'll help you to remember, next time some trashy 'breed comes nosing around your privates." Belle wheeled around. "Sam, you get one of the boys to saddle up Venus and a fresh mount for Pearl. I'm going to ride Baby to Chickalah to visit Betsy and Toler. She can stay out of trouble for a while up there, two, three months, maybe. Do her a world of good to sit around thinking about what kind of man her mama wants her to marry, when the time comes."

She strode off toward her own cabin, her calico skirts clearing the ground but her boots raising dust like powder.

Sam stirred from his impassive tilt against the porch post of the cabin and moved toward the corral. Pearl felt as rooted as a stump, felt she had been growing on this waterless spot for all of her nineteen years and was as dry and withered as a twig.

Two months passed before Pearl returned from Chickalah. During that time Sam Starr had been killed at a Christmas party at Lucy Suratt's cabin on the Briartown Road. A deputy of the Indian police, shot by Sam Starr as the conclusion of an argument, dying, had as his last act discharged his pistol into the breast of his murderer and killed him instantly.

"I am doomed," Belle Starr said, "to lose all my husbands through acts of violence. What is a woman to do in times like these?"

Jim July came forward to help Belle answer that question. He was a handsome Creek boy almost twenty years younger than the woman who was now in sole possession of the land and property known as Younger's Bend. He had been educated at mission schools and unlike Sam Starr he could read and write some, enough to impress Belle, to whom all the outlaws on the dodge at the Bend brought their Wanted posters for interpretation. "She is a truly wonderful woman," John Jason had once said. "She can read off things as quick as a rattler strikes, don't take her no time at all."

Jim July moved into the cabin at Younger's Bend to console the widow Starr. At Belle's request he added Starr to his name: Jim July Starr he was known as throughout the Indian Territory and in Arkansas, especially in Fort Smith, where he and Belle often jollied through the night. When they went dancing in Fort Smith's saloons, Jim Starr—as finally he came to be called—would sit astraddle a chair near the faro tables and observe with black oblique eyes his wife, as he liked to refer to Belle in the manner of a properly educated mission boy, rollick across the saloon floor in the arms of many a musical outlaw. He would bring her the whiskey she liked to drink and when she had drunk far too much of it to continue dancing, he would half carry, half lead her out of the saloon and down the street to one of Fort Smith's first-class hotels: "Don't you ever, Jim July Starr," Belle had more than once said, "take me drunk into anything but the best hotel there is to be had. Belle Starr, Queen of the Bandits, don't put up, even for the night, at any rum house, and you forget that at your peril." Jim Starr never forgot. He watched and he listened and he remembered everything that Belle Starr considered important. When Pearl returned from Chickalah, he was firmly in possession of the cabin where once Sam Starr had lain, gleaming as brightly as a knife, at Belle's side.

"Why did you stay so short a time?" Belle said, stirring China Po's stew. "You could have visited on for another month or so with Betsy and Toler. Don't you like town life, baby?"

"Chickalah ain't big enough to be a town," Pearl said. "It's just a bunch of shacks out on the prairie. It's dull as dirt."

Belle shrugged and stirred, then tasted the stew. "I'm glad you're home, anyway. Younger's Bend is never the same without you. Nothing is ever as nice without my baby Pearl around, and my boy Eddie." She looked sorrowfully into the stewpot as though she saw there the head of a friend. "My poor boy Eddie," she said.

"Will he be home soon?" Pearl said.

"I got him a real fine lawyer," Belle said. "Things are moving along nicely. But it takes money, my God, it does take money."

"You got plenty," Pearl said. She sat down at the long table behind her mother. She pushed her red hair away from her face over and over as though she were a distraught lady from a penny dreadful. She sighed.

Belle turned to her, holding the stew spoon in midair. "What's the matter with you?" she said. "You been sighing like wind through the sycamores ever since you came back to the Bend. Has your blood gone all thin like it did once before? Do I need to give you some of those iron pills again?"

Pearl shook her head. "It ain't my blood, Ma."

Belle dropped the pot lid back on the stew, threw another piece of wood into the stove and looked out the window, searching the grounds for signs of Jim July Starr. "Well, what is it, then?" she said with her back to Pearl.

"I'm gonna have a baby, is what it is," Pearl said quietly, watching her mother's back. She saw the back stiffen. She saw Belle turn. She saw the familiar dark eyes go blacker still and first narrow and then expand with fury.

Belle walked with studied calm over to Pearl and leaned against the table where her daughter sat and brought her face very close to Pearl's and said in a hushed voice, "You are going to have a baby?"

"That's a fact, Ma," Pearl said. "No mistaking it."

"And who," Belle said, still leaning over Pearl, her voice still low and almost friendly, "is the proud father of this infant you are carrying around?"

Pearl flushed. She pulled her head up as high as it would reach. She elevated her chin slightly, despite the proximity of her mother's dire face. "I really could not say," she said.

"You really could not say?" Belle straightened her body and gazed down upon Pearl with a strange, bitter smile. "You really could not say?" she repeated.

"No, ma'am," Pearl said. "I really could not."

"Would the reason for that ignorance be the one that comes most readily to mind?" Belle said.

"Ma . . ." Pearl began.

"Amid this collection of shacks out on the prairie, in this dirt-dull place that wasn't big enough to be a proper town, you managed to find several young men to amuse yourself with?"

"I just didn't see any reason for everything to be so tiresome every minute of my life . . . you don't believe in putting up with tiresome things, Ma—so why should I? So I didn't."

Belle grabbed her by the shoulders and shook her until Pearl felt that something in her head had come loose and was banging against the sides of her skull. "You stupid shit girl!" Belle shouted in Pearl's face. "Until you've lived out here at the Bend among these lads that can't find their privates in the dark and can't make out how to rob a bank that's got its doors open and its money hanging out to dry, you got no idea of tiresome." She struck Pearl such a blow across her face that the girl fell back against the table with everything turning white and whirling around in her head with the loose part that had broken off earlier. "We'll get you a first-class doctor and finish off this one," Belle said, staring at the cabin wall as though a list of first-class doctors was written there. "Dickens in Dallas," she finally said. "He'd do it for me, he owes me a favor or two."

Pearl took a deep breath. Her head had stopped turning white and spinning. "I won't," she said firmly.

Belle looked at her curiously. "You won't what?" she said.

"I won't get rid of this baby. I want to keep it."

"Oh, you want to keep it . . ." Belle said. "And what would be the reason for that wayward desire, my girl? You just feel like you are suited to be a mother? You feel real maternal, do you? Is that it?"

"I want to keep my baby," Pearl repeated, stubbornly setting her chin. "I don't want to kill it."

"You don't," Belle said. She walked over and took the lid off the stewpot and peered in. Then she stirred the stew again, contemplatively. "And who's going to take care of this little baby?" she said, still stirring. "Is it your intention to bring it here to Younger's Bend and leave it with its grandma? Who's going to buy it food and clothe it and school it? You think I'm going to care for this little bastard whose father could be anything from that half-breed Willie Brownleg to some dirt farmer's barefoot son from Chickalah?" She stopped stirring and put the spoon down carefully on the stove top. All her motions were studied and slow. Pearl watched mesmerized. These were the moments before the outbreak of the killing wrath. Dear God, Pearl thought, why did You make me daughter of this wicked woman I never can please?

Belle raised one arm to heaven. "God," she shouted, drowning out Pearl's question to Him, "has in His wisdom seen fit to give me slut for a daughter! But I don't have to just lie down and accept that like it was Holy Writ. I can fight against baby Pearl's whoredom, I can do that." She threw the stirring spoon at the window with such force that it cracked the glass. "You're going to finish off that baby like I say," she continued, turning irresolutely this way and that, trying to decide on a suitable expression of her anger, "or the two of you can get the hell out of here and never come back again." She upturned the stewpot with both hands; the contents ran sluggishly, thick with potatoes, over the top and sides of the stove and cascaded onto the wooden floor. "One way or the other," she whispered hoarsely into Pearl's alarmed face, "I will never set eyes on that brat you got in your belly."

Pearl arose, whiter even than usual. "All right, Ma," she said. "I'll go. I'll take my baby and go. The Reeds will take me in, I know they will. Eddie's always loved me and Jim papa was like my own daddy."

"You go where you like, missy." Belle stared at her, breathing heavily, her eyes so black no pupil could be seen and so large they looked like volcanoes into which Pearl might fall and be burned alive.

The house in Rich Hill, Missouri, was a small white frame with a live oak growing in the front and sparse brown grass. Grandma Reed, Jim Reed's mother, was five feet tall and fat as a Thanksgiving gourd. Her white hair had turned the color of an old bruise at the sides of her head and across the top. The other Reed children, Jim Reed's three brothers and two sisters and their mates, kept the old lady supplied with the cheap brandy she liked to tipple after supper. Her grey eyes were rimmed in pink and never seemed to close entirely, even in sleep: some said that was age and some said it was drink. The townsfolk of Rich Hill believed that although Grandma Reed lived modestly in her small white frame house, she was very probably a wealthy woman: her whole brood were outlaws of one kind or another and her long-dead husband, Hiram Reed—discontent with the rewards of his ministry—had been the first convert to the wicked ways his off-spring followed.

She embraced Pearl Younger without quite knowing how they came to be related. She gave her a little musty-smelling room at the back of the house, just large enough for a single bed and a chiffonier and a marble-topped table upon which a porcelain washbasin sat. Hanging on the wall in an oval gilt frame was a sepia photograph of a young man about nineteen with a blond mustache. He stood with his left arm dangling and the fingers of his right hand in the pocket of his tight trousers. Spanning his vest was a heavy watch chain with a little winding key hanging from the end and a fob charm. The photograph was not clear enough for Pearl to discover what the charm was, although she studied the question almost nightly. She never knew who the young man was.

Pearl grew larger and larger with child. She spent most mornings vomiting into the hand basin and then scurrying outside to dispose of the vomit behind the pecan trees in back of the house. Afterwards she washed the basin at the hand pump and sat weakly on the back stoop for an hour. She slept away most afternoons, dreaming fitfully of Belle Starr and Willie Brownlow and Jim July and the farmer boys of Chickalah.

In early April of 1887 Grandma Reed, picking at her oatmeal one morning, said, "I'm gonna go to Siloam Springs to take the baths. I go to Siloam Springs ever' year at this time, keeps me goin' for another year, keeps me young." She laughed, rubbing her bleary eyes in order to see Pearl more clearly. "You gonna come with me this year, child. You act sick. Them waters at

Siloam will cure whatever ails you. Cure or kill, that's what Hiram used to say. Cure or kill. Give this here oatmeal to the dog, it's got lumps in it the size of horse apples."

So a week later Grandma Reed and Pearl—both waddling and sweating and puffing—and a large box trunk were delivered by buggy to the stage depot and after four days of travel, stopping three nights on the road at feed stations and small, airless hotels, they were finally set down a hundred and fifty miles south at the Excelsior Hotel in Siloam Springs, Arkansas.

Grandma Reed went off at once to a nearby marble-floored bathhouse with tall sea-green wooden pillars on either side of the front entrance. Pearl had never seen a woman of Grandma Reed's weight and age lying naked in a marble bathtub, stream rising densely from the therapeutic waters: it was like looking at a great white decaying fish. She was fearful that Grandma Reed's flesh would be rubbed away by the fierce ministrations of the black woman attendant; she expected to see meaty lumps of skin floating in the water and afterwards swirling down the drain hole. But somehow the old woman remained intact.

Pearl began to feel a little better. She ceased vomiting, although whenever she rose up quickly from her lounge chair in the lobby of the Excelsior Hotel, her head seemed to spin around with a high-pitched whine. The sensation only lasted a minute, so Pearl didn't worry that it presaged a hard birth or a long convalescence. She went every day to the bathhouse with Grandma Reed and soaked in a huge marble tub of hot water that smelled reminiscent of a well in which a polecat had died. Submerged up to her plump chin, she gazed down curiously upon the mammoth belly that no longer seemed hers. Perhaps, she thought, it really wasn't hers any longer, being now a house for some male or female child who would be born, grow up and eventually leave her, as she had left Belle. Whenever she thought of Belle, she wept softly or bitterly, depending on the anguish of the moment.

"Dear God, child," Grandma Reed said, "you don't have that babe real soon, you gonna bust. It's gonna get itself out one way or another." She laughed and wiped her eyes and poured another brandy and one for Pearl. "Drink oils you up for birthin'," she explained. Over her brandy she focused her weak eyes on Pearl. One day she set her glass down and sighed heavily and labored up from her padded chair. "It's time I told Miz Simpson to be on hand," she said.

"Is it time?" Pearl put down *Fox's Police Gazette* and stared at the old woman in disbelief. Surely she herself would be the first to know when her child was ready to be born? But of course Grandma Reed had given birth to six children, so perhaps she knew things, could read signs Pearl was blind to.

Grandma Reed smiled faintly and puffed toward the hotel desk. "I'll get 'em to send a girl on over for the woman," she said. "We best go upstairs."

The midwife came to the Excelsior within the hour, carrying her little bag of tools, and that night in April a large female child was born to Pearl. It was the day for it, just as Grandma Reed had said. Pearl called the girl Flossie, a name she had always liked, although she did not know where she had heard it or read it.

Pearl stayed in bed for two weeks, feeling very thin and empty. Miz Simpson the midwife brought Flossie several times a day and deposited her at Pearl's milky breasts, where the child—its eyes closed, its fingers like the pistils of flowers softly kneading Pearl's rosy white skin—would ecstatically feed.

"Rest up while you can," Grandma Reed said. "You'll quick enough get the full care of the infant." She came every day to lean over the bed and gaze at Flossie and poke her with a fat index finger. "She don't look like a Reed," she would always say, but in such a way that Pearl never knew if that was a good or a bad thing. She was somehow loath to point out to the old woman that since there was no blood relation, Flossie's resemblance to the Reeds would have been nothing short of miraculous.

Pearl lay swathed in a white muslin gown and dozed the afternoons away, never sure if she was dreaming the images that passed like a shimmer of sunlight through her head. Now and then Belle would appear mysteriously at the foot of her bed, smiling, Jim papa sometimes at her side with his little nervous frown. Once she thought she caught a glimpse of Willie Brownlow standing on the far side of the room, his white teeth gleaming. One early evening she woke with a start to discover at her bedside a strange man in uniform with hair like winter grass. "Hello, little Pearl," he said in a heavy accent. And then he fell across the bed with a soft moan. A red-and-yellow fluid seeped from his chest and climbed up the bedsheet like oil climbing a wick. Pearl opened her mouth to scream, but before she could utter a sound, the body vanished.

"It's the laudanum," Grandma Reed said.

"What's laudanum?" Pearl said, tracing Flossie's delicate cheekline with the ring finger of her right hand.

"Helps you sleep," Grandma Reed said. "Makes you crazy in the head, but helps you sleep. I'm goin' home next week, you can come with me or stay another week."

So the following week Pearl and the old woman and baby Flossie returned to Rich Hill.

At the end of that summer a letter from Belle was forwarded to Grandma Reed by her daughter Emiline Thatcher in Wichita. Belle wrote that she was trying to discover Pearl's whereabouts, so that she could send her some important news; news, she wrote, that Pearl would be sick not to know of. Pearl read the letter with trepidation: was this a trick of Belle's to find out where she was and then ride into Rich Hill like a storm sweeping down from the Northern Plains? Or would she send Jim July creeping in Indian fashion to spirit her away in the middle of the night? Or was Jim July murdered? Or Belle sick?

She wrote to Aunt Emiline in Wichita, who in turn sent a letter to Belle saying that she, Emiline, would be pleased to deliver safely into Pearl's hands any important message her mother wished to impart. In a week's time another letter was forwarded to Pearl from Wichita. In it Belle wrote that her dear boy Eddie had been shot during a fracas with some whiskey peddlers and that if Pearl ever again wished to see her brother alive, she must come home at once. Belle added: "Conditions are such here at Younger's Bend (and I will not go into these ugly circumstances) that it would be impossible at the present time to care for an infant, so you must tell Pearl to come alone."

"Well now, if Eddie don't sound just like his daddy," Grandma Reed said, sipping her brandy and rocking away in her tall-backed chair next to the kitchen table. "All shot to hell, now there's a Reed for you. They never could get theirself out of a bullet's way if the blamed thing sang a little ditty before it struck 'em in the gullet."

Pearl packed at once. She nestled little Flossie in her arms and kissed her over and over on the eyes and across the forehead and at the corners of her tiny red mouth—admonishing Grandma Reed to see that Miz Leafly took the best of care—and set off for Younger's Bend. She hoped that God would allow her one more glimpse of her dear brother alive.

When she reached Briartown in Indian Territory she hired a horse for speed and left her suitcase behind to be sent out by the first wagon traveling the road to Younger's Bend. When she passed the familiar hills at the far side of the Briartown Road near the Watson place, she heard the firing off of a shotgun and knew she had been sighted by the lookout and that now Belle would know someone was approaching. Pearl crossed over the Canadian at the shallows and then rode like the wind for Younger's Bend, which was hidden in a grove of trees between two limestone outcroppings.

Two men she didn't know stood idly in front of the cookhouse, picking their teeth and squinting into the sunlight. "Water this horse," Pearl said, handing the reins to the taller of the two men. She made a dash for the main cabin. On the way there she thought she caught a glimpse of Jim July leading a horse from the corral. But she didn't stop to wonder why he wasn't at Belle's side. She threw open the door of the cabin and rushed in.

Belle stood at the end of the room, her head haloed by cigarette smoke. Eddie lounged on her bed with his boots propped against the footboard and his hands folded behind his neck. Pearl had the feeling they had been right in the middle of a sentence when she entered.

"Baby!" Belle cried, opening her arms and smiling broadly. "My God, I've missed you!"

Eddie swung his boots onto the floor and grinned up at Pearl. "Well, big sister," he said. "Ma knew you'd come. I wasn't so sure about it, but Ma said you'd for sure come to say goodbye to your baby brother."

Pearl backed away from Belle's embrace and leaned breathless against the washstand. She pressed her rib cage to steady her wild heartbeat. "I don't believe it," she said. "All this lying . . ."

Belle laughed. "Just a little white lie," she said. "Nothing a preacher would frown on."

"A little white lie?" Pearl said, incredulous. "Here I am thinking that Eddie's dying, that he maybe won't last through the night, and I ride from Rich Hill and I don't hardly eat or sleep or stop until I get here, praying every minute to God that He won't take Eddie till I come, and then I discover that not only ain't he dying, he don't even look sickly."

Eddie rose from the bed and hitched his pants up a little higher over his thin hips. He went on grinning at Pearl. "Well, I feel sickly, you just ain't looking at the sore whites of my eyes. I drank too much whiskey last night and God knows I feel today like I got a dirty old Indian squaw making buffalo stew in the back of my mouth. Don't that sound like sick to you?"

Pearl stared at him. "You ain't by no means dying," she said.

Eddie pulled a wry face and looked at his mother with mock sorrow. "And that makes her sad, Ma," he said. "Makes Pearl sad that I ain't dying."

Belle embraced Pearl and kissed her on the lips and said, "I would have done anything to get you home again, baby. You and Eddie and me, we're a family, we got to stay together. I can't have you off in Missouri someplace, living with a bunch of Reed yokels who can't put their coats on in the dark. You're Belle Starr's little Pearl. You got a lot to live up to, ain't that so?" She patted Pearl's face and smiled fondly.

Why can't I hate this woman? Pearl asked herself, looking curiously from Belle's dark eyes to Eddie's crooked smile and back again. Why can't I just tell her that this time she's made a real bad mistake, that I'm not ever going to stay here at Younger's Bend without my Flossie? She stood up. "I got to go," she said. "You lied to me and now I know Eddie ain't dying, I got to go. My little Flossie needs me."

Belle's brown eyes went as cold and hard as the barrel of a gun. "What your little Flossie needs is a decent mother and a nice pa who owns a haberdashery in some respectable little town in Kansas. Maybe then she'd have a chance to grow up to marry somebody proper and be a lady like I always planned her mother would be but God knows that didn't work out."

Pearl began to weep bitterly. Eddie drew a large dingy handkerchief out of his shirt pocket and handed it to his sister. "Now, don't carry on," he said. "Ma means the best for you."

"Flossie . . . Flossie . . ." Pearl moaned. She lay back on the bed, feeling sick. When she closed her eyes she could see a small pink bundle from the end of which protruded a rosy-cheeked head covered with a fine mist of red hair. The bundle bobbed up and down on a wave, drifting out to sea. Where had she seen the sea?

Belle leaned over and began tugging off her daughter's boots. "You just lie back there and have a little sleep," she said. "A little sleep will clear your mind, that's what I've always found to be true." She threw a light quilt over Pearl, who lay on the bed with her eyes closed and her face white as milk. "We'll talk about it again later on when you've rested up from the hardship of your recent travel," Belle said. She kissed Pearl on the eyes and grasped Eddie by the arm and the two of them, duplicitous mother and son, left the cabin.

For two weeks Belle and Pearl quarreled over Flossie. Belle remained contemptuous and adamant: she would not set eyes on the child, no matter how she was implored to do so. She wanted nothing to do with a grandchild whose father was undetectable, whose mother was unrepentant. She insisted that Pearl's mother love could best be demonstrated in leaving the child with a responsible person who could see to its adoption into a fine Missouri family whose members would indulge the babe, dress it in silks and ribboned lace, perfume the soft web of red hair, send it off to the best schools and finally celebrate its marriage into another fine Missouri family. "If you can't see what's as plain as the nose on your face," Belle said, "then I despair of your future wherever it may take place."

Pearl began to drink more than her usual one brandy before bed, a habit she had come to while living with Grandma Reed, who said she would never again need laudanum if she calmed her head nightly with Boll's Best Peach Brandy. Jim July brought her pint bottles of apricot brandy from Briartown. Often she would finish a bottle in two days, hiding the sticky empty container under the down pillow she had slept on since she was a child. The bottle made a lump like a dead baby under the pillow.

"What the hell are you hiding there, missy?" Belle said. "Lemme see." She threw the pillow aside and stared at the flat, oval, shouldered bottle as if it were the still-wriggling remains of a snake. She turned icy eyes on Pearl. "You're getting to be a souse, baby Pearl," she said. "I didn't bring you up to be a souse. But then I didn't bring you up to be a whore and a mother of whores, either."

Pearl wept and drank more apricot brandy and longed to see Flossie.

"Then why don't you go and see her?" Eddie sensibly asked. "If she's so goddamn important, why don't you go on back to Missouri and live with her. Ma won't like it, but what's she gonna do—hogtie you and string you up in the barn? You can do what you like. You're a growed woman."

That's true, Pearl thought. I am a grown woman. I am twenty-one years old. Ma has no business treating me like I was twelve and still going off to school. I am twenty-one and the mother of a sweet child named Flossie who is waiting for me to come and fetch her from a house in Rich Hill that smells like coal oil and cabbage.

Dear God, she prayed nightly, give me a vision of the Right Way. Tell me what is the best thing to do for my little Flossie.

"You think some rich, respectable man's gonna come along and want to marry a red-haired whore with a baby hanging round her neck?" Belle asked. "Why, he'll take one good look and then offer you two dollars for the night but no justice of the peace to make you Miz What's-His-Name. Men don't marry spoiled goods with little babes as evidence of all their sins. God knows I'm speaking the truth. You ever want a life of your own, Pearl, you got to get rid of Flossie. Best thing for the babe, anyway. Even you got enough sense to know that, when your head's clear enough of strong drink to know anything at all."

Dear God, Pearl prayed, is that the vision of the Right Way I asked You for?

Finally, after weeping for two days until her eyelids were as thick as shoe tongues and she looked out at Younger's Bend through narrow blue slits, she sat down at the small table in Belle's cabin and wrote: "Dear Grandma Reed, My heart is breaking but I must write you now and tell you that I have decided to give over my fatherless baby Flossie for adoption. The Good Lord has shown me the Way in this matter. My poor Flossie would have no chance of advancement and respectability in this life if I was to keep her at my side, which Lord knows is what I would like to do. I am going to leave everything in your hands. I am sure you and Emiline will find my dear baby the best parents in the whole state of Missouri. I will bless you both and sweet Flossie every day that remains to me. I will never grow too old to remember your kindness to me. Your own, Pearl."

In a month's time she got a letter from Rich Hill written by Grandma Reed's daughter-in-law Rubymae. It said: "Ma Reed wants you to know that we found a real nice couple in Wichita to adopt little Flossie and that the babe is happy and healthy. Ma says, Good luck to Pearl."

. . .

In July 1888, Eddie Reed was arrested in the Territory for stealing horses. He was picked up, drunk, in Briartown by a deputy of Judge Parker, before whose bench in Fort Smith he appeared in two days. The judge shook his head sadly: "Generations of outlaws . . . will there never be an end to it?" And sentenced Eddie to seven years in the Ohio State Penitentiary. In three months he was paroled; no one could say why, since his behavior had not been exemplary (he had set alight the straw mattress of his sleeping cellmate; he had almost garroted a black cook with strong twine). A few gossips speculated that Belle Starr had made an arrangement of some kind with Judge Parker. Linus James said it was common talk in Fort Smith that Eddie would never have been sentenced in the first place but for his ma: "She said the boy needed a taste of prison life to calm him down. He'd got as wild as a pony in loco weed."

In October, Eddie returned, sullen and explosive, to Younger's Bend. He refused to do any chores around the place. He needed, he said to Belle, a rest and a good time. A good time did not include feeding and watering and currying horses. It did not include killing and hanging beef or pulling up root vegetables like an Indian squaw. A good time was Briartown on a fine horse, money in the pocket for whiskey and faro, a Mexican whore with bracelets and bright eyes and shiny white teeth. And men standing at the bar whispering, "That's Belle Starr's son Eddie. And Jim Reed was his daddy. Ain't he something to see?"

"You are not taking Venus into town," Belle said. "That don't even come into the question. Nobody rides Venus but me, you know that goddamn well."

"You'd think the damn horse was made out of gold, way you carry on," Eddie said.

"Better than gold," Belle said. "I wouldn't take all the gold dust in California for that mare. She's better than a sister to me and God knows more loyal to me than any husband's ever been, or any son, come to that. There are plenty of good horses to choose. Take Beauty."

"Beauty don't compare with Venus," Eddie said.

"I know that," she said. "And you know that. Anybody who knows a damn thing about horseflesh knows that. But that little Briartown floozie you're hoping to bed down tonight, she don't know anything about horses. Beauty will look to her just as handsome as Venus. I don't want to hear anything more about it. You take Beauty and go on off to your dance in Briartown or you don't go at all and that's an end to it."

But that wasn't the end of it for Eddie Reed, who like his father and all the Reeds before him was a little headstrong and willful and now and then stupid. While Belle and Jim July and Pearl and two outlaws on the dodge were enjoying China Po's cottage pie in the kitchen cabin, Eddie saddled Venus and rode away on her to Briartown for the dance at Chapman's barn. He was the envy of all the young men at this event, since he not only enjoyed the celebrity of being Belle Starr's son but outside, tethered to the hitching post, was her favorite mare, easily the best-looking horse in the Territory. Eddie stayed very late at the dance and afterwards paid a visit to the graveyard at the edge of town with a whore named Gladys who had come all the way from Fort Smith. He was in high spirits going home: he rode Venus hard from Briartown to Younger's Bend; the mare was in a foam when he led her into the barn, but Eddie was too drunk to brush her down and dry her out. He threw her saddle over the stall side and stumbled into the hay to sleep.

Not ten minutes had passed before Belle threw open the barn door. She wore her nightdress and carried a lantern. Her hair was unpinned and cascaded into two streams, one falling forward over her breast and the other across her shoulders and down her back. Her eyes were as black as the inside of a coal scuttle.

She ran her hand along Venus' sides and across her fine wide neck, stroked her broad forehead, murmuring softnesses to her. She wiped the flecks of white foam from the mare's mouth and brow, brushed her flanks and belly dry and threw a blanket over her back. She watched Venus attentively for several minutes, then turned and picked a twelve-foot bull whip off a nail on the wall.

She stood briefly over Eddie's sleeping body before she drew her arm back, arched the whip high and let the buckskin tip of it pierce Eddie's chest like the point of a knife.

The boy woke with a howl and staggered, dazed, to his feet. He ran, half falling, first toward Venus and then toward the distant stalls and then back again toward the open door on the other side of the madwoman who stood flicking her bull whip over the boy's body with deadly accuracy, razoring the back of his neck, carefully missing his eyes as she sliced his cheeks, drawing thin lines of blood across his chest beneath the shirt she had cut into loose threads. When he turned and leaned forward to protect his lacerated bosom, she struck him again and again across his back and shoulders until he was bloodied from waist to skull and streamed like a fountain. He dropped to his knees and then fell forward on his face.

"Ma!" Pearl screamed from the barn door. "Stop it, Ma! You're gonna kill him, you're gonna kill Eddie!"

Belle stopped. Her face was white, her cheeks shone as if they had been brightly rouged, her eyes were black and flat like holes in her skull that went all the way through and emerged in some dark place underneath the river. She trembled with each rasping breath. She threw the bull whip into the hay, wheeled about and strode from the barn without speaking a word either to her son or to her daughter.

Pearl, who was bigger than her mother and a strong girl, dragged Eddie onto a pile of straw, drew a bucket of water and washed his wounds. But he continued to bleed. Finally, weeping, she lay down beside him on the damp, red straw, embraced him, feeling his blood creep like a warm hand between her breasts and legs, and fell asleep.

The next morning when Pearl awoke—curled in the straw and stained with her brother's blood from neck to hem—her arms were empty. Belle stood over her, looking down expressionlessly, holding a black cigarette in her left hand. "Go change your clothes," she said. "You look a sight."

Pearl labored to her feet, feeling sick at her stomach and heavy as an old woman. "Where's Eddie?" she said.

"Gone."

"Gone?"

"He rode off on Beauty early this morning," Belle said. "A born horse thief, that boy." She laughed shortly.

Pearl pulled straw from her red hair and studied it as though it was some queer thing she had never seen. "He'll die of his wounds, going wherever it is he's going," she said.

Belle shrugged. She went over to Venus' stall and stroked the mare around her soft eyes. "Eddie's a healthy young lad, he'll heal up quickly."

Pearl looked all around the barn curiously, remembering the night before as though it were something she had read about in *Fox's Police Gazette;* and yet there was the red-tinged straw, her nightdress stiff with blood, the sound of the whip she could still hear whistling through the early-morning air. "And if he dies?" she said. "Is any horse worth Eddie dying?"

Belle turned with her hand on Venus' forehead and looked coolly at Pearl. "One of these days, baby Pearl, I'm going to be able to stop telling you this. You're going to get it properly fixed in your head: men of whatever kind come and go through a woman's life like tumbleweed through a desert . . . lovers and husbands and brothers and sons, all of them. But a fine horse endures. You can't dance with one or hold it in your arms or go drinking and gambling with it. But when a woman gets done with all that and she's tired to the point of dying, then she can come home and put her head down on that warm flank and stroke that silken mane and listen to that soft, wet muttering in her ear, maybe a little flick of a fond tongue along the side of her face— and all the weariness goes out of her and she's comforted as she never could be comforted by any man, no matter if he was the handsomest buck in the Territory." She ran her hand down the length of the horse's neck one more time and then dropped her arm, but her eyes were still fixed intently upon Pearl. "Cole

Younger don't mean more to me than Venus," she said. "And Eddie came near riding her to death last night."

"But you would have whipped him dead!" Pearl said. "You would have killed him—your own boy!"

"Maybe," Belle said. "I've got an evil temper. It runs away with me sometimes. But maybe I would have stopped whipping Eddie just this side of dead."

Pearl moved slowly toward the barn door, her head aslant in earnest consideration of the question. When she reached the door she turned to Belle and, wonderingly, said, "You don't know for sure, though, do you? . . . whether you would have killed him."

Belle smiled a very slight smile. "That's what maybe means, baby Pearl," she said.

Winter at Younger's Bend that year of 1889 was bitter. A cold north wind from the Plains blew ceaselessly, freezing the ground so brick-hard that not even an Indian could follow horse tracks. Belle Starr and her daughter Pearl and Jim July huddled miserably by the fire in the kitchen cabin, eating China Po's bean soup and sipping rye whiskey. The outlaws who came and went from the hideout caves of the Bend drew their necks, red-skinned from the cold, down into the scant collars of their greasy cowhide jackets. They broke through the Canadian ice to water their horses and stamped their boots to keep warm until their spurs rattled like Mexican music. Indian relations of Sam Starr or Jim July banked glowing cow chips in the horse corral and stood with their backs to the harsh wind and their hands outstretched to the fire.

On Saturday, the second of February 1889, three days before her forty-first birthday, Belle—a heavy poncho draped over a warm woolen dress—rode off on Venus to accompany Jim July part of the way to Fort Smith, where he was to appear in Judge Parker's court to answer charges against him of horse thieving and assault. At San Bois, a town still in the Territory, Belle leaned over from Venus, threw an arm around Jim July's neck and kissed him squarely, passionately on the mouth, not caring that the townsfolk watched, agape, nor that Dickie Henderson jabbed old Weatherstone in the ribs and said, "Wisht you was a redskin, do you? You could get a little of that, if you was a redskin."

She turned back toward Younger's Bend, walking Venus, taking her time since the roads were deep in mire from heavy rains. She stopped overnight on San Bois Creek to visit with an old friend. The two women stayed late before the sitting-room fire, happily reliving early Missouri days and sipping peach brandy.

"I'll be forty-one in two days," Belle said, smiling, shaking her head. "I can't believe I've come to be so old."

"That's poppycock, Belle," Betsy Nail said, filling their glasses again. "You're not old."

"Not as old as I ought to be, considering what I've done in my span," Belle said. She laughed. "Considering just the men I've loved, I ought to be sixty."

"Now you're just bragging, Belle Starr," Betsy Nail said fondly. "You always was immodest, even as a girl in Carthage when we was together at the Masonic Hall school. You was such a bright girl, I remember that so well. But you was *fierce*, Belle. And you saw no use at all in hiding your light under a bushel."

Belle stared into the amber heart of her brandy. "Lights are meant to blaze out," she finally said. "They're not meant to be hidden away like shameful things. I always wanted the world to know that Belle Starr was in it." She sighed. "I'm a woman who has seen much of life, Betsy—you tell them someday that I said so."

The next day, Sunday, February the third, the two women kept late to their beds—the peach brandy, Belle said, laughing. It was afternoon before she mounted Venus for the last lap of the ride home to Younger's Bend. She leaned down from her saddle to embrace Betsy Nail one last time. At the first bend in the road, where four live oaks clustered, she turned to wave and then rode on, her gloved arm still lifted in salute.

Betsy Nail stood a long time before her house looking down

the road after Belle Starr. "I'm always looking where she's been," she said aloud, shaking her head. "Like I expect to see her shadow left behind to comfort me."

The first charge of buckshot hit her in the back, the force of it throwing her off Venus and into the wet, muddy road. The mare bolted and ran for haven, ears flat as paper against her head. She didn't stop until she reached Younger's Bend, foaming and snorting, wild-eyed.

Pearl hung over the corral fence watching a Creek boy break a horse. She ran forward screaming for help when she saw Venus rush into the clearing between the cabins and the barn with her reins hanging loose across her broad breast. Two men came out of the barn with their guns drawn. A third appeared on the stoop of the kitchen cabin with a shotgun aimed from the hip.

"Where is she? Where is she? Where's Ma?" Pearl shouted over and over, chasing after Venus, grasping at her reins, failing each time as the horse shied to the right, to the left, bolted toward the caves, then the corral, in spasms of fright. Pearl heard her voice in her own ears unnaturally loud: "Where's Ma? Where's Belle? Where's Belle?"

"Yonder comes Milo!" Tom Evans yelled, pointing to the distant figure that came on foot across the Canadian shallows, arms waving wildly, shouting something no one could yet understand.

Pearl stood rooted before Belle's cabin, arms hanging down limply, mouth slack, watching Milo Hoyt come clearer and clearer until his face seemed to be only inches from hers—a face larger than any human face she ever remembered seeing, chasm for a mouth, eyes like plates and black with fright. He could not contain himself: he leapt right and left, backed up and came forward again, his mouth opened and closed over the same words again and again—"They've murdered her! They've gone and murdered Belle . . . they've gone and murdered Belle!"

Pearl groaned and fell back against a porch post. Tom Evans

put out his hand to steady her. "Easy girl," he said. "Easy, now." And, grimly, to Milo Hoyt: "Where is she? Where's Belle?"

Milo pointed south across the river and east toward Briartown. "Down there," he said. "Briartown Road, lying there with her face in the muck . . ."

Pearl stared at him. Wisps of hair blew unimpeded across her face. Her tongue slid again and again across her dry lips. She struggled to form a picture. "Her face in the muck?" she said. "Belle's face in the muck?"

She leapt bareback upon the first horse she reached in the corral and, with her skirts above her knees, forded the Canadian at such speed that the water splashed high above her like a white curtain, almost concealing her from the startled gaze of the men left behind at Younger's Bend.

At her first sight of the figure in the road, she began to dismount. By the time her horse reached Belle, Pearl was already touching ground. She knelt next to the body stretched out in the mud. She touched the wide hole in Belle's back which had already turned dark and crusted at the edges. She turned her over and stared with disbelief into her mother's face: the right side of it had been torn away, her right arm and shoulder shredded by the same shot. Blood mixed with mire from the road clotted in the wounds. Pearl clasped Belle's head to her bosom, leaned near her face, groaning, rocking with pain. She heard a sound like a faint hiss from the face next to hers. She drew back, astonished.

"Ma?" she said. "Are you still alive . . . Ma?" The eyes in the white face did not open, did not flutter. But there was a barely perceptible movement of the lips. Pearl put her left ear against these lips: she could feel a wisp of breath, she heard a word spoken. She leaned back on her heels, looking at her mother's body, shaking her head. "No," she said. And, again, "No."

Tom Evans and Ed Starkey drew their horses up in a violence of mud. They pulled Belle's body away from Pearl, who went on sitting in the road as if she had been struck by lightning there and paralyzed.

"That bastard," Tom Evans said. "He wasn't content to shoot her in the back. He had to come up close and shoot her in the face and chest, just to make sure." He studied Belle's ruined face, the woolen dress already crisp with old blood. "Just look what some bastard has done to poor Belle."

Pearl continued to gaze across the road into the twisted trunk of a mesquite.

"Goddamn whoever done such a thing," Tom Evans said, struggling with Ed Starkey's help to strap Belle's body across his little mustang.

"I'll tell you who done it," Ed Starkey said. "Was Edgar Watson, no doubt of it. Ain't he threatened her many a time? Ain't they been at odds for years—disputing over property lines and Belle letting the horses graze on land Watson said was his? Who else would of shot Belle?"

Pearl stood up, still staring at the mesquite tree. Later on, Tom Evans said that he thought she was going to go on standing there all night, looking like she was thinking about something she couldn't quite get into words. "I went over and put my arm around her," Tom Evans said. "And I patted her and hugged her, real tender like she was my own girl, and I said to her, Now, you come on home with me and Ed, Pearl. You come on back home now. You can't just stand out here in the road, it ain't safe. And she turned around and looked at me like she didn't have an idea who I was. And she just went on shaking her head over and over, it was like her head was on some kinda spring and the damned spring had broke. And she kept on saying, No. Every few headshakes she'd say, No. Finally I asked her, I said, No what, Pearl? But she wouldn't say nothing else. Finally Starkey got her onto his horse, and we went on back to the Bend, me leading the unsaddled mustang with Belle's body tied on it. I put a blanket over the body, account of it was such a bloody sight and made us all so sorrowful to see."

She left no wealth behind her. A few hundred dollars in paper money and Younger's Bend, which because it was Sam Starr's headright could not by Cherokee tribal law be sold. Ed Starkey, who had known Belle for fifteen years, said she was a spendthrift, always had been improvident: Never spared a penny, he said, when it came to the best whiskey, and he'd known her to eat and drink nothing but champagne and raw oysters for days at a time, with a great slab of broiled Kansas City prime every third or fourth day. And the costumes, he said. All them clothes made up in St. Louis or Chicago or some such place. No wonder there's nothing left, Ed Starkey said. She had herself too good a time to worry if she'd leave four bits behind. Still . . . it was a shame about poor Pearl being left with nothing but two sticks to rub together against the cold.

Pearl drank a good deal of rye whiskey in the weeks following, ate little despite China Po's insistence on remaining at the Bend to cook the thick beef and potato stews Belle had always loved, and watched dispirited as the inhabitants of Younger's Bend departed, to come no more. Even the Indians took their ponies and rode away: there was no Belle now, no Sam Starr, no Jim July. They galloped into the Territory and vanished like dust in a desert. Finally one day even China Po: he appeared at Pearl's side with his carpetbag and an apologetic smile, and murmuring incomprehensible sounds, bowing continuously, he backed through the door of the kitchen cabin and disappeared as silently as he had, ten years before, materialized. Does he ride nothing? Pearl wondered, hearing only the silence—no neighing, no hooves across the hard earth. Has he got no horse? Does he walk everywhere with those tidy little steps? But looking right and left from the cabin door, she saw no sign of the Chinaman. It was as though he had turned into cloud and floated away as he passed through the cabin door. There was only one person visible to Pearl: a young man stood just inside the corral watching her. At least she thought it was a young man she saw, although she was never too sure of her eyes these drunken days.

"Who's that?" she cried out. "Who are you, over there in the corral?"

The young man crossed the clearing toward her, removing his hat as he approached the cabin. "It's just me, Miz Pearl—Will Harrison." He stood at the edge of the porch looking at her steadily, as unblinking as a bird. "You know me, Miz Pearl," he assured her. "Will Harrison? Your ma took me on some months back, for chores and general handy work. Here . . . let me help you, Miz Pearl. You're looking real peakid." He caught her swaying body just as it began its slide to the cabin porch, helped her back inside, set her down carefully on the bed. "I'm gonna make you some coffee now," he said decisively. "That'll make you feel better, good as new."

"I'll never feel good as new," Pearl said. "Ma's dead. Eddie's run off for good. My Flossie's gone forever. I got nothing left but my own nasty skin."

"You shouldn't oughta talk that way about yourself," Will Harrison said, watching the coffee come to a boil in the pan. "You got the prettiest skin I ever seen, in the Territory or in Fort Smith or anywheres else. Prettiest red hair too. And prettiest blue eyes."

Pearl grasped the wooden footboard of the bed and considered the rarity of this perception. How long had it been since a man had paid her a compliment? Was it way back in Chickalah? One of the dirt farmers' boys, Belle would have said. Maybe Flossie's daddy had had a fair way with speech . . .

"You're a nice boy," Pearl said. "But I think you're some kind of dream. I'm all alone here now. Everybody's gone away, even old Slade and China Po."

"Not me," Will Harrison said, bringing her a cup of boiled coffee. He watched with a serious face as she drank it. "I'm real as anybody could be. I stayed on because you didn't have nobody else. Seemed to me you needed somebody to help out, some man to kinda look after this and that."

Pearl studied Will Harrison's earnest face. It was a plain face with light grey eyes and a boyish mouth that looked downy instead of whiskered. He had hair the color of pale milk chocolate. She began to weep. Will Harrison looked surprised. "Why are you doing that?" he said.

"You remind me of somebody," she said.

"Who?" he asked.

"I don't remember," she said. "Some boy. Some boy I loved."

He frowned but said nothing. He refilled her cup with coffee. He leaned over and brushed her red hair from her eyes. His hands were surprisingly soft. "Will you be all right if I go away from the Bend?" he asked.

"No," Pearl said with conviction. She held out her hand to him. "I think you ought to stay here with me. I think we ought to stay together."

He considered this proposal. "What if you was to marry me?" he said. "How would it be if you was to marry me?"

"Would you take me away from Younger's Bend?" she said. "Someplace like Tamaha, maybe? I been to Tamaha, it's a nice little town. Away from here . . . I hate this place now that Ma's dead. Everywhere I look, I see her. I sleep in her bed and eat at her table. She's buried out there near the hideout cave. Dear God, I tell you, Will, when the wind blows some days I can hear her speak to me . . . I can hear . . . I tell you, Will . . ."

He leaned down and plucked her off the bed and hugged her to his breast until she was calm again. She felt comforted, like a child with a father. "Tamaha is a nice little town," she repeated quietly, resting on his chest.

"Good," Will Harrison said. "We'll go there, then."

There was hardly anything Pearl wanted to take with her from Younger's Bend: a basket of cookpots, a few blankets, a chocolate box in the shape of a red heart that had Belle's keepsakes in it (old photographs, a letter or two—one from Cole Younger), and the brace of pistols Belle had always worn on her hips and died wearing.

Pearl rode away on Venus. Will hitched two Morgans to a small wagon and rode ahead of them on a good Appaloosa, holding the bridles of the draft horses. A fine stolen Palomino was tied to the back of the cart. Thus they traveled to Briartown, where they stopped long enough for a preacher to marry them. Then they rode on to Tamaha on the Arkansas River, still in Indian Territory, but far enough from the Bend for Pearl to be able, for the first time in months, to erase from her mind's eye the image of her mother lying in the Briartown Road with half her face shot away and her woolen dress heavy with blood.

Tamaha was not a nice little town, the way Pearl had remembered it. It was as drab as calico and as uneventful as a church supper. Perhaps it had always been so, Pearl thought. "I'm like a woman waking up from a dream," she told Will Harrison. "Seems to me I've been asleep most of my life."

"Funny sleep," Will Harrison said, spreading dripping on his corn bread. "You got up to a thing or two at the Bend . . . and in Chickalah too. That's what I heard."

"Never mind what you heard," Pearl said. "You don't know what I'm talking about. You're as dumb as goose grease. You got no more imagination than pig at trough. It's just like Ma always said—if you want yourself somebody with fancy and a little color to their thinking, you got to get yourself a whore from a good hotel."

"Your ma had some queer ideas," Will Harrison said with his mouth full. "You shouldn't oughta follow her example too close."

Pearl stood up from the dining table and threw her crockery plate on the floor with such force that it broke into two slabs. "Don't you insult Belle," she said.

Will Harrison had stopped chewing. He sat with his napkin hanging from his neck like a flag and his greasy fingers propped in the air by his elbows. His face was startled. "I ain't meant to insult her," he said. "But it's a fact that what might be just fine for Belle Starr is the wrong thing entirely for Pearl Harrison."

"I'm not Pearl Harrison," she said.

"Oh no?"

"I'm Pearl Younger and my daddy was Cole Younger, who is famous in all the border states and throughout the South and West."

Will Harrison shrugged and resumed chewing. "Your daddy's sitting in the state pen in Minnesota. He's already been sitting up there for a dozen years and he's got hisself a dozen more to sit. He may be famous but he ain't very smart."

Pearl took a deep breath and clenched her fists and then picked up a cookpot and threw it against the window, breaking the glass.

"And throwing things around the way your ma used to do when she was in a temper ain't gonna help nothing anyways." Will Harrison's grey eyes were unperturbed. He went over to the cookstove and refilled his coffee cup. He turned with a thoughtful expression to face the enraged Pearl. "Truth is, I didn't much like your ma. She never give nobody any kind of a rest. Everybody at the Bend was in a state of uproar the whole time, on her account one way and another. Some kinda thieving she wanted to do or some kinda joke she wanted to play or maybe some man she wanted to bed. Everybody in a state of uproar . . . I don't want no wife carries on so. I like a restful kind of place."

"The graveyard's a restful kind of place," Pearl said. "But I don't plan to go there until I'm a very old woman and I've done everything there is to do and maybe one or two things I made up just for myself and I've had me a fortune, because Belle always said that maybe the most important thing for any female creature to possess was a fortune. Then she could do what she goddamn pleased in this life."

Will Harrison put down his coffee cup, pulled the napkin out of his collar and threw it down next to his empty plate. "Seems to me, Pearl," he said, "that you do more or less what you goddamn please right now, without a penny in sight."

"Not always," Pearl said. "But I'm going to start now. First off, I'm leaving Tamaha because living here is just like living in ditchwater from last week's rain. And when I leave I'm going to leave by myself because I can't stay married to somebody that's got no more color to himself than boiled oats. Why, in a couple more years of living with you, nobody would be able to see me, I'd just vanish into the landscape like one of those lizards that looks like a rock."

Will stood unmoving next to the table as though he were about to make a speech of some import and was collecting his notions and then rejecting them. His mouth opened and closed silently several times before he said, "I thought you wanted to settle down in some nice little town like Tamaha and live a quiet kind of life.

After the way you been living since you was a little girl, I thought you wanted something different."

Pearl paced up and down the cabin and then stopped in front of the broken window and looked out contemplatively. "I told Willie Brownlow once that what I wanted was for us to have a few cows and a place of our own. But that was a long time ago, when I was still asleep. Before Flossie was born. Before Ma was murdered. I don't believe in cows anymore. And I want a place of my own in Fort Smith where all the big money is. Not in this piss-poor town."

"You talk like some kinda cheap woman," Will Harrison said. "I don't know why you got to have such a cheap mouth."

"You're such a little church boy," Pearl said. "If Ma had known what a little church boy you was, she'd have given your balls to China Po for the stew. They wouldn't have added any flavor to it, though, is what I think. Wouldn't have made any more difference than a little tiny dash of salt. Now, that's pretty sad, Will Harrison. I think that's a real sad thing to say. Imagine having balls that don't afford any more taste than a little bit of salt sprinkled in."

Will Harrison stared at her with his earnest grey eyes. Finally he said, "I was purely wrong. You're a deal like your mama, Pearl. You like keeping a man in an uproar." He sighed. "Well, I'll miss you, I vow. A man can come to miss even a burr in his britches, if he lives with it day after day and it always sticks him in the same damn place."

Pearl pulled a stool up to the table and sat down and poured herself a large cupful of rye whiskey.

"What are you doing?" Will Harrison said, squinting at her as though he were trying to get a glimpse of her soul.

"Drinking rye whiskey," Pearl said.

"It's too early to drink rye whiskey," he said.

"It's never too early to drink rye whiskey," Pearl said, cup to her lips. "Ma used to drink it sometimes before breakfast, to clear her mouth up for China Po's brown biscuit."

Will Harrison picked his hat off the top of the bureau and set it resolutely upon his head. He stopped when he reached the door and turned back to Pearl. "I'll tell you one thing for very sure, Pearl Younger. You're gonna come to a bad end, just like your mama did. Sure as God made sunsets. And you won't deserve no better."

Pearl swallowed down her whiskey in one gulp and uttered a great gasp of pleasure. "Ma deserved better, but she didn't get it. Deserving's got nothing to do with anything. And if I make a bad end like Ma, then dear Jesus I hope I got a rich life to look back on, like she had."

Will Harrison laughed and Pearl realized when she heard it what an unfamiliar sound it was. "You think that was a rich life?" he asked. "You gonna sit there and tell me you think Belle Starr had herself a rich life?" He shook his head disbelievingly, turned and went out the door.

It was so quiet in the cabin after his leave-taking that Pearl could hear her heart beating. "Dear God," she whispered aloud, "is Will Harrison the Right Way? Were You trying to show me the Right Way again, and I threw it back in Your face?"

Standing on the Iron Mountain Railroad overpass in Van Buren, Pearl could see across the Arkansas River into the wild heart of Fort Smith, where she passionately longed to be. Fort Smith was to Van Buren as Van Buren was to Tamaha: with each move, Pearl strode nearer the lights and the music and the money of life as it should be lived.

But for the present, this year of 1890, there was little music and less money. Pearl had secreted a few of Belle's bank notes— her inheritance. Even Will Harrison hadn't known of them, and if he had known, he would have laughed his musty laugh again to imagine that Pearl thought they would pay for very much in a place like Van Buren. They had so far, in the few weeks of her residency, bought Pearl an egg every morning, a bowl of stew every night and a shot of rye whiskey early in the evening. It was not much to nourish a large girl with a hearty appetite. She had more than once had to accept the favors of some stranger in the saloon to appease her desire for whiskey and her taste for steak.

Two weeks after her arrival in Van Buren she saw Eddie Reed walking through the streets with a large flashy man in a planter's hat and diamond stickpin. Her first inclination was to call out his name and, when he turned to look, fall upon his neck with hugs and kisses as she always had done. But she didn't follow this first impulse. She hung back in the shadowed doorway of a haberdashery, watching Eddie move through the streets with a kind of easy confidence and grace she had never seen in him before. She marveled at this. She wondered if the flashy man with the diamond stickpin had something to do with Eddie's newfound ease. Or maybe, Pearl thought, it was only that Belle was no longer alive, that there was no longer Belle's mocking laughter like a nail in the heart, Belle's ready contempt, Belle's displeasure.

The next morning Pearl rose early, her heart already beating unsteadily at the thought of Eddie somewhere nearby. Bathing and dressing, she fell continually into a trance of recollection. She would find herself back on the Briartown Road a year before, holding Belle in her arms, listening to Belle whisper Eddie's name in her ear. Coming to herself again, she would run her fingers gently over her face as though to ensure that she was not dreaming, to prevent slipping back again to that other awful time. "He was her only son," she said aloud, looking at herself in the mirror. "It's natural she should die with his name on her lips. It's natural she should call out for this only son of hers." But the image in the mirror stared back at her, unmoved. Pearl leaned over the bureau and the tears came suddenly and wildly. "Oh, Ma!" she cried out between paroxysms of weeping. "You couldn't even get yourself killed without making things terrible for your baby Pearl . . . why couldn't you just of died like everybody else—dirt stopping up your mouth and nothing to say, no words to say, no names . . . just scream out in pain and fall dead . . . just your dead body left . . . nothing else to think about but putting your dear body in the ground."

She dried her eyes and gazed at the image in the mirror, who looked pale and dim-eyed and sorrowful beyond speech.

Eddie was staying at the Eureka Hotel. Pearl had seen him coming and going from that establishment, sometimes alone, sometimes in rapt conversation with a swarthy man who might have been—and Pearl knew something of these matters—a half-breed Indian, sometimes with the large rich man in the planter's hat, who now and then laid his well-clad arm companionably, perhaps even affectionately, across Eddie's shoulders. Today he was alone, eating oysters at the bar of the Eureka, looking brightly, avidly around the room, listening to parts of conversations on all sides of him in the noontime bustle of the room.

Pearl stood transfixed near the entrance to the bar, watching Eddie a while before she seemed to awaken, shaking her head as if clearing it of a dream. When she reached him she stood in silence at his elbow for a moment breathing in her brother's familiar odors: lye soap and hair oil, leather and gunmetal, and underneath it all a persistent aroma of nervous sweat. He turned finally and saw her. For a moment he did not react. His eyes remained distant and slightly unfocused. Pearl saw him escape suddenly from whatever faraway net had held him. He hugged her against his chest so hard that her breath was taken, crying her name over and over, tears springing to his eyes. Pearl kissed his cheeks and his eyes and his lips and held his face between her two hands to study it.

"Big sister," Eddie said, smiling, leaning back now against the bar rail.

"Baby brother," Pearl responded, smiling too.

Eddie studied her face intently, as though he had forgotten it and must memorize it again. "I can't believe it's you, Pearl. I thought I'd never see you again. I thought everybody from the old days was dead or in jail or gone off God knows where."

"Not dead," she said. "Only Ma dead. Oh, Eddie, why didn't you come home when Ma was killed? I almost died from it. If you'd come home, I would of had somebody to lean on, I didn't have anybody to lean on."

His eyes went flat and he looked down attentively at an empty oyster shell.

Pearl seized his hand and held it to her cheek. "Never mind, Eddie. Never mind that. I've found my dear brother, that's what matters."

He brightened again, pulling her close to him. "How about a whiskey, Pearl? Or something to eat? Where you living? How long you been in Van Buren, for God's sake?"

She patted his face. She laughed because she felt the tightness in her chest which had begun to grow from the first moment she had seen Eddie again break like thin twine stretched too far. "I've used up all my money, Eddie. I had a few dollars, but they flew off like sparrows and now I don't have a red cent. Ain't that rich, Eddie? Ain't that a laugh?"

He held her hand and caressed her cheek. "That's all right, now, Pearl. Don't you be distressed. Everything's going to be all right, I'll see to that. Eddie's going to take care of his Pearl. I got myself some money now, plenty of money. We'll find ourself a place to move into, a nice place, I can afford a nice place. And we'll eat steaks and eggs every breakfast and drink the best whiskey in town and play faro at the Archer Saloon or here in the Eureka. I'll show you the good life, Pearl. You ain't never seen the good life before, living out there at Younger's Bend or in that little wide spot in the Missouri road. I'm going to show you what the real good life is like."

"Oh yes," Pearl sighed, relaxing into his arms. "Yes, yes. Oh yes."

The large flashy man Pearl had seen with Eddie was Johnson Culpepper, who—as everybody knew—had become rich selling illegal whiskey to the Indians in the Territory and trading various contraband to whoever desired it. Some said he would gladly sell his grandfather a shotgun to blow off his grandmother's head, if the price was right. Culpepper had become so wealthy that he no longer delivered his goods in person (those who were there in the early days of his enterprise remembered him astride an intractable mule) but employed a number of reliable runners, among whom was Eddie Reed. He paid these runners well: Eddie Reed ate handsomely, drank extravagantly and rode a fine horse. After Pearl appeared, Eddie moved from his one large room at the Eureka to a suite, and brother and sister settled into the good life he had promised. He was away in the Territory for two or three weeks at a time, but he always left Pearl a roll of bank notes to pay for her food and drink and amusements until he returned. Pearl slept late, took breakfast in the sunny corner of the suite in front of the windows overlooking the hurly-burly of the streets below, which entertained her as she washed down her grits and eggs and pork sausages with pots of strong coffee. She played faro every evening at the Archer Saloon and won handily; it seemed to Pearl that Lady Luck had finally decided to smile on her and that whatever she did from now on would be blessed by that smile. Occasionally when she thought such a thing, she would hear a sound in the back of her head a little like Belle Starr's soft, mocking laughter. But since life went along so well, Pearl came to imagine that she was mistaken: Ma's dead, she would say to herself. Dead as a doornail. She's got no opinions anymore. She don't laugh these days.

But after six months of the good life Eddie did not return as promised on the day expected, and Pearl worried about this. She worried for five days. She sought out Johnson Culpepper in the dining room of the Eureka Hotel. He listened to her worries, chewing his Kansas City steak and swilling his beer. Then he wiped his mouth and his fingers and smiled and patted Pearl on the arm and said, "Don't you give it another thought, little lady. He's just having hisself a good time with some 'breed girl. He'll show up in a couple of days."

But after another ten days Eddie still had not appeared. Pearl no longer left her rooms at the Eureka. She sat by the windows anxiously watching the streets below. She had all her meals sent up, until the money began to run low. She would pace the bedroom until the early hours of the morning, smoking the black cigarettes Belle used to favor until the air in the room was thick and sweet-smelling as swamp flowers, and then, coughing, she would fall exhausted into bed.

One day just before noon, as Pearl sat hollow-eyed over the remains of her breakfast—the one meal a day she now allowed herself—a man who called himself Billy Dickinson appeared at her door. He carried his hat in his hand. His hair was flattened and shiny with grease and he smelled of cheap cologne. He said Eddie had sent him. Pearl looked out the windows for a minute, feeling strangely absent.

"Where is he?" she finally asked Billy Dickinson.

"Over to Fort Smith. Judge Parker's deputies done picked him up in the tumbleweed wagon and took him back there and tried him before he could say Jack Robinson, and the judge give him seven years in the Ohio State Pen. Now Eddie says to tell you that if you want to see him one last time, he'll be through Van Buren in two days, on his way north to the penitentiary."

"Why'd he get seven years?" Pearl said. "What did he do?"

"It was the whiskey peddling," Billy Dickinson said.

"Nobody gets himself arrested for peddling whiskey to the Indians," Pearl said. "People been doing that since the Union began. Nobody cares."

Billy's thumbs continuously crawled around the brim of his hat, turning it like a cartwheel. "I reckon Judge Parker cares," he said.

Pearl leaned back in her chair by the window, feeling dull and empty. "In two days you say?"

"Yes, ma'am."

"Where'll he be?" Pearl said. "Where'll I see him?"

"I don't rightly know," Billy Dickinson said. "I expect you'll notice when he gets here. They're transporting a goodly number of prisoners."

After several minutes of Pearl's silence, Billy Dickinson decided she was not going to speak again and so he left, quietly closing the door behind him. He refrained from resettling his hat on his greasy, scented head until he was all the way down the stairs and crossing the lobby of the Eureka. He wondered why he did this, because nobody had died.

Two days later, on a Friday afternoon, Pearl was awakened from a fitful, half-drunken sleep by an unusual sound that she thought at first was lodged in her dream: it was the sound, she lay thinking, that a man with a pegleg of iron would make were he to drag that leg along a boardwalk and then through the dust and then, again, along a boardwalk. A certain crippled rhythm, she thought. She had known men shot, men lamed who walked that way. But it wasn't in her dream at all. The sound rose to her windows from Van Buren's main street below. She pulled her heavy body up, pushed her hair back from her forehead, rubbed the crusts from her eyes. She staggered to the windows and peered down into the street.

A dozen men in single file, their arms shackled behind their backs, manacled together by chains on their right legs, moved slowly down Van Buren's main thoroughfare. People on either side of the street stopped their business in mid-sentence to watch them pass. Women moved back from the street and sheltered their children. With each step of the chained men the manacles clanked flatly in the dust and then without resonance against the next chain. Midway down the tethered row Eddie Reed staggered forward, his head bowed. As the prisoners neared the Eureka, Eddie lifted his head and searched the windows for sight of Pearl, such a look of anguish on his face that Pearl felt her heart snap.

She threw open the window and leaned so far out that the wind took her chemise and billowed it like a flag. "Eddie! Eddie!" she screamed. "Come back, Eddie! Don't leave me!"

The file of men had already moved from beneath the hotel windows. Pearl thought she saw Eddie turn stiffly and try to look back, try and fail to raise his shackled hands. She thought she heard him cry out her name. Then the dozen chained men disappeared around a corner. Pearl watched, waiting, sure that when the dust settled, Eddie would be walking down the street toward the Eureka, grinning and waving up at his sister. But all she saw when the dust settled were two men near the blacksmith's shed who were observing with interest her state of undress.

She fell back from the windows and collapsed into a nearby chair. Her heart raced as though she had run all the way to Van Buren from Tamaha and she found it hard to draw a deep breath. She closed her eyes and waited for the spell to pass.

When she opened her eyes again, the sun had set and she could hear the night's piano music from the Archer Saloon across the street. Where have I been? she wondered. Did I faint? Is that what fainting is like? She got up and studied herself in the mirror. Tears had dried on her face, making clear fresh channels through the white rice powder covering.

She leaned away from the mirror, still looking at herself. "I got to get over to Fort Smith," she said aloud to the image in the looking glass. "That's where all the money is. I got to have money, it's like Ma always said. And I got to get Eddie out of the penitentiary. That'll take lawyers. Ma always said if you could afford to get yourself a real costly lawyer, he could make the Devil give up a villain right out of Hell." The image in the mirror looked back at her and smiled. She reached out and touched her reflection in the mirror, as though she doubled her strength in this gesture.

"Pearl will find a way," she said.

She went to bed believing this, but despite that she wept herself to sleep.

SECOND INTERLUDE

Queenie James,
Proprietor of Madam Van's Bordello,
Van Buren, Arkansas

She came to see me, as I recall it, in early spring of 1891. Called herself Rosa Reed. Good-looking girl, that was the first thing I noticed, of course. I wouldn't be in business long without an eye for a good-looking woman. A big girl. Fleshy. Nice round, meaty shoulders. Good breasts. Trim through the waist and then substantial hips. A man does like substantial hips and buttocks. She had red hair and good skin. She didn't have all those freckles that you sometimes get with redheads. She had milky skin, smooth and clear as a window. And blue eyes. With the red hair and white skin, the blues eyes were nice. I thought to myself—when she came around asking for work—well, this one will make you a dollar or two, Queenie.

Her story was that her brother had just been taken off to the penitentiary and she didn't have no money or prospects and she was gonna go hungry any day—and the way she put it was, hungry was just no damn way to make a trip. She said she was from the Territory originally, but she'd been living in Van Buren at the Eureka for some while. She didn't have no experience in my line of work, but she said she was a real quick learner and she was sure she could please me. I said, Honey, the thing is, can you please a man? She smiled a nice bright smile—put me in mind of a sunflower, that smile did—and said, I been pleasing men since I was just a young thing, didn't know front from back. Now I know front from back.

I laughed and I said, That's fine, Rosa Reed. You come on over here and we'll just see.

It was no time at all until Rosa was number one girl at my establishment. She just had a way with her. It wasn't just that red hair bright as a new penny or the white skin or the blue eyes. It was that sunflower smile of hers that really made the difference. She was a good-looking girl with a smile that made a man feel like if he'd come all the way from the Grand Canyon on a mule, it was worth every blister on his backside.

I used to have to insist now and again on Marybeth or Grinella or one of the other girls. Give them a little shove forward, you know. Make up a little story once in a while about how Rosa was already spoke for or was gonna be busy all evening or some such tale. My other girls got their feelings hurt more than once on Rosa Reed's account. I said to myself, Well, Queenie, this one's gonna make you rich. I didn't hardly dare say it. I'd waited a long time since MacGonegal's Saloon for somebody to make me rich.

And then after about six months Rosa came to me and she said, Queenie, I'm leaving you, I'm going over to Fort Smith to make my fortune.

I asked her what made her think she could make some kinda fortune in Fort Smith. She just smiled and said, Queenie, you know damn well I'm the best whore you ever had. But I'm not going to be a whore forever. The money don't lie in whoring, you know that's true. The money's in having your own house. That's what I'm going to do in Fort Smith. I been saving up my money and I got considerable put aside now. I'm going to have the biggest, finest, most expensive whorehouse in Fort Smith. And before I get to be forty years old, I'm going to be a rich lady—you wait and see.

I just sighed and smiled—what else could I do?—and wished her luck.

I never been able to keep the best things I run across in this life. Men or women. I spot them and I know they're the best and then before I get a couple of minutes to appreciate them, they're on their way out of the picture. Some of us just got that kinda luck. Some of us got to stay in Van Buren, while others get to go off to Fort Smith. God give me the wisdom to see the

truth of this, and I guess I ought to thank Him for saving me
the grief of wanting something I never could have. But it's worm-
wood, I tell you that. Bitter as gall.

Maud McGrath,
Well-Known Madam of Fort Smith

When she leased the big house on Water Street in 1891, I said
to myself, Now, who the hell is *this* floozy? And I went over to
find out. There she was with her sleeves rolled up and running
around the place telling everybody what to do about this and
that and where to put the piano and how to lay the carpet just
so and every little detail. Sweating like a horse. Looked like a
housemaid and strong as an ox. And I thought, Now, do I need
to worry about this one or not?

She said she was Pearl Starr, Belle's daughter. And I said,
My dear God, I knew Belle Starr real well, she was a particular
friend. You coulda knocked me over with a feather. I didn't even
know Belle had a daughter. I knew she had this no-'count son
who was always giving her a hard time, even though she loved
him good as she loved his daddy. There wasn't no question that
Pearl was Belle's own girl, though. We sat in her private parlor
and sipped some mighty good rye whiskey and talked over old
times, and Pearl knew all about Belle and Jim Reed and Sam
Starr and old Jim July. She cried a little bit over her rye whiskey. She said her brother Eddie was in the pen in Ohio and she
had to get up a deal of money to buy some fine lawyers to get
him pardoned. And she cried a little bit more and said would I
help? Now, what could I answer to Belle Starr's little girl? Besides, there was plenty of business for all in those days in Fort
Smith. Why, I ain't ever seen such a sporting city before or
since. You couldn't hardly get through the streets for the men
rolling in from the Territory and parts east and north, all with
silver in their pokes and a ready way of spending it. Some used
to stand out on the street corners in broad daylight making deals
to run whiskey to the Indians or steal horses, or selling places in

wagon trains that wasn't going to Colorado or California or anywhere else or tickets for steamboats going down the Missouri,
only the steamboats was just made up, like everything else about
men like that, like their histories and their addresses.

Dot Parker,
an Equally Well-Known Fort Smith Madam

I didn't much like the whole thing and I told her so. I said to
Maud, What if we help her out and then in a year or two times
get hard and cutthroat and she's taken the place over? We'll be
out in the cold, you and me and Laura. I'm too old to think about
how cold cold can get. But Maud just shrugged and smiled in
that way she had and said, She's Belle Starr's little girl. You
know how they loved Belle in this town? Why, it was hers top to
bottom whenever she wanted it. All she had to do was ride in on
that big black mare of hers, dressed to the nines, wearing those
pistols underneath that velvet waist, smiling to the right and left
like she was Queen of the May, and my God—Maud said—Fort
Smith went down on its big callused knees!

Maud said, How's it gonna look if we gang up on Belle Starr's
little girl Pearl?

So I said to her, I said, You always know what's best, Maud.
We'll do whatever you think's right.

And Maud said, It's not a question of right, Dot girl. It's a
question of good business.

Laura Ziegler,
Who Completes the Triad of Famous
Fort Smith Madams

Pearl didn't know much when she started out—a real greenhorn,
over from Van Buren. She had a good instinct, but she wouldn't
have gone very far without Maud and Dot and me to help. We
got her some of the best girls out of Memphis and Hot Springs.

We told her how the whole system operated. We took her down with us on Monday mornings to city court to pay the tax: fifteen dollars to operate the bawdy house and five dollars for every boarder (that's what city court used to call the girls). She didn't even know about the weekly medical inspection of the girls and the health card they had to get if they hoped to entertain in one of our establishments. We all ran clean houses, we took pride in that. We didn't have no disease running through our places like the smallpox, and we didn't let no man in who looked like a dirty pig or had sores anywhere visible on his parts. We told our girls, You see something looks like a running sore, you get up and leave and come right then and tell us about it. When that happened, we'd have the fellow throwed out in the street, no talk about it. We never had had no disease. It was real important to keep a clean house, that way we could attract the best clientele in Fort Smith.

Pearl caught on fast. In no time at all she was the star of city court: men—women too, for that matter—would come and hang around in the streets to catch a glimpse of her arriving with her tax money on Monday morning. Now and then one of those Reform ladies would rush up to Pearl's carriage and throw a nasty old rotten tomato at her, splatter her dress maybe. Pearl would put her red head back and roar with laughter like it was the funniest thing since the last vaudeville come through town. I'll say this for Pearl, she had real style.

And real money too. Every day we could see her growing richer and richer: oxblood ponies and a carriage done up in cherry-colored silk. It was like Maud said, there was plenty of business for us all—but Pearl took the lion's share. Pearl's Place was about as well known as Judge Isaac Parker's hanging court and that was saying some. When the Reformers got to going real good once and it looked like we was in for it, Pearl put her up a sign on top of her house: it was shaped like a star, with red and white electric lights outlining it, and in the middle of the star it said "Pearl's Place." My God, you could see it for miles around! Even when it was so foggy on the Arkansas bottoms that a man had to feel his way across the railroad tracks from Garrison

Street to the Row, he could see that red-and-white star shining like a beacon! Now, here was the rest of us lying low and keeping quiet as could be in the circumstances. But not Pearl. That wasn't Pearl's way.

When Maud saw that sign for the first time, she put her head back and laughed almost as big a laugh as Pearl's, and when she was done laughing, she shook her head and said, I tell you, Laura, that girl's got the yellowest brass in town, there's no doubt of it. No doubt of it at all.

Desmond Murphey,
Attorney-at-Law, Fort Smith

Pearl was devoted to her brother Eddie, now that's a fact. She said it was for him she was doing all the wicked things she got up to. She smiled a little when she said that, but I think she mostly meant it for the truth. She came to me in 1892, not long after she arrived on the Row. She said she'd heard I was one of the best lawyers of my kind in the whole of Arkansas. I asked her what she meant by "my kind." She laughed and said, The not too particular kind. Pearl and I got along fine from the beginning.

She asked me what it would cost to get Eddie Reed out of the Ohio Penitentiary. I said I couldn't tell her that nor how long it might take, neither. But I promised her there'd be no taking advantage, that if I saw I couldn't do nothing for the boy, I'd tell her so. She thought that was fair enough.

Over the next year she paid me maybe two thousand dollars. Some of that was my fee, of course, but a great lot of it went to grease the proper palms in Washington and points north and east along the way there. It takes a bloody great lot of wicked money to extract a soul from a state penitentiary. Pearl worked like a Dublin doss-house maid to get me that money. That house of hers on the Row was lit up like the world's electric works night and day and Pearl didn't manage it all from her private parlor, not a bit of it. She was right in there bedding down with the best-paying gents who came in. God deliver every young lad in need into the hands of such a woman. So say I.

But in the end everything went as smooth as a buttered pig through a fence. I went up to Washington in 1893 with a full purse and a few choice words for Johnny O'Neill and lo and behold! there it finally was, looking like some kind of school-leaving certificate from a holy seminary: that sweet pardon for Eddie Reed, all nicely signed and sealed by his very self, President Benjamin Harrison. When I finally got it into me own two hands, Pearl gave me a lingering kiss and an evening at her place, everything on the house. Oh, it was a great night for us all!

Then no more than two weeks later Eddie Reed arrived in town, smiling ear to ear he was and ready to take on the world. I met the train he came in on, and when he knew who I was, he embraced me like a brother. He stood there at the depot with this little valise at his feet and he spoke about the goodness of his sister Pearl, who at that moment he thought of as nothing short of a saint. Without her, he said, he would just have rotted away in the Ohio pen, not a soul anywhere in the world caring a damn. His eyes teared up and he had a good blow into his handkerchief. I patted him on the shoulder and assured him that, indeed, he had a wondrous sister.

On the way back to my offices, however, the lad caught sight of Pearl's great electric sign that was so bright the dead in the graveyard could get up in the pitch black and walk away by the light of it. Eddie went white as a ghost, I thought he'd gone ill. What can I do for you? I hollered as I stopped my carriage in the street. He pointed to Pearl's Place without speaking. It never had occurred to me that he didn't know how Pearl raised all the money to buy him free. He was a young man with an amazing capacity to turn a blind eye to any logical deduction he might happen upon. I said to him, Come now, laddie—did you think she paid your way out of the pen selling needlepoint to church ladies? Took in laundry—did you think that? Taught school maybe? Why, you'd still be breaking rocks in Ohio five years from now! You'd have served out your whole damn sentence and there's an end of it. I sat in my carriage and said all this to Eddie Reed, but God knows it didn't help a bit. He went from white with grief to white with rage. By the time we got to my offices, he was in a fit of indignation the likes of which I hadn't seen since the priest discovered the poor-box theft in Kilkenny.

I pointed out to him that if it was logic he was hoping for, he was missing it by a country mile. Your mother, I said to him, was a notorious outlaw, likewise your father. Yourself's never drawn an honest breath—if it isn't horse thieving, it's another piece of skulduggery. And you sit there objecting to Pearl running a brothel—and mainly running it so's she could pay you out of the pen?

Whoring's different, he said. It ain't like outlawing and it ain't like horse thieving. Pearl wasn't raised up to be no whore.

I suggested to him that no young woman was raised up to be a whore, but that now and again she happened to find herself in circumstances . . .

But Eddie Reed wasn't interested in an intelligent discussion of prostitution. He was interested in being offended to the depths of his soul because his sister had bought him his freedom by selling her body and managing the sale of other bodies. Finally he jumped to his feet and announced that he was leaving Fort Smith as soon as he could find suitable employment.

And Pearl? I said. Surely you'll see your sister before you take your leave . . . she deserves at least a thank-you before you say goodbye.

And the young bastard shook his head and pressed his lips together like a stubborn child and said he'd got nothing to say to Pearl, that he was purely ashamed of her and that I could tell her this when I saw her.

I said to him, Eddie, you're hypocritical, ungrateful dog dung, I doubt a man could find ranker shit anywhere in the state of Arkansas than what's standing there in your boots. I think Pearl's well rid of you.

He got as red in the face as a fellow on the booze since age three, and I could see passing over his face an inclination to draw a pistol on me or flail me with his fists or some similar act.

But he thought better of it. I think he feared that maybe through some legal maneuver of mine he might find himself back in Ohio, languishing in a cold cell and sleeping on straw again. He turned on his heel and left my offices. I never set eyes on him again.

I went straight off to see Pearl and told her the entire story. I knew there was no use trying to deceive her. Sooner or later—and I suspected sooner, considering her contacts in Fort Smith—she'd learn the truth anyway. Or maybe, I thought, a garbled version of the truth that would be more painful than the honest truth I had to tell. All the time I was telling my story, she stood looking out her parlor window at the brown Arkansas River that ran along very nearly parallel to the Row. When I finished speaking, she turned to me with such a sad expression on her face that it almost broke my heart. And she said, I never ever blamed him for anything, you know, Desmond—though I had good reason to. Better reason than he'll ever find in me whoring.

About a week later Wallace Kline told me he'd heard that Eddie had hired out as a deputy marshal for Judge Parker's court and that he'd be operating in Indian Territory. That was an old story in this raw country: outlaws changing sides and policing other outlaws and then changing back again when the villain's fever came over them.

And so I had myself an extra Irish whiskey that evening and in me cups I thought about the queer forms revenge can take and how there's a kind of stupidity in men that can never, not even in God's time, be schooled out of us. And because of that observation I wept a tear or two into my whiskey and went off to Maud McGrath's to refresh my spirit.

The Row:
25 Water Street, Fort Smith

Laura Ziegler said the good life agreed with Pearl, but Maud McGrath said she thought maybe it wasn't the good life that was making Pearl heavier and more florid and never anywhere in her establishment without a glass of whiskey in her hand. Maybe it was sorrow, Maud said. Dot Parker found that hard to fathom, but Maud said, without further explanation, that sorrow often looked a lot like pleasure, if you just took a quick glance and didn't think too hard on it. Dot Parker didn't understand any of this, but she didn't pursue it: Maud was always saying things that Dot didn't pursue, mainly because she knew when she tracked the thought down, she wouldn't understand it any better, only she'd be tireder. Now, what's the point in all that trouble for nothing? she would ask. She let Maud and Laura work things out. Just give me the high points, Dot Parker would say about any matter that arose. Give me the main idea.

"Just the Mississippi and no tributaries," Maud McGrath would say to Laura Ziegler, smiling. "Dot just don't understand that you can't have a great big river without a hundred little streams feeding it."

Pearl's tall black maid Festina confided to Maud McGrath that most nights Pearl could not get to her bed without assistance. "If she had to uncorset herself," Festina said, "she'd sleep in her clothes ever' blessed night. She don't know which end of the bed be up."

This heavy drinking distressed her friends more than the sight of Pearl fattening. Fat, after all, could be removed if necessary, but alcohol ruined your liver and aged a woman twenty years in one. Pearl was only twenty-six, but no woman in her line of business, so they reasoned, could afford to do anything that would coarsen the skin or induce blue puffs under the eyes or cause the flesh around the cheeks to slacken. The sight of any of this occurring in one of their own undermined the sanguine congeniality with which the three celebrated Fort Smith madams customarily viewed life: it was as though Pearl reminded them that not even the riches of the sporting life would protect against decay.

Maud resolved to speak to Pearl.

"Is it Eddie going off?" she said as she and Pearl sat on opposite sides of a small heart-shaped table in Pearl's private parlor one evening before the main crush of business began. "Is that what's turning you into a drunk?"

Pearl looked at Maud for several minutes in silence and then she smiled. "That's what I've always liked about you, Maud. Not a bit of this beating around the bush. You're just like Ma in that respect. Ma never wasted a minute trying to put things in some nice way or another. She had her thought and she just spoke it out, devil take whoever didn't like it."

"Some people say you're gayer than you ever was before," Maud continued. "Just the other night Johnnie Whitestone said to me that you was the greatest fun of any woman he ever knew." She stretched herself up from her corsets, so that her white breasts swelled like custard over her low-cut gown. She sighed. She scrutinized Pearl. "I just don't happen to think it's gaiety I'm looking at," she said. "I think you're trying to get that no-'count brother out of your mind and you think whiskey is gonna help with that. I'm here to tell you it's not true."

Pearl arose from the chair covered in rose satin next to the heart-shaped table and crossed the room to search in the drawer of a polished mahogany chest for her cigarette makings. She carefully rolled the thin black paper around the dark tobacco.

"What's true," Maud pursued relentlessly, "is that you always sober up, next morning or the morning after that, and it's just like it always was—nothing's changed. Oh, your body's going to hell in a hand basket—your stomach and your liver and your hair and eyes and skin and all the parts; they're all going down-hill as fast as water through a sluice. But the drink don't change anything else. And for sure it's not gonna bring Eddie back."

Pearl smoked, filling the unventilated parlor with aromatic fumes. She sat down again opposite Maud. "What should I do, you think?" she said.

Maud shrugged. "Women do different kinda things when they feel real bad. Me, I tend to get myself a man. Men ain't good for much except their pocketbooks. But now and again they can give you a mite of comfort if you don't expect them to be too clean or too loyal."

Pearl laughed. Maud—later on, when she was recounting this episode to Laura Ziegler—said it sounded almost like the old Pearl, that laugh. Not too garish, not louder than it ought to be: just right, she said. Just a big, open laugh from way down in the belly. "It kinda relaxes your backbone to hear it," Maud said.

Johnson Mayhew was the only son of a rich Fort Smith family that consisted of the banker Franklin Mayhew, his wife, Vera, and two daughters, both older than their brother, one of whom had married a well-known surgeon and the other a prominent merchant. Johnson Mayhew himself, in his early forties, had not yet seen fit to marry, although he counted among Fort Smith's most eligible bachelors and was constantly sought out for dinner parties and galas. He was a tall, greying man whose brows arched elegantly over slightly hooded, often amused eyes. A heavy, carefully clipped mustache did not altogether conceal lips as opulent as a quadroon woman's. He had traveled extensively in Europe: there were those who said that Johnson Mayhew was a little more peculiar, a little more conspicuously eccentric with each return from his haunts in Paris or Vienna or Budapest. Rosalind Brown, who had once hoped to marry him, expressed the opinion that Johnson Mayhew would never marry anyone because this kind of alliance would, as she put it, "interfere with his nasty little pleasures across the seas." She never identified these, probably feeling that nobody in Arkansas would have any idea what she was talking about, anyway.

Franklin Mayhew had always expected that his only son would follow him into the First State Bank of Arkansas, which he had founded and of which he was president. But from the beginning of his life, through early manhood and into middle age Johnson Mayhew had expressed no single moment's interest in the banking business. When Franklin Mayhew tried to speak to his son of what he construed as the undeniable excitements and intricacies of this occupation, Johnson would smile politely until he could manage without offense to leave the room.

Once Franklin Mayhew—lunching in the spring sunshine on the veranda of the Mayhew mansion—had asked, provoked, "Must I leave the bank to strangers when I die?" And Johnson, picking small delicate oysters from their shells, contemplated his father for several minutes before replying that in his opinion there was no choice in the matter, since "we are all strangers, each to the other."

Such reflections, while perhaps philosophically apt, struck Franklin Mayhew as completely irrelevant to the lending of money and the taking of profit. But they were all he was ever able to extract from his son. Franklin was compelled to set his faith in First State's future into the hands of a small, dry nephew with eyes like screws, whom he did not like but whose efficiency and skill were indisputable and who was, after all, blood kin.

Johnson Mayhew, meanwhile, took no interest in any other business, either. Neither medicine nor the law enticed him. He made, now and again, amused and contemptuous observations about politicians. When he was in his twenties, his father asked him how he intended passing his life.

"I had thought," Johnson replied, "that I would luxuriously cultivate my tastes."

"I see," Franklin Mayhew said. "And who will pay for this cultivation?"

"Why, you will, Father," Johnson Mayhew replied, smiling. "Thereby making amends for your exorbitant profits and your merciless foreclosures."

He had been known to travel as far as New York City to hear some European diva with whom Fort Smith was unacquainted sing German songs. He would be weeks at a time lost from sight in Boston or Philadelphia. When at last he would reappear in Fort Smith, Vera Mayhew would inquire of him what delights he had found in his northern retreats. Smiling fondly at his mother, he would breathe a long sigh at the end of which he would utter the phrase: "Ah . . . now . . ."

"Johnson is a very secretive boy," Vera Mayhew said to her husband. "I can't think where he got it from."

"It's not like blue eyes," Franklin Mayhew said. "No doubt he has things to hide."

"What kind of things would he want to hide from us?" Vera Mayhew said.

"Every goddamn thing he thinks is important," Franklin Mayhew said. "That'd be my guess."

Pearl always remembered the night she met Johnson Mayhew. Deacon was playing the piano in the front parlor, something soft and sweet and slow because it was a very late and somnolent time. Two men were still playing cards for high stakes at the small octagonal table near the north-facing french windows, which were heavily draped in scarlet velvets. Several men sprawled on the satin-covered sofas, ties loosened and glasses propped against their bellies or thighs, staring into space or speaking quietly and aimlessly to each other. In the blue brocade chair a man sat with his arms neatly folded across his stomach, his head back and his eyes closed—Pearl wondered idly if he was dead and decided to check on that later, just before closing, so as not to alarm anyone with the thought of death in the midst of pleasure. She pulled the east draperies slightly apart and watched the first pale wash of the dawn. Behind her, someone said, "I wonder you're not too sick of us all to enjoy a sight like that."

And she turned to discover—or so she always said to Maud

McGrath—the nicest eyes she had ever seen: "Like huge black-berries rained on a little and hanging in the sun."

"Why, honey," she said, "it's you nice lads that give me the ease to notice a sight like that and keep me up late enough to see it."

He laughed, then took her hand and held it while he studied her face. "What is it goes on under that façade?" he said, almost in a whisper as though he were not speaking to Pearl at all. "I've been wondering about that all evening."

She touched his cheek lightly with her free hand and smiled. "I remember Ma saying once that only a fool wondered about what didn't meet the eye, since what met it was generally inter-esting enough to keep any soul busy for years."

Johnson Mayhew went on holding her hand and scrutinizing her face. Pearl allowed him to do this, feeling strangely at ease and a little excited all at the same time. Finally she took her hand away and said, "Maybe you'd like some of my very special brandy to round off the evening. I have it brought in for me from St. Louis. It tastes just like gold looks."

"I'd like that," he said.

"I keep it in my private parlor," Pearl said. "You go on ahead—it's that door yonder behind the palm plants. I'll just have a word with Glory about closing up for me."

He nodded and moved away toward the parlor door. Pearl looked after him for a moment and then sought out Glory, who was in the kitchen at the back of the house with her shoes off and her feet propped on the table. She was eating honey and dark bread.

"Put on your silver shoes again, dearie," Pearl said. "And go on out front in about half an hour and tell the gents we're clos-ing up. Jolly them along and remind them we're open again tomorrow late afternoon."

Glory sighed and put down her bread and honey. "You know you close up the place better than anybody else, Pearl. You say just the right thing, and nobody gets mad and spits in your eye."

"I got somebody waiting in my parlor," Pearl said.

"Somebody special?" Glory grimaced as she stuffed her swollen feet into her silver shoes.

"I wouldn't be a bit surprised," Pearl said, and turned and glided down the hallway to the front of the house again. She opened her parlor door upon the pale pink light she left burning there constantly.

Johnson Mayhew was standing at the window, watching the early light brighten the brown Arkansas River into copper. He turned to Pearl with a quizzical expression: "I heard some music once, in London, that sounded just like the river looks right now, this moment. But I can't remember the name of it. Is it age, you think, makes me forgetful? Or is it perhaps the thought of you coming any minute through that door that drives everything else out of my head?"

Pearl stood transfixed by the heart-shaped table upon which the brandy decanter glistened in the faint light. Of all the voices she had ever heard, there had been none like this: no tone easy and graceful as a horse loping through the high grass of a plateau, no words that sounded like some kind of music she couldn't understand right away, that she would have to put away in the back of her head to take out and listen to later on. She had never done that before, never kept words the way she kept diamonds or gold dust, saved away for a rainy day.

Johnson Mayhew came to Pearl's Place every night for the next two months. He came in late, after hours, through Pearl's private entrance, to which he had a key. He brought flowers: blue cornflowers, which he said were the color of Pearl's eyes, or bunches of Indian paintbrush—almost as vivid, he said, as her splendid hair. Festina would have been sent out earlier to fetch fresh oysters and some culinary delicacy Pearl had ordered in advance from the kitchen of the Hotel Biscayne, whose chef was French and highly thought of in Fort Smith. Some Sunday afternoons Johnson would call for Pearl at her private door in a closed carriage drawn by a stallion so black that in the sun he shone blue, and they would drive slowly into the countryside, find a green meadow with a few old, fat trees and spread the feast that Johnson had brought in a wicker case: champagne, cheeses the names of which Pearl could neither pronounce nor remember, eggs deviled with white wine, bread the color of clover honey with a delicate water crust. At the end of the day they would lie in each other's arms and watch the blood-red sun drift beneath the horizon, while Johnson, in a soft clear tenor, sang snatches of old French songs. Pearl would shiver with delight and fall, finally, into a light sleep from which Johnson would awaken her with kisses upon her eyelids soft as butterflies.

Pearl didn't understand why he loved her, and she told him so. Not in any sense to demand an explanation, merely to express her amazement at the remarkable pass to which things had come. She saw photographs in the newspaper of Johnson Mayhew at some social event or another; usually he was in the background, his face a blur, identifiable only because of the caption. But there was always a woman nearby, listening to him, looking up at him, reaching out for his arm.

"All these society women," she said to him one night in her pink-lighted parlor as she refilled his glass. It was late. Her hair hung down upon her shoulders, her bodice was unlaced. She sipped her brandy and studied his face earnestly. "You could have any one of them you wanted, for just as long as you wanted. Why do you come here to me? Half the time I don't even know what you're talking about. It must matter some to you, speaking to a woman who understands what you're saying. You're always making fun of people who don't know what you're talking about. But I hardly ever know, myself. And it don't seem to matter to you."

He laughed and took his brandy down all in one swallow. "There are different ways of not understanding," he said. "Mabel Oxford, for example. Now, if Mabel lives to be as old as one of those ancient turtles that acquire maybe a hundred years before their end comes, she won't understand anything any better than she did when she was four years old and clinging to her mother's plump knee. That's because Mabel is inattentive. Everything escapes her, rushes by her in a stream of color. She never tries to distinguish the elements. She just gets tired and goes home and lets a servant girl rub her feet and put her to bed. And then her old mother, who still has plump knees after all these years, comes in to tell Mabel good night and reassure her that the stream of color is really all there is and that no nice girl gets so attentive that she can pick out one tint from another, that being man's work." He held out his glass for Pearl to fill again. He gazed at her fondly across the small heart-shaped table. "Now, you," he continued, "you pay attention. That's your stock in trade: telling one color from another in that rushing stream you live in. Nothing much escapes you, my Pearl. You turn that bright blue eye of yours all the way around in your head, like a chameleon."

Pearl sighed. She got up and passed behind Johnson's chair, where she stood gently burnishing the shoulders of his dark silk shirt. "I don't care much if I know what you're saying all the time," she said quietly. "I like to hear your voice. It calms me. It's like when Ma would speak to Venus—that wonderful mare of hers. There'd be Venus with her eyes rolling back in her head and her lips drawn up tight to show all those long teeth, and Ma would say something to her—not touch her, you know, just speak to her—and Venus would soften. You could see that horse's backbone relax, and she'd focus those big eyes on Ma's face and drop those tight lips and whinny this little love song. That's how I feel sometimes when you speak to me. That string so tight through the spine just broken in two."

Around Christmas that year Pearl began vomiting now and again in the early mornings, and a continual sense of nausea interfered with her usual evening good humor. She inquired of Hiram Tucker, who attended to her medical needs in exchange for a free run of the house on Saturday nights, and he lifted his shaggy white eyebrows and pursed his soft, pink lips and said, "Sounds to me like you might be on the nest. But we'll check it." And he did check it. And, indeed, Pearl was almost three months pregnant.

Somehow she had always thought Flossie would be her only child. No matter what she did or with whom, there would be no other conception—only this one rosy child from another time. A fever of excitement she had never known before seized her: this was Johnson Mayhew's child. A child to be loved as no other.

Johnson didn't come to Pearl's Place every night now. He was sometimes away, in the East to listen to the music he adored, or detained by some undeniable occasion on Fort Smith's social calendar, which to have missed would have caused his mother a degree of unnecessary pain; he liked to spare his mother whatever suffering he could, although he seemed never to mind inflicting emotional hardship upon his father. "He's not a vulnerable man," he told Pearl. "His suffering is limited by his vision. With Mama it's different." But unless he was out of town, Johnson always came to Pearl at least twice a week. And he had never missed a Sunday afternoon: on one of these he was informed of Pearl's condition.

They were sitting in the private parlor, their feet resting on petit-point stools in front of a great clamorous fire well-laid and started by Festina before she went off to collect cold turkey sandwiches and warm puddings from the kitchen of the Hotel Biscayne.

"I'm very happy," Pearl said at the end of her announcement. "I know it'll be a boy and that he'll have his pa's good looks and maybe even his pa's good sense, if I can keep out of the way." She laughed at this, but Johnson was silent, rolling his long, thin cigar between his fingers, contemplating the white veil of smoke that rose before his face.

"A child," he said, the same way he might have said "a leaf," "a redbird," "a live oak."

Pearl rose and filled their glasses with champagne. Her hand shook. She studied the back of Johnson Mayhew's handsome head. "Are you any way pleased?" she asked, her hand flying of its own accord to her throat to still the fierce pulse beating there.

He considered this question. Then he said, "There's a child of mine, a daughter, in Budapest, and I have a son somewhere in Vienna, although I never saw him and don't know if he's even still alive. But this will be the first born right here in the Mayhew domain." He spoke quietly, looking into the fire. Then he leaned forward in his armchair and turned to Pearl, who still stood next to the heart-shaped table upon which two crystal glasses of champagne waited. "If it has its mother's good heart, I'll be a happy man," he said, smiling. "If it also has its mother's blue eyes and hair like sunrise, I'll feel blessed."

Pearl kissed his forehead, his large hooded eyes, his full mouth sheltered inside the mustache that always felt to her as soft and delicate as fur. "I was afraid you'd hate it, having a baby born in a sporting house. A sporting house is no place for a Mayhew babe to come into this world."

Johnson laughed. "Why, on the contrary, my Pearl. It's just the place. Payment in kind for the whoremongering of decades. Father, grandfather, uncles, brothers-in-law, cousins . . ." He threw his cigar into the fire and leaned back again in his chair, pulling Pearl gently down upon the petit-point footstool before him. He stroked the back of her neck.

Pearl turned on the footstool to embrace his knees. "I know you don't want anybody to know whose child this is," she said. "I know why we always go out to the country in a closed carriage and why we never go out together in public in Fort Smith. I'm a good many poor things, Johnson, but not a fool. I don't expect anything from you. You're not obliged in any way."

His eyes seemed to shutter. "But I am obliged, Pearl. It's my bairn, I must look after it. I can do no less."

"I won't have you feeling bound," Pearl said. "I knew from the first—"

"Hush, Pearl!" He had never spoken to her sharply before. He got up and began to pace about the room, distracted and far away from her. The sudden distance between them made her uneasy. He stopped pacing and leaned tensely against the mantel, staring into the fire. "I won't marry you, of course. It's nothing to do with you. I won't marry anyone. But I want to establish an apartment for the child and find it a reliable keeper to live in and look after it. I'll settle some money on you for all the child's needs. It will want for nothing, I promise you."

Pearl nodded. She fixed her eyes upon the pale pink flowers in the carpet.

"Do you want to go away from Fort Smith until the birth?" he said.

"No," she said. "I want to stay here where I belong. This is home now. Besides, I got a business to run. If I'm not here, everything will go to ruin. I've worked too hard to let that happen." She looked up at him, studying his profile as he gazed toward the window and the river outside. "Long after you're gone, Johnson, this place here will take care of me."

He turned his eyes from the window toward Pearl. She couldn't see them clearly enough to know what expression was in them. "That's true," he said. He lit another long, delicate cigar, rolling it between his lips. "What will you tell them here when you get very large with child?"

Pearl rose from the footstool, sighed, swept her hair away from her face. "Nothing. It's none of their business if I get to be three hundred pounds and Festina has to use a shoehorn to get me through the door."

Johnson laughed. He held out his arms toward Pearl, and she crept gratefully into them and rested her face against his shirt-front, closing her eyes. He stroked the back of her head.

"Poor Pearl," he said softly. "How different things might have been. You could as easily have been one of those society ladies preening themselves under the Chinese lanterns in a garden with artificial waterfalls." She raised her head and looked at him curiously. "But I suppose," he continued, smiling, "that had you been born into such a respectable family, you'd not have your great good heart that makes all the cold of my life recede."

In February 1894, Johnson Mayhew announced to his father that he was going abroad and had no idea when he might return.

"Am I to take it," Franklin Mayhew said, "that you are planning to stay in Europe permanently?"

Johnson was standing with his back turned to the gargantuan fireplace in the sitting room of the Mayhew mansion. He lifted the tails of his frock coat. "It's very cold in here these days," he said, frowning. "The heat from this fire seems to die on the hearth."

"It's not cold in this room," Franklin Mayhew said. "Try to keep to the subject, Johnson. If that's not asking too much of you. All I want to know is whether I can expect to see you again in this life."

He gazed at his father steadily, without expression. "I think there must be some answer to these questions that plague me somewhere in the world," he said. "I can't sit in Fort Smith and turn to dust without trying to find out."

"What questions are you talking about, Johnson?" Franklin Mayhew said.

"I'd like to know what this is all about," Johnson said. He turned and held his hands out to the fire as though he were blessing it. "I have some small light, now and then. But the larger light eludes me."

"I will never understand it," Franklin Mayhew said.

"What will you never understand?" Johnson faced him.

"How your mother and I could have produced such a creature as yourself," he said. "All I ever wanted was just an ordinary son who liked a fine Havana cigar and good rye whiskey and knew the ins and outs of compound interest."

"I need a favor from you, Papa," Johnson Mayhew said.

"When have you not?" Franklin said.

"I have established an apartment here in Fort Smith," he said. "There's nobody living in it at the moment, but come sometime next June, there'll be a child living there, along with a woman to look after it. I want a sum of money paid to this woman every month for herself and for the child, who is mine. I'd like to rest easy that this will be done until the child is eighteen."

"My God, Johnson!" Franklin Mayhew said, letting his cigar go cold. "Who's the mother of this child?"

"Not the woman who will be living there," Johnson said.

"Well then, who? For God's sake, Johnson, I've a right to know who the mother of my grandchild is!"

"You have no such right," Johnson Mayhew said. "No such right at all. I tell you that it's my babe. That's all you need to know. Will you see the woman gets the money each month? I ask this of you because I know you'll keep your word. There's nobody else I can trust."

Franklin Mayhew relit his cold cigar and studied with some attention the smoke emanating from his mouth. "I'd like your child in my house," he finally said. "It may be all I'll have left of you. I'm a man of more sentiment than you know, Johnson. Let me take the babe in June. It might comfort your mother for the loss of her only son."

Johnson Mayhew shook his head. "No," he said. "It won't do."

"Why not?"

"Its mother will want to see it, be near it, come to call on it. She wouldn't come here. You wouldn't want her to, but even if you did, she wouldn't come here. She'd be at the same time too proud and too ashamed."

Franklin Mayhew stared at his son for some moments. Then he nodded, got up and threw his cigar into the flames: it was suddenly hot and tasteless and scorched his lips. "I'll do what you ask, Johnson," he said. "Not gladly. But you're my son, whatever else you're not."

And so in February 1894, Johnson Mayhew traveled away to Vienna, from which exotic location his mother received an occasional letter for the first year of his absence, each communication a little stranger than the one before. Vera Mayhew suggested to her husband that perhaps Johnson was ill in ways no one could clearly see.

"I think you ought to go over there and bring him home," she said. "I don't like the sound of him at all."

"Just because you can't understand what he says doesn't mean he's sick," Franklin Mayhew said. "You never have understood what he said. And if I showed up in Vienna and insisted

he come home with me, I leave it to your imagination what he'd
say to me after he finished laughing in my face for twenty, thirty
minutes. Johnson's not a child, Vera. He can't be told what to
do, like he was a boy of twelve."

Vera Mayhew rolled her napkin and inserted it into her gold-
plated napkin ring. She rested her hands at either side of her
plate and gazed with slightly narrowed eyes through the immac-
ulate french windows at the darkening chimney tops of Fort
Smith. "He's sick," she repeated. "We'll never see him again.
He's gone from our lives, Franklin. We haven't got a son anymore."

Franklin Mayhew sat across the heavy oak, linen-covered dining table from his wife and stared at her through the twilight,
struck by how like she was to the old fortune-teller he had consulted when he was yet a very young man and had just come
west from Illinois: the same certain tone, same faraway look in
her eyes. Old Syl had been right about everything important.

But then he must remember that Vera Mayhew was not Old
Syl. Somebody in the Mayhew family, he said to himself, must
keep reality in mind.

The last four months of Pearl's pregnancy were hard ones for
her to bear. She covered the heart-shaped table in her parlor
with such quantities of food that the platters sat touching each
other, and it was troublesome to lift one delicacy without up-
ending another. She secluded herself and ate and grew enormous
—Hiram Tucker said she was far too heavy, that she oughtn't
to let herself go like that. Never mind, Pearl would say. When I
birth this baby, I'll give up being an elephant, I'll be horse-sized
again. But not till then, Hiram. Not till then.

She left the running of Pearl's Place more or less completely
in Glory's hands, and whereas business did not thrive as it had
when Pearl herself moved nightly through the parlors and rooms,
dispensing advice and raucous laughter and aged whiskey, the
receipts were ample and the profits good.

"But you don't much care about that, one way or another, do you?" Maud McGrath said to her one evening as they sat sharing a plate of oysters in the private parlor. "Since Johnson went away, you don't much care about anything, way it looks to me. Ain't that so?"

Pearl lit a long, thin, black ready-made cigarette. "Now, don't start in on me, Maud," she said. "I'm not in the mood."

"You never are in the mood to hear me say something that needs hearing," Maud said. "You can't eat yourself and the babe to death because some goddamn man runs out on you. A woman's a prouder creature than that. You got to pull yourself together, Pearl. You knew from the first that Johnson Mayhew was no way gonna marry you and most likely wouldn't even be visiting on no permanent basis."

"I knew that," Pearl said, drawing deeply on her black cigarette. "Of course I knew that."

"And he done what he said he'd do. Didn't he? There's a nice place waiting for this babe, with a caretaker and all. It ain't gonna grow up in no sporting house—bastard child running around the place emptying spittoons and carrying messages and seeing more than any child oughta see. It'll have a nice place and pretty things to wear and good schooling." Maud sucked an oyster out of its shell and drank the juice down noisily. She wiped her mouth. "Johnson Mayhew is an honorable man. There's not too many of them around, and that's the truth."

Pearl studied her friend's face for some minutes. "I miss him, Maud. I never missed Ma this much, or Eddie, or even little Flossie. No matter how much I eat or smoke or how much whiskey I pour into myself or how much of the day and night I can manage to sleep away—nothing helps."

"You've had heartache before, Pearl! What about when that husband of yours run out on you . . . that Will fellow . . ."

"I never loved Will Harrison," Pearl said. "He came along at just the right time, that's all. He saved my life when I didn't know how I was gonna do it by myself. But I never loved him. And when he left, I was glad. Scared to be all alone. But glad, anyway."

Maud was silent. She squinted over the plate of empty oyster
shells. She wiped under her fingernails with her napkin.

"I never thought Johnson would leave so sudden," Pearl said.
"Like the wind turning in a norther."

"It's better for awful things to be over quick," Maud McGrath
said. "It's lingering that kills you sometimes. Besides, how do
you know he won't come back? He's gone away before, and he's
always come back."

Pearl shook her head. "Not this time, he won't," she said.
"He went across the water, far away. And that last day we were
together—he kept studying me all the time like he was trying to
get me down by heart, so he could remember me."

Maud stood up and sighed and adjusted the stays in her corset.
"You just recollect this, Pearl honey, whenever you get blue—
men, even the best of them, ain't worth warm spit. No one knows
that better than we do, in our line of work. You got the best part
of Johnson Mayhew right there in your belly."

On the twenty-ninth of June 1894 a closed carriage called at the
private entrance and took Pearl—half led, half carried by Festina—across Fort Smith to a narrow, three-story building with
a paved walkway in front and a garden in back. In the ground-
floor apartment a midwife awaited her, standing next to a large,
freshly made bed into which Pearl crawled still wearing the silk
wrapper she had put on when she rose from her own bed with
the first birth pains upon her. Festina fluffed the pillow under
her head and patted her comfortingly on the shoulder and then
left the room. Pearl could hear Festina speaking to someone in
the hallway outside.

"Who else is with us?" she asked the midwife.

"The child's nurse," she replied, gathering instruments and
towels and bowls of steaming water upon a cloth-covered tray.
"A woman named Rooney. She's kinda hard on the eyes, but
she seems a good sort."

"But you never know, do you?" Pearl said, watching the midwife fold back the bedsheets and pat them smooth. "People can look kindhearted, and then in a little while you find out you got a wasp at your bosom."

"That can sometimes happen," the midwife said. "Now, take a few deep breaths. I calculate we're almost ready."

It was just like when Flossie had been born, Pearl thought wonderingly. And old Grandma Reed had known before she did that the birth was upon them. She was mystified how these women read the secret workings of her body quicker, easier than she did herself.

But the midwife was right, just as Grandma Reed had been right back in Siloam Springs seven years before: about six o'clock in the morning, just as the early-summer heat was beginning to shimmer in the air, a female child was born to Pearl Starr. She called her Ruth and gave her Reed for a last name. "We'll hide you out," she whispered to the baby in her arms. "Your pa would like that."

It was in September 1895 that Pearl read in the Fort Smith *Independent* of Johnson Mayhew's death in Bucharest. The announcement was made by his father, Franklin Mayhew, president of the First State Bank of Arkansas. It was reported that the bereaved parents and the eldest sister of the deceased would depart immediately for New York City, whence in two weeks they would embark on the S.S. *Gripsholm* for Europe to arrange memorial services for their son and brother, who by the time of their arrival would already be buried in Rumanian earth. Hospital authorities in Bucharest said Johnson Mayhew had died of a "sudden cessation of the heart."

Maud McGrath had handed the *Independent* to Festina and told the black woman to take it to Pearl. Something about Maud McGrath's face made Festina ask what might be in the newspaper that her mistress would need to see.

"Never you mind," Maud said grimly. "You take it in to her, folded just like it is now."

"It be something bad," Festina said with certainty.

"It's something bad," Maud confirmed, opening and closing her beaded bag over and over. "But she's got to know about it."

Festina shook her head, holding the newspaper with just two fingers as though it were hot. "Not me," she said. "You tell Miz Pearl."

"You get in there with that paper, girl, or I'm gonna beat you with a stick," Maud said.

Festina stared desperately at the newspaper. "What do it say there?" she asked Maud. "You tell Festina."

"It says that Johnson Mayhew is dead," Maud said.

Festina opened her two fingers, and the newspaper fluttered to the floor. "No'am," she said. "You beat me with a stick wide as a bed, I ain't gonna take that piece paper to Miz Pearl. No'am."

So it was Maud McGrath who bore the tidings to Pearl and stood hardly breathing while she read it and then read it again.

Pearl finally stood up and threw the newspaper violently down on the table and wheeled to face Maud McGrath, her face very white, lips drawn back over her teeth. "Goddamn son of a bitch!" she said, sounding strangled. "Goddamn him for a filthy whoremongering son of a bitch, may he rot in Hell!"

"Now, Pearl . . ." Maud began, moving forward to touch her shoulder.

"Goes off to some godforsaken place and hides himself and then dies! Lets his heart stop! That bastard . . . that awful bastard," she cried. "His heart never would have stopped if he hadn't let it . . ."

"Pearl, now, you're raving, girl . . . get ahold of yourself! Festina!" Maud screamed. "Get in here this minute!"

And Festina, skulking outside the parlor door, came at once. Efficiently, she grabbed Pearl in a tight embrace, pinning her arms against her sides.

"Buried in some goddamn godforsaken foreign place!" Pearl's face grew whiter despite her vehemence. "Where is this god-forsaken Bucharest . . . God alone knows where this shit town is!" Her voice filled the front parlor, where the few men who had

come early for their amusements turned away from their con-
templation of neatly turned ankles to stare toward Pearl's rooms.

Glory hurried to the door, which Festina had left slightly
ajar. "What in God's name is going on?" she said, her eyes
alarmed. "Sounds like somebody's getting killed in here."

"Get out, Glory, and close that door!" Maud shouted, pushing Pearl so that she sat down heavily, falling like a stone from
Festina's arms. Pearl went suddenly very still and silent. She
stared for several minutes at the crocheted cover draped across
the table. Then she raised her head to look at Maud McGrath,
who leaned down and tenderly swept the disheveled red hair
away from Pearl's eyes, back across her forehead.

"I keep losing people," Pearl said quietly.

"I know that, sugar," Maud murmured, stroking Pearl's forehead.

"One of the first things I remember in this world is some
man, I don't even recollect his name, I don't even recall where
it was I saw him. Guts dropping out, he was so full of shotgun
holes. I found that out later in my life, what big holes shotguns
make. He couldn't keep his guts in, all this bright red blood and
yellow stuff. Sometimes late at night when I'm in bed, I wonder
who he was, where he was . . ." She sighed and closed her eyes
and let her head drop back on the stem of her neck. "It don't
seem right to me. Some people live all their lives and die and
never lose anybody, same souls from beginning to end."

"Some are lucky like that," Maud said. She motioned Festina
toward the brandy decanter. The black woman poured a cupful
of the liquor and handed it to Maud. "Now, you drink this,
sugar. It'll make you feel better." She pressed the cup against
Pearl's white lips.

Pearl grasped the cup without opening her eyes and drank
down the brandy in one swallow, coughing afterwards. She stood
up. "I'm gonna drive out to the country now," she said. "Festina, you tell Willie to bring my small buggy to the back door.
I'm gonna drive myself."

"You think you oughta do that?" Maud said anxiously.

Pearl nodded. "That's what I'm gonna do," she said. "I'll be back sometime tonight. Don't come looking for me. I'll come back when I'm ready."

The buggy with the one bright black mare hitched to it was brought to Pearl's parlor door. She climbed in, laid the whip gently to the mare's back and drove away toward the open countryside. Finding the meadow with the few old, fat trees she remembered—the meadow not its soft, rich green now but stiff and brown with early fall—she dismounted from her buggy and went to lie in the grass and gaze up at the drifting clouds that seemed always to be the same ones.

The money from Johnson Mayhew for Ruth Reed's upkeep and her constant nurse, Bertha Rooney, had always come to Pearl through her lawyer Desmond Murphey. This had been agreed from the beginning, so that Franklin Mayhew would have no way to trace the whereabouts of his grandchild or the identity of its mother.

"He's not to get his hands on this child," Johnson had said. "This will be your babe, Pearl. You'll teach it to have a large, golden heart and be as uncorrupt as a doe in the woods."

For three months after Johnson Mayhew's death the money had continued to be delivered to Desmond Murphey at its usual time. And then one day Franklin Mayhew himself called on the lawyer.

"Sir, this is an honor," Desmond Murphey said. "Sit yourself down. Let me pour you a drop of the finest Irish whiskey ever distilled in the old country."

Franklin Mayhew sat down, at the same time lifting his arm in a negative gesture. "I'll forgo that, I'm afraid. My doctor, you see—won't let me indulge my taste for spirits these days."

"You won't mind, I hope"—Desmond Murphey smiled at the banker over the broken red veins in his cheeks—"if I have a small dram myself . . ."

"Not a-tall, not a-tall," Franklin Mayhew said, settling himself into the huge leather chair on the far side of Desmond Murphey's desk. He consulted the watch that gleamed at the end of the heavy gold chain spanning his waistcoat. "However," he said, "my time is very short today, so if I may soon come directly to the point . . ."

"Please, sir . . . please, sir . . ." Desmond Murphey swallowed his small dram all in one gulp and sat down at his desk, arranging his face into what he supposed was its most attentive expression.

"For something more than a year," Franklin Mayhew said, "a quite respectable sum of money has been paid to you each month for the purpose of supporting and maintaining a child of my son Johnson."

Desmond Murphey nodded. "True, sir . . . entirely true."

"My son is now dead, as you no doubt know."

Desmond Murphey bowed his head briefly, closed his eyes an instant in acknowledgement of that loss.

Franklin Mayhew ran his soft white hands over his silver hair and pursed his lips, appraising for a moment this attorney with a reputation no better than it should be, taking in at one swift glance the quality of the furnishings, the cut of the suit cloth, the dusty, rain-splattered windows; the smell of whiskey pervaded the room like old flowers. "I want his child," he said quietly.

Desmond Murphey, who had been leaning forward across the desk, smiling, conciliatory, recoiled into the interior of his chair, his face going for a moment as blank as a plate, then turning red. Franklin Mayhew perceived that the man's eyes began to water somewhat.

"Yes," Franklin Mayhew repeated, "I want my grandchild. It's all I have left of my son. Its mother could not possibly be so unreasonable as to refuse this child what my wife and I can offer it. Advantages, as you must know, beyond any easily available elsewhere."

Desmond Murphey nodded and nodded again, reddening still further, wiping his eyes with a large pocket handkerchief. "No doubt that's true, sir . . . no doubt a-tall."

"Then I trust you'll take this message to the child's mother?

Of course, I'm prepared to settle a very substantial amount upon the woman, provided she gives the child up wholly to my keeping and makes no attempt to see it again. A very generous amount . . . she will never want for anything again."

Desmond Murphey cleared his throat and said, "Well, sir, now, I am only the lady's representative, you see. I can't speak conclusively without her instructions, and that's a simple legal fact of the matter. However, my educated guess would be, that is to say, sir, having known the child's mother for several years, my educated guess would be that she would refuse your offer without a second thought." He got up and slowly, with a certain relish in the sound of the liquid splashing and the look of it in the dirty glass and the smell of it drifting into the room, poured himself another Irish whiskey. "Without so much as a second's second thought."

Franklin Mayhew sighed and leaned back in his chair. "Perhaps you can persuade her, Murphey—for a suitable emolument."

"I'm well paid by my client, sir," he said. "I've no complaints."

"It's a far cry from well paid to rich," Franklin Mayhew said. "Come on, man—what will you want for bringing me this child? If it's any way at all reasonable, it's yours."

Desmond Murphey poured himself yet another Irish and sat down again in his swivel chair, facing Mayhew. He sipped his whiskey and contemplated his guest. "The child's mother," he said, "is a friend of mine. That's one thing. Another thing is that even if you made me a rich man, I couldn't persuade her to give up her child. And a final thing is that even if I might be able to, I wouldn't do it. Your son wanted this child to remain in its mother's care, and I'm sure he had good reason for desiring that. The mother wants her babe, because she loved its father, you see. For some of us, you see, sir, love is triumphant."

Franklin Mayhew rose stiffly from his chair. He gazed down with fierce scorn upon the head of Desmond Murphey. "You are a little insignificant, untalented lawyer, regularly in danger of disbarment," he said. "Contest with me at your peril, Murphey. You'll lose."

"Not this time," Desmond Murphey said. "Not a chance of it, sir."

"I'll stop the money instantly," Franklin Mayhew said. "Not another penny will she get from the Mayhews."

Desmond Murphey smiled. "Ah, the siege," he said. "Well, sir, now in this case, it won't work, though it's got a long history of working well time and again, and I can see where you'd naturally want to try it on. In this case, the lady in question don't need your money, never has needed it. She agreed to take it because your son insisted on providing it, you see. But the child's mother can look after the offspring perfectly well. She's got plenty of money in her own right." He stood up, swaying a little after so many Irish whiskeys so early in the afternoon. "Now, if you'll excuse me, sir, I believe I have a luncheon appointment at the Biscayne."

"You'll be hearing from me again," Franklin Mayhew said.

Desmond Murphey shook his head, leaned heavily over his desk. "Fruitlessly, sir," he said. "Fruitlessly."

And fruitless it was.

Franklin Mayhew hired the best Pinkerton operative from the Chicago head office to track Desmond Murphey until he led them to their quarry. But the Pinkerton man reported after two months' hard work that the lawyer went only four places: to his offices, to his apartment (in a somewhat shabby building that barely skirted disreputable Garrison Street), to the Hotel Biscayne (where the lawyer enjoyed leisurely meals accompanied by copious drink, and where he appeared to transact most of his business), and to a house of ill repute run by a madam named Dot Parker (at which iniquitous place the lawyer spent at least four out of seven nights). Murphey's offices had been entered by stealth and searched, but no list of clients had been discovered nor any file pertaining to Mayhew. Every female entering Murphey's offices had been investigated, but in every case a Mayhew connection had failed to materialize. The Pinkerton operative was frustrated. He offered to continue the pursuit. The woman is somewhere to be found, he told Franklin Mayhew. It is merely a question of time. Pinkerton's is never defeated.

Meanwhile, Pearl, who met Desmond Murphey when the need arose in Dot Parker's private parlor, ensured Bertha Rooney's loyalty and secrecy with a large increase in salary and three months in Hot Springs, during which time she was to be the widow Rooney, taking the waters against the depression of her recent bereavement, accompanied by her only child, Ruth, and the child's nurse—a tall, thin black woman called Festina.

Sometime in the spring, as she and the banker Mayhew sipped iced mint tea on the veranda of their great red house set far back from the clamorous streets of Fort Smith below, Vera Mayhew said, "Johnson came to me in a dream last night."

Franklin Mayhew set down his glass of iced tea on the small, ornate marble table between them. "Did he? . . ." He gazed out over the vast sweep of his green lawns.

"He spoke to me. He said, Mother, leave my child be! I heard him say this as clear as I hear you speaking now."

Franklin Mayhew turned away from his elegant trees and looked at his wife. He waited patiently for whatever would follow, this time, from her nonsense.

Vera Mayhew sighed and leaned back in her cane chair, closing her eyes for a moment. She looked very tired. I must take her on a holiday, Franklin Mayhew thought. I must give her a change of scene.

"He cried," Vera Mayhew continued, opening her eyes and looking at her husband with trembling lips. "I had never seen Johnson cry since he was a little boy. Tears ran down his cheeks, and he said, Leave my child be, Mother! Clear as life, he said it."

"We've only just begun the search," Franklin Mayhew said. "The Pinkerton man says—"

"I don't care what the Pinkerton man says," Vera Mayhew interrupted. She had never, to the best of Franklin Mayhew's recollection, ever interrupted her husband. This event so startled him that he sat staring at his wife for some minutes, speechless.

"It's base, Franklin. Dealing with shabby little men like this detective, paying him to follow people around and ferret out their secrets . . . it's base, unchristian work. I thought so from the beginning, Franklin. And now Johnson has come to tell me there must be no more. He doesn't want us to go on, you see, Franklin. That's very clear to me."

"People can't make important decisions on the basis of dreams, Vera," Franklin Mayhew said. "Savages in jungles do that, not smart people in cities."

"Didn't I know he was sick?" Vera Mayhew asked, leaning forward in her chair, fixing Franklin with a sharp bird's eye. "Didn't I know we'd lost him?"

Franklin sighed. "Yes," he said. He rubbed his eyes. "Yes, you knew all that."

"And I was right!" Vera Mayhew said triumphantly. "There are many ways to be right, Franklin. Mine is one of the ways. You just never have realized it. Now I say to you that we will stop all this business of looking for the child. We will put it out of our minds. Johnson is dead, and he left nobody behind. We've got no son and no offspring of that son. We've got daughters, Franklin. Just daughters." She leaned back again, pale as a camellia.

"But we know a child of Johnson's exists!" Franklin Mayhew stood up in his agitation, leaned over his wife.

She shook her head. "Johnson doesn't want us to have that child, Franklin," she said. "My belief is that you could hire Mr. Pinkerton himself to look for that babe, and he will never have a particle of luck because he is running athwart a Spirit Force."

And so Franklin Mayhew, feeling old and used up and threatened for the first time by death, resigned himself to the bitter taste of failure and sent the Pinkerton operative back to Chicago. He never recovered from this defeat: when, two years later, he lay dying, he said to those daughters and sons-in-law and grandchildren surrounding him that they had gathered merely to witness the formal conclusion of an event that had occurred on that day he had abandoned the search for Johnson Mayhew's child.

THE MUSICIAN: 1896

One Monday morning after their weekly visit to city court, Pearl took Maud McGrath to see the three-story frame apartment house on South Fourteenth Street which she had christened "the Flats."

"You mean to tell me this is yours?" Maud said wonderingly.

"Seventeen thousand dollars of it is mine," Pearl said. "And I got a mortgage for eight thousand dollars. When I get too tired and old to tend to business on the Row, I'm gonna move to the Flats and live like a lady. I may even get Ruth over to live with me. She'll have nothing to be ashamed of in this place."

Maud McGrath strolled about the spacious, unfurnished second story, leaning over as far as her corsets would allow to investigate the condition of the wooden flooring, stopping by the windows to gaze out over Fort Smith. "You was always real smart about money," she said. "If I'd of put my affairs into your hands years ago, maybe I'd be rich now." She smiled at Pearl. "Maybe *I'd* be Queen of the Row."

Pearl put an arm about Maud's shoulder, and they both stood looking down at the hurly-burly below them. "I wish Ma was alive to see this place—and the Row house. My God, she'd be amazed! Her baby Pearl being such a businesswoman, owning property . . ."

"And whereas you ain't exactly law-abiding," Maud said, "on the other hand, you ain't stealing horses."

Both women laughed, and Pearl kissed Maud McGrath on the cheek and, taking her by the hand, led her down to the street again, where a carriage waited to take them to the Silver Dollar for a leisurely breakfast of grits and eggs, pork sausages and pots of coffee.

Speaking of this interlude later that day to Laura Ziegler, Maud McGrath said she thought perhaps Pearl was finally beginning to recover from the heartbreak of Johnson Mayhew. "And she dotes on Ruth," Maud said.

Laura Ziegler shrugged, buffing her nails. "She's gonna make a regular hothouse flower out of that kid. Keeps her all shut up in that house with that great ax handle of a woman, face that'd sour milk. Child don't live a natural life."

"Well, for Jesus' sake, she's only two years old!" Maud said. "You want Pearl strolling around her place with the babe on her hip? You think it'd be natural to let the girl toddle around the parlors at night, do you? Pearl don't want her ever to know what kinda work her ma does, what's wrong with that? You know, Laura, sometimes I do believe you ain't got the best sense in town."

Laura Ziegler studied her shiny fingernails. "A child oughta know some other children," she insisted. "Not just this woman with an eye like a chicken hawk watching a fat little pullet. And her ma coming to see her two, three times a week . . . Anyway, she's bound to find out about Pearl one of these days. She'll be asking questions later on, like kids do."

"When Ruth's older, Pearl's gonna send her off to St. Louis to school," Maud said.

"It won't be soon enough," Laura said.

"You got second sight?" Maud asked, growing increasingly irritated at Laura Ziegler's certainties. "Maybe we don't need to guess what's gonna happen to us in the future, maybe we can just come on over and ask you and you can tell us all about it."

Laura Ziegler put her nail buffer back into its mother-of-pearl case and stood up. "It ain't necessary to be such a snot," she said with dignity. "All I meant was that when people go to such pains so somebody or other won't find out something, well then, it almost always happens that that somebody is exactly the one who finds out."

"Is that so, Miss Know-It-All?" Maud McGrath said. "Is that the way it is, Miss Can't-Tell-You-a-Thing? Why do you suppose it's like that?"

Laura Ziegler looked sorrowful for a moment. Maud McGrath couldn't remember that she had ever seen Laura Ziegler look sorrowful: her friend's face became suddenly unfamiliar and made Maud feel afraid. "I just always thought it was God's way of saying He don't want no secrets kept, that secrets is wrong," Laura said.

"Now, you're a one to talk about keeping secrets," Maud said. "Where would we be in our line of work if we didn't keep secrets?"

Laura Ziegler sighed. "That don't mean God likes it," she said.

In November 1896, Desmond Murphey came by Pearl's Place late one night just before closing. His face was even redder than usual, and his pale grey eyes looked dim and unfocused as though he had been drinking for several days.

"I'm afraid I got to speak to you, my girl," he said, nodding toward the private parlor. "It's a bastardly errand I'm on, but some man's got to undertake it, and that's true."

Pearl led the way to her parlor, closed the door carefully, and poured two brandies. She handed one of these to Murphey. "Sit down, Desmond," she said. "Warm yourself a little."

The lawyer sat down in an armchair, holding his hat and his brandy. He shook his head. "You're a very self-possessed woman, Pearl Starr," he said. "There you stand, looking as collected as if you was about to set off on a Sunday social."

Pearl drank her brandy down all at once. "The thing is," she said, "I don't want to hear what you got to say, Desmond. I know I don't want to hear it. And I'm standing here right now pretending that I'm somewhere else. When they killed Ma, I did that. I squatted out there in the Briartown Road for the longest time, pretending I was a tiny little thing running along a sandy beach holding Jim papa by the hand."

Desmond sighed heavily and rubbed his pale eyes. "He's dead, Pearl. Your brother. Eddie Reed. Dead as a mackerel. Killed by a couple of disgruntled saloonkeepers in Claremore."

"Dear God," Pearl said. She sat down very suddenly, as though her spine had broken, in a chair next to the small heart-shaped table in the middle of the room.

"He was still working as one of Judge Parker's deputies," Desmond said. "He killed Zeke and Dick Crittenden to keep them from shooting the town of Wagoner into small bits, and people were busy, you know, congratulating Eddie for this derring-do. Folks came from all around to buy the boy whiskeys and pat him on the back, which Eddie loved, you know how he bloomed like a bloody flower when he had a whiskey in him and somebody gave him a pat on the back into the bargain. Anyhow, he got to be a local celebrity and never drew a sober breath, on account of all those congratulatory drinks people kept buying him."

Pearl listened attentively. It seemed to her that if she followed each word very carefully, as it was spoken, not lingering over one already spoken or rushing ahead to one not yet spoken, she could delay the horror lumbering already toward her heart.

"Then this month," Desmond continued, speaking into the fireplace, avoiding Pearl's eyes, "Eddie went into the Two Bar Saloon in Claremore to have himself a whiskey or two just to pass the time. John Whitty and Elias Chain, the proprietors of the Two Bar, passed an inelegant comment or two about the mostly besotted deputy, and Eddie drew his pistol and chased both of them out of the Two Bar and beyond the town limits."

Pearl stared at the back of Desmond's head as though it were a puzzle whose solution must immediately be found.

Desmond rose and poured himself another brandy, focusing only on the decanter, as though it were a lodestar, seeing nothing else in the room. He steadied himself against the mantel and spoke into the flames warming his shoes. "They weren't about to sit still for that, as you can imagine. John Whitty and Elias Chain were not men to be trifled with and, sure, that had to be shown to one and all. They went by the residence of John Whitty's brother-in-law and acquired sidearms from that gentleman and returned to the Two Bar. Where they killed Eddie Reed, who, they say, was still standing at one of the two bars, gulping down rye whiskeys and telling all assembled how it was he had done in those villainous Crittendens."

"There's no end of it," Pearl said.

Desmond Murphey didn't know precisely what she was referring to, but he knew there was no end to anything, and so he nodded.

Pearl rubbed her hand again and again across the surface of the heart-shaped table, polishing it until it was a mirror. "No end of goodbyes. I'm twenty-nine years old—not an old bawd with no tooth in her head. And the goodbyes I've said, why, I can't count all the goodbyes. Everybody I love disappears like water on a hot griddle."

"You've got little Ruth," Desmond Murphey said. "You'll have little Ruth forever, that's what I predict. She's sturdy, body and soul. I know that child."

Pearl stopped rubbing the heart-shaped table and leaned back in her chair, closing her eyes. "The child's not enough," she said. "It ain't enough having somebody come after. You got to have somebody who went along with you, who saw what you saw. Otherwise you lose it. It gets mixed up in your head with dreams and stories and such, and you can't remember anymore if it really happened or not. Eddie was the last of the ones who saw what I saw." She opened her eyes and stared across the room at the uncurtained window, where she could see the first light of dawn. "Eddie's the end of it. God's untethered me now, Desmond. I got no more ties to anything but today. I'm just gonna float around like trash in the Arkansas River."

When Deacon quit playing the piano in Pearl's front parlor and went off to New Orleans, Glory put out the word around Fort Smith that the house needed another piano player right away: good pay, two meals a day and all the whiskey he could drink without ruining the music. Two black men came the first day, but one of them trembled badly from dope or drink, and the other had a red, murderous eye and spoke insolently to Glory, who was attending to the hiring.

At the end of the week Count Arthur Erbach appeared, removed his slouch hat when Glory entered the room, smiled at her sweetly and played three short waltzes with a lot of what Glory called "flowering." When he finished playing, he stood up next to the piano and bowed, as though he had just presented a recital. Then he smiled radiantly at Glory and said, "Shall I play further?" His voice was deep and resonant, his English lightly, handsomely accented. Glory's ear was charmed at once.

She told him to wait in the parlor for her return. She found Pearl in her private rooms, looking over the accounts. "You gotta come see this," Glory said. "Some foreigner, pretty as can be. He wears a cape—can you picture that? A cape? He wants to be your piano player."

"Can he play worth a damn?" Pearl asked without looking up from the accounts.

"Oh, he plays nice," Glory said. "Not like Deacon played. But nice. Sort of . . . elegant."

Pearl rose from her ledgers and went into the front parlor to meet Arthur Erbach, who now stood next to the piano smoking a molasses-colored cigarette in an ivory holder. He dropped the cigarette into a dish on the piano and bowed to Pearl. "Madam . . ." he said, lifting his head, smiling.

His very large eyes were as dark as chicory coffee and looked slightly wet, as though he had just been thinking of a long-dead mother. He had a wide, grave mouth and a fine, straight nose. Curls of shiny dark hair fell at random across his forehead, embraced his small, well-formed ears, rested on the nape of his neck atop his starched linen collar. His skin was as smooth as caramel. He was somewhat taller than Pearl and as slender as a young boy. Glory was right, Pearl thought: he's pretty as can be.

"I hear you play the piano right well," she said.

"I am, you understand, not a professional," he said. "But since I am a small boy, I play the piano, and so I am, as you say"—he hesitated a moment—"not bad." There was something soft and indifferent in his voice, as though it insisted that the listener make an effort to hear it, bend close to hear it, and if she did not, then Arthur Erbach would shrug and smile and not mind at all.

"Play me something," Pearl said.

"With pleasure," he said. He played two little songs Pearl didn't recognize. They sounded sweet and sad and made tears spring to her eyes. When he had finished, she said, "Do you play any happy melodies? Early in the evening, when things are just getting started, we like the piano man to play happy tunes."

"Like this, perhaps?" he said, and played a song so light and gay—his delicate white fingers moving easily and quickly up and down the keys—that Pearl felt like dancing.

"Yes! I like that," Pearl said. "I think you'll do nicely, very nicely. What was your name again?"

"Erbach." He stood up. "Count Arthur Erbach."

"Oh?" Pearl said. "Count, is it?"

He smiled. "Of the Hamburg Erbachs. I am only just come to this country. But, please"—he briefly lowered the heavy fringe of his dark lashes over his great black eyes—"call me Artie." He looked up again at Pearl with such directness that she felt the breath catch suddenly in her throat. "In this country many people call me Artie."

"No, no," Pearl said. "Artie's not good enough for a real, honest-to-God count. Around here you'll be Arthur."

"As you like," he said. "May I smoke?"

Pearl had never been asked such a question, and she savored it for a moment before nodding assent. "Can you start tonight?" she said. "We're in sore need of some music in this place. We been silent but for loud voices and drunken talk for a week."

He placed another molasses-colored cigarette in his ivory holder and lit it. "Tonight, yes," he said. "At what hour?"

"Make it six," Pearl said. She held out her hand to Arthur Erbach, and he pressed the fingertips gently to his lips. Then he turned, gathered his cape from the brocaded love seat and disappeared into the shadowed foyer. Pearl heard the front door close quietly behind him.

Their love affair was the talk of the Row. All along Water Street and across the tracks on Garrison Street people said that

Pearl Starr had herself a new German fancy man. Played the piano, they said, and had eyes like a woman. More than one person suspected that Arthur Erbach laughed at them—not in a friendly way—but then no one could be sure, and no one wanted to challenge the lover of Pearl Starr, who had been known in the past to take such offense at comments on her personal life that she struck the offender with the butt end of a pistol and barred him from entry into what was now clearly the best whorehouse in Fort Smith.

Pearl referred to him as the Count and addressed him as Arthur. He moved into her apartments at the Flats, and every night he appeared at Pearl's Place to play a series of mostly melancholy songs which induced tears among many of the patrons. When Glory complained to Pearl about this propensity of Erbach's, she said, "That's what he likes to play. That's what pleases him. If the clients don't like it, they can bring their own organ grinders."

After three months, Pearl began introducing Arthur Erbach as her husband. Arthur would nod and smile and shake hands and say it was a pleasure to meet whoever it was he was meeting. People said Pearl thought this German fancy man hung the moon, that's how besotted she was with the fellow. Glory said, "Well, if he was mine, he could do whatever he liked to do, and I'd say it was all right, it was just fine. Pretty as that you don't get more than once in this life," she said. And if someone laughed at this, Glory would just smile and say, "You ain't a woman."

Some people on the Row who discussed the matter said that Pearl and the Count were not really married, that it was all just another of Pearl's fantasies. Like who the father was of that child born dead two, three years back, Eli Grass said. Rumors had gone around the Row—doubtless inspired, he said, by Pearl herself—that the pa was some socialite, some muckety-muck. In actual fact, Eli Grass said, that babe was like as not fathered by some down-and-out roustabout for the Southern Pacific, stopping over on his way to Memphis. I do like Pearl Starr, Eli

Grass said. God's truth, I do. She's the lightest-hearted woman I ever knew, and I never passed a truly boring evening in her company, but she's a damned great liar, couldn't tell the truth for diamonds.

But when Dick Kincaid asked Pearl if they ought to call her Countess now, on account of her being married to a count, she said being the daughter of Belle Starr was royalty enough for her.

Dot Parker said she thought the whole thing was a little on the disgusting side. "It ain't only that he's foreign, though I do wonder why it is Pearl couldn't find herself a nice fellow from around these parts. After all, we got a lot to choose from now. It's not like the old days when all we saw in a week was six, seven cowboys smelled like old dogs had died in their britches."

Maud McGrath replenished Dot Parker's bourbon, topped up her own and Laura Ziegler's. She winked at Laura. "You got some additional objection, I take it," she said to Dot Parker. "I mean, you said it ain't just that he's foreign."

"He's too young," Dot Parker said, throwing back her whiskey and smacking her lips in appreciation afterwards. "Pearl's a good deal older than he is."

"Five years," Laura Ziegler said. "He's twenty-five. That ain't exactly in the cradle, as I see it."

"Belle always had a taste for the young ones," Maud McGrath said, settling down amid the soft cushions of a chaise. The three madams were enjoying their monthly meeting for drink and relaxation and gossip. Pearl usually attended, but that—as Dot Parker had pointed out—was before the Count came along. Nowadays, Dot said, she don't have time for nobody but Pretty Boy. "I recall," Maud continued, "that Jim July was a deal younger than she was. Fact of the matter is, I think they was all younger than Belle. I remember her laughing once and saying, Well, you know, Maud, if you can get yourself a young cock instead of an old rooster, you got a kinda moral obligation to do it. And I said,

Moral obligation, Belle? And she laughed again—she was always laughing in those days—and she said, Happiness is a moral obligation, my way of thinking." Maud shook her head, sipped her bourbon, her eyes caught in old memories. "She was quite a woman, that Belle."

"Well, her little girl is getting to be quite a woman too," Dot Parker said sourly. "Making a scandal of herself, is what I think. Hanging on that fellow like the world's gonna end if he gets out of her sight. Why, I never seen the like."

"Oh, sure you've seen the like, Dot," Laura Ziegler said. "Remember when you was in love with Elmo? Now, you talk about disgusting . . ."

Dot Parker glared at Laura Ziegler from the deep comfort of her armchair. "Elmo was different. How can you say he was disgusting?"

"I didn't say *he* was disgusting," Laura Ziegler said. "We was speaking of hanging on people and making a scandal. I thought that's what we was speaking of."

Dot Parker fumed into her bourbon. "You're getting to be a real bitch, Laura . . . you know that? Real unpleasant. Not at all like you used to be. Why, you used to be sweet as jelly. Now you're always bad-mouthing somebody, mostly me."

"I'm not bad-mouthing you," Laura Ziegler said. "Maud knows I'm telling the truth. Elmo Jones couldn't hardly go pee without you tagging along." She yawned, took a mouthful of bourbon and swished it around for a moment before swallowing it. "Everybody laughed at you," she added. "I remember Dick Kincaid said once that he bet old Elmo thought when he left his mama that was gonna be the last little round woman who was gonna feed him his oatmeal."

Dot Parker rose in wrath from her cushions, fists clenched. "I ain't gonna sit here and be insulted like this! Maud . . . I ain't . . . You can't think I'm gonna sit here and let her say such things to me!"

"Now, now, Dot," Maud McGrath said, imperturbable. "Don't get your tail in a crack. You know damn well you did everything but chew Elmo's biscuit for him. So what's it matter if some folks laughed about the way you treated him? You loved him, that's the thing. You loved him a long time."

"She loved him till he up and run off to the Yukon Territory," Laura Ziegler said insouciantly. "Desperate to find gold and spoon his own oatmeal, was my guess."

Maud McGrath laughed in spite of herself and said, "Now, stop it, Laura. Give Dot a rest."

Dot Parker stared from Maud McGrath to Laura Ziegler and back again, her eyes wide and hurt, tears threatening to spill over onto her plump cheeks. She seized her brightly beaded handbag, extracted a lacy handkerchief and dabbed at her eyes. "I never thought it would come to this," she said. "My two best friends. . ."

"Oh, shut your face," Laura Ziegler said calmly. "We all know how it was with Elmo. Maybe I'm just jealous because I never had an Elmo. The same way you're jealous now because Pearl's got her Pretty Boy."

Dot Parker grew red in the face. "I am not jealous of Pearl and that boy! Why would I be jealous of them? I could get a boy like that if I offered him the Flats to live in and oysters and champagne every day of his life and a fine horse and buggy to travel around in and all the spending money he needed, and then when he got the least little bit jaded, I'd send him off to Hot Springs for the baths . . . why, we could all have ourself a new lover every single year till we was eighty, ninety years old!"

The madams were silent for a few minutes, studying the ceiling and each other and their cups of bourbon. Finally Maud McGrath said, "I guess the best thing in this life to be is a good-looking man."

Laura Ziegler smiled and sighed.

Dot Parker took a deep breath, adjusted her stays and resumed the deep cushions of her armchair.

Hiram Tucker said, "I don't understand why you want to do this, Pearl. You know it ain't necessary. I could fix you up easy as pie."

Pearl smiled and shook her head, relacing her silk wrapper. "Arthur would like a son," she said. "I'd like one too. So far it's just been girls."

"But is Erbach gonna stay around to help with this son he wants?" Hiram Tucker insisted. "You always get left alone to fend for yourself, that's what I don't like. It's gonna be little Ruth all over again."

Pearl poured the doctor a whiskey and looked out the window for a while at the early-afternoon sunshine on the river. Then she turned to Hiram Tucker again. "Ma wanted me to get rid of Flossie the same way you think I ought to get rid of this one. She threw me out because I wouldn't do it. Well, in the end, you know, I didn't keep her, after all. I was young then and didn't know how to do things, and Ma was always after me to give the babe up for adoption . . ." She smiled wistfully, brushed her hair away from her face. "I never forgave Ma for that. I remember swearing to myself when I wrote that letter telling Grandma Reed to find some nice family for Flossie—I remember swearing that I'd never again give up a baby of mine, no matter what happened."

The doctor gazed contemplatively into the glass Pearl had handed him. "All right, Pearl. You have it your own way. But I tell you, it ain't worth all the heartache, this birthing of babies whose papas don't take no more notice of them than if they was little burros on a Colorado trail."

"Arthur's not like that," Pearl said. "He wants this child, Hiram. You wait and see."

He nodded. "Not too long to wait," he said. "Five months, Erbach'll have himself his son."

Pearl stayed most of the day now at the Flats, leaving Glory and one or two of the older boarders to lay in food supplies and quantities of rum and whiskey, replace worn playing cards, tune the piano, change the bed linens, sweep the carpets and beat the dust from the heavy curtains. At midevening Pearl and the Count would arrive, received like visiting royalty. Erbach would play his sorrowful European songs, and Pearl would stroll through the house greeting old friends, welcoming newcomers, pouring rye and corn whiskey, embracing this man, comforting that one, telling another a joke she'd had from a fellow just in from St. Louis, all the while subtly and skillfully managing the disposition of girls and clients.

But her eyes never strayed far from Arthur Erbach, who sat at the piano with a faraway look in his eyes, squinting delicately against the smoke rising from the dark cigarette in the ivory holder between his teeth. Now and then he would lift his head and focus his huge black eyes on Pearl with an intensity that brought her immediately to his side, to kiss his lips, to press his head lightly against her bosom. Often she would stand for a long time next to the piano watching him play—with an expression on her face, Jim Grover said, like she was looking at the Hanging Gardens of Babylon or one of the other Seven Wonders of the World.

As Pearl grew larger and larger with child and Arthur Erbach remained at her side, smiling coolly, saying little, people began to believe that this one was going to stay—as permanent (Desmond Murphey said) as men get before they die into true changelessness. That contrary to the expectations of those who said that men too handsome and foreign to boot could never be trusted, the Count intended to acknowledge both marriage and child.

Eli Grass said it was nice to see Pearl looking happy again and that no one deserved it more than she did, but he couldn't fathom a man who thought so well of himself as Erbach settling down in Fort Smith with a plump whore.

In August 1898, Pearl went off to St. John's Hospital early one morning and after only three hours of travail gave birth to Arthur Erbach, Jr. He was a thin, yellow-hued infant with eyes like sacs of pink jelly, and when Pearl saw him, she rose up from her sweated sheets (hair in disarray and still glazed from ether) and said to Hiram Tucker, "Is this poor, weak little creature my own?"

Hiram Tucker nodded sadly and assured her that it was.

"I've seen healthier babes," he confided to Maud McGrath, who waited in the hallway outside. "It's a delicate infant."

"Like its papa, I guess," Maud said. "The Count could in no way be thought of as sturdy."

Hiram Tucker sighed deeply. "Too bad the little thing couldn't of took after its mama."

"Maybe it'll grow into a resemblance," Maud McGrath said. "Maybe every birthday it'll get brighter cheeks and bluer eyes, and its little body will get stronger and stronger until it's got the constitution of an ox, just like its ma."

Hiram Tucker lifted his white eyebrows very high on his smooth forehead and said, "Well, why not? They say Lazarus took up his pallet and walked."

But Maud McGrath's hopes for the newborn Arthur Erbach, Jr. —known to all as little Artie—were not fulfilled. Hiram Tucker said he didn't rightly know what the trouble was—"just born a weak little thing," he told Pearl. "God sends some creatures out kinda unfinished, seems to me." He prescribed an iron tonic and cod-liver oil. And patience. "He's just a mere babe," he told Pearl. "Hardly sprung out of his mama's womb. Things change with time. Give him a little time."

But time, as Pearl said to Maud McGrath later on, is one of those things you always think you have a lot of until you find out you don't have any. Not an hour more. Not even a minute.

Three weeks after the birth of his son, Arthur Erbach fell into a paroxysm of chills and fever and, despite the best efforts of Hiram Tucker, slipped rapidly into the stupor of typhoid-malaria. He lingered for several days in this quiescence, and then he died —without a cry, without even a murmur—his head cradled by Pearl, whose disbelief in the reality of this event kept her dry-eyed for two days. And then such an extremity of bitter tears and lamentations came upon her that Hiram Tucker was forced to administer draughts of laudanum and put her to bed. For ten days Pearl refused to eat or to rise. She made no inquiries about little Artie or Ruth. She did not ask how Pearl's Place fared. She lay upon tear-soaked flannel sheets and gazed at the ceiling or closed her eyes and slept a white-faced, motionless sleep during which she did not appear to breathe.

"Grief like this ain't natural," Dot Parker said to Maud McGrath. "She's got to get up out of that bed. She's gonna waste away."

"Who would of thought it," Maud McGrath said, shaking her head in wonderment. "Twenty-six years old! Who'd of thought that somebody hardly alive long enough to get sinful was gonna die!"

"She can't just go on lying there looking at the wall," Dot Parker insisted. "It ain't like Pearl." She peered anxiously at the half-open door behind them leading to Pearl's apartment at the Flats.

Maud McGrath studied Dot Parker's nervous face. "Maybe Pearl's gonna change," she said. "Maybe we oughta get used to the idea of some kinda different Pearl."

"Different?" Dot Parker sounded alarmed. "How do you mean different?"

"I don't know how I mean," Maud said. "Just . . . different. She's always been such a big jolly girl, laughing all the time, telling jokes to all the boys. And real capable at running things, nothing ever got her down . . . took everything in her stride . . ."

"You mean," Dot Parker whispered, "you think she ain't gonna be capable anymore?"

Maud took a handkerchief out of her beaded handbag and mopped her forehead. Too much fat, she thought. Makes me sweat unseasonable. "You have too much grief, you can't go on being jolly. It's too damn hard."

"Dear God," Dot Parker said.

"But we got to pray she don't start getting sorrowful like Laura. Laura used to be nice and sharp as a lemon, and now every year she gets sadder. Mouth's started turning down in the corners, and some mornings she's got pink eyes like a mouse from crying all night. Just the other day Will Foley said to me that nothing made him wearier than a sad whore."

"I don't want to hear any more, don't tell me any more!" Dot Parker said, putting a hand up to ward off knowledge, moving toward the stairway. "I want to go back to my place and sit in the parlor and drink a little bourbon before the evening trade starts. I got to collect myself. I ain't as strong as I used to be. Takes me a while now to collect myself."

In a commotion of petticoats and camisoles and fat thighs in silk stockings, Dot Parker descended the stairway of the Flats. In a moment, sighing, Maud McGrath followed, casting a regretful glance over her shoulder toward the door behind which Pearl Starr lay in drugged and dreamless sleep.

But on the eleventh day Pearl rose from her bed, put on her wrapper of flowered China silk, smoked two black cigarettes with the coffee Festina brought her and then went into the nursery. She leaned over the crib in which little Artie lay and studied the small sleeping face, pale as the moon. She said nothing, nor did she pick the child up. She returned to her room and sat next to a window looking out at South Fourteenth Street until nightfall.

The following day she dressed, with Festina's help, and was driven in her buggy to Pearl's Place, where Glory embraced her fervently and fluttered about making her comfortable in her private parlor. Pearl asked to see the accounts and spent the afternoon slowly turning page after page of the large ledger books, making occasional notes and now and again murmuring to herself. In late afternoon she drank brandy and ate little cakes Glory had baked herself. She returned to the Flats before the lights were turned on in the public parlor.

Count Arthur Erbach's funeral had taken place two days after his death: September was too warm in Fort Smith to delay the planting of bodies. Arrangements had been made by Desmond Murphey for interment in Oak Cemetery. The ceremony had been brief—the Twenty-third Psalm was read and a hymn sung in an uncertain, out-of-tune fashion by Murphey, Glory, three of the girls from Pearl's Place, Maud McGrath and Laura Ziegler (Dot Parker had refused to attend, since burials made her sick and she would never again, she swore, go to any funeral but her own). A simple wooden marker was erected until something more suitable could be decided on by Erbach's widow.

Three days after her return to the world, Pearl drove alone in her buggy to the stonemason, where she spent most of the afternoon. She spoke to no one about this visit, but three weeks later the simple wooden marker was removed from Arthur Erbach's grave, and in its place there appeared a pink marble monument eight feet tall—higher by far, Dot Parker pointed out (proudly, as though it was all her own doing), than any other monument in Oak Cemetery. The statue depicted a slender angel with a cunningly attached halo, a beatific expression and a large harp. Around the strings of the harp were carved the words: Play on, play on, my Beauty! On the angel's base, just below the dainty pink feet, was inscribed: Count Arthur Erbach, 1872–1898, Beloved husband of Pearl.

Maud McGrath said it was a work of art the likes of which she never expected to see again in this life. Dot Parker told everybody who came to her place for a month that the viewing of this monument would more than compensate anyone for the long drive out to Oak Cemetery. Laura Ziegler wept when she saw the statue, but as Maud McGrath said, Laura weeps nowadays when the sun don't come out by noon.

Pearl drove out to Oak Cemetery after the angel had been installed and looked it over carefully, touching the harp, running her fingers over the carved letters, gazing up into the saintly face for some long while. And then she reentered her buggy and drove back to the Flats. She paid no more visits to Arthur Erbach's grave.

It was as Maud McGrath suspected it might be: Pearl changed, but it wasn't in the fearful way some had expected. The laughter lost a little of its scale but none of its frequency. The voice was less boisterous but more lyrical: visitors to Pearl's Place said she'd gone from brass to yellow gold. Perhaps, some said, the gleam of the blue eyes had diminished, but no one could say they were sorrow-struck. It's not that she's subdued, Desmond Murphey said. (Dear God, the day Pearl grows subdued—he said—we can all of us kiss sweet time goodbye!) It's that she's withholding.

"Withholding what?" Maud McGrath said.

"Herself, m'dear," Desmond Murphey said. "Her own fine self. She's going to hold this little bit back, is what I think." He sighed and studied his Irish whiskey as though he could read in it the saddest of tales. "There's been too much taken away for her to go on giving like no matter how much you drank from her, she'd replenish herself like a deep well."

In early December of that same year the nurse who lived at the Flats woke Pearl before her customary rising hour of eleven with a cry of alarm. Pearl pulled a wrapper about her shoulders and accompanied the nurse to the small room where little Artie lay in his crib as though he had faded in the night—even his blue eyes seemed bleached.

She sent Festina in the buggy to fetch Hiram Tucker, who within twenty minutes appeared at Pearl's side, tieless, hatless and without a collar underneath his frock coat. He examined the child quickly and then instructed that he be wrapped in warm blankets for the trip to St. John's Hospital. "Move, woman!" he yelled at Festina, who was already moving like a frightened snake through the grass.

"What's wrong with him, Hiram?" Pearl asked quietly.

"What ain't wrong with him, is more to the point," Hiram Tucker said. "Just at this moment, I'd say he's got congested lungs, and if he don't get some oxygen pretty damn quick . . ."

He and Festina, carrying little Artie, started downstairs. Hiram Tucker turned just before his head disappeared below the stairs and looked back curiously at Pearl, who stood fixed near the entrance to the child's room. "Are you coming, Pearl?"

She nodded. "You go ahead, go on . . . I'll be just behind you, I got to slip into a dress, I can't go out in my wrapper, I got to . . ." Her voice drifted away, but Hiram Tucker was already out of sight, anyway.

Pearl went into her own rooms and sat down next to a small escritoire whose mahogany sworls she studied for some minutes. She took a photograph out of the drawer of the writing table: Arthur Erbach, smiling his grave smile over the swaddled body of the son cradled in his arms; Pearl stood next to him—one arm lying across his shoulders, she gazed adoringly at the man holding the child. Pearl stared with terrible intensity at this sepia photograph and then crossed the room to her wardrobe, from whose shelf she took down Belle's old chocolate box in the shape of a large red heart. She returned to her chair next to the escritoire and opened the chocolate box. Inside were photographs of Belle: several with Jim Reed; a few of Belle posing with men— mostly Indian-looking—whom Pearl didn't know; two in which Sam Starr stood next to Belle staring with narrowed, inexpressive eyes into the camera; one in which the Oriental-looking Jim July smirked at the camera as he embraced Belle. There was one picture Pearl had always especially liked; she didn't know why: Belle and Jim Reed sat on the porch of some house Pearl didn't recognize. Pearl herself, hardly more than a baby, leaned lazily against her mother's knees. Jim Reed sat very erect, proudly holding a bundled quilt from which an infant's head projected. They were all windblown and squinted against the sun. Their heads were turned slightly away from the camera: they stared into the distance as though something fascinating lay there.

There was a photograph of Eddie Reed at seventeen: thin, smiling broadly, a sombrero caught at the back of his head, one boot heel hooked into a railing as he leaned back against a corral with both arms lifted like wings. There was also a clipping of Johnson Mayhew from the Fort Smith *Independent*, three letters in Belle's flowery handwriting and one in Cole Younger's fast scrawl.

Into this heart-shaped chocolate box Pearl dropped the photograph of Arthur Erbach and his son. She returned the box to its shelf in the wardrobe. Then she began to dress, slowly, as though she had just risen from a long illness and must take care.

By the time she reached the hospital her small, frail son was already dead. Hiram Tucker met her at the entrance, shaking his great white head. Festina lurked behind a pillar in the corridor, afraid as she always was in the presence of death. Whether it was the death itself or the passion of grief left behind that frightened her, Pearl never knew.

"We did all we could," Hiram Tucker said, "but the little thing just didn't have no resistance. Its lungs was full to overflowing with fluid. It's hard to know how it lived through the night."

Pearl nodded. "Little Artie was just passing through. Like his pa, only quicker."

She motioned Festina to her side. "You call Sam Peguees to come collect that little body, will you do that, Hiram?" He nodded. She turned toward the door, Festina following along behind with head bowed and arms clasping each other. When the door closed behind them, Hiram Tucker shook his white head again and said, to no one in particular, "Not a tear shed . . . not a single tear shed. Dear God, that ain't natural, that ain't a bit natural."

With the briefest of ceremonies little Arthur Erbach, Jr., was buried in Oak Cemetery next to his father. A tiny replica of the Count's angel, minus the inscriptions, was placed at the head of the grave that was no longer than a cradle. At the foot of the grave a marble tablet the size of a foolscap sheet identified the inhabitant as "The Son of an Angel, an Angel Himself . . . Never at Home in This Cruel World."

Pearl Starr did not weep at the graveside. She stood very straight and dry-eyed and watched them plant little Artie in the earth the same way—Maud McGrath said—she might have watched somebody plant spuds in a garden. "She patted my arm and said, Don't you worry, Maud . . . everything's all right, don't you worry. Like she was consoling me. Like *I* was the mama of that poor dead baby."

Laura Ziegler and Dot Parker stared at Maud McGrath speechlessly after hearing this story (neither Laura nor Dot had attended the burial: Dot never went to funerals, and Laura, at whose bedside the other two madams now sat, was sick with the grippe).

"What could be wrong with her, you suppose?" Dot Parker finally asked, almost whispering.

"You mean besides burying her man and her son in the same year?" Laura said, blowing her nose fiercely. She lay back, groaning, upon a heap of pillows. "I don't know why a little thing like that would upset her."

"I don't care if you *are* sick," Dot Parker said. "I'm not gonna take no smart lip off you today, Laura Ziegler. You might as well know that right now."

Laura Ziegler lifted her eyebrows and smiled with her mouth turning downward in the corners ("Nobody but Laura can smile down," Maud had said once). "If you don't expect no smart lip off me," she began sweetly, "then don't make such pig-dumb remarks that any woman with a lick of sense would have to puke in her sickbed."

"There she goes doing it again!" Dot Parker rose up, going beet-red in the face, and turned to Maud McGrath imploringly. "You see how she insults me all the time? You see the kinda thing she says to me? What kinda friend says that to another friend?"

Maud looked thoughtfully from one to the other of the two women. "Maybe you ain't friends at all," she said. "Maybe you never been friends. We're just all whores together. Not friends. Had you considered that?"

Dot Parker put her hand over the round circle of her open mouth. Laura Ziegler, forgetting for a moment the discomfort of her grippe, laughed aloud. Maud McGrath got up and kissed both women on the cheek and poured all of them a stiff brandy—for celebration or consolation, she couldn't have said which.

THE GAMBLER: 1899

In 1899, when Pearl was thirty-two, she met Dell Andrews.
He had come to Fort Smith a year earlier to look things over,
and the things he looked over seemed so promising that he had
stayed on to play the faro tables at the saloons and hotels and to
engage the local gentry in private games of poker. He was a very
large, amiable man with a small, soft voice who never took
offense even when some heavy loser called him a sonuvabitch
card sharp during the evening's play. Dell Andrews would just
smile and shake his head a little and murmur that he was sorry
the man felt that way—and could he maybe buy the gentleman a
drink, just to show there were no hard feelings as far as he was
concerned? Occasionally a sore loser would take a swing at Dell
Andrews or indicate that it was his intention to brandish a pistol,
at which time Dell would take the man firmly by the elbow, step
up very near his face and speak a few words to him in a low voice.
Then Dell would lead him out of the room in a kindly way, as
though the man were the sudden victim of an embarrassing
seizure or had become dangerously weak upon receiving bad
news. In five minutes Dell Andrews would return to the table, at
which five or six men sat silently gripping their cards, and play
would resume. He always politely apologized for these interrup-
tions. Some people, he would say, got no idea how to behave.

Men who played poker with Dell Andrews often speculated as
to what it was he said to these troublemakers with his lips very
nearly touching their sweaty faces and his voice so low that it was
a wonder the man being addressed could hear it.

Finally one night when this scene had just repeated itself,
Robert Pickens carefully folded up his five-card poker hand and
laid it down in front of him and said, "Say, Dell, just what is it
you say to these bastards that draw on you or do some other
damn fool thing—I mean, what is it you whisper in their ears
that way?"

And Dell Andrews laughed his big, soft laugh and said, "I just
tell them that if they don't behave themselves and come on with

me real peaceable, I'm gonna dispose of them in such wise that not even their old mamas would be able to pick them out of a dead crowd of three."

Robert Pickens' smile turned a little queer and uncertain. He studied the girth and height of Dell Andrews for several moments. "I guess that'd calm anybody down," he said.

Dell Andrews lowered his bulk into the empty chair next to the felt-covered table and picked up his poker hand. "Seems to," he said. He smiled his amiable smile. He spread his cards at about the level of his collarbone. "Now, what I'm gonna do, gents, is I'm gonna raise that bet twenty-five dollars."

But Dell Andrews was a man who believed in a variety of diversions, and so he quickly located the Row and the choice houses upon it. He called first at Maud McGrath's place, where he sat for an hour and some in a large wing chair with his vest and collar unbuttoned and his bow tie dangling down his shirtfront, drinking corn whiskey and smiling benignly around the parlors as though he intended the smile to fall equally upon everyone.

Since he was a newcomer, Maud welcomed him personally. "Hello there, big feller," she said.

He rose to his feet as though, Maud later reported, he weighed no more than a few ounces and held out a huge hand upon which a diamond the size of a musket ball glittered. "Dell Andrews is the name."

Maud's hand disappeared almost completely into Dell's. What remained visible was covered immediately by his other enormous hand. Maud McGrath, who was herself not a petite woman, felt tiny and girlish and almost as though she might at any moment giggle flirtatiously. "Well, Dell," she said, "and what's your line of work, you don't mind me asking . . ."

"I gamble," he said, releasing her hand but still looming over her like a mountain.

"Cards, is it?" Maud asked.

"Just about anything, ma'am," he said. "If you're a gambling

man, you gamble on whatever chance gives you—maybe two
turtles racing over a Turkish carpet, maybe how quick a man full
of gunshot is gonna pass on over to the other side."

Maud laughed and said, "I get the feeling you're pretty good
at what you do."

"I got no complaints," he said, caressing the big diamond with
his clean, well-tended hands. "Now, if you was to come and sit
with me over there"—he gestured to a divan recently vacated—
"we could get ourselves better acquainted."

So Maud McGrath found herself sitting on a divan with Dell
Andrews for almost the whole of one evening, during which time
—she told Pearl Starr with amazement the next day—she confided in him all manner of sinful recollections which it had never
occurred to her before to speak out to anyone. "I don't know
what it is about that man," she said to Pearl, "that makes you
want to tell him things, but by God you do tell him things! And all
the time you're telling him how you really feel about this, and
how at one time in your life you got up to this particular thing
. . . he's sitting there looking at you like everything you say is as
fascinating as the Jersey Lily. And when you get through with
one tale, he just smiles and leans over to you and says in this very
confidential voice, Well, what about this? Or what did you do
after that? Or how come this or that? And you go off on some
other tale."

Pearl Starr laughed. "Watch he don't get all your secrets."

Maud McGrath looked rueful. "That could happen real easy
with this feller. And you know the funny thing? At the end of the
evening I didn't know any more about Dell Andrews than I knew
at the beginning! I knew he was a gambler and that he ain't been
long in town—that's all I knew."

"He's a smart man," Pearl said. She poured herself another
whiskey and leaned back in the armchair. The two women were
in Pearl's private parlor in her house on the Row: she had moved
out of the Flats just after little Artie's death and not been near
the place since. Laura Ziegler had speculated that Pearl might
even sell the big South Fourteenth Street house, but Maud
McGrath's opinion was that Pearl would never get rid of the

Flats. "Too many memories in that house," she said. "Too many to live with now, but there'll come a day when she wants to renew their acquaintance."

"Real smart, my way of thinking," Maud agreed. "You oughta get to know him, Pearl. You two'd get on like a house afire."

Pearl shrugged. "Maybe so, maybe so."

"He asked about this place," Maud said. "Said he'd heard you was Queen of the Row." Maud pulled an exaggeratedly mournful face. "I confessed it was true, but I assured him it was temporary."

Pearl laughed again, got up and hugged her friend. "You're a tonic, Maud. You do more for me than those goddamn iron pills Hiram is always stuffing down my craw. I wonder sometimes what I ever would have done without you."

"Works both ways," Maud said. "I've had a lot of pleasure from you, Pearl Starr. A lot of good times. It ain't all been heartache."

Pearl lit a cigarette and went over to the window to watch the Arkansas River glide past. She seemed to forget Maud's presence.

"I think I'll ask old Dell Andrews over for a meal," Maud McGrath said to Pearl's back. "I'll get something real special in from the Biscayne, and we'll have dinner upstairs in the Blue Room at my place. And you got to come, because I ain't entertaining this gent all evening on my own. You can get Glory to take care of everything here. Maybe I'll even ask Dot to come over and bring that funny little man she's crazy about now, that Caleb Hickson. And Laura too. Make a real party of it."

Pearl turned away from the window, pulling herself back from the distance she had occupied. "A party would be nice," she said, smiling. "It's been a long time since we had one of those."

Caleb Hickson, who came with Dot Parker to Maud McGrath's party in the upstairs Blue Room of her place a week later, was a thin-faced, scrawny little man barely as tall as Dot herself, and eighteen years younger. (Laura Ziegler said she guessed it was Pearl's pretty count that helped Dot overcome her natural disgust for young lovers. "But, Jesus, twenty-two years old!" she said to Dot. "Does he know where to put his foot to miss the shit?") He had small eyes so black that no pupil could be seen and a face so pale it always prompted people to inquire after his health. He smiled hardly at all and spoke in an intense voice so quietly that people had to lean forward to hear him. He had ridden with the Daltons as a boy and could not stop reliving the disaster at Coffeyville, Kansas, from which he had unaccountably and mercifully been spared. "I shoulda been there," he would always say, with a look of amazed preoccupation. "I was with them all the time in those days, always riding along behind Grat. Just a kid, but they let me go along everywhere—they was teaching me all those outlaw skills I was gonna need when I growed up, if I wanted to acquit myself real well. I shoulda been with them in Coffeyville when they tried to take the Condon Bank and the First National both on the same day. But I was sick with the dysentery, and Bob Dalton said I should stay behind." Caleb viewed this illness as a heavenly dispensation, a sign of God's grace: he gave up the outlaw game after that, not wanting to test God any further. But he knew and was happy to report the caliber of every bullet that had struck Grat and Bob Dalton, Bill Powers and Dick Broadwell. He could describe every entry and exit wound in the four bodies. Upon slightest provocation Caleb Hickson would produce a worn photograph of the four dead men lying neatly arow on the boardwalk of Coffeyville, their heads propped at awkward angles against the wooden wall of a store behind them. Caleb Hickson would grab a man by his lapels and shove this photograph into his face and point to a little space to the right of the dead Bill Powers: "I shoulda been lying there," he would whisper intensely, staring unblinkingly into the man's eyes as though waiting for him to explain why Caleb Hickson was still alive and selling grain at Carson's Feed Store in Fort Smith.

"Why the hell you like that little cow chip of a man is something I can't understand," Laura Ziegler said. "All he ever talks about is the Daltons. Who gives a damn about the Daltons anymore?"

"He don't just talk about the Daltons," Dot Parker said, bristling. "He talks on other subjects from time to time."

"The price of chicken feed by the pound is not a whole lot more interesting," Laura Ziegler said.

"Sometimes," Dot Parker said in her most serious voice, "he talks about God."

"Oh, I've heard him talk about God," Laura Ziegler said. "All he ever says is he can't understand why God spared him at Coffeyville. I can't understand that myself, unless God knew Carson's Feed Store was gonna have a pressing need for a clerk a few years later."

Dot Parker would have liked to slap Laura Ziegler at times like these, but she never did. It wasn't just that Laura was larger and stronger than Dot, which she indisputably was. It was, as Dot told Maud McGrath one day when she was discussing this provocation and temptation, that she feared breaking their union: "If we ever start attacking each other, setting on each other in whichever way—why, then we'll just fall apart. Then those Reform ladies will have the last laugh."

So when Laura Ziegler was rude about Caleb Hickson—as she almost always was—Dot Parker would just frown and narrow her eyes like knives at Laura, and if that didn't shut her up, Dot Parker would finally leave the room, fanning herself in agitation and swearing under her breath at the fates that had cast her with such a sour-tongued woman.

But Laura Ziegler did not come to Maud McGrath's party, since she had already made arrangements at her own house for what she called a "soiree" in celebration of Robert Pickens' promotion to head teller at the First State Bank. Dot Parker was not too upset about this prior engagement of Laura's.

Pearl came to Maud's party on the arm of Desmond Murphey, whose pale grey eyes seemed to have grown paler through the years until they now seemed colorless spaces in his florid face. His step was nearly always a little uncertain, like a man making slight, rapid adjustments to the pitch and roll of a ship.

And Dell Andrews appeared, large and sweet-smelling, voice

soft as eiderdown. He shook hands with Caleb Hickson and Desmond Murphey and bowed slightly to the three women. He smiled his benevolent smile, showing his small white teeth that looked as clean and well tended as his hands. Maud said to Pearl —as they poured brandy punch into blue crystal glasses—that she couldn't understand how anybody Dell Andrews' size could have such a small voice and small teeth. Pearl reminded Maud of Dot's Elmo Jones—a tiny man with a voice like a church organ and teeth the size of piano keys. They were both laughing at this recollection of the natural disparity of things when Dell Andrews approached the punch bowl.

"Ladies," he said, "I hope I ain't interrupting some private moment. I thought I might try a little of that smoked hen and maybe a spoonful or two of the fish roe."

Pearl heaped his plate with the cold delicacies from the Hotel Biscayne and filled his glass with the strong brandy punch. "A big man like you ought to eat a big plate," she said. "That's what suits. Little appetites don't go with substantial men." She smiled, handing him the laden plate.

"I got in every respect a big appetite," he said. He picked up between his fingers a slab of ham lathered with mustard and took a bite. "Now, that's delicious," he said. "Man'd be a fool not to say straight out how delicious that is. I got to compliment you ladies on the fine table you set."

It seemed to Pearl that Dell Andrews' warm blue eyes were studying her with an intentness he directed nowhere else, that whereas he had not rudely turned away from Maud, his glance somehow excluded her. Maud sensed this too and walked away from the table toward Dot Parker and Caleb Hickson, who stood near an open window. Dot fanned furiously, offsetting any advantage of the cooling evening air.

"Pearl, I would sure be pleased," Dell Andrews said, putting his half-finished plate down on the table and carefully wiping his fingers, "if you'd come to dinner with me at the Creole Palace tomorrow night, maybe a little faro afterwards, if that suited your taste. But if games of chance ain't your style, there's other ways to entertain ourselves."

"I been playing games of chance all my life," Pearl said. "One kind or another. I don't know if you'd say it's my style, but it is sure my habit. You can call for me at eight o'clock. I guess you know my place?"

Dell Andrews laughed. "I met a gent yesterday said his wife would sure like to burn Pearl's Place to the ground. Seems she thinks it's one of the main sources of evil in Fort Smith. Her husband, now, he don't agree. He thinks your place is the finest location in town for a man to amuse himself. Looks to me like a clear contest between good and evil."

"And where are you left standing in a contest like that?" Pearl said.

"I'm a gambler by profession," he said. "Gambling's always been thought an evil occupation by all good Christian ladies. I just stay in towns and practice my trade until those sweet gentlefolk run me out. Then I find another town."

Desmond Murphey, who had wandered up to the serving table in time to hear this remark, said, "We're all gamblers, sir, ain't that so—in our separate ways . . ."

Dell Andrews inclined his head slightly to indicate agreement. "That'd be my feeling," he said. "The law, now, the law is maybe the biggest game of all. Whether you win depends a good deal on who's playing the hand, ain't that so, Murphey? And the luck of the draw when it comes to who is judging the case? And it's God's truth that one jury will hang a man and another let him go free—and that's just luck. Why, if you was to say that the law is no better than the roulette wheel, you wouldn't be far off."

Desmond Murphey's pale grey eyes had turned pink at the edges and were watering badly. Dell Andrews noticed this, and it surprised him a little. He was a quick, astute judge of men, and he had not imagined the lawyer to be so emotional. "Maybe we oughta change the subject," he said quietly to Pearl. "I think this subject distresses your friend here."

Pearl put her arms around Desmond Murphey's neck and kissed him lightly on both cheeks and then the lips. "Eat something, Des," she said. "Nourish your dear self and then go on home."

The lawyer wiped his wet face and smiled at Pearl. "I've lost all hope of dignity," he said. "I was a half century old before I discovered justice don't exist. Oh, I always knew you could *use* the law, bribe it, grease its greedy palm, stand the damn stuff on its head, but it only came to me one day late in life that the using and the bribing and the greasing was all there was to it. No great idea called Justice hovering behind it all like a wonderful angel." He studied the large, damp handkerchief crumpled in his fist. He blew his nose into it with abandon. "I used to think that wonderful lady wept when we disappointed her."

Pearl stroked his face affectionately. "Go on home now, Des," she said softly. "I'll call round and see you tomorrow. We'll have a good talk. I'll take you to see Ruth. She misses it when she don't see you for weeks at a time."

"Ah, Ruth . . ." Desmond Murphey smiled and looked wistful. "Dear little Ruth . . ." The tears began to flow unchecked down his cheeks. Pearl drew a lace handkerchief out of her handbag and wiped the tears away, murmuring comforts. "Punishing a child . . . There was no way I could stop old Mayhew, nothing in the law to help me. He could buy the law, you see—like it was a suit of clothes or a pair of shoes."

"It didn't matter, Des," Pearl said. "We didn't need anything from the old man, you know that."

"But if you had, it would have been all the same to him." Desmond Murphey sighed deeply. "He would have withheld, no matter the need. The rich only know getting their own way." His knees sagged perceptibly. He put one hand out flat upon the blue linen-covered serving table to stop his descent.

"Could I maybe help the gent home?" Dell Andrews said, grasping Desmond Murphey's elbow lightly. "I know what it's like to be full of drink and sorrowful. Makes navigation painful and uncertain."

Desmond Murphey looked at him appraisingly. "It does that," he said finally.

"I'm sure Pearl here will excuse us," Dell said.

Pearl nodded, kissed Desmond Murphey again on the cheek

and turned away from the two men toward the window in front of which Dot Parker and Caleb Hickson were seated upon a small, bright blue divan. Maud stood behind them, gazing down upon busy nighttime Water Street.

Dell Andrews steered Desmond carefully through the Blue Room door. Just before the two men disappeared from sight, Dell looked back over his shoulder and said to Pearl, "Tomorrow at eight." She smiled agreement, watching them go and wondering how it was that such a soft voice as Dell Andrews had could carry so clearly across the room that it was as though he stood at her side and whispered into her ear.

Caleb Hickson sat glumly with his chin cradled in his hands. Pearl could never get over how old he looked for twenty-two. Tonight he looked forty. Was it worrying about why God had saved him? Was it thinking maybe God had saved him for something nearly as bad as the Coffeyville massacre?

"I'm so hot I could perish," Dot Parker said, tugging at her bodice as though it chafed her. She cast a reproachful glance at Caleb.

"Poor old Desmond," Maud said, still gazing down upon Water Street. "When I first met him I didn't think he gave much of a damn about anything. Then later on I found out he cries himself to sleep most nights like a baby." She shook her head, sipped champagne.

"What's wrong with Caleb tonight?" Pearl asked Dot, as though the boy were somewhere else.

Dot Parker shrugged. The velocity of her Chinese fan increased. "He says he's having a crisis," she said.

Maud McGrath laughed and went over to the table to refill her glass. She emptied it at once.

"What kind of crisis?" Pearl said.

"He don't say," Dot Parker replied.

"What kind of crisis, Caleb?" Pearl addressed the glum boy.

He raised his thin, despondent face to Pearl and said, "I think I got to leave this town. But I ain't sure."

"What makes you think you got to leave?" Pearl said.

"He thinks some fart of an old marshal from Kansas is after him," Dot Parker said, palpably offended by the ridiculousness of the idea.

Maud McGrath—champagne bottle poised in midair—laughed again.

"Now, why," Pearl said, pulling a blue brocaded side chair up near the divan and seating herself on it and leaning over toward Caleb with an expression of intense interest, "would some fart of an old marshal from Kansas be chasing you, Caleb?"

Dot Parker leaned back against the divan; her eyelids fluttered as though she might faint with irritation.

Caleb Hickson stared at Pearl, his small black eyes as fixed as bullet holes in a wall. "I rode with the Daltons," he said simply.

"And seven years later, with most all the Daltons dead and Emmett locked up in the Kansas Penitentiary, the marshal's gonna come looking for you?" Pearl said. "Now, why would he do that, Caleb? You weren't at Coffeyville, trying to rob the banks. You were home nursing your dysentery. Dysentery's not against the law."

"He can't grasp it," Dot Parker said, propelling herself forward again to the edge of the divan, "that nobody anywhere on God's green earth gives a poor damn about the Daltons or Coffeyville or Caleb Hickson. He's got this notion that every lawman west of Philadelphia is looking to string him up because he rode around some behind Grat Dalton when he was fifteen years old." Dot groaned and fanned and grabbed a lace handkerchief out of her sleeve to dab at her upper lip and forehead. "It's hard to credit a man having such a want of good sense."

Behind her, Pearl heard Maud McGrath say, "Thank God Laura didn't come tonight. Poor Dot would never hear the end of it."

The next night Pearl and Dell Andrews went to the Creole Palace and ate gumbo soup so thick with small, tender, rosy shrimp and sea-green okra that a spoon would stand in it. Then they ate crayfish tails slathered with lemon juice and dipped into pots of melted butter. To finish there was deep-dish apple pie sprinkled with cinnamon and crisp with burnt butter. They washed every-thing down with champagne. Dell Andrews said it was the best meal he had eaten since he was last in New Orleans five years earlier.

All through the evening—butter running down his chin and glistening on his fingertips—Dell Andrews told Pearl stories of his adventures all over the country.

How he had gone West during the later gold strikes in Colorado and then up North to the Klondike mines, not to prospect but to try out the skills he had learned at his uncle's knee: five-and seven-card stud and draw poker, blackjack and assorted games of chance.

"He was a wonderful old man, my Uncle Jake," he said. "Never sweated for a dollar a day in his life, except when he was trying to fill an inside straight. He always said to me, Dell, he'd say, that's a fool's game—don't ever go for an inside straight. Fold up and get out while the getting's good. But Uncle Jake never could forgo such a thing himself. He'd consider and sweat and reconsider and sweat some more, but in the end he'd go for it, and by God if he didn't draw to it most of the time! He was kinda magic that way. Inside straights was his specialty. But to me he always said, Don't be a damn fool, Dell. Just because God favors me, don't mean He's gonna feel the same way about you."

How he had made and lost two or three fortunes along the way, thereby learning to appreciate but not adore money, to value high living but survive the low life that accompanied a run of bad luck. "You learn not to consider a clean, soft bed and steak and eggs for breakfast as right and natural things like drawing a breath of fresh air. You look in your pockets every morning to find out what your rights are that day."

How he had been forced to run for his life from this town and been very nearly strung up in that one. "What's always been funny to me," he said to Pearl (emptying his glass, refilling it), "is how a man who would normally never think of breaking the law—why, he wouldn't even consider spitting on the sidewalk—will try to shoot you down like a dog if you take his money in an honest game of chance."

"And disgruntled wives," he continued, "have set upon me like harpies when I bested their husbands in poker. Like I'd forced them to gamble, held a gun to their heads and said, Okay, boys, ante up!" He shook his head in wonder. "Gamblers don't see the finest side of a human being. You got to learn to smile."

When they left the Creole Palace late that night, two women rushed at them from a dark doorway, cawing like wild birds. A stout female in a large black hat with wings cried, "Get out of town, whore! We don't want your kind in Fort Smith!" She hurled an overripe tomato at Pearl's head; it split against her shoulder and spread its pips and juice down the back of her cape. The stout female's accomplice ineptly cast another tomato, which fell upon the sidewalk short of its target. Both women darted into a carriage waiting at the corner and were spirited away.

Dell Andrews tenderly wiped away the clinging tomato seeds and juice stain from Pearl's cape with a large linen handkerchief, whispering soft reassurings as though Pearl were an injured child. He seemed neither astonished nor inquisitive. Pearl usually would have laughed at this Reformist behavior, but tonight she found it impossible. She felt tears spring to her eyes. She leaned lightly against Dell Andrews' enormous bosom. She closed her eyes and let his soft murmur spread over her like grease over a burn.

When Maud heard about this attack, she looked grim. "These old Reform hags are getting completely out of hand," she said. "First thing we know, they'll be coming right into our parlors with their dirty vegetables."

"They're getting braver all the time," Pearl said. "Why is it?"

"It's Indian Territory," Maud said. "Some people want to make it into a state in the Union. All nice and official. They think it'll be easier to do that if Fort Smith ain't so wild, don't look so much like a frontier town."

Pearl smiled and lit a black cigarette. "You know how you can tell when an old dog is gonna die? All its fleas jump off and run away. When we close up our doors and leave this place, Fort

Smith'll be dying. No spirit left in it." But she felt uneasy. Her smile faded. She and Maud exchanged anxious glances over their late-night whiskeys.

"All the men I've known," Pearl said to Maud McGrath, "thought I was too big for my britches, too ambitious, wanted too much. Ate too many oysters, drank too much rye whiskey, wore colors that were too bright and painted my face too heavy. Stayed up too late at night and kept to my bed too long in the mornings. Too much all the time. Now, Dell—he don't say that at all. He likes that about me. He laughs and says to me, Pearl, you're a wonderful natural force. You're like a hurricane or a tornado. Nobody ever heard of a tornado blowing just a little bit."

"I like Dell Andrews more than most men I know," Maud McGrath said, "but it's a fact to face that he's a rolling stone. He comes and goes like the wind. You might say he's a natural force himself."

"Maybe that's why I like him," Pearl said. She laughed. "Maybe together we can do everything twice too much."

And indeed Pearl Starr and Dell Andrews lived to the outside limit of their large selves. They ate like two children discovering the wonders of nourishment after prolonged deprivation: they spent hours every week at the Creole Palace, had food sent in to Pearl's Place regularly from the Hotel Biscayne, sent Festina scurrying here and there about Fort Smith for one delicacy or another. Pearl blossomed, and her skin grew taut over her cheekbones and thick under her chin; Dell Andrews became even more mountainous: Laura Ziegler said his suit jacket alone could provide shelter for two orphans.

They drank quantities of champagne, brandy, rye whiskey and bourbon—seemingly without losing either control or humor. Pearl smoked black cigarettes until her fingers yellowed, and Festina brought bowls of hot water and lemon oil to soak them in and fresh lemon to rub on them every morning. Dell Andrews smoked Havanas with the same abandon. Festina told Maud

McGrath that there were evenings in Pearl's private parlor when
the air was too thick to fall over if you was to faint.

They often went out to gamble after the Place closed. Dell's
carriage would reappear at dawn in a great lather of neighing and
hooves and cries of instruction to the horse and roars of laughter,
and Dell would climb down out of the conveyance and turn and
catch Pearl as she half fell, half soared from the carriage into his
arms. On the Row they said they'd never seen two people enjoy
themselves so much. Dot Parker said that in her opinion Pearl
was too old to carry on like a silly girl and that she was going to
burn herself out real quick, if she wasn't careful.

"You ever seen Pearl be careful?" Laura Ziegler asked. "You
ever see a thing like that, why, then, you look up real quick
because the Pearly Gates is gonna be just over your head."

Three months after their first meeting at Maud McGrath's
house, Dell Andrews moved into Pearl's bedroom back of the
private parlor, and Pearl began introducing him around Fort
Smith as "my husband, Dell." Dell Andrews referred to Pearl
directly and in conversation with others as his wife. Maud
McGrath looked skeptical and said, "You really married to Dell?"

And Pearl smiled, plump and sleek as a goose being fattened
for a Christmas feast, and said, "Sure, we are." Desmond
Murphey said they probably weren't formally married, not before
a justice of the peace and all, but they were certainly officially
married.

"Well, now, what the hell kind of answer is that?" Laura
Ziegler said.

And Desmond Murphey, in his cups but still (he assured them)
in possession of a few basic facts, explained the concept of
common-law marriage to Laura Ziegler and Maud McGrath, who
later conveyed this information to Dot Parker. Dot Parker looked
confused. "You mean to say that all you gotta do to be officially
married and legally bound is to go around telling folks that so-
and-so is your husband or wife?"

"Would you credit that?" Maud McGrath said. "Law is a
passing strange thing, my way of thinking."

Laura Ziegler said, "Desmond told us that Pearl asked him about this very thing, this common-law marriage thing, when she was living with the Count. She'd read about it somewhere, about how it made things legal and all the rest."

"Now, why," Dot Parker said, "would Pearl all of a sudden be so interested in being married legal? I mean, she never has give a poor damn about being legal in any respect."

Maud McGrath and Laura Ziegler squinted their eyes in consideration of this point, but remained silent. Dot Parker said that it was maybe because Pearl wanted to have legal babies, although she herself couldn't for the life of her think why anybody would give a fat stuff about a thing like that.

After two months of living at Pearl's Place, Dell Andrews and Pearl moved back to the Flats. Pearl said the Water Street accommodations were simply too small for people their size: "When Dell walks into that bedroom, it just disappears. It could be a necktie inside a coat for all you see of it." And so they occupied the entire first floor of the South Fourteenth Street house, staying carefully away from the upper stories where Pearl had lived with the Count and little ephemeral Artie.

Dell spent part of each day practicing his trade: he played poker or monte every night in private games with the lastingly or temporarily rich of Fort Smith; afterwards he dropped into the Biscayne for roulette or blackjack. Occasionally he traveled off to Hot Springs for the horse races, and several times he journeyed all the way North to Saratoga for the races, coming home with his pockets full of money and his arms laden with gifts for Pearl. Because Dell Andrews was, mostly, a lucky man who won the games he played, whose horses crossed the finish line first or, at the least, second.

Pearl, meanwhile, continued to manage her establishment with acuity and care. Laura Ziegler said that Pearl read her ledger books with the same attention some folks gave Holy Scripture;

every penny had to be accounted for, and though she was generous—some said overgenerous—to her girls (when Glory fell
sick with pneumonia, Pearl sent her off to a private room at St.
John's Hospital, paid all her expenses and moved her into the
Flats to recuperate), to steal from Pearl or withhold revenue
meant instant dismissal from the best-run house on the Row.

Pearl refurbished her parlors and bedrooms whenever any
slight degree of wear became visible. The exterior of Pearl's Place
was painted every two years: except for the neighborhood, it
could have been a fine old family home.

Pearl spent money unstintingly on fine food, the best whiskey,
gambling (often losing), clothes specially made or imported from
Chicago or St. Louis, extravagant presents for Dell Andrews—a
solid-gold pocket watch, a ring for his little finger with a diamond
in it the size of a grape. Bertha Rooney remained Ruth's well-
paid nurse-companion, and little Ruth herself was sent—stylishly
dressed and bountifully fed—to an expensive private school. The
child, now six, and Bertha still lived in the same sedate, unnotice-
able house chosen by Johnson Mayhew.

But there were those on the Row who said that for all her
spending ways, Pearl was a rich woman from the proceeds of her
house and from clever speculation in Fort Smith real estate.
"Don't you worry about Pearl," Maud McGrath said. "She's got
enough all nicely tucked away to keep her until she's too old to
chew drippings."

When the century turned to the twentieth, the ladies of the Row
gave a party that lasted four days. The girls weren't free, but the
whiskey was. And tables in the front parlors of Pearl's Place and
Maud McGrath's and Laura's and Dot's groaned under the weight
of continuously replenished platters of roasted chickens and
baked hams and baskets of bright yellow ears of corn steamed in
their shucks. "After all," Pearl said, "how many other turns of
the century are we gonna see?"

Everybody in Fort Smith, it seemed to the four hostesses, passed through the Row at some time between New Year's Eve and the third day of January. The girls were very busy, but care was taken that they were not overworked.

In the fifth of January edition of the Fort Smith *Independent* there appeared an editorial headed: "Blatant Disregard of Public Morality." The ladies of the Row were castigated, their services deplored, their four-day New Year's party abominated. "We can do without this infamous flaunting of vice and corruption!" thundered the anonymous editorialist.

Two days later the *Independent* printed a Letter to the Editor from Mrs. Bayard Harrington, wife of a prominent Fort Smith businessman. This letter read, in part: "Fort Smith will never take its place among modern, civilized cities like St. Louis, Philadelphia and even Little Rock—habitations where children can be raised in decency, and women can safely perambulate in the company of their families without danger of observing a scene unfit for tender Christian eyes—until we have rooted out and destroyed such obscenities as that area of town known as the Row, and made it clear that we will not tolerate the presence of such persons as that notorious woman who calls herself the Daughter of the Outlaw Queen."

Pearl had never before been the subject of public obloquy, and she was startled and somewhat alarmed by the editorial and by Mrs. Harrington's letter. Dell patted her arm and said she was not to give the matter a second thought. "Those old biddies have been trying to close up pleasure houses since long before we was even tiny tots, since before we was even twinkles in our papas' eyes, come to that."

But when Pearl made her usual trip down to city court on Monday morning, Lemuel Smith, the clerk who always took her weekly payment for each "boarder," gave her a nervous glance, looked up and down the hallways and told her almost in a whisper that if she was smart she would lie low for the next few weeks and not call any attention to herself. Pearl looked at Lemuel speculatively for several minutes, and then she laughed and said,

"Why, Lemuel, I can scare up some of my best clients in this very building."

Lemuel nodded and cleared his throat. "Don't say I didn't warn you," he said, carefully wiping his eyeglasses.

The following Saturday night, as Pearl strolled with smiles and jocular greetings through the parlors of her house, she collided with three uniformed members of the Fort Smith Municipal Constabulary who burst through her front door just as she arrived at the palm plant in the foyer. The leading constable was Ed Raines, red-faced with embarrassment underneath his small blue cap.

"Why, Ed," Pearl said, "what are you doing here in that getup?"

"Doing my duty, I'm afraid, Pearl," he replied miserably. "Just my goddamned silly duty."

Ed Raines and his two cohorts, all three looking uncertain and even more abashed as the catcalls and curses from the many patrons of the house grew in volume, chopped halfheartedly with shiny new axes at the side table and chair and hat rack in the foyer. One of the constables, a young boy about sixteen, even took a few swipes at the palm plant, looking as though he felt a bit foolish.

Pearl screamed and fell back against the arched doorway to the front parlor, into which the three constables were by then thundering. Ed Raines wore a look of dogged determination and avoided glancing either to the right or left at any of the clients of the house. He swung his ax vigorously, as though the derisory hoots from the men in the parlors merely incited him in this performance of his duty. Two inlaid wooden card tables fell apart under the onslaught; the brocade of a divan was ripped asunder, the stuffing exposed, the legs at the right side hacked away, so that the divan listed badly; the piano stool collapsed in two blows. But none of the ax wielders seemed able to attack the piano itself, standing in its well-known mahogany splendor almost in the middle of the room.

The mayhem ceased after only a few clamorous minutes, and Ed Raines—his face a lather of sweat and beet-red with exertion and chagrin—said, "You're under arrest, Pearl. You gotta come along with me."

Pearl still stood transfixed at the parlor entrance, her hand over her heart as though she meant to protect at least that organ from the ax handlers. She finally dropped her hand, gazed around the room with openmouthed disbelief and then approached the head constable. With her flushed face only inches from Ed Raines's, her breath emanating with such fierce intensity that Ed could feel the heat of it against his nose, she hissed, "What is the meaning of this?"

He looked down at the ax he still grasped with both hands and sighed. "Prostitution is against the laws of the city of Fort Smith. I got to take you in and charge you."

Pearl's face recoiled slightly from Ed Raines. "Two nights ago you were enjoying the company of Maybelle in one of my upstairs bedrooms," she said.

Ed Raines reddened still more. "That's neither here nor there," he said. "I got my duty to do. I was sent here to distress your premises and to take you back to jail."

"*Distress* my premises?" Pearl looked at him incredulously. "*Distress* . . . ?" Her mouth opened and closed wordlessly over any attempt to describe the condition of her parlors. "Why, you've damn near distressed my place to pieces, Ed Raines! You and your little helpers here . . . Now, you get the hell out of here before I have some of these boys throw you into the street!"

Ed Raines raised his eyes from the floor. His jaw was clenched. He shook his head slowly. He looked around threateningly at the men in the room, some of whom moved forward menacingly as Pearl spoke. He unfastened the top strap of his holster but left his gun sheathed. "No, ma'am," he said. "I cannot leave here without you. If you won't come along peaceable, then all three of us here's gonna carry you off by force."

Pearl stared at him with narrowed eyes. Her color was still so vivid that her eyes looked pink. She wheeled about suddenly, crying "Festina!" at the top of her voice.

The black woman materialized behind the palm plants before

the entrance to Pearl's private parlor. She knotted both hands at the base of her throat and waited.

"You go get Desmond Murphey!" Pearl shouted. "You tell him they're taking me down to jail, and he should get his tail over there pronto!" Then Pearl turned and marched out into Water Street—shoulders back and head high—leaving the three constables to shuffle after her through the wreckage, looking hangdog and muttering unintelligible sounds to the floor.

Desmond Murphey appeared at the Fort Smith jail within an hour, but he was not allowed to make bail for Pearl until the next morning: the sergeant in charge simply shook his head over and over in response to Murphey's legal niceties and demands. "She gotta stay here overnight," he said. "No two ways about it, she gotta stay here overnight."

Festina brought Pearl a small reticule in which there was a flask of brandy, some sugared fruit and three heavy linen handkerchiefs. The sergeant took her belowstairs to the celebrated Fort Smith dungeons and locked her into a cell by herself and went away again, leaving her with a dim yellow lamp just outside the steel bars.

Pearl looked at the dirty, decayed walls, upon which desperate messages had been written by generations of the condemned, and the filthy straw mattress, at one end of which there was an imperishable, uncleansable bloodstain. She smelled the air, putrid with excrement and piss and sweat. She sat upon a small beige stool and closed her eyes and thought of Belle Starr and Sam in the Detroit House of Correction, and Jim Reed locked away in Texas, and Eddie in Ohio. She thought about Cole Younger rotting away for the past twenty-four years in a Minnesota prison. She remembered Belle saying that whatever you had to do to stay out of jail was worthwhile: murder, she had said—any kind of killing of any kind of soul—you do what you got to do, but you stay out of jail.

She remembered with what passion Belle always tried to keep Eddie out of jail and, once he was in, how arduously she would try to get him released. "No man," she had once said to Pearl, "can live in a jail for more than a night or two. After that, he goes crazy with pain and humiliation. You know what that word humiliation means, Pearl? You find out. You remember what it means."

Pearl sat all night on her small beige stool, holding her skirts off the damp floor. She did not sleep at all. She kept her eyes closed, thinking of Belle and Jim papa and Eddie and Cole Younger, of Sam Starr and Jim July. Even Jim July, whom she hadn't thought of for a decade. She kept her eyes closed, and she wept large, slow tears. Toward morning, as the dawn began to turn the pocked, rotten walls a pale yellow, she opened her eyes.

"Dear Ma," she said aloud. "Oh, dear Ma."

Early the next morning Pearl appeared in court before Judge Henry Follet, who looked her over with a cold eye and fined her two hundred dollars for running a house of ill fame. "Don't let me see you here again, Pearl Starr," the judge said. He closed his eyes momentarily as though meditating briefly on the gravity of justice, and then he arose and left the courtroom in a crisp swirl of black robe.

Desmond Murphey led Pearl from the courthouse through a side entrance to avoid a horde of irate Christian women and one or two excited reporters from the *Independent* who had taken positions in front of the building. He drove her back to Pearl's Place in his small carriage with the side curtains drawn. Festina met them at the back entrance to Pearl's private parlor.

"You draw me a bath," Pearl said to Festina as soon as she entered the parlor. "Draw me the hottest bath you ever made. I want to be scalded just this side of death."

Festina nodded. "And when I'm done bathing," Pearl continued, unlacing her waist, easing her corsets, "I want to find in here a plate of fried eggs, some rashers of bacon, buttermilk biscuits and a pot of chicory coffee."

"Yes'um," Festina said.

"And bring Mr. Murphey a platter of oysters and a pitcher of beer."

Festina was already at the door.

Pearl unbuttoned her shoes and kicked them across the room. She slumped into the chair next to her heart-shaped table. "I don't think I ever felt so dirty or so hungry."

Desmond Murphey nodded, patted her shoulder consolingly. He stood, hands in pockets, in the parlor entrance studying the front rooms. "Some of the girls cleaned up most of the mess late last night. It's a beginning."

"It'll take weeks to put right," Pearl said. She went to stand at Murphey's shoulder, surveying the damage. "Those bastards . . . And, of course, they waited until Dell wasn't here."

"That's their way," Desmond Murphey agreed.

Glory appeared down the hallway from the back kitchen. She embraced Pearl, making small comforting sounds. "We're all so sorry," she said. "They shouldn't of kept you all night in that filthy jail. That wasn't right. That Ed Raines oughta be horse-whipped."

Pearl kissed Glory on the cheek and said, "It wasn't Ed Raines's fault. He was just the poor fool they sent. You go on about your business now. Tell the girls it'll be business as usual tonight. Tomorrow I'll get in old Stritch and his helpers to put things right, and I'll speak to Maud and Laura about borrowing some furniture to tide us over until we can get things replaced and reclothed. For tonight we'll just drape what we can't do anything about."

"We gonna carry on tonight as usual?" Glory said, surprised.

"We are," Pearl said resolutely. She disappeared into the back bedroom, slipping out of her waist and attacking her camisole ties as she went. "Nobody's gonna run Pearl Starr out of business as easy as that," she shouted over her shoulder as she closed the bedroom door.

. . .

Desmond Murphey smoked a thin cigar and watched Pearl finish her fourth buttermilk biscuit and wash it down with coffee. She wiped her hands on a large cloth and leaned back in her chair, sighing, rubbing her tired eyes. "What's happening here, Des?" she said. "Is this the kinda thing I can expect from now on?"

He shrugged. "Now and again, Pearl," he said. "They may not come again for two weeks or two months, but they'll come again, all right. You won't be the only one to suffer, m'dear. Maud'll feel the sting of it, and Laura and Dot too. You'll get more callers than them because Pearl Starr is Queen of the Row. But you'll all suffer, until you give up and go into hiding."

"I thought my hiding days were over when I left Younger's Bend."

"The handwriting's been on the wall since there was first talk of statehood for Indian Territory. Sure and I warned you about that years ago. Then when Isaac Parker, the old Hanging Judge himself, was removed from the courts of Fort Smith—when Washington says to him, Well, old man, no more gibbet for you, no more public shows with six men kicking their heels in the air all together on one sunny afternoon, with the missus packing a picnic lunch and the kids drinking lemonade and perching on their dads' shoulders for a better view of the gallows—well then, the end is for a fact in sight."

Pearl poured warm beer from the pitcher into Desmond's glass and into one for herself. She sighed. "The end of the sporting house in Fort Smith . . ."

"The end of the frontier," he said. "Passions and lust going underground like little burrowing animals. Happens everywhere, finally. Men give up their open pleasures and learn to creep around in the dark. Indian Territory becomes a bona fide state of the Union; Fort Smith gets to be a civilized metropolis. You can't have people settling their quarrels anymore with Colts and Winchesters, slugging it out in muddy streets, running guns and whiskey, whoring around openly in front of all these women who go off to church every Sunday and say prayers to a wonderful, tidy God who's against the excessive consumption of alcohol and women who sell themselves. Not to mention gambling and dancing and any form a-tall of tiny pleasure we might find at the end of a sorrowful day."

Pearl swallowed her beer down in one draught. "How long you think I've got left here?"

"Well then, I'm no prophet, you see," Murphey said. "My guess would be it's gonna take a bit of time. They're not expecting to close the Row in a couple of weeks. But, on the other hand, they won't expect to wait ten years for it, either."

Pearl nodded, looking tired and sad. "They'll wait twenty, if I got anything to do with it," she said. "I'll fight them every day, tooth and nail—until I got no nails and no teeth. They expect to get rid of me, they're gonna have to work hard at it, harder than they ever worked at anything before. No old biddy with a rich husband who sneaks around and visits me on Saturday nights and then preens himself in church on Sunday mornings is gonna close me down without a fight that looks like one of the Indian wars. I'm not Belle Starr's daughter for nothing."

Desmond Murphey looked at her with his dim grey eyes shining. "You're a real pleasure to me, Pearl. One of the few remaining in my depleted life."

She rose and kissed him lightly on the lips. She drew her loose wrapper tighter around her. "I'm going to bed now. I may stay there all day. Clients tonight will just have to remember how splendid the front parlors used to look."

Desmond Murphey stood up and slipped his arms into his rumpled suit coat. "I got to say one thing to you, in good conscience. I got to warn you that it's best you do things from now on more quietly than you done them before, with less fanfare maybe. Everything will last longer that way. You rub their noses in it, Pearl, and they'll feel obliged to enforce the laws already on the books, you see. You try being a little more circumspect, and they won't bother you so much."

Pearl laughed and said, "I'm kinda like my ma in that respect, Des: never anything halfway. She used to say to me, There's no such thing as a *little* style, Pearl. You got to sing so loud that God'll hear you and laugh and decide to keep you alive for a while longer, just for the hell of it. It was the same way with loving somebody. If you love a man, Ma would say, then you love him just this side of the gallows. If she was alive now, she'd say, Pearl, if you're gonna be a whore, then don't go creeping around in the dark like some kinda crib girl with a dirty mattress; be the best goddamn whore in the whole state of Arkansas!"

She disappeared into her bedroom and closed the door. Desmond Murphey swallowed the last dregs of his hot beer and let himself quietly out the back entrance of the parlor.

In 1901 Pearl became pregnant again and on the eighth of November 1902—when she was thirty-five—gave birth to her fourth child, Jennette Andrews, a fine, blond, healthy girl who ate well, slept long and peacefully, cried little and charmed everyone with her ebullient laughter and her bright blue eyes.

Pearl said, "All my girls are strong and merry."

"It's as well they're strong," Maud McGrath said. "Kind of world we live in . . ."

Dell Andrews picked up Jennette's tiny hand and examined the fingers with careful, wondering attention. "I never saw anything so small that worked," he said. "Do they work? Can she hold things with these little soft fingers—why, you'd think there was no bone in them at all, they're so soft!"

Pearl laughed and said, "Give her your own big finger, you'll see." And laughed even louder when the child grasped Dell's first finger and held it with such tenacity that the huge father turned red in the face and sweated profusely under his small, pleased eyes.

But when Jennette was four weeks old, Pearl awoke early one morning at the Flats feeling that something was not as it should be. She lay for a while in her bed, studying the ornate molding that joined one wall to another in the corners of the ceiling. And then she arose and put on a pale blue wrapper and crossed the hallway to Dell's bedroom. The bed was neatly made. Two suits

—his favorites—were missing from the wardrobe. Underlinen
and shirts had vanished from the bureau, along with his gold
watch and his diamond rings. His valise was nowhere to be found.
Pearl went downstairs.

In the kitchen, propped against the coffeepot, was a letter:
*"Dear honey, I am going away for a while. I have been longer in
Fort Smith than I ever have stayed anywhere, and that is entirely owing to my love for you, but now I feel I got to move on.
I am for a fact a gypsy at heart, and gypsies, you know, do not
always do so hot as husbands and fathers. I hope you will understand, honey, that it is my intention, if the Good Lord spares me,
to return to your sweet bosom in the near future. Your sweetheart, Dell."*

Pearl burned the letter in a skillet that sat at the back of
the stove with a thin layer of sausage dripping covering its
bottom.

The harassment of the madams of the Row was occasional and
unpredictable, as Desmond Murphey had said it would undoubt-
edly be. Maud McGrath and Laura Ziegler and Dot Parker all
had raids similar to the one against Pearl's Place which had
signaled the beginning of the legal onslaught. There was, however,
as Pearl pointed out, less breakage than at her place, less havoc
wreaked. "I suspect too many husbands and city officials were
inconvenienced," she said. All the madams continued to run
their houses, though with more discretion and less rowdiness
than before. Except for Pearl Starr, whose sole concession to the
Reformists of Fort Smith was to remove the towering Pearl's
Place sign—outlined with its colored electric-light globes—from
atop 25 Water Street.

Monday mornings were no longer devoted to entertaining
outings to city court, at which time, in earlier days, men who
had stood for an hour in a shop door or leaning disconsolate
against a lamppost would applaud the arrival of the carriages
bearing the celebrated madams of Fort Smith. Nowadays the

money paid to the city for house rights and "boarder" privileges was sent to city court covertly: Jimmy Rose was chosen as messenger for all four of the famous Row houses. Jimmy was a little bit simpleminded, and the madams felt that this defect would prevent the boy from working out a scheme to steal all the money until long after he had delivered it to city court.

In 1903 Dell Andrews reappeared in Fort Smith: he looked much the same, except for a trim beard which followed the outline of his substantial jaw and joined in its midsection with a neat mustache. His heft had increased somewhat, although there were those who said this was mere illusion brought about by simply not remembering how monumental he had always been.

He took a room at the Hotel Biscayne and went to Pearl's Place on his second afternoon back in town. Pearl, busy in the private parlor with her accounts, had been informed of Dell Andrews' arrival as soon as his foot had touched the train station platform, and so she was not surprised when the very large man walked through her door and said, in his usual small, soft voice, "Hello, honey. I've come home again."

Pearl put down her pen and looked at him with a slight smile. "You're looking good, Dell."

He leaned down and kissed her lightly on the forehead. He smelled fresh and slightly fragrant with rose water. "I feel good," he said. "I been to Oregon and the north of California, a few other little spots along the way. It all set me up fine. Why, I feel like a young man again!"

Pearl poured two brandies and handed Dell one, motioning him to the wing chair. He sat down and put his feet on the petit-point stool Pearl had crouched on at Johnson Mayhew's knees all those years before. "If you're feeling like such a young man again, Dell, then maybe what you need is a young woman, ain't that so?"

Dell looked at her speculatively, the way she had often seen him appraise a poker hand, trying to work out what it meant and what he could do with it. He drank down his brandy all in one turn of the wrist and afterwards studied the wall over the fireplace for a few minutes, as though he were collecting his thoughts. He handed Pearl his empty glass. "I'll have another of those," he said.

"I can recommend you a good hotel bar," Pearl said.

He sighed and caressed his hair from forehead to nape of neck. "I can see I ain't forgiven," he said.

"You see clear," Pearl said.

He pulled his chair closer to the writing table where Pearl sat. "It's only been a year," he said. "A man needs to go off by himself once in a while—catch himself a little breath, you know that, honey. Especially a gypsy man like me who's spent his entire life gambling on one thing and another. It's a hard thing for men like your old Dell here to settle down. But I come back, you see? I told you I would and I did."

Pearl poured herself another brandy. She looked at Dell's gargantuan hands lying on his well-tailored knees: they were soft and clean; the diamond she had given him—big as a grape—still gleamed on his smallest finger. The diamond he had worn when he first came to Fort Smith had vanished—some turn of the wrong card, she guessed.

"A year is a long time, Dell," she said. "It's a hell of a long time when you got a new infant on your hands, and the father of that babe is nowhere in sight when you got a need for him."

"Pearl . . ." he began.

"I am sick and tired"—her voice rose; she stood up and loomed sharp-eyed over Dell Andrews—"of men coming and going from my life like I was some kind of stage depot! I run a whorehouse, but that don't mean you can come and lay your head on my pillow when it pleases you, and when it don't, you can run off to carouse around and gamble and enjoy life, all by yourself, just about as faithful as a hound dog in rut, and you won't have to worry a thing about me because I'll be a happy woman got this babe on my knee to remember you by!"

She slammed her ledger shut with such force that the book spun off the table and crashed at Dell's feet. "No trips to Chicago or St. Louis, never mind Oregon, for Pearl! Pearl's breath don't need catching, like old Dell's! Pearl can get her a new lungful behind the whorehouse, while she's waiting for the next man to come along and share her bed for just so long as it pleases him and not one minute more for Pearl's sake!"

Dell looked down thoughtfully at the ledger on the floor near his feet and then up at Pearl. "I never thought I treated you so bad, honey."

Pearl closed her eyes and shook her head, as though disputing with some unseen person. "I don't want to turn out like Belle. Falling into bed drunk with any horse thief showed up at Younger's Bend, because she was a passionate woman, and there wasn't a good man would stay around long enough for her to love him and be loved back." She paused, eyes still closed, head thrown up, hands grasping the back of the chair, remembering. "She had one or two good men: got themselves killed or put away in the penitentiary to rot like Cole Younger for a lifetime. What's the answer to all this? I can't work it out, hard as I try." She opened her eyes and stared across the room, as though the answer was written on the far wall. She seemed to have forgotten Dell Andrews.

Dell sat staring at her, waiting, hands lying again on his knees. Finally she looked down at him, struggling back from some distant place. She smiled slightly, and because Dell did not notice the expression in the eyes that accompanied this smile, he smiled in return, feeling hopeful again. But then she spoke: "I'm not having any more lovers living under my roof nor any more husbands. That's all finished and done. I'm not gonna rely on anybody ever again but Pearl herself. My heart's been broken so many times there's scars on it everywhere, scars on top of scars, some of them so old you could hardly see them if you was to look in, they'd have gone heart-colored again, and still they pain me and they're likely to go on paining me till I'm dead. But my heart's not gonna get broken again, not if I can help it. No fresh wounds in it. Not from you, Dell. Not from anybody. I live at the Flats now with little Jennette and a woman to look after her when I can't. That's how it's going to be. You can come and see

Jennette once in a while, if you want to. And maybe now and
then you can stop over for the night, we'll see about that when
the time comes. But we're not to be thought of as married anymore—by you or by anybody else. That's all finished, like I
said."

He nodded, stroking his head from front to back again. He
looked pale, and his small eyes shrank to points and vanished
under his heavy brows, leaving his face all beard and mustache
and side whiskers.

Pearl pitied him for a moment, but then the moment passed.

Four years later, in 1907, Indian Territory became part of the
new state of Oklahoma, and Fort Smith was delirious with excitement at this further evidence of the establishment of civilization
along the Arkansas and Red rivers.

Oklahoma had its own courts and its own judges. A ruined
old man in his fifties, Judge Isaac Parker had died half a dozen
years before for want of that empire where he had flourished
for two decades as sole custodian of the law from western Arkansas to Colorado. "Oh yes, yes," Robert Pickens had said
when Parker died, "broke him, that did. Why, you take away the
scaffold from a man thinks he's the Avenging Angel, it's like as
if you cut his heart out."

Desmond Murphey and Pearl sat drinking rum together near a
fire laid in the private parlor. They had been comfortably silent
for a while. And then Pearl said, "I'm gonna send my babies
away, Des."

Murphey set his glass down carefully on the small round
table that stood between their chairs. His pale grey eyes widened.
"Dear God, you can't be thinking of that!"

Pearl nodded. "I've already enrolled them in Convent Marietta in St. Louis. Bertha Rooney will take them up on the train. It'll be the last job she does for me."

"But little Jennette's only six years old, for God's sake!"

"That's why I want her to go now," Pearl said. "Before she suffers any, like Ruth's done."

"But nobody knows about Ruth!" Desmond protested. "We been at great pains since she was born fourteen years ago to see to it that nobody knew she was yours. And around here everybody thinks she was born dead, except for me and Hiram Tucker and the other three ladies of the Row. And we've all been silent as the grave, Pearl—you know we'd never tell around a thing like that."

"I'm not accusing anybody, Des—I don't know how these things happen. Maybe life's just one great big loose net, and everything finally slips through and escapes. I've wondered about that often enough. Fact is, somebody found out last year, or suspicioned it, and suspicioning is good enough for most people. Some little snot girl said something ugly to Ruth at her school. What you pay for a school's got nothing to do with how many ugly souls you got in it, and that's the truth."

"And since then?" Desmond asked.

"Since then it's got worse," Pearl said grimly. She poured two more rums and studied the reflection of fire through her glass. "Ruth didn't know, you see, Des, until that happened. She didn't know what her mama did. I was just this mystery woman who came visiting two, three times a week, bringing presents. She was heartbroken."

"Ruth's a real sensible girl, Pearl. She wouldn't stay heartbroken about something like that. She loves her mama."

Pearl shrugged. "If she suffers from her mama long enough, she may stop loving her. I got to get her out of here. And I don't want the same thing happening to Jennette. I want them both safe somewhere they ain't known as the whore's girls and they won't ever be."

Desmond Murphey swished his rum slowly around in his mouth, considering. "You'll be all alone, m'dear. You won't like it. No little ones at home, no man . . . What'll become of you, then?"

"God alone knows." Pearl sighed. "Seventeen years on the Row . . . I'm a rich woman, Des—like I always planned to be. Ma always said how important it was for a woman to be rich if she could any way be. But it don't keep me a good man on the premises or my babies at my side." She leaned back in her chair and made a sound that Desmond Murphey thought might be weeping; in the half-light he couldn't tell.

"There ain't any good men nowadays," he said, getting up. "Is this the end of the rum?" He held up the empty bottle.

"Change to bourbon," Pearl said indifferently. He had been mistaken about the weeping: her voice was sad but dry. "There's a whole bottle sitting right above your head on the mantelpiece."

Desmond filled their glasses and sat down again, sighing "yes yes yes" under his breath. "Not a good man anywhere to be found," he repeated.

"Except you, Des," Pearl said, smiling at him. "You're a good man."

"I'm a drunk," he said flatly. "We don't anyways count."

"A man like Cole Younger or Jim Reed," Pearl said, as though she were pursuing a conversation in her head. "A man with some gumption, knows how to enjoy himself, knows what a woman likes. I thought I'd have me a man like that. Only he'd never leave me because I'd be a rich woman, there'd be no cause to leave."

"A man don't need a cause to leave." Desmond Murphey pressed his glass against his forehead. "I got a misery in my head."

"I'd give him everything he wanted, you see. There'd be no cause to go off on his own and get shot or taken by the law and shut away forever or hung . . . My God, Desmond, the anguish she lived through, the terrible pain! She lost them all . . . she lost everybody, even me and Eddie . . . even . . ."

Murphey cleared his throat and took another swallow of bourbon. "Some things don't much change, been my experience.

Anything permanent in this life, it's losing people: mothers and fathers and lovers and babies and friends. Dear God, it's a sad story! I don't know why any of us consent to live in it." He blew his nose in his large linen handkerchief. He dabbed at his eyes. "I got to go. You don't need a weeping Irishman to keep you company."

"Don't go just yet, Des," Pearl said. "I don't want to be alone just yet. I'm not quite drunk enough for that."

He relaxed into his chair again. They studied the deep red embers of the fire in silence. Then he said, "Did you tell little Ruth yet she's leaving?"

"I did."

"What did she say to it?"

"She don't want to go," Pearl said, sighing again. "She wants to stay here with me in Fort Smith. I asked her why she'd want to stay here. I said, You're not happy here, baby, God knows I can see that. They don't know you in St. Louis, you wouldn't be anybody's daughter in St. Louis . . . you'd just be Ruth Reed. You could study to be happy." Pearl paused, drank down the rest of her bourbon. "You know what she said to me, Desmond? She said she thought it'd be too hard to be happy. I said, What do you mean by that, baby? And she said she just didn't think she had a gift for it."

"Ah . . . ah . . . dear God . . ." Desmond Murphey said. "Poor child . . . I never heard nothing so sad as that."

Pearl was silent for a while, and then she rose and leaned against the mantelpiece and stirred the last embers. "Go on home, Des," she said, turning to her old friend, leaning down to kiss the top of his head. "I'm drunk enough now."

Bertha Rooney attended to the efficient packing of a good-sized trunk for Ruth Reed, and on the appointed day in August 1908 she went with her charge by carriage to the train depot, where Pearl awaited them. Jennette sat perched on a trunk of her own on the station platform. Pearl paced up and down in front of the child, smoking furiously and occasionally patting Jennette distractedly on the arm as she passed.

"Where have you been!" Pearl greeted Bertha Rooney. "My God, the train'll be along through here any time . . ."

Bertha Rooney looked at Pearl coolly, as she had always looked at her for nearly fifteen years, and said, "There's plenty of time." She looked down at Ruth, whose hand she held. "Stand up straight," she said. "Don't slump. You'll get a curvature like somebody from the lower classes. Say hello to your sister."

Ruth emerged from behind Bertha Rooney's skirts. "Hello, Jennette," she said.

Jennette was trying to pry off a brass corner of her trunk with a short, blunt pencil. She looked up at Ruth with her mouth open, blue eyes preoccupied. Both girls wore light traveling capes and little hats. Ruth turned and studied the tracks in front of her, avoiding her mother's eyes.

"Dear God . . ." Pearl said.

"Don't worry about a thing," Bertha Rooney said. "I'll look after them proper. I won't leave them for a minute until they're safely at the convent."

Pearl nodded several times. "I trust you, Bertha. I know you're as reliable as sunrise. It's me I don't trust."

"You?" Bertha looked surprised. "I don't follow the meaning of that."

"It don't matter," Pearl said. "Come here, Ruth." The girl was at the edge of the platform staring down at the cinders between the rails. She moved reluctantly, eyes averted, to her mother's side. "You're gonna write your ma, now, you promise that?" Ruth nodded. "I paid a lot of money so you could learn to write real good. Now I want to see some evidence, you hear me?"

"I hear you, Mama," Ruth said.

"And you watch out after Jennette," Pearl said. "She's just a baby, not a nearly grownup woman like yourself. When you write, you tell me about Jennette too."

"Yes, Mama."

Pearl thrust a packet into Ruth's hand. "Your aunties Maud and Laura and Dot sent you some chocolates for the train. They're shaped like little hearts. Don't eat them all at once."

Ruth nodded, pressing the packet against her chest. She stared at Pearl with wide, frightened eyes. "Mama, I don't . . ." she started. "I don't feel good. I feel sick."

Pearl put one arm around the girl's shoulders. "I know you do, baby," she said. "But you're gonna feel better and better, the closer you get to St. Louis. No time at all, you'll feel fit as a fiddle. Why, I expect the first letter I get from you is gonna say how wonderful everything there is and how you don't miss your mama at all, not a bit, because you're having such a fine time."

Tears sprang to Ruth's eyes. She shook her head, biting her lower lip until she drew blood in one corner. Pearl kissed the girl quickly on both cheeks and then turned and lifted Jennette up and embraced her tightly, kissing her all over her face until the child protested. She set her down on the trunk again.

"Goodbye, Bertha." She held out her hand, and Bertha Rooney took it very formally. Pearl turned quickly and left the platform, walked through the depot and climbed into Desmond Murphey's carriage. He embraced Pearl with one arm and with the other he lightly stroked the flank of his horse with the whip and directed the carriage toward Water Street.

"Years ago I told Dell I wasn't gonna be heartbroken again," Pearl said quietly. "That was a lie."

THIRD INTERLUDE

Maud McGrath

When Pearl came bringing me the poster to look at that day in early September 1910, I couldn't believe my eyes. Cole Younger, it said—big, bold type—and underneath that, written in fancy script with lots of curlicues and such, it said: "What Life Has Taught Me." At the bottom of the poster was written: "Little Rock Tent Grounds, September 20, 7 p.m."

I said, My God, Pearl, when did he get out of the penitentiary?

She shook her head and said she didn't know. She just went on staring at the poster and repeating Cole Younger's name. I thought he was dead, she said. I thought for sure he was dead.

I said, Are you going to Little Rock?

She said she was afraid to go. I don't know how I'll feel or what I'll do, she said. It'll be like seeing a ghost.

I told her I wouldn't mind a short trip to Little Rock, if she needed some company. She seemed grateful for that and hugged my neck. I don't know why I offered to go. I guess it was just because she looked so miserable.

Come the nineteenth of September, we set off on the train. Pearl left Glory in charge of her place, and I left Mattie in charge of mine (with Hannah to keep an eye on Mattie, since Mattie was no way so experienced and reliable as Glory was and sometimes took a little too much to drink and got so busy strutting her stuff that she forgot to look after things proper). We only took a small valise apiece, since we was only planning to stay overnight in Little Rock.

There was about fifteen of us in the tent, mixed about equal, maybe one or two more women than men. At exactly seven o'clock, just like the poster said, he came out from behind the curtain, and in about two steps he was over at the podium. He just stood there for a couple of minutes, not saying anything, not smiling. It was like he knew we wanted to look him over before he started, and he was giving us a chance to do that. Pearl leaned forward in her seat and stared at him real hard, like she had just a second or two to see everything. She turned pale as curd and pink around the eyes like she was gonna start crying. But she didn't. She leaned back in her chair, but she didn't take her eyes off Cole Younger for a minute.

He was a big man—tall, maybe two hundred pounds. I expect he'd been even bigger when he was young, before he shrank some from sitting in the Minnesota Penitentiary such a long time. He'd gone kinda round through the shoulders, but then he was sixty-six years old when we went to hear him speak—a little stoop-shouldered was normal at that age. Still good-looking, though. Pearl used to say she could remember a man with golden blond hair and the bluest eyes. Well, the hair was mostly gone—just a little left around the sides—and although I wouldn't of said golden anymore, it was still a pretty color. The eyes was kinda weak-looking, like maybe he needed glasses, and there was heavy puffs under them. But when he smiled, they just gleamed like blue diamonds. He had a nice smile, a lovely smile. Just like Pearl had said.

He stood at the podium. He put his hands in his pants pockets and looked like he was meditating on something serious. Then he said that it was his intention to use himself as an Object Lesson, to maybe make it clear to us all that even a life full of evil and wrongdoing could serve a worthy purpose by preventing some young man from stepping onto a wicked path which would lead him to the penitentiary or worse. And then he cleared his throat once or twice and poured himself a drink out of a small pitcher on the podium (I guessed it was water, it was supposed to be water), and then he said, Ladies and Gents, you are looking at a man gone astray in his youth, who has now seen the Error of his Ways. But only the dear Lord knows (and here he cast his blue eyes upwards) what that error has truly cost him. For I was only released from the state penitentiary at Stillwater, Minnesota, nine years ago, after wasting twenty-five precious years of my life in that godforsaken place.

When he said that, the audience gasped in horror. Pearl drew a handkerchief out of her sleeve and mopped her brow: it was fearsome hot for September, and although they'd left the flaps open for air, it was almost too close in the tent to breathe.

Well, he went on from there. He told all about his early life as an outlaw. About when him and Jesse James rode with Quantrill during the great War Between the States, and how it was after-wards when the James brothers and the Younger brothers raided and killed and generally played hell in Missouri and Kansas during the terrible border war. Everybody was real still and quiet, listen-ing to all this: you coulda heard a pin drop, even on the dirt floor in that tent.

Pearl held her wadded-up handkerchief over her mouth, and she had her eyes shut. Now and then I'd hear her make a strange little noise like she was trying to draw a deep breath and couldn't. I knew she was laboring under heavy emotion, but I didn't know what to do about it, except wait for it to pass. There wasn't a whisper of air in the tent. Some woman sitting a few seats back of us fainted dead away and had to be carried out by two other women. I felt real light-headed myself.

Finally, at the end, Cole told about the fateful raid on the First National Bank at Northfield, Minnesota. He said, I seen Charlie Pitts take a bullet right between the eyes and stand there firing his Colt for another five minutes before he fell down dead. He recounted the famous story of the three Younger brothers being taken back to Madelia by the victorious posse—Cole with eleven bullet holes in him. When they came into the little town, Cole stood up—blood streaming from all those holes—and took off his hat and bowed to the ladies standing on the sidewalk watching the wagon pass with the shackled, wounded outlaws in it. Every-body repeated that story about Cole Younger for years and years. That night in Little Rock he said it was a true story. He smiled that wonderful smile and said, I was quite the dandy in my day, and for sure and certain I did like the ladies. And he put his head back and laughed this big rich laugh. And for a minute his whole face changed: it got handsome and bright in a new kind of way. It was like somebody turned on a light behind it. I could see that women would've loved Cole Younger. That Belle Starr would've thought he hung the moon.

Then he got serious again and said that the Lesson he'd learned from Life was that crime did not pay, that a man had to make his way by honest toil—not by thieving and robbing banks and harming innocent folks—and that God could look into each heart and know True Repentance when He saw it. (I hoped that God didn't look too close at Cole Younger's heart: I know he was sorry about the twenty-five years in Stillwater, but I didn't get any feeling of real strong regret about all the hell-raising.) He thanked us all for coming, and then he made a little bow from the waist and waited for us to finish clapping, which took a minute or two, and then he disappeared behind the curtain again.

I turned to Pearl and said, You are gonna speak to him, you're not gonna stay silent after you went to all this trouble . . .

She stood there with her eye fixed on the empty stage like she could still see Cole Younger up there. Then she looked at me with this faraway expression like she didn't know exactly who I was, and she just got out into the aisle and walked down it toward the stage. I followed along behind her, because I wasn't sure what else to do.

She went around behind the stage, and there he stood. He was in his shirt sleeves by then—handsome yellow suspenders—with his jacket over his arm, and he was mopping his forehead and face with a wet handkerchief. There was a kinda nervous-seeming boy standing to his left, holding the glass with the clear liquid in it. Pearl went right up to Cole and just stopped there in front of him. He went on wiping his brow for another minute, and then he took the glass from the boy and drank it dry and gave it back to him, keeping a wary eye on Pearl all the time. Then he said, Now, what can I do for you, little lady?

Pearl was forty-three years old that year. I don't think she'd been called "little lady" in maybe thirty years. She laughed that great big roar of a laugh of hers and she reached out and touched

Cole Younger's arm and she said, I'm Pearl. I'm Belle's little girl Pearl.

Up close he seemed even bigger than he did on the stage. He was huge. He made Pearl look small, like a girl. But he looked older, close. You could see the wrinkles around his eyes and alongside his mouth and across his forehead. It seemed like these very bright blue eyes was buried inside all this crumpled-up skin. You just got a quick glimpse of them now and then when he turned his head this way or that and the light caught them just so.

He said, Belle?

Just that way: Belle? Like it was a question. Like he couldn't recall this name.

Pearl said, Belle Starr. You was the first man she ever loved. I was the first babe she ever had, and I was yours.

He stared at her with his eyes so tiny and narrow you couldn't tell what color they was, they coulda been yellow for all you could see of them. He stared at her that way for what seemed to me along about an hour, but of course it wasn't an hour, it was maybe two minutes. Then he said, Belle Starr . . . when God made your ma, he throwed away the mold. Goddamned wonderful woman. And he started to cry. He didn't cover his eyes the way most men do when they feel like they got to cry. He just looked at Pearl, and the tears started rolling down his wrinkled cheeks, through all those channels in his face, and they rolled over his lips and his chin and dropped onto his collar until it was dingy-looking with the damp. He didn't put up his hand or wipe the tears away. He just went on looking at Pearl and crying.

Pearl had started to get some of her rosy color back by this time, but when he began to cry she turned pale again. She opened her arms, and Cole Younger walked into them and put his head down on her shoulder. She stroked his bald head and patted his back like he was a baby that had hurt itself. And he said, Dear Jesus, it wasn't supposed to be like this, none of it was supposed to be like this. It was supposed to be . . .

And then he drew back and looked at Pearl again, shaking his head, the tears still falling over his cheeks like water. And Pearl smiled at him and said, I know, Daddy. I know what it was supposed to be like.

He clung to her hand. He said, I'm old, dear God. Look at me! I'm old.

She pressed his hand to her bosom. She said, I'm old too, Daddy. Your baby Pearl is old. And Belle is dead. I swear there are some days I still can't believe that.

I'll never forget the way he looked when Pearl said that to him. He looked like poor Charlie Pitts at Northfield with that bullet between his eyes so unexpected that for five minutes he didn't know he'd got killed. Cole's blue eyes went as dead as fish on a plate. He stopped crying, and he let go her hand. After a minute he said, I don't know who you really are, but don't you come round here telling me these goddamned lies. I ain't had so much gin I don't know a lie when I hear it. You can't deceive a man been sitting in Stillwater twenty-five years.

He grabbed the empty glass out of the boy's hand and filled it up from a flask he got out of his back pocket. As soon as he uncapped the flask, I could smell the aroma of gin even from where I stood. He drank it down all at once. Then he made a kind of a strangled sound, like the gin had taken his breath, and he said, Not a day passes but some shit fool tries to tell me some damn lie or another.

He sat down on a packing box in the corner. He blew his nose. I swear he looked about eighty years old. You couldn't see any color of whatever kind in his face or his eyes. You couldn't even tell anymore where he was looking.

He said, Dear Jesus, ain't I paid You enough? Ain't twenty-five years of shit enough? You got to send me these miserable liars every day till I'm dead . . .

Pearl just stood there looking at him, not saying a word.

He filled up his glass again from the flask. He didn't pay no attention to Pearl at all. It was like he didn't notice anymore that she was there. Then he said, She had this wonderful hair—it was like sunset but darker than sunset. From where we stood, high up, you could see the ocean. My God, it was beautiful . . . the ocean.

Hot Springs: 1920

I saw the Mississippi Delta one morning at dawn, on my way to St. Louis to visit my babies. It looked like the sun was coming up through it, it shimmered like gold leaf, I felt almost blind from the shine of it. Water and plants and marsh flowers. That's what the Delta is, really: shining mud, full of the remains of everything that ever crossed it or settled on it or lived near it. Skeletons of little animals. Footprints way down at the bottom, you can see every toe on these feet because there's no water moving in the Delta to carry anything away. Something makes a footprint in the mud, it sinks down and down, but it stays, it don't wash away. Skeletons and footprints and broken bits and pieces of everything that anyone passing over the Delta ever threw out—trash.

I am a good deal like the Mississippi Delta. Nothing moves in me anymore to carry off anything. From the insides of my bones all the way through the veins and the fat, right out to the skin I am full of the remnants of skeletons and footprints and trash left by somebody passing over me. If you could open me up and poke around in my mud and plants and flowers, you would find some souvenir of every minute of my life: a bone, a footprint, some piece of trash.

I was twenty-five years on Water Street. Jesus, I can't believe it, even now as I say it. Twenty-five years. Belle never lived five years in one place—on the move all the time, on the dodge (that's what she used to call it) from the law, some marshal, some posse, a Pinkerton man. When I was a girl, I moved around considerable. But when I came to the Row, I stopped, mainly so I could make my fortune. That was important to me. Belle always said that no matter what else I had to warm me, I'd end up cold without a fortune. Nothing heats a woman's blood like gold dust—I heard her say that, God knows, a dozen times. It'll keep you warm long after a man's gone cold as a slab of beef. I believed her when she told me that. She was right about a good many things in her life. Oh, she was wrongheaded about so much I can't recall it all. But she was generally right about men and money. Although she ended up with a poor specimen of a man and no money at all.

Fort Smith was like a carnival when I first went there back in '91. People were in the streets till dawn, milling around, making deals of one kind or another—mostly illegal—drinking, gambling, looking for women, eating. Oh, there was lots of eating going on all hours of the day and night. Best eating, anyway, between the Gulf Coast and Chicago, except for New Orleans. Men coming through from the east and the north on their way to Colorado or California or Oregon, looking for gold or silver or land. Wanting to own their own land, the way I wanted to own my own house. Not beholden to anybody. They were a rowdy, free-spirited bunch of men, those days. Sometimes too free-spirited. I'd have to get Lester to throw some bastard into the street now and then for mistreating one of my girls. I never allowed that, no matter how much money or inclination a man might have.

But things change. It's like Desmond Murphey used to say: the good things change, the bad things go on forever. Desmond was a wise man. Not just smart, you know. Wise. Maybe the only wise man I ever knew. Most people thought he drank too much to be wise, but that was wrong: he drank just enough to say what it was he saw as clear as his own hand in front of his own face. Some people see things very plain, but they won't speak them out. Maybe they're afraid of frightening the rest of us. Maybe if we all said what it is we truly see, there's not one of us would get out of bed in the morning.

Fort Smith got respectable. After Indian Territory became a full-fledged state, people got to thinking they ought to behave better. Or at least they ought to *seem* to behave better. In the early days men'd stand around in my parlors—this was after they'd spent a considerable part of the evening upstairs, you understand

—chatting among themselves and with the girls that weren't busy, listening to old Deacon's piano music, playing faro or dominoes. All nice and sociable. Everybody comfortable and easy. No frowns and worried faces. All that changed after statehood. People got concerned about Fort Smith being such a wild frontier kind of town that respectable folks with families wouldn't come and settle there.

Official people kept showing up at my house and bothering me—that was the main reason for all those worried faces in my front parlor every evening. Men never knew when a constable or two would come busting into the place and drag some of them off to jail. Well, of course, they didn't hold the men very long, but they took down their names, and nobody in those days wanted his name taken down by anybody connected with the law. (I doubt that's changed much.)

Sometimes these constables would bring along their little axes and wave them around the place, doing what damage they could: one night somebody even managed to break off some of the ivory keys of my wonderful piano. I'd had that piano in my front parlor since I opened the house. I cried for a week over that piano.

I asked Desmond one night if he thought trying to stay open was worth all this grief. He said it depended how rebellious I was feeling and how alone I was prepared to be.

Maud McGrath and Laura Ziegler were still open for business —this was about 1915. But Dot Parker had already closed her place and gone off to Denver, to retire, she said. Knowing Dot, I think she probably just opened another place in Colorado, some kind of discreet little place nobody would take any notice of. Because Dot liked socializing, and I don't think she knew any other way to do it but whoring. Where would she go for friendly chats and a good laugh? A church social? Wednesday-night prayer meetings? I never heard anything from her after I left Fort Smith in 1916. I had one short letter before I went: she wrote that Denver was nice but that she was freezing her butt off in the snow, and that I should tell Caleb Hickson he'd missed a good thing not coming along when he was invited. I never could understand what she saw in that scrawny little boy, but whatever it was, she went on seeing it for fifteen years.

Maybe Dot's dead by now. If she's not dead, she'd be about sixty.

Maud and Laura were both getting very uneasy, though, I could see that. I could see it was just a matter of time until they closed up their places like Dot had done and went off somewhere else where they didn't have to go through all that grief every day and night. You won't credit how bad it got. People would throw nasty things at us in the street—ripe fruit and suchlike, animal shit wrapped up in little muslin bags. Even in Garrison Street this would happen—why, they used to get up to just about everything known to a man in Garrison Street! Women would pass out insulting broadsheets in front of our houses. I even had some women singing hymns once in front of the Flats!

Life in Fort Smith wasn't tolerable those days for a whore, not even a first-class whore like me or Maud McGrath or Laura Ziegler.

Then one night Desmond Murphey came to see me, and he said, Pearl, they're gonna padlock the Flats. And I said, Why, you got to be crazy! I live there, that's not a place of business!

But Desmond told me they were saying I kept the Flats for immoral purposes. Judge Follet told him that very morning that a party of good, respectable Fort Smith ladies had called on him the day before and said that I got up to all kinds of evildoing in the Flats, and that all this wickedness was bad enough when it was confined to the Row, but they were not gonna permit it to spread over to South Fourteenth Street. Judge Follet had to promise these nice ladies with their delicate feelings that steps would be taken.

Desmond said I had to give an undertaking, make a solemn, binding promise, that I wouldn't for any reason or at any time use the Flats for immoral purposes. Otherwise, they were gonna lock it up so I couldn't use it for anything at all, even to live in all alone.

So I gave the judge such a promise. What else could I do? And Desmond said that, anyway, it would give us time to think about what to do next. Or to study if there was time left to do anything at all.

Come to discover, there wasn't. Like I always said, time is one of those things you always think you got a lot of until you find out you don't have any. None whatsoever. Time was always catching me unprepared like that.

I remember it like it was yesterday, even though it was four years ago. I was entertaining a gentleman friend name of Thomas Freed one night at the Flats. He was an old friend—why, I'd known Thomas since the first day I came to Fort Smith. We'd had ourselves a fine meal—oh, a first-class meal—and we were finishing it off with some brandy up in the sitting room on the second floor, when these men came busting into the room and said I was under arrest for practicing prostitution. Well, I wasn't practicing prostitution just at that instant. It's true that my blouse was unbuttoned a little ways down the front and that I had loosened my camisole, but I wasn't practicing prostitution. I was digesting my supper with an old friend. I was feeling very full and content at that exact moment.

Jesus, I was mad! I was so mad I thought I'd have a stroke. The blood was pounding so loud in my ears I could scarcely hear over it. I yelled, What do you bastards think you're doing in my house where I am entertaining an old friend?

One of the constables smirked ear to ear and said, We're just here to see you don't do any more of this "entertaining" of yours.

They took me off to jail. They gave me a minute to straighten myself up a little bit and get a warm coat on, and then they took me off. Thomas just stood there looking absolutely dumbfounded, still holding this glass of brandy in one hand and his cigar in the other. I don't think he uttered a word from first to last. As I was leaving, I hollered over my shoulder at him to go and tell Desmond Murphey where I was and to come right away. I guess he must have done that, because Desmond was at the jail almost the same time I got there.

He said, Pearl, you promised me you wouldn't get up to nothing at the Flats. And I said, Goddamn it, Desmond, I wasn't up to anything! I was eating and digesting my meal, is that immoral? Is that against the law in Fort Smith?

Desmond went off for a while and left me waiting in this little room off the vestibule of the jail. When he came back, he looked so tired he was chalky. His eyes were even dimmer and redder than usual. He said it was no use this time, it was all over. I said, What do you mean, all over? He said they had three witnesses that I was in a state of undress when they'd broken into the Flats. He said Follet told him they could put me in jail for ten years if they wanted to. I thought Desmond was gonna cry. His cheeks turned scarlet, and he put his head down in his hands. I asked him what I could do, what he would advise me to do. He said, If you promise to leave town right away—bag and baggage within a week's time—they'll drop the charges against you. But he said I had to promise never to come back to Fort Smith. Because if I ever showed my face there again, they'd arrest me on the spot and put me in jail and throw away the key.

Yes . . . I do think I'll have another rye now. I better drink it while I can, and that's God's truth. The Prohibitionists are gonna stop all that kind of fun too—any day now. Ain't it odd how some people just cannot let other people get on with their lives in their own peaceable way? They always got to interfere with the rest of us, even when our sins are just small, private things.

Where was I . . . ?

Oh yes, I remember. Sad time. Maybe the saddest time of my life. But that would be hard to say, I guess. So many sad times. It's like Belle said to Betsy Nail on the day she was murdered, I'm a woman who has seen much of life. Betsy told me that at the funeral.

So first week in March 1916, I left Fort Smith for Hot Springs. It was raining and cold. I'll never forget that day. I felt a chill strike my soul, and it hasn't warmed up since—not entirely, not right there in the middle of it. I don't think I ever had felt so alone, not even after Ma died.

I didn't bring Festina with me, even though she'd hardly been out of my sight for twenty years. Well, the reason why is that

Festina had a man of her own in Fort Smith, a Baptist preacher name of Granville, handsome buck; big, deep preacher voice; always smelled wonderful, like good soap and lilac water. They'd been lovers a long time, ten years anyway. I don't know when they got together: an hour here, an evening there . . . Every time I needed Festina, she was there—and I needed her a good deal—so God knows when she saw her preacher man. Anyway, I couldn't take her away from Granville. I couldn't drag her off here to watch me die. The morning I left, she stood out in front of the Flats and cried like her heart would break. I left her well fixed, and Desmond has instructions to see she gets whatever she needs. But that didn't stanch the tears.

I loved Festina. I do think Festina loved me back. I miss her.

So now I been four years in Hot Springs. It's a lively enough place in its way, but it's not Fort Smith's way by no means. It's all these sick folks who come here for the mineral baths. They don't want to listen to music and dance and gamble and do all those other amusing things that healthy people in Fort Smith used to stay up doing until sunrise. Oh, you can find all those entertaining things going on somewhere here, if you got a mind to. But it's all going on slower than in Fort Smith. Two or three shades darker and two or three beats slower, I always say. Still . . . I'm not in jail.

I started in eating with real attention from just about the moment I arrived. I got rooms straight off right here at the old Majestic, and they always have laid a nice table. Three times a day that big serving table down the middle of the dining room groaning under the weight of all those dishes . . . Then there'd be afternoon tea: all those wonderful breads and cakes and honey fresh from the hives and pots of tea and coffee. I ate a lot in those first days here. You might almost say I ate professionally, if there was such a thing. I was sorrowing almost to the point where I couldn't swallow sometimes, but that just made me want to eat more. If I couldn't swallow cake or whatever it was I had in my mouth because I wanted to cry and the tears were in my throat, then I'd just sit and hold the cake in my mouth until it dissolved in my tears and slipped on down my throat. It felt awful, awful.

It felt like a solid gob of tears. I thought once or twice I'd choke to death. Then I had to laugh. Imagine Pearl Starr finally coming to an end because she couldn't catch her breath over a piece of cake! I thought to myself that of all the ways we had died over the years—all us Starrs and Reeds and Youngers and Jameses— Jesus, that would be the shabbiest. So I stopped stuffing cake into my mouth like it was a towel to blot up tears.

In no time at all I weighed about two hundred pounds (I'm not too scant of that now). I was this big, ugly thing like a crooked building. I'd sit out here on the veranda of the Majestic, looking out at the green mountains all around, watching the rain fall, rocking in my cane chair. And I didn't know who I was anymore. You can't imagine how terrible it was, losing Pearl that way.

Partly it was the drink too. Not just the food. I drank everything I could get my hands on, and I started doing it early in the day. One thing I did take away with me from Fort Smith was most of my fortune. Desmond Murphey helped me see to that. I had a good deal of business sense from the beginning—where I got it, I don't know—but I learned early on how things worked with money. The house was always a paying proposition, and I invested in real estate and bonds and whatever else Desmond recommended to me. When I left Fort Smith, he closed Pearl's Place for me and sold everything, including the property. He sold the Flats too, eventually—when he could get the right price. Disposed of everything, that's the way they put it, I think. He disposed of everything. And when you added it all together, it made a considerable amount. Desmond was of the opinion that I could probably live just on the interest from my investments for the rest of my life, without a worry in the world.

So I didn't worry. I had my fortune. I'd done that, anyway. Not like Belle, dying without loose change in her pocket. Rich three or four times over, she was, but all gone when she came to die. But then she came to die early—just turned forty-one—so she didn't need it for her old age anyhow, not shot down in the Briartown Road like she was. They never found out for sure who did that terrible deed. Most thought it was that neighbor of hers, Edgar Watson. Maybe it was. They'd been on the outs for years.

Common knowledge that he hated Belle. But nobody knows for God's truth, except the man who shot her dead, may he rot in Hell no matter who he is . . . but I'm digressing, I'm getting off the subject here . . . it's harder and harder these days for me to end up where I think I'm going when I start . . .

When I think about old age and dying early, I always remember Cole Younger—tippling gin, handsome blue eyes turning dim as milk glass, the golden hair—what was left of it—gone white. Living in the past . . . I guess one of the saddest things in the world is to be born beautiful and grow old. I sometimes think it would have been better for Cole to come early to grief, like Jesse and Jim Reed. I don't think Cole recognized himself later on. I think it made him drink harder, living with an old man he didn't know.

Anyway, I didn't worry. I drank the best brandy and champagne and the smoothest rye and bourbon there was. And I ate the fanciest meals I could get into me without busting right through my skin. I sat out here on the veranda and slept away the afternoons in a drunken stupor while the rain fell. I guess most people who saw me then just thought I was one of the sick folks who come to Hot Springs for the mineral baths.

I did take the baths two, three times a week. Just for something to do. But I'd grown so big I could hardly fit into one of the marble tubs anymore. And I knew the black girls who shifted around the sick people at the bathhouses used to pass comments on my size: I was wrapped up in hot sheets one day in a little cubicle, and I heard two of them talking outside my door; one of them said moving me around was like shunting a train with no tracks. But I didn't mind. I don't know why I didn't mind. In earlier days I would have minded—dear God, I would have minded! But not here in Hot Springs in 1916, 1917. As long as I could eat and drink and sit on the veranda and sleep and rock—that's all I cared about then. I sorrowed. I didn't have time for anything but sorrowing.

I recollected everything. I remembered, oh Jesus in such detail, in such little particular detail sometimes that I couldn't believe any head could hold such an abundance of tiny particles of memory. Just like the Delta . . . like I said.

Once I spent an entire week, every waking moment of it, it seemed to me, remembering Siloam Springs and Grandma Reed and Flossie. I remembered lying in the marble tubs at the bathhouse with the sea-green columns outside its doors, looking down at my huge stomach where little Flossie was floating around waiting to be born. Poor little Flossie, who I never got to know at all. Little strange Flossie, living somewhere in Wichita still, I guess. Married by now. Children of her own. Maybe even here in Hot Springs, taking the baths against the rheumatism or some such thing. Never knowing that her own ma was this sad woman size of a mountain, rocking away on the veranda of the Majestic Hotel . . .

Grandma Reed would be dead by now. Oh, yes . . . dead for years. Pickled in peach brandy, but dead anyhow. Finally God notices you, no matter how well preserved in alcohol you are.

I recollected and I wept—these two naturally going together like champagne and little fat shrimp in pink shells. I wept until I thought I'd never again know what a dry sleeve or a dry handkerchief was. I cried over Johnson Mayhew until I couldn't eat for two days. I nourished myself with corn whiskey for that period.

I couldn't even bring myself to remember poor little Artie. I still can't. He wasn't in this world long enough to find out what a sad shit thing it is. Not even alive long enough to get acquainted with his pa and ma. Maybe that's better, in the long run. I knew my ma and pa—what in God's name that got me, I can't truly say. Grief, for the most part. I can truly say grief. No matter what else I could add to that after taking some thought of it.

Dell Andrews made me happy for a while, but even remembering that didn't stop the tears. He ruined it all, in the end. He didn't know how to stop ruining things. None of them did. I never could understand it. It all looked so clear to me sometimes: all they had to do was go on loving me and stay where I could see them when I had the need to. Not anybody I loved could manage that simple thing. To this very day I can't get to the bottom of that incapacity.

I used to ask myself: Was it something I did or said? Some disgusting habit I couldn't recall? Was I not pretty enough or lively enough? Didn't I have enough wit about me? Was I too forthcoming? (Dot Parker used to say I was too forthcoming; I never really knew what she meant by that. Maud McGrath said to pay no attention to anything Dot Parker said, because she was dumb as a stump about almost everything except the location of a man's privates.)

Maybe I just always loved people who were not suitable. Like Johnson Mayhew. (Like Belle Starr and Jim papa.) I knew from the beginning that Johnson Mayhew was not a suitable man for me to love. But I went right ahead and loved him anyway. Until he left. No one ever mentioned to me how to go about picking out somebody suitable to love and then loving that person. Nobody ever explained how to do that—not even Maud McGrath, and she explained a helluva lot of things to me in twenty-five years. I got this stupid heart that just dashes around the place bumping into walls and falling downstairs like a silly child, and I never can make it mind. Oh, I say things to it, like: Now, you be careful, it won't do to love that one, that one's gonna be pain and despair, that one's gonna break you. But it just goes on feeling grand and full and batting around inside my chest like a happy bird, until the end comes. And the end is pain and despair and heartbreak, just like I knew it would be in the beginning. What can I do about it? There was never anybody to give me advice on these questions.

Even Maud McGrath . . . I was very fond of Maud. You get fond of a person in twenty-five years. I used to hear from her once in a while after I left Fort Smith. She and Laura Ziegler were hounded out of business not too long after me. Maud went off to Little Rock, bought a little house and took to serious drinking. The last letter she ever wrote me, she said how she missed me and how dull and musty everything seemed. She said, Is it old age makes me feel this way? Because if it is, I'm not gonna put up with it. I never knew what Maud meant by that. Maybe she had it in mind to drink down a big draught of opium or suchlike and just float away to heaven. I never knew, because she never did write again after that. It was strange to me. We'd always been so

close, and then not another word. How could you love somebody
and never want to speak another word to them—and them still
alive and longing to hear that word?

Laura Ziegler married a man name of William MacIntyre last
year and went off with him to live in Chicago. He's about seventy
and has a deal of money. She wrote me a very amusing letter a
few months later about how people would see this nice old couple
together at the theater or out to some nice restaurant, and they
would smile in that sugar-sweet way they smile at old people and
lunatics and other folks you don't have to take serious, and Laura
was sure they were thinking what a sweet old couple they were
and how many years they'd been married and how many sweet
children and grandchildren they had. And Laura wrote that she
always longed to yell out to them, Darlin', I was the best whore in
Fort Smith, next to the Queen of the Row herself!

Even Desmond Murphey don't write as much as he used to. But
then his sorrow is almost as abundant as mine. And he's drunk so
much of the time . . . I could hardly make out the last couple of
letters I got from him. He says Fort Smith is getting to be dull as
ditchwater. In one letter he said, Dear girl, the fleas have all
jumped off this town, the old dog is dying.

My babies, now . . . I think maybe my babies are suitable
people to love, although God knows it may be too soon to know
that yet. I hear from Ruth regular. She was always a good girl, and
she still is. She lets me know what's going on in St. Louis. She's
twenty-six now, works in a shop that sells cards and geegaws. She
never has married, and she don't say anything that would lead me
to believe she's strongly considering it. Maybe I turned her against
the whole institution, although I don't know how that could be so.
I never said anything against that arrangement. I just always told
her the same thing Belle told me—that regardless of who came
and who went, if she'd somehow get herself a little gold, she'd
never be just a cold, poor thing not worth spit to herself.

Jennette don't write often. She's eighteen and lives in Chicago.
Ruth said she thought Jennette was in some kind of show business or musical entertainment or suchlike. She was kind of vague
about it. My babies ain't especially close to each other, which

makes me sad, but I guess it's natural since they had fathers different as meat and milk. Jennette was always an odd kind of a child . . . I don't know exactly how, just odd. Always coming out with some funny remark. Not funny ha-ha.

Ruth's very quiet. She was always quiet and well behaved. She was always taking thought, I think that's what made her so quiet. I see a lot of Johnson Mayhew in her. I guess in that case there's hope for the child. I know if I ever really need somebody, if it gets down to a question of life and death, I can call on Ruth and she'll come. Don't ask me how I know that, but I know it. I hope it don't come to that, but then you never know, do you? You get old, you get infirm. In my case, maybe I'll just get too fat. I'll eat so much one night that I'll founder like a cow turned over in mud with its feet up in the air—and they'll have to call little Ruthie to come move her mama, the way you'd call a mechanic to come and move one of these big Pierce-Arrow automobiles out of the road, so the other traffic can get by.

So I'm going to Denver come spring. A few months ago it came to me that there were only two things I could do: I could leave Hot Springs for some other town, or I could die here where I sat —just expire one afternoon in my rocking chair, breathe my last like some sick old woman with gout. Let the undertaker worry about how to remove my gigantic carcass from the veranda of this hotel. So I decided to go. It was the first time I had felt like Pearl in four years.

I think it'll be better in Denver. It's high up and the air is dry. It don't rain until you feel like the mold has grabbed you around the ankles and is rising slowly and changing your whole body into a mushroom. And people don't go to Denver when they're sick to get well again. Or at least it ain't so obvious if they do.

Thing that worries me some is how cold it gets in those mountains. My body don't take too kindly to the cold. I grew up in the warm country. Born in Texas, spent some of my childhood in California—high up, where I could see the ocean—and some back in Texas and some in Oklahoma. Warm country, all of it. Not like Colorado.

I had thought maybe San Francisco would be a nice spot. If I get too cold in Denver, maybe I'll go on out there next winter. They say it's very lively: music, dancing, clubs . . . amusing things. A port city, so you get all kinds of people coming and going from faraway places—different, interesting kind of people.

Belle always said she loved California. Eddie was born there— poor Eddie, no old age for him, either. Murdered like all the others. Maybe he deserved killing, I never was sure . . .

Belle said she could have lived in California forever, she thought. High up, with the Pacific Ocean on the horizon. But something happened . . . I don't know what it was exactly . . . she and Jim papa had to leave. Something was always happening in those days. Not like now. Nothing ever happens now. Maybe if I get to San Francisco I'll discover things are happening. Maybe I'll even study to be happy again. Belle always said that happiness was a moral obligation, to her way of thinking.

A NOTE ON THE TYPE

The text of this book was set on the Linotype in a face called Times Roman, designed by Stanley Morison for The Times (London) and first introduced by that newspaper in 1932.

Among typographers and designers of the twentieth century, Stanley Morison has been a strong forming influence, as a typographical adviser to the English Monotype Corporation, as a director of two distinguished English publishing houses, and as a writer of sensibility, erudition, and keen practical sense.

Composed by The Maryland Linotype Composition Corporation, Baltimore, Maryland. Printed and bound by The Haddon Craftsmen, Inc., Scranton, Pennsylvania.

Designed by Mark Argetsinger.